10723031

HIGH KING
BOOK 3

THE CARNYX

S. M. DAVIES

The Carnyx copyright © S.M. Davies 2024

First published in the United Kingdom by Sylfa Press 2024

The right of S.M. Davies to be identified as the author of this work has been asserted under the Copyright, Designs and Patents Act 1988.

All rights reserved.

No part of this publication may be reproduced, stored in a retrieval system, or transmitted, in any form or by any means, without the prior written permission of the publisher.

The Carnyx is a work of fiction. All characters are the product of the author's imagination, and any resemblance to persons living or dead is entirely coincidental.

ISBN 978-1-7396726-6-9 (paperback)
978-1-7396726-5-2 (ebook)

Requests to publish work from this book should be sent to:
smdavies@sylfapress.com

Cover and Interior design: JD Smith

Preface

At the close of the 5th Century, the Greek historian Zosimus wrote about the decline and fall of Rome's Western Empire. 'The Britons had freed their states from the barbarian threat …and set up a native constitution of their own,' he said, referring to the earlier part of the century. If Zosimus and his readers were surprised, they had good reason. No other western region could claim similar success. In defeating the Picts in the North, Vortigern and his allies succeeded where generations of Roman commanders had failed. The frontiers were as secure as they had been in living memory. The foundations of a state which Zosimus described as 'affluent, with abundance beyond the memory of any earlier age', had been laid.

Such a state should endure and prosper, at least for a while, but all Vortigern's achievements are jeopardised by his feckless allies. His attempts to secure the future defence of the kingdom come to nothing when most of them refuse to contribute to the cost. Complacent and self-assured after the victory in the North, they are too short-sighted and tight-fisted to see what the consequences of their actions might be. Vortigern's devoted companion and chief warrior, Kerin Brightspear, has even to sequestrate the money and goods promised to their Jute mercenaries. Soon Vortigern's enemies will seize on the rift between the king and his oldest son, Vortimer, to undermine him and make their own play for power.

This, the third part of Vortigern's story, begins in a time of fragile, illusory peace. The king has returned home with his young wife Rowenna, daughter of Hengist, his Jute captain. Kerin, now universally known as 'the King's Right Arm', has carved out a position of responsibility he could scarcely have dreamed of, sealing his happiness with marriage to his beloved Gael. But the peace which the two men have fought so hard to win is shattered when Vortigern's rivals proclaim his son king and threaten his strongholds in the West, tipping the kingdom into civil war. Violence explodes in Kent when they drive Hengist's people from the land granted to the mercenaries for their military service.

Little is known about the conflict between Vortigern and his oldest son. That it happened can be deduced from the semi-historical and legendary sources, but detail is scarce, and the chronology often confused. *The Carnyx* is the story of what might have happened, when two men with vastly different agendas and resources fought for control of the kingdom. In the end there could only be one King of all the Britons; and Vortigern was not going to surrender his power without a fight. The tragedy of it, as Vortigern himself says from the outset, is that they should not have been fighting each other at all, but standing together against the far greater threat awaiting the survivors of a brutal and needless war.

Characters

Those marked * are recorded in history or legend

Cambria
* Vortigern, Lord of Cambria and the West, King of all the Britons
* Rowenna, his second wife, daughter of his mercenary captain Hengist
* Vortimer, known as Rufus, his oldest son
* Katigern, his second son
* Paschent, his youngest son
* Sevira, his late first wife, daughter of Roman emperor *Magnus Maximus

Vortigern's household and associates:
Cenydd, his principal servant
Cynfawr, his bard
Ashur, his Parthian stable boy
Claudius Custos, harbourmaster of Isca

Kerin Brightspear, 'the King's Right Arm', Vortigern's companion and confidant
Gael, his wife

Kerin's household:
Cheldric, his Saxon cook
Dimos Bekuh, his scribe and teacher
Catula, his servant
Morvid, aged healer
Marc, Morvid's grandson
Cambrian warriors and their associates:
Gwyndaf of Craig Goch, Vortigern's standard-bearer
Derfyn, Leil and Cadfan, Gwyndaf's young warriors
Mari, Gwyndaf's wife
Lud, Vortigern's chief warrior
Macsen, Lud's oldest son
Custennin, Lud's second son
Elir, Lud's youngest son
Mora, Lud's wife
Bened, their nephew
Hefydd of Carneddlas, warlord, Vortigern's ally
Mabon, Hefydd's son
Branwen, Hefydd's daughter
Hefin, Hefydd's younger brother
Tirion, Hefin's wife
Brwyn, former warrior
Idris, Brwyn's son, ally of Rufus
Aron, Brwyn's younger son, ally of Rufus

Craftsmen and villagers:
Cilydd, silversmith
Edryd, smith and skilled metal-worker
Gwydion, blacksmith
Gwynfi, weaver
Mabli, Cilydd's daughter
Eleri, Macsen's girl
Anwen, wise woman, cousin to Mora

Londinium

Publius Luca, formerly of the Second Augustan
Legion, friend of Vortigern
Titus Luca, lawyer, his son
Gaia Fulvia, his wife
Marcus Fulvius, his brother-in-law
Marcellus *magister*, physician and soothsayer
Elissa, Marcellus's wife
Gallus Mercator, merchant, friend of Vortigern
Lucius Arrius, commander of cavalry, friend of Kerin
Marcus Arrius, Lucius's stepfather
Livius Gaius, Lucius's second-in-command
Valerius Dio, new praetor of Londinium
Ariadna, his wife
Severus Maximus, disgraced former praetor
Alberius, his acolyte

Glevum

*Eldof, Lord of Glevum
Bertil Redknife, Gael's father, Eldof's kinsman and
rival
Balin, Bertil's chief warrior
Malan, elderly village headman, loyal to Vortigern
Berget, Malan's daughter
Runo, Berget's husband
Flora, Malan's granddaughter
Pedr, alehouse-keeper

Other warlords and their associates
*Gorlois of Kernow, Vortigern's loyal supporter
Gerdan, his younger brother
Varro, Eldof's former chief warrior, now pledged to
Vortigern
Eliud and Danius, Varro's young warriors
*Garagon of Kent, ally of Rufus
Livia, Garagon's sister
Batraz, Sarmatian mercenary captain, Rufus's chief
warrior

The Jutes
*Hengist, leader of Vortigern's mercenaries
*Horsa, his brother
*Aelle, his nephew
Oswi the Horseman, a leading warrior

Priests and monks
Father Paulinus, abbot of Venta Belgarum, Rufus's
mentor
Brother Padarn, of the same monastery, 'the warriors'
priest'
Father Iustig, abbot of Caerwenn
Brother Cadog, his associate
*Bishop Eldadus of Glevum, brother of Eldof
Father Septimus of Glevum, loyal friend of Gael
Caradog, archdruid of Henfelin, Vortigern's capital
Cynan, archdruid elect, son of the bard Cynfawr

Glossary of horses' names and other Welsh terms

Annwn - the Underworld

Blaidd - the Wolf

Eryr - the Eagle

Gwalch - the Osprey

Hebog - the Hawk

Seren - a Star

Calan Gaeaf - literally, the First of November; equivalent to Hallowe'en or the pagan Samhain

Calan Mai - literally, the First of May; equivalent to May Day or the pagan Beltane

anwylyd - beloved

uchelwyr - the high-born

Glossary of place names

Abona - Sea Mills, Roman river port

Aquae Sulis - Bath

Ariconium - Weston under Penyard

Armorica - Brittany

Blestium - Monmouth

Bononia - Boulogne

Caerwynt - Winchester

Calleva (Atrebatum) - Silchester

Camulodunum - Colchester

Corinium - Cirencester

Dubris - Dover

Durobrivae - Water Newton

Durovernum - Canterbury

Eburacum - York

Gallia - Gaul, France

Glevum - Gloucester

Glywysing* - The Glamorgans

Gwy - River Wye

Hafren - River Severn

Hibernia - Spain

Isca (Silurum) - Caerleon

Kernow - Cornwall

Lacobriga - Lagos, port in southern Portugal

Lemanis - Lympne

Leucarum - Llwchwr, Loughor

Lugdunum - Lyon

Lusitania - Portugal

Moridunum - Caerfyrddin, Carmarthen

Nidum - Castell Nedd, Neath

Rutupiae - Richborough

Segontium - Caernarfon

Tanatus - Thanet

Vectis - Isle of Wight

Venta Belgarum - Winchester

Venta (Silurum) - Caerwent

*Glywysing was the name of the ancient Welsh kingdom which included all the Glamorgans; its boundaries changed over time, but it generally extended from the Tywi in the west to the Wye or the Severn.

Cheviot Hills
HADRIAN'S WALL
EBURACUM
SEGONTIUM
Eryri
VIROCONIUM
DUROBRIVAE
CAMBRIA
Hafren
Gwy
Preseli
CAMULODUNUM
ARICONIUM
MORIDUNUM
Bannau Brycheiniog
VERULAMIUM
GLEVUM
BLESTIUM
CORINIUM
LEUCARUM
ISCA
LONDINIUM
NIDUM
VENTA SILURUM
RUTUPIAE
ABONA
Tamesis
Tanatus
ABER HENFELIN
AQUAE SULIS
CALLEVA
DUROVERNUM
KENT
DUBRIS
Plains of Sarum
LEMANIS
KERNOW
SARUM
VENTA BELGARUM
TINTAGEL
VECTIS
BONONIA

To Anna and Hunter

1

'Close your eyes,' Kerin said, to his wife of six days.

'When I'm riding a horse?' Gael said sceptically.

'Yes. Come on, humour me. Give me the reins and close your eyes. I want to surprise you.'

Gael laughed as if she thought he was completely mad, but complied. This was the road on which they always returned home after travelling eastwards; an ancient track worn hard and smooth over centuries by feet, hooves and wagons. Kerin steadied Blaidd as the hill grew steeper.

'This had better be good,' Gael said.

'Wait.' Kerin reined in on the ridge, looking down over the sunlit country below. 'Now open your eyes. This is your home.'

Gael gave a little gasp of astonishment. Kerin clasped her fingers briefly as he returned the reins. Nothing in his experience resembled the feeling which always filled him when he and his companions returned home after a long absence; the quickening of the heart which came as they rode up over the high ridge of Crib Garw and saw before them the moors and valleys of Henfelin, rolling towards the sea. 'Over there is our home,' he said, pointing. 'Can you see the citadel, looking down over the valley?'

Gael shaded her eyes. 'Is that where your house is?' She smiled. '*Our* house.'

'Yes,' Kerin said. 'Right there. But everything you can see

is Vortigern's country. You're free to go wherever you like.' His gaze moved from the cleft of the valley across rippling grassland where cattle grazed as thick as sparrows round a corn bin, to the windy blue ridge of the Cribin. Beyond lay the sea, shimmering under the sun. They both turned at the sound of an approaching horse. Gwyndaf was riding up the track, the dragon standard resting in a sling fixed to his saddle. Gael waved to him and rode off along the ridge for a better view of her new home. Gwyndaf reined in beside Kerin and they sat, listening to skylarks singing high in the spun clouds and the wind rattling through the bog cotton.

'I don't know about you,' Gwyndaf said, 'but it seems so long since we fought the Picts, I'd almost forgotten what we did it for. It's strange to think that people here have thought of nothing much else. I wonder if they'd cheer if they knew what had happened since?'

'I expect so,' Kerin said. 'All they care about is that we've won, and they're safe, at least for now.'

'Well, that's true,' Gwyndaf said, 'and they'd cheer Vortigern if he'd murdered his mother, so they're not going to worry about the Saxons having a few cornfields in Kent. I've got better things to think about, anyway, and a few things to do.'

'What do you mean?' Kerin asked. Gwyndaf smiled, warmly and without reserve.

'It took me all of a minute to find out that I loved my first wife. It took nine years and a battle to make me realise that I loved the second, and my greatest fear in the North was getting killed before I could tell her. That may sound strange coming from me, but it's the truth. You should look after that girl of yours.'

'I intend to,' Kerin said, as Gael whirled her horse and galloped off to meet Rowenna, who was riding up the hill with Vortigern.

'Come on, come on!' she cried. 'Come and look at this. You see? Now we'll never want to leave, even if we get tired of our husbands.' With a burst of laughter, they rode off downhill through the bracken. Gwyndaf chuckled.

'Isn't that girl afraid of anything?'

'Not that I've noticed,' Kerin said. He glanced over his shoulder and grinned. 'Certainly not of him.'

Vortigern arrived beside them. 'Thou shalt not take the name of the Lord in vain,' he said.

'We're not,' Gwyndaf said, and nodded towards the women. 'Perhaps they are, though.'

Vortigern watched the two women careering around, Gael's tall hunting horse dwarfing Rowenna's white pony. 'They can do what they like,' he said. 'Let them have fun while they can.'

As the king's company rode down from the high moors, two shepherd lads appeared on a limestone outcrop. One jumped on his pony and galloped off towards the settlement. The news would spread like a gorse fire now. Kerin watched Gael and Rowenna jogging along side by side. Thrown together, two lone women in a band of warriors, they might have been expected to draw comfort from each other's company; but there was something more than that going on. Sometimes they spoke in hushed voices. Their conversations were punctuated by laughter. Now and again one of them would look anxious, and the other would reach for her hand. In a vague but obtrusive way, it worried Kerin. He had not supposed that there was more than one honest position to hold about Hengist's daughter. Today, though, it was easy to push misgivings aside. The women plucked long trails of honeysuckle and hung them round their necks like garlands. Brother Padarn sang lustily about ale and gambling, and Lud appeared quietly content, despite the prospect of explaining why two of his sons had not come home with him. At the crossroads where the valley broadened out, hundreds had gathered. Gwyndaf raised the draco, and everyone cheered hysterically as the tattered banner streamed out in the wind.

'Enjoy it, Kerin,' Gwyndaf said. 'Just enjoy it. I know you can't stand the girl, but for today, let it go. I know what I'm talking about, believe me. Just let them live. It wasn't even her father's idea, was it?'

'Not in the first place,' Kerin said. 'But Hengist will grab any chance that comes, never mind the piece of Kent he's already been granted. Can't you see what's happening?'

'Yes,' Gwyndaf said. 'And what I can see looks very simple and obvious, but it's no good telling you that, is it? Remember what I said about your girl.'

As people crowded around him, shouting, singing and weeping, Vortigern drew rein. All the warriors sensed a significant parting. The procession halted. Gwyndaf lowered the draco and rode forward.

'You will be leaving us now,' Vortigern said.

'Yes,' Gwyndaf said. He furled the banner, kissed the dragon's head and held out the standard.

'No,' Vortigern said. 'You are the dragon-bearer. Will you carry him again for me, if the need comes?'

'Probably,' Gwyndaf said. 'But I'd still need a damned good reason to fight on the same side as you.'

'I wouldn't ask you otherwise,' Vortigern said. 'And I won't raise the dragon again unless I have to fight for this country. For Cambria and the West. Now, pass him to a man you trust, and go home to your family.'

'I'll give him to Derfyn, then,' Gwyndaf said. 'He's as good as a son to me, and you of all men should know what

I mean by that.' He presented the draco to Derfyn, then gathered his warriors and rode away. Kerin watched them bobbing up the steep track which would take them over the flank of Crib Garw towards their home on the Cribin. Derfyn looked down at the draco with a mixture of pride and trepidation.

'He won't bite you, boy,' Vortigern said. 'Now, raise him up. When you've been carrying that thing for a while, you'll find that Gwyndaf is even stronger than you thought he was.'

They turned south on the good, hard road which led down beside the river. Kerin could hardly wait to lead Gael up the steep track to the citadel, carry her into his house and make love to her in his own bed. He turned and saw her laughing with Rowenna. They noticed him watching them, looked at each other, and attempted to stifle the laughter.

'What's the matter?' Vortigern asked as they rode side by side. 'You shouldn't have a care in the world, as far as I can see.'

Kerin hesitated. Vortigern looked so much at peace that it seemed criminal to say anything, but in the end prudence got the better of him. 'Lord, you know there's going to be trouble,' he said.

'Yes, Kerin. I know there's going to be all kinds of trouble. But trouble is for kings. Today I'm an ordinary warrior again, and I want no more than to get home, drink a jar of ale and lie with my wife. Tomorrow I'll be a king, and you can be my right arm and tell me what to do. But not today.'

Kerin watched the two women riding ahead. 'Lord, I wish you nothing but joy of all this,' he said.

'Then please, allow me some peace,' Vortigern said. 'Some simple, common pleasure. God knows, I've waited long enough for it.' He had spoken without a trace of harshness. Perhaps of all of them, Kerin thought, he was most in need of their homecoming, and all it promised.

'You're right, lord,' he said. 'Tomorrow will do.' He caught Gael's eye and smiled. 'I've got better things to do with my right arm today, anyway.'

2

It was not tomorrow. It was not even the day after that, since fate permitted them a few weeks' respite before everything began again. On the morning of Midsummer's Eve, Kerin woke to the sound of the sea and the crying of gulls. Shafts of sunlight streamed in around the door of his house, motes of dust dancing along the beams like fireflies. For a while he lay quite still, listening to the familiar, beloved sounds of the settlement; children shouting, the slow, rhythmic clang of the smiths' workshops, the faint cries of sheep on the high moors. He turned over and looked at Gael, lying asleep beside him. She lay on her back, hair tumbling back from her face, her breasts rising and falling gently with the rhythm of her breathing. Kerin smiled and lifted a strand of her hair. It would have seemed heartless to disturb her. He got up, pulled on his tunic and breeches and went outside.

Marc was squatting beside a fire, cooking bread on a flat stone. Cheldric was peeling roots into a cauldron. Otherwise, there were few signs of life amongst the houses of the *uchelwyr*. Lud and Mora were sitting outside their door enjoying the sun as their daughter hung washing out to dry. Their grandchildren had disappeared off somewhere, but Catula's little white dog, Hadrian, was snoozing on Mora's feet. Ashur was grooming the Pike. The chieftain's hall was silent, the door barred from within.

'Bread, lord?' Marc asked.

'Please,' Kerin said, stretching and taking deep breaths of the sharp sea air. He sat down beside the fire. Marc passed him hot bread and filled a mug with cool water from a pitcher. 'Where have all the children gone? They're usually running around here like a flock of chickens.'

'Oh, that man's got them,' Marc said. 'Dimos, is it? The one who's teaching you to read and write. That's what he's doing with the children. He's moved in with the Lord's bard, Cynfawr. There was a spare room, and it's nice and big, so that's where they have their lessons. He did ask me, but I said I had more important things to do. He's a good man, though. Kind and funny. I like him.'

'I'm glad you do,' Kerin said, 'because you're going to spend some time with him soon, like it or not, or you'll end up an ignoramus like me.' Marc grimaced, but knew better than to argue.

'Good morning, lad,' a voice wheezed. 'Come out at last, then?'

'Hello, Morvid,' Kerin said. 'What have you got there?' The old man sat down on the warm ground beside him, nursing a canvas bag and a little earthenware pot full of a greenish mixture.

'Something for the fever,' he said. 'Gwynfi's wife is on fire with it.'

'Will it cure her?' Kerin asked.

'I expect so. Oh gods, she's mad, though. Funny things happen to women when they're expecting children, something you'll find out about before too long, the way you've been carrying on. Not to mention that young ram Derfyn, who's hardly been out of Mabli's bed since you got back.'

'What's in it?' Marc asked, peering into the pot.

'I'll teach you one day, boy,' Morvid said. 'It would be a pity for all this to die with me.'

'Die?' Kerin said. 'You'll see us all in our graves, you old buzzard.'

Morvid sniffed. 'Probably, if you wear yourself out on that girl.' He took a handful of fresh leaves from his bag and pounded them into his pot. 'Are you going to Kent to fight Rufus, then?'

Kerin sighed. 'Who have you been talking to?'

'Lud. He tells me that his boy Macsen's there, keeping an eye on things. Hefydd's brother Hefin too, and a bunch of good warriors.'

'We didn't have a choice,' Kerin said. 'No one in Kent knew about Vortigern's marriage to Rowenna. The Kentishmen spat on us and went home after the victory in the North. None of them knew that Vortigern had granted more of their land to the Jutes. And Oswi the Horseman was travelling there overland, with a wagon train. He's one of the best Jute warriors, but anyone's at risk when he has women and children to protect. Someone had to go with Oswi and his people, to keep the peace and prove that their new land's been given to them in good faith. What about it, anyway?'

'Lud's worried about his son,' Morvid said. 'He's afraid there'll be a scrap, even if our side don't start it. He'd go charging off to Kent, if he could.'

They heard the soft thud of a bolt being drawn. The door of Vortigern's hall opened and Rowenna peered cautiously out. Her Saxon clothes had been exchanged for a dress of the soft grey cloth woven further up the valley by Gwynfi and his family. She closed the door and looked out across the headlands. The sea had been her life, but the sight of it seemed to stir no painful memories. Closing her eyes she threw her head back and stretched her hands up towards the high sun. An ecstatic smile transformed her face, as if the warm, healing light had flooded through her, making any trace of unhappiness impossible. Her whole being glowed with it.

'Well,' Morvid said, 'he brought home a princess of the Jutes, but I think the Cambrian air has turned her into a princess of the Celts.'

Kerin wrinkled his nose. 'She'll never be that,' he said. Rowenna looked round. Whether she had overheard or not, nothing seemed able to dispel the look of pure joy. She came across to the fire carrying her well-worn green dress and seafarer's clothes, threw them into the flames and watched them burn.

'Why?' Kerin asked.

'I have already explained,' Rowenna said. 'For our people, when a woman marries, she must live as her husband lives. I will not need these now.'

Kerin looked at the smouldering bundle. 'You can't make yourself a Celt by burning your clothes,' he said. Rowenna's eyes flashed.

'For you, nothing is enough,' she said. Kerin did not respond. He couldn't warm to her, but it was impossible to ignore the courage with which she had borne the long journey home. It had tempered his hostility with a grudging admiration.

'Have you eaten?' he asked. Rowenna shook her head. 'Sit down, then.' Kerin said. 'Marc, fetch more bread.' Rowenna sat, arranging the skirts of her dress carefully so that they covered all but the tips of her toes. She looked around her at the sea, the valley and the green hills.

'Will you like it here, do you think?' Kerin asked.

'It is beautiful,' Rowenna said. 'If you saw where I come from, you would understand why my father wants something better for his people.'

Kerin leaned forward. 'I hope you're not telling me that you want all this for your people.'

Rowenna's forehead creased. 'How can you say this?'

Kerin shrugged. 'Your father wanted Kent for them, didn't he?'

'Kent is different,' Rowenna said. 'And please, do not tell me that Kent is something to you. This is Vortigern's country. How could I wish anyone else to have it?'

'You love your father, don't you?' Kerin asked.

'Of course I do,' Rowenna said indignantly. 'I am Hengist's daughter, and he is a good father, even if you hate him. But now I am Vortigern's woman first. How could I betray him?'

'Easily,' Kerin said. 'Others have.'

'Then I spit on them,' Rowenna snapped. She too leaned forward, so that the tip of her nose almost touched Kerin's. 'I know what you think. I know what they say. They say I do this because it was good for my father to make this marriage. So, Vortigern is King of all the Britons. I can tell you, it is nothing for me. One day, you will see.' She leaned back again and folded her arms.

'What does that mean?' Kerin asked.

'I hope you never know,' Rowenna said. Her eyes moved to the closed door of the hall and a shadow crossed her face, slight but unmistakable.

'What?' Kerin asked. 'You've got what you wanted, surely.'

'Yes,' Rowenna said. 'But it is not what you think.'

Marc came out of Kerin's house with a wad of dough, shaped it into flat cakes and set them to cook on the baking stone. Rowenna peered past them into Morvid's pot.

'What is it?' she asked. Morvid, who had been listening silently, cleared his throat.

'A potion for the fever, my lady.'

'Vortigern has told me about you. You are the old man who heals the sick.'

'Well, I do what I can,' Morvid said. 'When it comes to things inside the body, Marcellus is your man. You haven't met him yet, have you. When you do, take good notice. He's got more knowledge in his little finger than most stupid arses have got in their heads, including me, more's the pity. But wounds and fever, I know about. My father taught me the herb lore. Some for bruises, some for dog's bite, some for battle damage. I could put a name to everything that grows around here.'

'Vortigern said you saved his arm,' Rowenna said. Morvid looked up.

'Did he, now. I assure you, that's not what he said to me when I was binding it up.' He chuckled and stirred the pot. 'No, indeed. He told me I was a horrible old bastard, and I should burn in hell with my pots and weeds.'

'Ah,' Rowenna said, 'but he tells me also that I am a heathen bitch, and I should go back home with my false gods. So please, teach me, Morvid.'

The old man looked at her blankly. 'Your pardon, my lady?'

'Teach me,' Rowenna said. 'Show me how to heal the sick and the wounded.'

Morvid frowned and scratched his head. 'I don't know about that. What would the king say?'

'The time may come when you will all thank me,' Rowenna said. 'And you will teach me, Morvid, or I swear I will have you sent home to get roasted with the pigs by Gael's father.'

Morvid raised his hands in resignation. 'Very well. But please don't blame me if Vortigern roasts both of us instead.'

Rowenna laughed. 'Come on, then, old man,' she said, jumping up.

'You haven't eaten your bread!' Kerin protested. Rowenna grabbed one of the hot loaves and skipped off down the grassy slope towards the valley.

'Come *on*, Morvid!' her impatient voice floated back. Morvid shambled off after her, muttering under his breath. Kerin got up, pulling Marc with him.

'Come on,' he said. 'It's Midsummer's Eve. Let's go and see how the druids' fires are getting on.'

They walked together down the steep, sandy road to the valley bottom. Even though many of its people would have described themselves as Christians if pressed, nothing in the church's calendar stirred them like the fire-festivals. The cornfields above the woods were deserted and the workshops were silent. A sweating procession was toiling up the steep path to the headland of Penrhyn Fawr. Some men were hauling branches large enough to have roofed a house. Children frolicked after them with armfuls of twigs. The archdruid Caradog was standing at the foot of the path, leaning on his oak staff and watching the proceedings with a critical eye.

'Hello there, Kerin Brightspear,' he said. 'Have you come to help us?'

'The *uchelwyr* don't carry wood,' Kerin said, trying to sound disdainful. Caradog shook his head.

'You're all the same,' he said. 'You sit up there and wave your little crosses, but you're glad enough to eat the bread when the corn grows.'

Kerin grinned. 'Do you really think it would die if you didn't light the fires?' he asked. Caradog folded his skinny arms.

'Shall we leave the fires unlit and find out?' he enquired. Kerin smiled uneasily. Caradog sniffed. 'No, I thought not. And before you ask, I know we usually keep the great fires for Calan Mai and Calan Gaeaf, but were you all here for Calan Mai and Calan Gaeaf? You were not. You were gallivanting in Londinium, or marching around the country killing Picts. So I decided that we should make a great fire for Midsummer's Eve too, to honour your return and ask for a blessing on the king's endeavours.' He picked up a stray branch and tossed it to Marc. 'Here. You're young and strong, and you live on his charity. Go on, before I find you a tree trunk.' Marc glared at him, shouldered the branch and started up the path. Caradog watched him go.

'Come with me for a moment, boy,' he said, patting Kerin's arm. They walked along the grassy track leading inland, until Caradog turned aside on a path which led steeply upwards through thickets of whitethorn. Kerin had never set foot on this path. Everyone knew that it led to holy places, forbidden to all but the initiated; the home of the priests, and the hallowed groves where they cast their circles and burned their sacred herbs. High up in the woods, the path levelled out on the rim of a hollow in the hillside. Tall oaks and ash-trees towered upwards, their green canopy casting a net of gleaming light down to the woodland floor. Trails of ivy and lichen hung from their branches like veils. A limestone crag bounded the hollow to the landward side, riven by gullies where ferns grew alongside tumbling waterfalls. Caradog smiled.

'The gods are bountiful,' he said. 'Do you blame us for keeping this to ourselves?' They went down into the hollow, where a group of youngsters in dark green robes had gathered beside a pool at the foot of the crag, washing clothes in the clear water. Caradog led Kerin to a bank cloaked in bright green moss.

'Well?' he said, as they sat. 'Is it true about Rufus? They say he's raised an army. That he's sworn to kill the Lord, and burn the Saxons – ' he squinted up at Kerin. 'You're his friend. Is it true?'

'Some of it is,' Kerin said. 'Rufus does have an army. Some are Christians, like he is. But most of them are there because they want a piece of Vortigern's power.'

Caradog stood up. 'Come. I have something to show you. If Rufus has any sense, he'll avoid starting a war against his father. But if it comes, we of the old faith will stand with you. And we have weapons of our own; not bloodletting weapons like the ones you warriors wield. Things which can freeze the blood and frighten men and beasts to their souls. Come.'

Kerin followed the archdruid to the foot of the crag. At the last moment a cave became visible; a black slash in the limestone. 'Wait,' Caradog said. 'This is holy ground. You may enter, but you must bring the sacred herbs. And it's dark, pitch dark, so I must light my lamp.' The darkness, all-enveloping only paces from the entrance, swallowed him entirely. Kerin heard the scratch of a flint. Caradwg came back, carrying a small, guttering oil lamp and a handful of greenery. 'Here,' he said, handing Kerin the leaves and twigs. 'Juniper and agrimony. Some eyebright, to protect you from malign spirits. Now, come with me.'

Kerin followed him into the deeper darkness within. The cave was narrow; he could easily have touched the walls on either side. Droplets of freezing water fell from an invisible ceiling. As the lamp threw its wavering light on the smooth rock, he saw pictures; beautiful, vivid pictures of running deer, boar and bison, some pursued by men with spears. Astonished, he stopped to gaze at them.

'Come,' Caradog said, touching his arm. 'These were

made by our ancestors and they have been here from the beginning of time, so they will surely be here when we come back. This is not what we have come to see.' They walked on. The cave sloped downwards and opened into a chamber whose size Kerin could only guess at. Caradog stopped and held out his lamp. 'There,' he said. 'In the corner, over there.' Kerin looked.

'My god!' he exclaimed, and stepped backwards. The thing was looking straight at him. A head, mounted on a slim wand of gleaming bronze; his own height at least, and possibly taller for it was leaning slightly forward, propped on a boulder which concealed its lower end. Water dripping from above in some earlier time had created a depression in which the neck rested. And the head – what was it, a serpent? A dragon? No, it was a boar. There was the snout, the bristled crest, the tusks set in a yawning mouth, the pricked ears. A monstrous boar, which looked as if it had every intention of eating him alive. Caradog chuckled and brought the oil lamp round.

'Well then, Kerin Brightspear, what do you think it is?'

'I don't know. Is it a battle standard, like the draco?'

'Oh no,' Caradog said. 'That thing has a voice. It can sing sweetly to the gods, but when it's angry, it's a thing of terror. A war horn. And it can make such a sound that men will think the gates of Annwn are opening before them. My old lungs can't make it speak, but Cynfawr and Cynan can do it. It's come down to them from their forefathers. The last time it spoke in anger, those men were fighting the Romans at the river. Afterwards they hid it here, for safekeeping. No-one knows about it but Cynfawr, Cynan and myself. Not even the Lord. One day we'll bring it out for all to see, but for now, keep it to yourself. It may be the only one of its kind remaining; most were destroyed, as far as we know, and who would make one now? Cynan comes in and cleans it now and again, just in case. Salt, flour and crab apple juice, I think.'

'Just in case?' Kerin asked.

'Just in case it's needed,' the archdruid said, eyes gleaming as brightly as the bronze. 'It's been waiting here, silent as the grave, all these years. And now its time is coming.'

Kerin reached out and, very gingerly, touched one of the beautiful pricked ears.

'Does it have a name?' he asked.

'Oh yes,' Caradog said. 'This is the carnyx.'

3

Kerin galloped his horse across the beach, scattering flocks of oystercatchers. After his encounter with the carnyx, he needed fresh air to clear his thoughts. It seemed incredible that a thing like that could make enough noise to frighten a Roman legion. Having no musical bent, Kerin found it impossible to imagine anything beyond the military trumpets he had heard in Londinium. Harsh and ear-piercing, but hardly enough to upset a soldier, or even a moderately well-trained horse. He wondered if Caradog was getting carried away.

Eryr was running like a youngster. Kerin had rested her on the way home, letting Blaidd take the strain; but the younger horse might have to face his first battle before long, and needed to save his strength. It was a pleasure for Kerin to be riding his old companion, but another horse was foremost in his mind this morning. A newcomer; a beautiful brown filly bred by Gwyndaf. She was hidden in Gwynfi's barn behind the woollen mill, and Kerin sneaked over there every day to talk to her and lead her around on a halter. She would be his marriage gift to Gael, although of course that was a secret. He turned inland towards the steep path which skirted the monks' wood, emerging high above on the lower slopes of Crib Garw. There he pulled Eryr to a halt. Out on the windswept hillside where the dead of Henfelin were laid to rest, a grey horse was grazing.

The Pike raised his head and whinnied to his half-sister.

Vortigern was sitting on a grassy bank, staring forlornly at the place where they had buried Sevira. There was not much to see; a cairn of smooth pale grey stones gathered from the beach and a simple limestone cross with no inscription, just a finely etched image of a little bird rising on outstretched wings. Vortigern did not turn as Kerin's footsteps came crunching towards him through the dry grass.

'Do you think she's angry with me?' he asked. Kerin sat down on the bank beside him, all misgivings submerged by compassion, at least for now.

'Of course not, lord,' he said. 'Sevira loved you more than life; everyone says so. She couldn't possibly be angry with you. And you know, if I were to die, I hope that after a while Gael would find herself some good, strong man who'd love her and look after her for the rest of her days. I couldn't wish anything else, loving her as I do.'

Vortigern looked round. 'Suppose he was a handsome pagan half her age?'

Kerin experienced a momentary twinge, grappled it down and laughed. 'Then I'd wish her joy of him,' he said, and found that, much to his own surprise, he meant it from his heart. Vortigern reached across and cuffed him over the head.

'Come on,' he sighed. 'I need a jar of ale.'

They whistled up their horses and rode down from the cliff, across the beach and inland to the alehouse beside the river. For as long as anyone could remember, Vortigern had made a habit of arriving there unannounced from time to time, to drink alongside his people. No-one remarked upon it; it was as natural to them as going to bed at night, and all the other mundane details of their safe, well-protected lives. Only when Kerin went to Londinium and became acquainted with leaders like Garagon of Kent and Severus Maximus did he realise that it was unheard of amongst men of power.

The alehouse was doing a brisk trade for the time of day. Most of the labourers and craftsmen had finished work early, on the pretext of helping to build the fire. There was a flurry of respectful greetings as the king and his companion arrived, and everyone at the benches outside moved up to make room. Their ponies and mules also moved up, with even greater nervousness and speed, to accommodate the warhorses. Caradog was sitting at the nearest table with the bard Cynfawr and his son, the druid Cynan. Next to them sat curly-headed Gwynfi the weaver and a bunch of his workmen, alongside a table crammed with tanners and horse boys. The bench by the door was an all-female affair where Mabli was holding court, regaling her companions with a tale both hilarious and filthy, judging by their shrieks of laughter.

Vortigern beckoned the landlord and spoke quietly to him before he and Kerin sat down with the bard and the priests. The general merriment went up a notch, because all the drinkers knew what happened when the Lord honoured them with his presence. Jugs of ale and cider began arriving on the tables, along with extra tankards for the new arrivals as word spread and the crowd swelled. Everyone drank to the victory in the North, to the spirits of those who had died, and to the courage of those who had survived; then Gwynfi the weaver climbed up onto his table and proposed a toast to the king's marriage, in all sincerity as far as Kerin could tell, although Gwynfi and his workforce were devout Christians most of the time and might have been expected to have some misgivings.

Everyone drank, nobody gave a fig, and even Kerin, for all his doubts, found himself wishing that Rowenna had been there to see it.

'It's a good fire,' Vortigern said. 'The biggest I've seen in years.'

'We thought perhaps you might need an extra benediction, lord,' Cynan said, smiling. He was startlingly like his father. The same pale blue eyes and fine, strong features; the same tendency to look absent on occasions, as if they inhabited another world entirely. Cynfawr's flowing locks were snow-white; his son's remained iron-grey. That was the only notable difference, give or take a few wrinkles.

'What with everything those Christians are up to,' Caradog could not resist adding. Vortigern sighed.

'Look, let's be clear. I have no quarrel with the Christians. They can believe what they like, as long as they don't try to foist it on the rest of you. But they shouldn't mix faith with politics. And if anyone else says anything else to stop me enjoying this jar of ale, I'm going to throw him in the river.'

He had spoken just loudly enough for the words to carry. There was a silence, punctuated by a few nervous chuckles, before all the merry conversations resumed. Mabli fell off the end of her bench, as if someone had given her a shove. She picked herself up and came skipping over.

'Hello, Mabli,' Vortigern said. 'What can I do for you, then?'

Mabli smiled shyly. 'Lord,' she said, 'the women are wondering. Should we call you "Lord King", now that you are one?'

'Not if you know what's good for you,' Vortigern said. 'Do you respect me any more than you did before?'

'No, lord,' Mabli said. 'That wouldn't be possible.'

'Good. We'll keep things as they are, then. Now, what

else do you want to ask? There is something else, I'm sure.'

Mabli's cheeks turned a delicate shade of rose. 'Lord, the women are asking, are you going to have a wedding feast?'

'No, Mabli. I'm sorry to disappoint you all, but neither of us wants one. Someone else will have to have one instead. When are you going to marry that no-good Derfyn?'

Mabli lowered her eyes. 'When he asks me, lord,' she sighed.

'Is that so? Well then, tell him this. Tell him that the church has given a special dispensation to the King of all the Britons allowing him to take two wives, and that if he doesn't marry you soon, you might not be there for the asking.'

Mabli's eyes opened as wide as plates, then a great gale of laughter arose, finding its way out as a stifled snort. 'If he's stupid enough to believe that, lord, then he'll probably be stupid enough to marry me.'

'He'll be stupid if he doesn't,' Vortigern said. 'Now go and tell those twittering birds what I said, and leave me in peace.'

Mabli tripped off to rejoin the women. A chorus of shrieks and giggles arose as she shared her news. The ale flowed, and Cynfawr began to sing in his deep, melodious bass; not one of his own hymns of battle and glory, but a simple love song, which the valley people had been singing for as long as Kerin could remember. A horse was coming. The grey colt came weaving through the houses, scattering chickens, dogs and children. Marc jumped off and elbowed his way to Kerin's table.

'Lord, riders in the valley,' he said.

'Who?' Kerin asked.

'Eldof of Glevum and three warriors,' Marc said, catching his breath. 'They're carrying a flag of truce.'

Kerin's eyes met Vortigern's. Already, so soon, it was time to put on the mantle he had laid aside for a few blessed weeks. 'Stay here, lord,' he said. 'I can deal with this.'

Lud looked up from sharpening his sword and frowned. Gael came out of the house, blinking in the bright sunlight.

'Eldof,' Kerin said, hurrying her back inside. 'Coming down the valley with three warriors.'

Gael started. 'My father?'

'I don't know.' Lud came in, buckling his sword-belt. 'Eldof,' Kerin said. 'With three warriors, carrying a truce-flag.'

Lud snorted. 'He isn't that brave or stupid on his own. Rufus is behind this.' He took Gael's arm. 'Come and stay with Mora and my girls.'

'Go on,' Kerin said, kissing her forehead. 'They won't pass us.' He put on his sword-belt, grabbed his spear and went outside. The riders had reached the foot of the hill. At least Bertil Redknife was not one of them. Eldof had brought his young son, Tullius, and two regular warriors. They rode up the track and stopped outside the hall. The Henfelin boys swarmed around as Kerin and Lud stepped forward.

'Where is Vortigern?' Eldof demanded. Drumming hooves answered his question. The crowd parted and closed ranks again as horse and rider passed through.

'Eldof, you're not welcome here,' Vortigern said. 'I respect the truce-flag, but I don't respect it that much, so say your piece and get out.'

Eldof braced his shoulders. 'First, there's something you should know. Macsen, Lud's son, and Hefin of Carneddlas have been taken. If we don't return safely, they'll hang as surely as the sun will set tonight.' Lud's fists clenched. A sound rumbled in his throat like an animal's growl. 'We're not jesting,' Eldof snapped.

'We?' Vortigern asked. 'Who are we?'

'I speak for the lords of the Britons,' Eldof said pompously. 'We crowned you King. It was a dark hour, we did as we thought best. But you invited a band of heathen savages into our country. You gave them land, you married one of their kind –'

'Enough.' Vortigern drew his sword and raised the point to Eldof's throat. 'I will say this once, and once only. Hengist came at *our* invitation, not mine alone. Titus Luca holds the document, signed by you all.'

Eldof blinked but did not flinch. 'What should we have done, then?' he said indignantly. 'We'd just made you king. Should we not have done our king's bidding?'

Vortigern began to laugh. He lowered the sword. 'Eldof, you did that very well,' he said. Eldof frowned. An uncertain little smile flickered. A yelp of surprise followed as Vortigern's sword flashed out and sliced off the tip of his bushy red beard. 'Now say your piece. I know you've come from Vortimer, so tell me what he wants and get out of my sight.'

Eldof fingered his chin and took a breath. 'Very well. You betrayed our trust, so we've asked your son to be king in your place. To lead us in the fight for Kent and the Christian faith.'

'Vortimer, king?' Vortigern said incredulously. 'You've asked that young crack-brain to be king?'

'Yes, we have. And there can only be one King of all the Britons. We've come to ask you to swear allegiance. Do it, and no harm will come to you or your people. But refuse, and I swear that when we've finished with the Saxons, we'll cross the Hafren and burn this hell-hole from here to the Eryri.'

'Never!' Lud bellowed. 'We owe allegiance to Vortigern, and to no other man!' The Cambrian warriors roared agreement and shook their swords.

'Never on God's earth,' Vortigern breathed. Eldof glanced apprehensively at the advancing men.

'A word with you in private,' he said, dismounting. He nodded to his son, Vortigern beckoned Kerin and they all went into the chieftains' hall. Eldof flung his sword down.

'Enough of this,' he spat. 'You don't want to fight your own sons, any more than I would.'

'What do you want me to do, then? Crawl to my son? Hang my wife's father?'

'Renounce the kingship and swear allegiance,' Eldof said. 'It's all we ask.'

All? Kerin thought. After the blood and risk and sacrifice of the North, it's all? He stepped forward and stood between the two men. It was done without thought. He had no idea what he would say or do. All he knew was that, bubbling away inside him like molten metal, was the same raging anger which had shocked him rigid in Londinium. This time he knew where it was coming from, and he had mastered it. He was standing so close to Eldof that he could feel the other man's rancid breath on his face.

'You miss the point,' he said softly. Droplets of sweat began appearing on Eldof's brow. 'You don't know what you're talking about,' he blustered.

'Oh, but I do. You speak for the high-born. For wealthy men with blood horses and fine houses. But you don't speak for robbers' bastards like me. And you don't speak for the people in the fields and the foundries and the corn-mills and the smiths' workshops, who outnumber you a thousand to one. So know this. If Vortigern crawled on his knees from here to Kent and kissed his son's arse, he would still be king in the hearts of all those people. The kingship isn't up to you. It isn't even up to the king. It's up to them.'

Eldof gaped. Having no response, he ignored everything Kerin had said and turned to his well-prepared speech. 'It was the new king's wish that you should have a day and a night's grace,' he blurted. 'If you accept, light a beacon on Crib Garw at midnight tomorrow. If we don't see it, there will be war between us from that hour.'

Vortigern smiled briefly, picked up Eldof's sword and handed it to him. 'In that case, Eldof, you'd better take this home and start sharpening it.'

'This is not what I want!' Eldof shouted, slamming the sword into its sheath.

'Of course it's what you want,' Vortigern said witheringly. 'You've been aching for this since the day the Romans left, but you've never had the nerve to take me on. Now Rufus has given you the excuse, and he's too blind to see it. Get out of my sight. There's no more to be said.'

'Oh, but there is,' Eldof said, popping with indignation. 'Bertil Redknife's daughter. Ten good men are dead because of this woman.'

'Leave it,' Kerin said. 'The woman's my wife now, and she's here of her own free will.'

'Enough,' Vortigern said. 'What's your price for Macsen and Hefin?'

'Safe conduct to the Hafren,' Eldof said. 'Once we're back in Glevum, I'll send a rider to Kent and they'll be released.'

Vortigern smiled and patted Eldof's son on the shoulder. 'Well, I think you mean it. But just to make sure, I'll keep this fine young man here until I know they're safe.'

Eldof started. 'No! For all I know, you'll lop his head off as soon as my back's turned.'

'And then they'll butcher Macsen and Hefin. Don't be a fool, Eldof.'

'I'll stay, father,' Tullius said, sounding far more confident than he looked.

Eldof threw his hands up. 'Alright. Keep your word, and I'll keep mine. But harm a hair on this boy's head, and on the holy cross I'll kill every last one of you.' He embraced his son and stalked out of the hall. Lud was waiting outside.

'Eldof's son is staying here until we get Macsen and Hefin back,' Vortigern said. 'Guard him well. No-one lays a hand on him. And see that these three treacherous bastards get safe conduct to the river.'

Eldof mounted his warhorse as Bened marched Tullius away and Lud picked the escort. The other warriors dispersed. Mora peered curiously from her doorway, blithely unaware of what had happened to her son. A voice echoed from the valley, sweet and clear on the warm wind. Rowenna came up the path, carrying a basket of herbs and flag irises on her arm. A child was skipping at her side; one of Lud's little granddaughters. Rowenna waved gaily. The wind lifted her fine hair and rippled her dress of soft grey Henfelin wool. She was singing her song of ships and the sea. For a moment, Vortigern forgot himself and smiled. The child reached up to clasp Rowenna's hand. She took one of the irises and fixed it in the child's hair. A horse whickered and stamped. She looked up and saw Eldof, and the song died.

'So,' Eldof said, alight with curiosity. 'This is the price of Garagon's inheritance.'

Rowenna kissed the top of the little girl's head and sent her to Mora. She stood in front of Eldof's tall warhorse and looked up at him. 'Who are you?' she asked suspiciously.

'This is Eldof of Glevum,' Vortigern said. 'And I'll tell

you why he's here. He wants me to swear allegiance to my son, the new King of all the Britons.'

Rowenna moved round to the shoulder of Eldof's horse. She did not look at all afraid of him, Kerin thought, although perhaps as things stood she should have been.

'Is this true?' she asked.

'Yes, it's true,' Eldof said, with unveiled contempt.

'Then I spit on you, Eldof of Glevum,' Rowenna hissed.

'Spit all you like,' Eldof said, with an ugly scowl. 'Your husband lost more than Kent when he took you to his bed.' Rowenna folded her arms calmly. She looked fearsomely unmoved by Eldof's attempt to frighten her.

'You are not fit to kiss the ground under his feet,' she said; then she turned her back and glided away into the hall. Eldof gathered his horse's reins.

'Come on, lads,' he said grimly. 'They're even madder here than I thought.'

Vortigern and Kerin stood at the top of the track and watched them ride away with their escort. Rowenna came out of the hall, still clutching her basket.

'Have they really made Rufus king?' she asked.

'Some of them have,' Vortigern said. 'In truth they're far fewer than the people who are loyal to me, but they're all in one place, and ready to fight at any time. My men are scattered all over the kingdom now. We probably have days to prepare. So perhaps you are no longer married to a king, as your father intended.' Rowenna took the irises from her basket and held them out to him. Vortigern frowned. 'I don't want these things.'

'A gift for the king,' Rowenna said. Vortigern looked down at the fragile yellow blooms.

'For the king? I told you what Eldof said.'

'I would not waste my time even to piss on Eldof,'

Rowenna said. 'But a gift for the brigand chief, if you like it better.' She shoved the irises into Vortigern's hands and went back into the hall. Vortigern picked up the Pike's reins.

'Where are you going?' Kerin asked.

'To Carneddlas, to tell Hefydd and his boys. Hefydd's no blood-drinker but Hefin is the man's only brother, he loves the air he breathes. And Hefin's wife, of course. With child after all these years, for God's sake.' He passed Kerin the irises. 'Here, give these to your woman. Do you believe what you said to Eldof?'

'Yes. With my heart and soul. But everything you said was true, too. Our loyal men are scattered everywhere. It would take months to rally them, and half of them are healing battle wounds. Some of Rufus's men are too, but I can promise you he was telling the truth about reinforcements. Paulinus and his friends in Gallia will have seen to that. And we'll have to fight with what we've got. Send to Gorlois and Lucius, by all means, but by the time they get here it may be too late.'

Vortigern looked out across the valley and the fields beyond, where tall green corn rippled and sleek-coated cattle grazed in the warm sun, switching flies.

'There's much to lose here, Kerin,' he said. 'Much to lose.'

Kerin could feel everything he had fought to preserve beginning to sag and slip. You'd let it all go if you could, he thought. The crown, the power; all worth less than a single day of peace in this blessed green valley. 'Lord,' he said, 'you know what would happen if you gave them what they want.'

'Yes, I do,' Vortigern sighed. 'They'd kill Rufus, once he'd outlived his usefulness. Then they'd all start cutting each other's throats. It would be just as it was before I became king. A few thousand stupid bastards too busy fighting each other to notice Hengist burning his way across the country. So we'll meet tonight. Summon them all. The leaders, the warriors, everyone down to the craftsmen and labourers. It's as you said. The kingship is up to men like them. They made me King of all the Britons. So let them choose.' He retrieved a single iris, twisted it round the stallion's browband and swung into the saddle. Kerin watched him go until the Pike was a pale speck on the lower slopes of Crib Garw. The door of Lud's house opened and Gael came out. He had come to know the look she had about her; composure hiding a deeper pain which only her eyes betrayed.

'Lud told us about Macsen and Hefin,' she said.

'Did he say what it would mean?'

'No. But he didn't have to. When will you leave?'

'I don't know,' Kerin said, drawing her close. 'We're meeting tonight to decide what to do.' He supposed that it must be hard for Gael to know what to say, when Rufus was no more than a name to her. 'Come on,' he said. 'Come in the house.'

Gael sat down at the table beside the fire. Kerin brought mugs and a flask of the sharp cider Mora brewed every autumn.

'I haven't met Hefin's wife,' Gael said. 'Does she have women around her, to care for her? Mora said she's with child. Is she a strong girl, to bear with this?'

'I don't know,' Kerin said. 'Hefin's a friend, we've ridden together in the warband for years, but Tirion's a quiet girl. Warm and friendly, but she's not like Mabli, laughing and chattering away with the other women. I'd say she's more like you.'

'Then I will go to her,' Gael said. 'Tomorrow morning. I'll take Marc and Ashur, otherwise you'll worry, won't you.'

'Yes,' Kerin said. 'You can be sure of that.'

'Does Rufus hate his father?'

'I doubt it,' Kerin said.

'He fought him, though. Would he have killed him, if he could?'

'Probably, in the heat of the fight. Whether he could kill in cold blood, I've no idea. You'd better ask God. That's what Rufus does.'

Gael folded her hands and studied them. 'Does it trouble you, that Rowenna and I have become friends?' she asked. Kerin was taken aback. It was not a question he had expected.

'Why raise this now?'

'Because I believe that it does trouble you,' Gael said. 'And because thinking about Rufus and his father made me wonder what's to be done, when love for one – whether a father or someone else, or even God – is at war with love for another.'

Kerin placed his hands over hers. 'Sometimes it means making a choice,' he said. 'That's what Rufus did, and for him the choice was simple. Painful, probably, but simple. Nothing before God. For that, he was prepared to sacrifice his place with his father. His friendship with me. But of course, it's not always simple.' Here he paused, because the memory seared him still. 'When I first told Vortigern about you – or rather, when I told him who your father is – I thought it was the end of everything. I'd picked a bad moment. I hadn't told him as well as I might have done. He absolutely forbade me to have you. I told him that nothing would stop me. I thought I'd have to choose between our marriage and my place with him. It took a much wiser man than I am, to make me see that it was not so. That there was a way to deal with things. So perhaps this is the same. You know I can't be easy with Rowenna, because I see her father's hand in everything. I believe that Hengist will betray us one day. And at the moment, I can't separate Rowenna from it.'

He felt Gael's fingers tighten around his. She bent her head to kiss his hands.

'Perhaps I see things in her which you don't see,' she said.

'It wouldn't surprise me,' Kerin said. 'And I don't expect to choose your friends, any more than I'd let you choose mine. But please, because she's Hengist's daughter, be careful.'

'And are you careful, because I'm Bertil's daughter?' Gael enquired. 'Do you think I'm an instrument of some grievous plan, nestling here like a little viper in the warm nest you've built for me?'

'No!' Kerin exclaimed. 'I hope – well, I believe – that you're here because you love me. And for no other reason.'

Gael withdrew her hands and smiled. 'Well, then,' she said gravely, and sipped her cider. Kerin found that he had nothing further to ask her. He was not even sure what the question should be. There was within her a depth of wisdom, profound, glowing like embers, whose edges he could barely touch. She would never ask him what his choice would have been.

4

'It's time,' Lud said. 'The sun's down. They're all here. The warriors, the priests, the people, everyone.'

'I'm sorry, Dimos,' Kerin said, as Lud marched out. 'My mind wasn't on our work today.'

'Not to worry, lord,' the scribe said. 'There'll be other days. And your progress has been remarkable.' He looked up. 'I saw what happened this morning with Lord Eldof. I find it all incomprehensible, to be truthful. Sometimes men don't know they're born.' He gave a sad smile and gathered his writing materials. Kerin buckled on his sword belt and followed Lud towards the hall. Warriors were spilling out through the door and people from the valley were jostling around outside, filling the gaps between the houses. Vortigern was pacing the dark passageway which ran the length of his private quarters. One look was enough to tell Kerin how things had gone at Carneddlas.

'What did they say?' he asked.

'What do you think? They'd ride to Kent tonight, if I let them. Hefydd was charging around like a mad bull, ranting about slaughter and revenge. For God's sake, Hefydd, of all people.'

Lud came in. 'It's getting hot out there,' he said. 'And Hefydd's stoking the fire. He looks ready to kill Brwyn.'

They rushed out into the main hall. The warriors had forced their way in until there was barely space to breathe.

Hefydd had Brwyn by the collar. He was unlikely to meet much resistance from Idris's father, who had been crippled with back pain for years.

'Any man who says he's going to hang my brother is my blood enemy!' he yelled. 'He can be Jesus Christ's son, for all I care.'

A rowdy chorus of agreement came from the warriors on the right-hand side of the hall. Kerin saw that Gwyndaf was amongst them. Vortigern pushed the two men apart, drew his dagger and hurled it at one of the massive oak roof supports. It lodged, quivering. The commotion subsided. Vortigern leapt onto the table.

'We have a choice,' he said, to the suffocating silence. 'Eldof and his lackeys have set Rufus up as king. They want me to renounce the kingship and swear allegiance. They say that if I agree, they'll leave us in peace. If I refuse, we can ride to Kent and make a fight of it, or we can stay here and wait for them to try and burn us out. You all know that I granted land in Kent to Hengist the Jute, when I married his daughter. The Jutes at least fought bravely with us in the North, but Garagon of Kent ran away like a scared rabbit, and his uncle Edlym refused to give a single denarius to our defence. And now Rufus has thrown in his lot with these shameless bastards. Be in no doubt, they have men and weapons, and will fight. And now they've captured Macsen and Hefin, and say they'll hang them if I refuse their terms. Macsen, son of Lud, my chief warrior. Hefin, the rock of my warband, brother of our loyal man Hefydd. The two men I sent to Kent with fifty of our finest, simply to keep the peace and see that my word is respected.'

'Blood!' Elir growled 'Blood of the bastards who want to hang my brother Macsen!'

'Calm it down, boy,' Brwyn protested. 'Rufus won't

hang his own. Do you want to see Cambria burning from end to end?'

'I'd like to see you burning from end to end, you gutless old coward,' Hefydd snorted. 'My brother's head is in a noose. A man who's fought for this land since he was old enough to lift a sword. And his wife Tirion about to bear their first child, after fifteen years of waiting.'

Brwyn began to weep. 'Lord, I'm a Christian in the ordinary way,' he stammered. 'Not like my boy, Idris. I know he's with Rufus's bunch of hotheads. The Sword of God, indeed. And now I've had to lock up my youngest to stop him coming here, because they've got at him, too. But it would break my heart to fight our lads.'

Lud reached for Vortigern's arm. 'Lord, please. Macsen's my son. You can't abandon him.'

Vortigern glanced around the hall. His eyes rested on the archdruid Caradog and his chosen successor, Cynan.

'Well, priests?' he said sharply. The archdruid coughed and stood up.

'Lord, we can't be ruled by those upstarts,' he said.

'You're only saying that because Rufus is a Christian, you old goat,' a voice shrilled. A thin lad with a shaven head and a scar bisecting his right cheek. Kerin had to look twice. Brwyn's younger son, Aron, had possessed a full head of black hair when he marched for Hadrian's Wall.

'Didn't lock him up too well, did you,' someone said. Caradog swelled with fury.

'Old goat?' he roared. 'The same old goat your brother begged to admit him to the sacred order?'

'He was deluded!' Aron protested. 'God came to me in the North, on the eve of the battle.'

'Aron,' Cynan said gently, 'I think you'll find that all men's gods came to them on the eve of the battle, whichever gods they called on.'

Aron threw his hands up. 'But there's only one! Only one god! And that's what Rufus and Idris are fighting for!'

'For the Christianity of the Empire,' Caradog said scornfully. He squinted up at Vortigern. 'They'll have the Romans back here tomorrow, you see if they don't.'

'The Romans washed their hands of this place years ago,' Vortigern said impatiently.

'Tell Ambrosius that,' the archdruid said. 'The young brother they wanted for king, instead of Constans the monk. What do they say? His family wears the purple?'

'Lord, please!' Lud murmured. His son Elir barged past him.

'Blood! Kill the savages who'd hang their own countrymen!'

'Kill!' the warriors roared, and the roar resolved itself into a continuous deafening chant. They rattled their swords and stamped their feet, and Kerin's blood screamed *Kill!* along with them, while the spectre of his love for Rufus choked the words in his throat. Vortigern stared at the stamping, chanting mob. There was a disturbance by the main door. Abbot Iustig forced his way through the crowd and stood panting in front of the table. Kerin hoped that the abbot, if anyone, should be able to speak for the Christians in his own community. At the moment, some of those Christians seemed barely able to speak to each other.

'So,' Vortigern said. 'The old buzzard has come down from his perch.'

'This is no time for mockery,' Iustig said. 'Come down from there, and hear me.'

Vortigern gave a cynical laugh, but he came down from the table. 'Well, what do you want?' he asked. 'How can a man of God come near a black-hearted sinner like me?'

Iustig folded his arms. 'All the more reason.'

'Aha! It's repentance you're after, then.'

'It's never too late for that,' Iustig said. Vortigern's face darkened.

'Then what should I repent, Iustig? How far back shall we go?'

'Constans?' Iustig suggested. 'The poor wretch you made king so you could grab the crown off his head?'

'Constans?' Vortigern said, in disgust. 'I've killed better men than him for less reason, and you haven't raised an eyebrow.'

'Constans was a monk and a servant of God,' Iustig said obdurately.

'Constans was a monk because his father could think of nothing else to do with him. You'll have to do better than that, Iustig.'

'The woman, then,' Iustig said. 'The pagan woman you've taken to your bed against all the laws of the holy church.'

'The woman,' Vortigern sighed. 'I thought we'd come to that. Well, Iustig, what do you want me to do? Hang her? Take a good Christian wife?'

'You know what I want,' Iustig said. 'But you'll do what you like, whatever I say, and there are worse things upon us tonight than the fate of one man's soul.'

'Throw him out, lord!' Hefydd bawled. 'He wants us to kneel to Rufus.'

'I do not,' Iustig retorted. 'I want no man to kneel to anyone but his Creator. But for the love of God, Vortigern, do what Rufus wants. Swear allegiance and let him have his way in Kent. Is your pride more important than the lives of these people?'

Gwyndaf, who had been listening with head bowed, suddenly looked up and smiled. 'Swear allegiance, lord! Every village has its warriors, but only Henfelin has a man who'd kneel to his own son.'

Vortigern flew for his sword. Iustig leapt between him and Gwyndaf. 'This is madness!' the abbot shouted.

'Get out of my way, Iustig,' Vortigern breathed. 'I'm not averse to killing the odd monk, as you've been happy to tell everyone.' The abbot seized his sword-arm and hung on like a terrier. Gwyndaf's lips tightened.

'Keep out of this, abbot,' he murmured. Iustig released his grip.

'Vortigern, hear me. I've known you from your cradle. I've ministered to your people, and I've never wanted any reward because it was God's work. But if it's meant anything to you, then please, don't go to Kent. Don't make war on Rufus. Nothing can justify that.'

Vortigern looked hard at him, and the flame of anger sank to a dull glow. 'Iustig, I know how much you love my son,' he said. 'But he'll never be Lord of the West while I live.'

'He won't fight you on this side of the river!' Iustig exclaimed.

'Yes, he will,' Kerin said. Vortigern turned. His lips framed an incredulous question.

'Lord, you can't leave Macsen to die,' Lud said, his voice rough with tears.

'Blood!' Elir bellowed. 'Blood, for the life of my brother and the honour of Henfelin!' The warriors took up the cry, and the sound swelled until the timbers of the hall shook to the stamp of feet and the howls of 'Blood!' Vortigern stared at Kerin. His eyes glowed with the unnatural brightness of fever.

'Go, then!' Iustig cried, in a rage of desperation. 'Have your blood. But it's the blood of Sevira's sons. You've spat on her memory; isn't that enough for you?' Vortigern's reply died in mid breath. He turned and fought his way through the chanting crowd. Kerin plunged after him, but reached the door too late. He felt the rush of wind in his face and heard the thunder of hooves as the pale horse flew past him into the darkness. The abbot arrived beside him.

'Damn you, Iustig!' Kerin shouted. 'Why that?'

'I'd say anything if I thought it would stop this.' Iustig looked quite unrepentant. Kerin turned, and found himself face to face with Gwyndaf.

'Are you pleased with yourself?' he roared.

'No!' Gwyndaf said. 'I feel like dog dirt, for what it's worth.'

Kerin left them in the hall and ran through the houses to the gap in the rampart. Dusk had given way to one of the darkest nights he had known. There was no moon, not even a star. The wind had died and the air was stifling. Kerin stared down into the black pit of the valley. They were lighting the torches already; he could see little blobs of light swimming in procession round the pasture. Caradog came out of the darkness on his red pony. He was carrying a great torch of willow-rods dipped in tallow, and his eyes gleamed crazily in its flaring light.

'What's passed, Kerin Brightspear?' he croaked. 'I just saw the Lord, riding like a madman for the sea.' They turned as a crowd of warriors came yelling and brawling out of the hall. 'Come on, lads!' the druid shouted. 'To the fires!' He shook his torch, and sparks showered down to the bare earth.

'To the fires!' voices echoed. Kerin looked at the warriors in dismay. Their blood was up and most of them were drunk. They ran to fetch the torches which lit their houses. Aron stumbled out of the hall, white-faced. Kerin saw that the scar extended over the crown of his head. Someone must have shaved it bald, to deal with the wound.

'Ha!' Caradog cackled. 'So much for the cross of Christ.'

Aron clenched his fist. 'Burn in hell, you old fool.'

Caradog stared up into the black windless air. 'Keep your puny hell, young Aron,' he murmured. 'The powers are abroad tonight, and your hell is like one of these little sparks falling from their great torch.' Aron seized his thin arm; then they heard hoofbeats. 'The Lord?' Caradog said.

'No,' Kerin said, straining eyes and ears in the darkness. The horse came up the steep track at the gallop. It was a dun mare, and she was spent. As she passed through the gateway her knees buckled. Her rider was thrown clear as she rolled on her side, flanks heaving. Bloody saliva trickled from her gaping jaws. Kerin seized the rider and turned him onto his back.

'Lucius! he exclaimed. Lucius Arrius's face was filthy and his breath came in harsh sobs. Kerin helped him to sit up. Lucius sank his head between his knees. 'God, what's happened? Where have you come from?'

'Londinium,' Lucius gasped. 'I've ridden for days and nights.' They both glanced sideways as the mare shuddered and died. 'Publius Luca sent me,' Lucius said bleakly. 'Kerin, they've hanged Hefin.'

Kerin stared down at him. 'Who?' he asked, aghast. 'Who did it?'

'Rufus's people,' Lucius said, coughing violently. Kerin heard Caradog muttering behind his back. Lucius's eyelids flickered and half closed.

'Macsen!' Kerin exclaimed, shaking him mercilessly.

'Alive. Things were getting out of hand. Publius sent us to sort it out. They tricked us. It was a trap. Oswi the Horseman got me out, I owe him my life.'

Elir ran out of the darkness, carrying a torch. He stopped short when he saw the dead horse.

'Traitors' work!' Caradog crowed. 'You'd better know that Rufus and his cronies have hanged Hefin. No doubt your brother will be next.'

Elir's lips twisted. 'What must be done?'

The archdruid gazed up into the blackness above. 'Blood calls for blood,' he murmured. 'We ask much of the powers tonight.'

Elir flung down his torch and ran. Mora came out of her house and looked in horror at the dead mare. Kerin jumped up and seized her arms.

'Macsen's alive,' he said.

'Oh, thank the gods!' Mora whispered. 'And Hefin?'

'Mora, they've hanged Hefin,' Kerin said. He felt a shudder run through Mora's stout frame. 'Please, look after my friend Lucius. He's ridden all the way from Londinium. And tell Gael what's happened. She means to visit Tirion in the morning. God knows what she'll find.'

Mora nodded dumbly and helped Lucius to his feet. Kerin ran for the gateway, fear growing within him. Elir had vanished. The citadel was alive. Men were running in all directions, waving swords and firebrands. The flames streamed behind them like wild hair as they rushed from house to house, rousing friends and families. Hefydd came out of the shadows with a dagger in his hand. He was laughing and weeping all at once, and his eyes were mad with bloodlust.

'To the fires!' Elir's voice, somewhere over by the rampart. Kerin made for the horse pens where a bay mare was standing by the rail, ready saddled. Leaping onto her back, he rode down into the valley and along the riverbank. The sea, Caradog had said; the sea. Fires were burning on the edge of the pasture. Little black figures were dancing in the pools of light around them to the dull, monotonous beat of a skin drum. The sound throbbed in Kerin's brain as the mare galloped on. From the corner of his eye he could see a procession of torches wavering up towards the head of Penrhyn Fawr. He crossed the river and skirted the sandhills. As his eyes became accustomed to the pitch darkness he saw the trail, leading away along the firm, pale beach to the water's edge, where hoof prints melted into wet sand. Behind his back he could hear men shouting and cattle bellowing in terror as they were herded towards the fires of purification. The tide was rising, lapping the foot of Penrhyn Fawr. Kerin gritted his teeth and drove the mare into the sea. She was wading belly-deep by the time they reached the headland. As they passed beneath its shadow the great fire burst into life high above them, and a roar went up from the men who had carried the torches.

The darkness beneath the trees was impenetrable. The mare stumbled up the rocky path. High on Penrhyn Fawr the fire was blazing, its flickering light dancing eerily in the high branches overhead. The confused shouting of the torch-bearers had resolved itself into a mesmeric chant. The clearing outside the monks' chapel was bathed in a dull glow, as if by some shifting orange moonlight. The mare whinnied loudly and a horse answered her. Kerin dismounted and crept to the door. His hands shook as he eased it open and slipped inside. The cold air made him shiver. Slivers of light flickered through the tiny windows. He trod warily forward, then his blinking eyes became accustomed to the darkness. He stared mutely at the stark cross and at the dark form lying prostrate on the flagstones before Iustig's altar. He felt a hand on his arm. He spun round, seized the intruder and forced him into one of the pools of fractured light. Marc's white face stared up at him. Kerin bundled the boy outside and slammed the door. Marc was shaking with terror.

'Lord,' he gasped, 'they're burning Eldof's son.'

'Oh God,' Kerin whispered. In four strides he was across the clearing and on the mare's back. He rode at a crazy gallop across the headlands. The chanting rushed to meet him, rising above the roar of the flames. Most of the women had come up to the headland with their men, and they had all formed a circle round the fire, a sea of fire-brands and flashing swords. Gael and Rowenna were there with the village girls. Caradog was standing on a huge flat stone, oak staff raised above his head, oblivious to the searing heat which was singeing his wild hair and scorching his skin. Iustig was at the foot of the stone, bellowing and waving a rough wooden cross while Brother Padarn and Cynan tried to remonstrate with him. Kerin elbowed his way through the crowd. Six warriors were parading round the fire, led by Elir and Dull Bened. On their shoulders they were carrying a cage of supple willow rods. Tullius was thrashing frantically about inside, tearing at the rods with hands and teeth. Kerin drew his sword and leapt in front of them.

'Put him down, you savages!' he roared. Elir laughed hysterically.

'Don't speak to me of savagery!' Hefydd wept. 'My brother is dead!'

'Stand aside, Kerin Brightspear!' Caradog bawled from his perch on the rock. 'Blood will have blood!'

A hand gripped Kerin's shoulder. 'Lad, don't cross them,' Lud pleaded. 'They're going to have blood one way or another. If you cross them, it may be yours. Let them have their blood. It's the only way.'

'Not like this!' Kerin exclaimed. He raised his sword, then a hammer-blow from behind sent it flying from his hand. Vortigern had come from nowhere. Rowenna ran towards him. Lud seized her by the arms. She struggled and twisted, trying to bite his hands.

'Alright,' Vortigern said, staring at the willow cage and the panic-stricken Tullius. 'What's going on here?'

Iustig barged forward. 'You know quite well what's going on,' he panted. Vortigern turned and sliced off the front end of the cage with one sword-stroke. Elir and Bened jumped clear. Tullius struggled out and ran howling into the darkness. Caradog leapt down from his rock.

'Lord, we will have blood,' he threatened.

'Life for life!' Hefydd sobbed. Vortigern frowned.

'Life for life? Whose life?'

'Hefin's life!' Hefydd burst out, weeping with rage and grief. 'My brother's dead, hanged by your son and his noble Christians!'

Vortigern seized him by the shoulders. 'This isn't true!'

Kerin touched his arm. 'Lord, it is true,' he said. Vortigern let Hefydd fall. He looked hard at Kerin, then laughed and walked away.

'So much for the power of prayer,' he said. Iustig turned on him.

'Go on, then,' he shouted, waving his arms at the druids and the fire. 'Blame all this on God, too.'

Vortigern followed his eyes. 'Rufus is God's servant,' he said. 'And Rufus hanged Hefin.'

'No!' Iustig said bitterly. '*You* hanged Hefin, the day you took Constans from his cloister.' Vortigern wrenched the cross from Iustig's hands, broke it across his knee and hurled the pieces into the flames. Caradog howled with glee and shook the oak staff above his head.

'Victory in Kent!' he roared.

'You'll burn in hell if you go,' Iustig said. Rowenna twisted from Lud's grasp and clung to Vortigern's arm.

'Please!' she sobbed. 'Please don't let them hang my father!' Vortigern shook her off and she stumbled back to the crowd. Gael caught her and hurried her away with a frightened glance over her shoulder.

'You heard me,' Iustig said. Vortigern stared into the fire, where the embers of the cross were throwing up a little yellow flaring light. 'Well?' Iustig demanded. Vortigern nodded to Lud.

'Do it,' he said.

'For the love of God!' Iustig breathed. Vortigern stared up at the leaping flames.

'I am done with the love of God,' he said, in a voice which held the bleak horrors of the night. Lud's face was taut and expectant.

'Lord?' he said calmly.

'No!' Iustig shouted.

'Find Eldof's son and hang him,' Vortigern said. 'We ride for Kent at dawn.'

5

Hefydd stood, shoulders braced, in front of Vortigern. All tears shed; white, composed. At the gates of the citadel four of his boys waited in the thinning darkness before dawn. Mad Mabon, a touch less mad after the carnage in the North, held his father's horse.

'I'm coming with you,' Hefydd said. 'My beard may be grey, but I can make a warband's pace.'

There was a brief, barely noticeable pause before Vortigern gripped him by the arms. 'No, Hefydd,' he said. 'I have other work for you, and no-one else can do it. You must gather the army of Cambria. Send a man to every village and hill fort within a day's ride, and tell them I need their swords. Tell them that blood calls for blood. Then raise the red stag of Carneddlas, and lead my army to Kent.'

A shiver passed through Hefydd's body. In the wavering light of the torches, Kerin could see tear drops glistening in his straggling grey beard.

'I will work this thing,' he breathed. 'For you and for my dead brother. For his widow and his unborn child.'

'Good,' Vortigern said, releasing him. 'And every leader your boys meet must send riders north and west with the same message. You won't have time to wait for those men. Leave Mabon in command, and tell him to lead them to Kent, by the plains of Sarum.'

'Done!' Hefydd said. As he trotted off and scrambled

into the saddle, shouting to his boys, Vortigern caught Kerin's eye. The look conveyed, all too clearly, the inadmissible truth. Vortigern did not want Hefydd on a forced march because it would kill him.

Gael was standing in the horse pen with the brown filly. Kerin had fetched the horse from Gwynfi's barn at dead of night, knowing that by daybreak he would be miles away. Gael had wept and laughed; she had kissed him, and then the horse, and now she was standing there in the half-darkness gently stroking the filly's arched neck, while all around her warhorses were saddled and checked. Eryr shoved Kerin with her nose. She was quivering gently, knowing what was afoot. He secured his spear to the front of the saddle alongside the pigskin bag which Morvid had given him. There wasn't much in there. A meagre amount of dried meat, a hoofpick, a sharp knife for gutting animals, a length of unbreakable twine. Vortigern was already in the saddle. Gael came out of the pen and into Kerin's arms.

'I'd give anything not to leave,' he said.

'I know,' she said. 'And you must know that I'd come with you if I could.' She drew back and pressed a finger to his lips. 'Don't speak. I know it can't be.'

'It can't. Although I know that you can ride and use a sword as well as most men.'

She gave her soft, throaty little laugh. 'You're a liar, Kerin Brightspear. But for the best reasons. Now I must go to poor Tirion. I expect she sees her life ending, child or not.'

There was nothing more to be said, so he simply held her tightly and kissed the top of her head. She seized his hands, then pressed into his fingers the ring with which she had now pledged her life to him. Hands shaking, Kerin threaded it onto the chain of his crucifix. As he mounted up Rowenna came from the chieftains' hall. Gael pulled her close. The two women stood in the gateway with their arms around each other, and watched the men they had married vanish into the dim blue light of dawn.

Gwyndaf was waiting at the crossroads by the water-mill. He was facing across the path, staring fixedly ahead of him. He had his spear, sword, and twin daggers, his sling and a saddlebag. Derfyn was with him. Vortigern drew rein in the middle of the track.

'What are you doing here?' he asked.

'I heard you were riding to Kent,' Gwyndaf said, stiff as a ramrod.

'Yes,' Vortigern said. There was a fraught silence.

'You're going for Macsen?' Gwyndaf asked.

'Yes. I put him there; it's for me to get him out.'

Gwyndaf stared at the side of the valley. 'We could come with you.'

'It's up to you,' Vortigern said. 'This is a forced march. You fall off, we leave you. We kill our wounded. If that's what you want, get to the back of the line.'

Gwyndaf nodded silently, turned his horse and rode to the tail-end of the warband, head high. Derfyn gave Kerin a wink as he passed. They rode up onto the open moors, on the track which led to the Roman road. The sun was rising ahead from a dark cloud-bank. Its brassy light already held premonitions of heat.

'The Jutes didn't start it,' Lucius said as they hit the Roman road. 'Don't ask me if they should be where they are, but they didn't start the fighting. Macsen said that as soon as they arrived in Kent, they spent their *annona* on cattle and timber and started building houses. There were a few arguments with the locals, but Hefin soon sorted them out. He offered the people good money, and most were glad to take it. They seemed to want to get on with the Jutes, not fight them. And then the burning started. Not the new houses; the old villages on the poor land Hengist was given before the North. Some young hotheads loyal to Rufus, Macsen said. The families soon turned up on Hengist's doorstep, women and children looking as if they'd been through a war. Things went mad after that. Publius had had spies down there all along. He called me in to talk it through, then sent me off with fifty cavalrymen and a hundred foot soldiers. That should have been enough to stop a half-hearted scrap between the Jutes and a few young lunatics.'

'More than enough,' Kerin said. 'What happened?'

'They tricked us. Rufus and Paulinus sent a messenger, asking for talks. We suggested meeting them in the middle of a bridge near their encampment. It seemed sensible. We could each muster on our own side and send a handful of people to do the talking. So that was the plan. Macsen, Hefin and I would meet Rufus, Paulinus and some Kentish dignitary in the middle of the bridge. But they'd hidden men under the bank on our side. As soon as we were all out on the bridge, they set fire to it behind us. God knows what they used, it burned like wildfire. Our boys couldn't possibly pass it. All the bastards had to do was drag us away and lob spears across the river.'

The sky was growing lighter by the mile now, and there were signs of life in the villages beside the road. People left their morning gruel to watch the Lord's warband pass by. They looked, and then shrugged their shoulders and went on eating; because they were Vortigern's people, and believed that he could save them from all their enemies, more surely than they had ever believed that God and his beloved son could save them from their sins.

'How did you get away?' Kerin asked.

'Oswi,' Lucius said. 'They tied me up and threw me in a shed. The next morning they hanged a Jute lad and made the rest of us watch. They told me I'd be next. Later on there was a hell of a noise outside. Shouting and banging. Someone ran in and grabbed me under the arms, and the next thing I knew I was in the river. I was as much help as a sack of corn because my hands and feet were still tied. There were spears flying everywhere, but the man holding me just kept swimming until we were back on our own bank. When he pulled me out I realised that it was Oswi the Horseman. He said they couldn't get near Macsen and Hefin. There was nothing I could do, so I rode back to tell Publius Luca. My God, you should see Oswi's horse go. Or is it Garagon's horse? It was like sitting on a thunderbolt.'

Kerin laughed. 'Ghazal! No wonder they didn't catch you.'

'I sent him back to Oswi,' Lucius said. 'Then one of your warriors turned up and told us that Hefin had been hanged. Publius got me a fast horse and told me to get here as quick as I could.'

'Hefin!' Kerin said, holding back tears. 'He was one of our best. A good friend. Married, with a baby coming. God, why couldn't they just have ransomed him?'

'Because Rufus and his people wanted to get Vortigern out of Cambria. It was an open secret. A trap from the beginning, and now Macsen's the bait.'

'Yes,' Kerin said; but he did not share the rest of his thoughts. It hardly seemed fair when Lucius had already half-killed himself. They would not be making a warband's pace. They would be riding at a speed most men would have thought impossible, to reach Kent in a time generally considered unachievable; and there they would try to rescue Macsen from an army they could not beat, through pure, blinding shock.

6

On the afternoon of the second day, east of Corinium, Gwyndaf came cantering back to the rocky knoll where the others had made camp.

'Someone's following us,' he said. It confirmed what Kerin had suspected since early morning. A movement of birds far behind; a barely perceptible uneasiness in his horse, only noticeable because he knew her so well.

'How many?' Vortigern asked.

'Just the one. A youngish lad. I only glimpsed him, but he stopped and looked for tracks by the stream we crossed.'

'Are you sure he's alone?' Kerin asked.

'Sure. You couldn't hide a mouse on that hillside.'

Vortigern reached for his sword-belt. 'It's a trick, or he's a spy,' he said, giving Kerin a nod. 'The rest of you, wait here and prepare for an ambush.'

They followed Gwyndaf down the narrow valley. Within a mile its sides fell away and merged into open moorland. They left the track, riding uphill through waist-high bracken, and tied their horses out of sight behind a clump of blackthorn.

'He can't be far away,' Gwyndaf said. They wriggled down through the bracken on their bellies and crouched amongst tall foxgloves and spikes of yellow archangel. The soft sound of a horse's hooves approached. Gwyndaf reached for his sling and fitted a smooth stone. The rider was a slight, straight-backed young man in a grey hooded cloak. Kerin stifled an exclamation of astonishment.

'The cheeky bastard! He's pinched my wife's horse.'

Gwyndaf balanced the stone in his hand. 'Well, he'll never pinch another.'

'You can have him later,' Vortigern said. 'I want to know who sent him first.'

Gwyndaf rose on one knee. His arm flicked out and the stone went spinning through the air, striking the lad a glancing blow on the back of the head. He gasped and pitched sideways out of the saddle. The filly plunged forward and crashed away into the bracken. Gwyndaf ran to catch her while Kerin and Vortigern drew swords and leapt down onto the track. The rider was sprawling on his face. Kerin prodded him with his foot. When there was no response, he drove his toe under the lad's shoulder and rolled him onto his back. The hood of the cloak fell away and a mass of corn-coloured hair tumbled out.

'Merciful God!' Vortigern whispered. He dropped his sword and gathered Rowenna up in his arms. Gwyndaf's stone had only stunned her, and her eyelids were already beginning to flicker as Vortigern laid her down and loosened the neck of her tunic. She sat up, blinking and rubbing the back of her head. Vortigern grabbed her by the shoulders.

'What the hell are you doing here?' he shouted. Rowenna twisted free and retreated up the bank.

'I told you I wanted to come with you,' she said mutinously.

'And I told you it was impossible. For the love of God, woman, we're riding to war. Do you think I've got time to waste on you?' He picked up his sword and slammed it into its scabbard. Gwyndaf came back, leading the sweating brown filly. 'Behold your mighty warrior,' Vortigern said sourly. Gwyndaf chuckled.

'What will you do?' he enquired. 'We can't take her with us. She'll slow us down.'

Kerin raised a hand. 'We can't send her back alone. This country's thick with cut-throats and robbers, never mind Eldof's spies.'

'He's right,' Vortigern said, tight-lipped. 'They'd knife her or worse.'

Gwyndaf regarded Rowenna dubiously. 'It won't please the warriors.'

'It doesn't please me,' Vortigern said, dragging Rowenna to her feet. Kerin trudged up through the bracken and fetched the horses. They rode slowly back along the valley. Kerin turned to Rowenna, bitter and furious.

'Why did you have to take that horse? It's Gael's horse, my gift to her. You could have had any horse in Henfelin.'

Rowenna's eyes flashed. 'I did not steal the horse. Gael gave it to me, of her own free will.'

'You're lying,' Kerin retorted.

'I am not. Ask Gael, when you go home. She will tell you if I lied.'

Kerin was mortified. He did not see how she could possibly be lying. To make matters worse, the decision must have been made mere minutes after the warband left Henfelin. The young horse was fast, but would have struggled to keep up with hardened warhorses. It looked exhausted already. '*Why?*' he said. 'The filly was my gift to Gael. My first gift. My marriage gift.'

Rowenna raised her eyebrows. 'You are a man. You would not understand this.'

Back at the camp, Kerin watched dismally while Lud paced up and down.

'A woman riding with a warband?' he growled. 'Lord, this is madness.'

'Then what do you want me to do?' Vortigern said, burning with resentment. 'Leave her here for Eldof's butchers? How will it look if the King of all the Britons can't even protect his own wife?' He looked at the silent warriors. 'Get out of here and kill our food.' The men took their spears and trooped off, muttering amongst themselves. Gwyndaf remained, sharpening his spear. Kerin did not move. Even now, he was disinclined to leave them alone together. 'Well?' Vortigern snapped. 'What are you waiting for? If we don't eat now, there'll be nothing for two days.'

Gwyndaf rose to his feet, examining the gleaming arrow head. 'A man can't hunt with a blunt spear, lord,' he said mildly.

'Go!' Vortigern said. 'The light's going, and even you can't spear a hind in the dark.'

Gwyndaf suppressed a smile. 'I'll leave that to you, lord,' he said, and strode off into the trees, spear on his shoulder. Vortigern watched him go.

'You see?' he said, white with temper. 'And that's only the beginning.'

'I am your wife!' Rowenna protested.

'You're a disobedient bitch,' Vortigern said, grabbing his spear.

'Where are you going?' Kerin asked.

'To hunt. You can stay here and play the nursemaid.' He marched off towards the trees. Kerin turned on Rowenna.

'Why? I know you want to see your father, but for God's sake couldn't it have waited?'

Rowenna laughed contemptuously. 'You think that's why I have come?'

Kerin ignored the question. 'The warriors say it's more fun to be a monk than to go on one of Vortigern's forced marches. It's enough to kill most men. And they do it, because they love him, and because he's never denied them anything that he won't deny himself. Now you've made it impossible for him. You heard Gwyndaf.'

Rowenna covered her ears with her hands. 'I did not come for that!'

'The warriors won't believe it,' Kerin said. 'And I know Hengist's work when I see it.'

Rowenna looked at him, head tilted, like a curious bird. 'You really believe this. You really believe that I do this for my father.'

'Why else? I think you knew what would happen here. And your father would love to see us slitting each other's throats. It would save him a lot of trouble, in the long run.'

'You know, I will tell him this,' Rowenna said. 'He will smile. But this is even a plan too clever for Hengist. In fact it is not a plan at all, but you are too stupid to understand, I think.'

Kerin swallowed his reply, walked from the clearing and found a bank overlooking the valley. Drawing his dagger he hacked a stout twig from a hanging bough, sat down and started whittling. Behind his back he could hear Rowenna singing softly as she gathered wood for the fire. He watched the sun go down over the valley, possessed by thoughts of a woman who had given away his love-gift, for reasons which, as Rowenna had predicted, he did not understand at all.

The warriors came back at dusk with two young deer which Gwyndaf and Elir butchered into small pieces for speed and set to roast over the fire. All the men munched silently, knowing that there would be no more food until they had crossed the plains of Sarum. Vortigern hacked off a hunk of meat and thrust it at his wife.

'Eat,' he said. Rowenna turned away. 'Eat,' Vortigern said, forcing the meat into her hands. 'We ride all night and tomorrow, and there'll be no stopping for food. You can't hide twenty armed men on the plains of Sarum.'

'Do we have to go that way?' Gwyndaf asked truculently.

'Yes,' Vortigern said.

'It's madness. Rufus has the place in his hand. They'll be watching every track.'

'Rufus's men are in Kent,' Vortigern said. 'And the few he can spare to look for us will be watching the Ridgeway.'

'Are you sure, lord?' Lud said uneasily. 'It does seem stupid to pass so close to Caerwynt, with it being Paulinus's home.'

'Of course it's stupid. That's why we're doing it.'

'Lord?' Lud said blankly.

'I taught Rufus about strategy,' Vortigern said, 'and on my mother's grave it wasn't easy, but I flatter myself that he learned something.' He picked up a stick, squatted down and drew some lines in the dust. The men joined him. 'Here are the plains of Sarum,' he said, pointing. 'This is Caerwynt – Venta Belgarum, to you – which any sane man would avoid. And this is the Ridgeway, where all the sensible men would go. We could follow it all the way to the east coast, then head south into Kent. Now, my son knows damned well that I'm not sensible, but he also knows that I might try to outwit him by doing the unexpected. By crossing the plains of Sarum, for example. But he thinks he's clever enough to second-guess me, so he'll be watching the Ridgeway. And we –' he tapped the blank centre of his diagram – 'will cross the plains of Sarum.'

Lud looked bewildered. Vortigern glanced up at Kerin. 'I'm right, aren't I?' he asked.

'Yes, lord,' Kerin said. 'I'd put my horse on it.'

They gathered the bones and buried them in the leaf-mould. The night sky was dull with drifting cloud.

'Sleep,' Vortigern said. 'After this, we don't stop. If you fall from your horses, we'll leave you where you're lying.' The information was intended for Rowenna, Kerin supposed, since all the warriors knew it already. Elir took the first watch as the others settled down to sleep. Kerin lay awake, staring up at the swaying branches. A wolf howled somewhere in the distance. Lud's snores reverberated around the clearing. Kerin picked up a clod of earth and hurled it at him. Lud spluttered and snorted and pulled his cloak over his head. Something moved in the shadows. Kerin's hand tightened round the hilt of his dagger, then relaxed as Rowenna glided past him and knelt at Vortigern's side. She touched his arm, and he sat up with a start.

'What are you doing here?' he whispered. 'I told you not to come to me.'

'I am your wife,' Rowenna pleaded. 'I want to share your danger as well as your bed.'

'You think so? We're warriors. Celts. We can cross sixty miles of moorland in a day. I should make you walk barefoot back to Henfelin.'

'No!' Rowenna whispered, fighting tears. 'I want to ride with you. I want to be like Helen of the Hosts.'

Vortigern frowned. 'Helen of the Hosts? What do you know about her?'

'Mora told me.' Rowenna stared at the ground. 'She told me that Helen was your first wife's mother, and she loved Prince Macsen so much that she used to ride with his army wherever he went.'

'Well, that's true,' Vortigern conceded. 'But Maximus didn't take her to war. And at least her daughter had the grace to stay at home where she belonged.'

'Then I will better her!' Rowenna cried. Vortigern cupped her chin in his hand.

'Go,' he said softly. 'Or I'll give you to Gwyndaf, and we shall see if he can practise what he preaches.' Rowenna ran from the clearing. Vortigern drew his knees up to his chin and sat staring at the remnants of the fire, until Elir came back from the woodland fringe to say that the moon was up and it was time to move on.

7

The heat was the worst of it. By day the sky was a sheet of blinding light. The nights were stifling and leaden with storms which would not break. The horses ran with sweat. The riders scarcely exchanged a word. Their clothes grew filthy with dust and clung to festering saddle sores. Rowenna's flawless white skin blistered and cracked. Her scorched eyelids swelled until she could barely see, and she rode with reins flapping loose, fingers knotted in her horse's mane. Lud, tight-lipped and sick with fear for his son, was the only man whose face betrayed any trace of feeling as they passed beyond exhaustion into a shadow-world where sleep and pain were memories.

They skirted the southern boundary of Venta Belgarum at dead of night and saw no-one. A thin veil of cloud obscured the moon. Kerin's raw eyes picked out distant lights glimmering from the Roman town. A few scrubby trees rose in the half-darkness ahead and they heard the faint sound of running water.

'Stop,' Vortigern said. 'Let the horses drink.' They reined in on the bank of a shallow stream. Drought had reduced it to a foul-smelling trickle. The horses dropped their heads and gulped. It was impossible not to feel on edge in Paulinus's territory, however quiet things looked. An owl flapped out of the trees and glided silently about over the parched cornfields. Elir slipped to the ground, flung himself flat and plunged his hands into the muddy water. Vortigern was out of the saddle like a lightning-bolt.

'Get up!' he shouted, seizing Elir by the shoulders. Elir turned on him, eyes rolling.

'I've got to drink, lord,' he choked.

'Drink that and you're a dead man,' Vortigern said, pushing him backwards with all his force. Elir staggered back into the flank of his father's warhorse. Lud grabbed him by the hair.

'Look over there, you young fool,' he croaked. Elir followed his eyes upstream. The bloated carcass of an ox, half eaten by wolves or carrion birds, was lying in the sluggish water. Vortigern leaned against his mare's shoulder, catching his breath.

'Get back on your horse, Elir. I can't afford to lose one warrior, even a stupid one.'

'I'm sorry, lord,' Elir mumbled. He looked close to tears as he caught his mare and struggled onto her back.

'We've made good time,' Kerin murmured. 'We could probably rest once we're clear of the city.' He glanced behind at Rowenna. 'This is enough to kill strong men.'

'I know,' Vortigern said. 'But we'll never get Macsen out alive unless we can take them by surprise.'

'Yes,' Kerin said resignedly. 'I know you're right.' His aching limbs didn't feel equal to taking a field-mouse by surprise. He rode alongside Rowenna as they moved out of the trees. 'Two more days at this pace. Then you can sleep on a goose-down bed in your father's hall.'

Rowenna glared at him. 'I am Vortigern's woman. What do I want with my father's hall?' She gathered her reins and Kerin noticed a thin, dark trickle running down her left arm from wrist to elbow. Rowenna saw what he was looking at. She opened her hand to reveal a fragment of knife-blade. 'I found it by the stream. Now, if I think I am going to sleep, I will go like this.' She closed her fingers and gasped. 'It will help me not to sleep. But you tell him and I will kill you!'

Two days later, evening found them riding towards a low, bare ridge. Kerin had only ever approached Kent on the Roman road from Londinium, but the position of the setting sun told him that they were still riding east. Vortigern clicked to his exhausted mare, suddenly eager. The steep slope flattened ahead. Before them, looking astonishingly close, lay the shining buildings of Durovernum. Gwyndaf gave a yell of triumph and punched the air.

'We rode well,' Lud said fervently. 'It couldn't have been done in less time.'

Rowenna smiled. 'You see? I did not hold you back.'

Vortigern scanned the country ahead. 'It's further than it looks, girl,' he said. 'We're not there yet.'

Rowenna stared reproachfully at him. Vortigern sat very still in the saddle, testing the air.

'Burning,' Kerin said apprehensively.

'Where's Rufus's camp, Lucius?' Vortigern asked.

'It was on the river north-east of Durovernum, lord. But I heard a lot of talk about driving the Saxons into the sea.'

'Alright, Kerin,' Vortigern said. 'Go and see what's happening. Find out where Rufus and Hengist are.'

Lud cleared his throat. 'Lord, I'm still your chief warrior. And Macsen is my son.'

'All the more reason for you to do something stupid. Kerin can speak some Saxon. And he's the only one of us Rufus won't hang.'

Kerin rode down from the ridge and through the sparse

woods below. The countryside was empty. In the corn-fields, half-ripe heads of grain nodded in the light wind. Sparrows and corn buntings fluttered on the tall stems, stripping them bare. After a few miles Kerin reached an abandoned farmstead. He remembered it from the spring and knew that the owner had kept his house in order, but now the few bushes which had not been uprooted were overgrown and straggling. Cherries rotted on the trees in the walled garden. A door banged somewhere in the wind. Kerin remembered a cluster of rough houses, inhabited by labourers. He checked his horse and advanced cautiously through a grove of apple trees. The stench of burning, though strong, was not fresh. Kerin's skin prickled as he sensed death in the air. A few thin drifts of smoke were still rising from the blackened ruins of the houses. A dejected old horse was pulling half-heartedly at tufts of dead grass. Kerin dismounted, then saw the old man, sitting on a pile of charred wood and drinking from a cracked bowl. His hair was white and matted, and his tattered brown tunic would probably have fallen to pieces if not for the rope binding it to his skinny body. His eyes were running and his nose was running, and he looked almost as old as Morvid. Kerin sat down on a ruined wall. The old man studied him for a moment then went back to watching the birds in the cornfield. The sight of an armed warrior seemed to hold no terrors for him.

'Who are you, then?' he asked. 'One of Vortimer's thugs, come for the pickings?'

'No,' Kerin said. 'I'm a warrior of Vortigern's following.'

'King Vortigern, eh?' The old man snorted and spat on the ground.

'What happened here?' Kerin asked. The old man sniffed.

'First the Saxons came. They told us your Lord Vortigern

had given them this land for helping him beat the Picts. So they raped our women, turned us out of our houses and killed half our young men. Then Vortimer's good Christians came. They said that if we hadn't died fighting the Saxons, we must be either cowards or traitors. So they raped our women, burned our houses down and killed the rest of our young men.' The old man drained his bowl. 'So you may as well tell Vortigern to go back to the West. There's nothing left here worth fighting over. And you'd best leave Vortimer and Hengist to it, because the sooner they put an end to each other, the better it'll be for the likes of us.'

'Where are the women and children?' Kerin asked.

'Gone away. And you'll kill me before I tell you where.'

'I don't want to kill you,' Kerin sighed. 'Tell me where Vortimer and Hengist are, and I'll leave you in peace.'

'That's easy,' the old man said. 'Vortimer's camped across the river – you know, the one north-east of here. And Hengist's people are out by the coast. They'll stay where they can reach their boats, if they've got any sense.'

'Won't that please you?' Kerin asked. The old man sniffed.

'It won't make much difference to folk like us. Garagon's a rotten master, and as for Vortimer, a Christian sword's as bad as a pagan sword when you're on the end of it.'

Kerin got up. He wanted to move before his limbs stiffened, and before the old man's conversation raised any more questions he preferred not to answer. 'Thank you,' he said, mounting up. 'I'll make sure you're left alone.'

The old man grimaced, as if he didn't believe a word of it. Kerin reached into his saddle-bag for the last of his dried meat, tossed it to the old man and rode away.

The countryside east of Durovernum was flat and unnervingly bare. A patch of scrubland came into view; a barren, rocky strip in the middle of a trampled cornfield where gorse and buckthorn had been allowed to grow unchecked. A flock of jackdaws rose cackling from the bushes and flapped away into the corn. The faint smell of smoke tickled Kerin's nostrils. Before he had time to think, he was hit from behind by a weight which knocked him clean out of the saddle. He crashed to the bone-hard earth, and a knife blade ripped through his tunic. Struggling, Kerin went for his dagger. He and his assailant rolled over and over, hacking furiously at each other. Strength sapped by the journey, Kerin was pinioned on his back. He found himself face to face with Horsa. The Jute's ferocious snarl gave way to a roar of delight.

'Odin's mercy!' he shouted, hoisting Kerin to his feet and dusting him down. 'I think you are one of Vortimer's killers!'

Kerin smiled weakly and retrieved his mare from the buckthorns. 'What are you doing out here? Where's Hengist?'

'I keep watch,' Horsa said. 'We expect another attack all times. And Hengist is east. Not far.'

'Macsen?' Kerin asked, dreading the reply.

'Alive,' Horsa said. 'If they kill him, they hang his body where we can see it.'

'And our men?' Kerin said. 'The warriors we sent with Oswi's company?' Horsa stared down at his boots. Kerin closed his eyes, breathing deeply. 'Horsa, where are they?'

'They are dead, Kerin Brightspear,' Horsa said, his voice barely a whisper. Kerin seized him by the shoulders, tears springing from his eyes.

'How?' he shouted. Horsa looked up. He was weeping, too.

'After we make our raid,' he sobbed. 'After Oswi gets out your Lucius. Hengist and Aelle go to protect our women, our children. The rest of us make a camp, your boys, our boys and some from Lucius. A good camp in a wood. We hide with branches and leaves. We make plans, look after wounded.' He cleared his throat. 'They come in the dark, when everyone sleeps. Maybe someone tells them where we are. They burn every man in his bed except me and Oswi, because we cannot sleep, so we go to find food. When we come back, all are dead. We find one young boy, one of ours –' he drew a forearm across his eyes. 'I do not know this word. The Christians, they say the unbelievers kill the son of their god. They say they take wood and nails –'

Kerin blinked. 'They crucified someone?' he said incredulously.

'Yes. This is the word. They nail him to big ash tree.' Horsa grabbed Kerin's arms and propelled him through the thick bushes to a small open space where a horse was tethered. He picked up a leather bottle and thrust it into Kerin's hands. 'Drink,' he said, mopping tears and mucus from his face. 'You deserve.' Kerin seized the bottle and poured the contents down his throat. The strong ale made his exhausted head reel. Horsa grabbed him under the arms and helped him mount up. 'You have how many men?' he asked.

'Just twenty,' Kerin said. 'The rest of our army is coming. We're near the village that Vortimer burned.'

Horsa laughed. 'The village that Vortimer burned? If I have a bag of gold for every village he burned, I sail away and buy myself another kingdom. Come now, I ride with you. This is bad country to be alone.'

Kerin did not argue. Under the circumstances he was glad to have another sword on his side, whoever was hold-ing it.

The shadows were lengthening as they approached the place where Kerin had left the others. The sun was on the ridge, glassy and brilliant. They pushed through tinder-dry undergrowth into a clearing. Kerin slipped from his horse's back, then turned, sensing movement. Vortigern seized him by the shoulders and embraced him. The warriors came crashing out of the brushwood and surrounded Horsa, slapping him heartily on the back.

'Well?' Vortigern asked. 'Where is he?'

'Still camped on the other side of that river,' Kerin said. 'And Hengist's out near the coast. Macsen's alive.'

Vortigern glanced at his warriors, still preoccupied with greeting Horsa. 'What's it like?'

'As bad as the north country after the Picts. Ruined corn. Burned villages.'

'Hengist's work?'

'Rufus's,' Kerin said reluctantly. Vortigern raised his eyebrows. 'Lord, they've killed our boys,' Kerin blurted. 'All the lads you sent with Oswi. They burned them in their beds. They crucified a Saxon lad, for God's sake.'

Vortigern stood completely still as he absorbed the news and all its implications. Amongst the warriors, the merriment dissipated as Horsa shared his account of the slaughter.

'And Rufus ordered this?' Vortigern said, his voice barely audible.

'I don't know,' Kerin said, blinking tears. 'Either he ordered it, or he couldn't stop it. I don't know which is worse. Horsa thinks they were betrayed. They'd gone out of their way to hide the camp. God knows who'd do a thing like that.'

Vortigern took a breath and steadied himself. 'Horsa!' he said sharply. The Saxon strode forward; then, without warning, let out a furious bellow. Rowenna had come out of the brushwood. Horsa stared at her wind-burnt face and scarred hands.

'Odin!' he roared. 'Is this how you treat your women?'

'Ask her how I treat her,' Vortigern said, with a look of disgust.

'Well?' Horsa shouted. Rowenna looked at him without a blink.

'I have no complaints,' she said.

'I'm your uncle!' Horsa cried, lapsing into his own tongue. 'You're the child who sat on my knee and sang for me. How can you say that you're happy with this?'

Rowenna's eyes filled with tears but she did not flinch. When she answered, it was in British. 'I love you, Uncle Horsa,' she said. 'But I have no complaints.'

Horsa turned away, shaking his head in bewilderment.

'Alright,' Vortigern said briskly, 'now take us to your brother before my son gets here with his Christian charity.'

'Wait,' a sharp voice said. Gwyndaf left the warriors and marched up to Vortigern. 'My boys Leil and Cadfan were with that escort,' he said. 'I know you didn't command it. It was their idea. You know what it's like. Young lads with no dependants. It's all a big adventure for them. I could have stopped them, but I didn't.'

Vortigern closed his eyes. 'Gwyndaf, I'm sorry,' he said. Gwyndaf's lips tightened.

'Like I said,' he snapped. 'It's not your fault. But don't complain when I rip out your son's liver and feed it to my dogs.'

They saw the village long before they reached it. Out on the flat lands between Durovernum and the sea; a miserable little huddle of huts, bleak, exposed, impossible to defend.

'Gods,' Lud grumbled, 'couldn't you have picked a better place?'

'Ask Vortimer,' Horsa said curtly. 'We work hard, build houses, and now they are ashes.' He kicked his tiring horse and trotted ahead. Hengist was waiting for them, standing on the pitiful mud rampart. His glittering eyes were colder than ever, and Kerin could see that his daughter's presence was no surprise to him.

'Lord, I gave you my daughter to grace your bed-chamber,' he said. 'Not to be dragged about like a common camp-follower.' He looked up at Rowenna. 'Are the Britons so short of warriors that they must drag their women on marches which would kill fighting men?'

Rowenna's eyes blazed. 'No man drags Hengist's daughter!' she shouted. 'No-one forced me. It was my plan. My choice. And it was not hard. I would ride from here to Cambria now, this moment. It's better than filling the tankards at your pestilent feasts.' She planted her hands on her hips. Hengist blinked. For the first time in Kerin's experience, he looked lost for words. Vortigern regarded his wife with the suspicion of a smile.

'What was her mother, Hengist?' he asked. 'An old warhorse?'

Hengist looked deeply affronted. 'Lord, my wife was a noblewoman of the Jutes,' he said haughtily. Vortigern chuckled.

'She played you false, then,' he said. 'No two Saxons could bear a warrior of the Celts.'

The colour flew to Rowenna's cheeks. Her eyes burned with pride, and with something which Kerin might have interpreted as love, had he not known better. Vortigern inclined his head respectfully. Rowenna's face illuminated. It was the same transforming smile which she had worn on a distant morning in Henfelin. Such ludicrous displays were not within Vortigern's compass, naturally. Gathering his reins, he winked at his wife and led his flagging warband over the rampart into her father's sad village.

8

There was only one building large enough to be called a hall. The warriors dismounted outside and the Jutes fought over the privilege of caring for them and their horses. Hengist was clearly embarrassed by his poverty.

'It's not much, friends,' he said gruffly.

'Don't worry, man,' Lud said, gripping his shoulder. 'The bare earth will do tonight.'

'Of course,' Hengist said. 'And we bless you. I know you come for your son, but perhaps you have also some thought for Hengist and his brothers. Horsa, show them to their beds. See that they have ale and meat, even if we must go without.'

Horsa flung one arm round Lud's shoulders and the other round Gwyndaf's, and marched them off towards a nearby hut. The other warriors trailed behind, stretching weary limbs. Kerin turned to follow them. He could almost feel the touch of rough blankets and the solid weight of a tankard in his hand. Vortigern's hand came down on his arm.

'Kerin, it must be done tonight,' he said quietly. Kerin's heart sank.

'For the love of God!' he said beseechingly.

'Look, you know I'm right,' Vortigern said. Kerin rubbed his eyes.

'Yes,' he said. 'I know.'

Hengist came out of his hall and beckoned. They followed him to a squalid shack near the rampart. Inside a skinny man in a threadbare tunic was squatting on the earth floor, sharpening a knife by the light of a candle. Thirty years old, perhaps, but privation had put years on him.

'A slave of Garagon's,' Hengist said. 'Some of them were sent up to serve Vortimer and his men. But this one hates them all enough to sell them to me.'

'Is this true?' Vortigern asked.

'Aye,' the little man said, picking his teeth with the point of his knife.

'Look at me when you speak,' Vortigern said. The slave regarded him without concern, as if nothing alarmed him any more.

'Don't kill him,' Hengist said. 'Vortimer thinks he's an honest Briton, spying on the wicked pagans.'

'What do you want, lord?' the slave asked.

'Vortimer's camp,' Vortigern said. 'Can we get in?'

The slave shrugged. 'If you can swim. There's a big village across the river. They kicked half the people out and took it over. Not the women, naturally. There's a ford, but they watch it all the time. Downriver, the bank overhangs on the other side. It's impossible to climb, so they don't bother to guard it.'

'The prisoner,' Kerin said. 'Well guarded?'

'So-so. Two warriors, day and night. They change the guard at midnight.'

Vortigern pursed his lips. 'Three men, then,' he said. 'Two to cross the river and one to keep watch and hold the horses. I'll take Oswi. He didn't have to save Lucius Arrius.'

'I'll tell him,' Hengist said. 'And I have fresh horses for you.'

'Fast ones?' Kerin asked.

'Of course,' Hengist said. 'They're Garagon's.'

They crouched in the tall reeds at the river's edge. The darkness enveloped them and water lapped around their feet. Nothing was moving in the village on the far bank. Lights glimmered here and there. Occasionally a slight thinning of the cloud allowed the moon to spread a faint, luminous glow across the sky, revealing the forms of the houses against a background of scrubby trees. The night was very still and they could hear nothing but the suck and gurgle of the water flowing sluggishly past. Kerin shifted position to ease his numbed limbs.

'How much longer?'

'Midnight,' Vortigern said. 'That's when they change the guard.'

'If the moon's in we won't see them,' Kerin said.

'Then you'd better pray that it isn't,' Vortigern said testily. The cold black water had risen to their knees. The tide was coming in. The faint sound of voices drifted across the gliding water. A momentary lightening of the sky revealed two hooded figures dawdling along the far bank, spears on shoulders. Their movements completely lacked the urgency which Kerin had learned to expect from men-at-arms. Two ideas crossed his mind. Firstly, that Rufus's warriors were accustomed to a loose rein; secondly that they had no fear of being attacked. The men reached a solid-looking hut. Two dark shapes came from the shadows. The four men greeted each other and fell into conversation. A few words floated across to the watchers in the reeds. Horses, women, the usual thing.

'Come on!' Kerin hissed. He was up to his ankles in the sucking mud and the water was still rising.

'Quiet!' Vortigern said sharply. Kerin scowled.

'Some of us get tired,' he said mutinously. 'Some of us feel pain.'

Vortigern looked round. 'If you must know, my body pains me so much that I wouldn't notice if Rufus put his sword through me.' Kerin stared at him silently. Ludicrous though it was, he felt as if someone had told him that the Hafren had dried up, or the whole of the Eryri had slid westward and fallen into the sea. 'God or the devil,' Vortigern said. 'The men think I'm infallible, and I'll lose them the moment they begin to doubt it, so don't enlighten them.'

Kerin felt his throat tighten. 'There's nothing to say, lord. The men are right.'

A shout came from across the water. 'Sleep well, lads!' Footsteps thudded softly away along the bank.

'Now,' Kerin murmured. Daggers gripped in their teeth, they slipped into the water and struck out for the far bank, letting the current carry them. In the central channel, the force of the water grew stronger. They struggled, swallowing water, as their little remaining strength ran out of them like grain out of a split sack. The bank rose high above them and Kerin's scrabbling hands found a tree-root. Clinging on with one hand, he leaned out into the current and dragged Vortigern clear. Downstream the river bent sharply to the left, and at the point of the bend the bank had caved in. The current drove them against a pile of mud and stones and they hauled themselves clear of the water. Vortigern braced himself against the bank. Kerin clambered onto his shoulders, scrambled over the top and lay gasping in the short, dry grass. He wriggled back to the edge and leaned down. Vortigern grasped his outstretched hands and Kerin hauled him up. The few lights had all been extinguished.

They drew their daggers and crept towards the village. The shapes of the houses became visible only when they were almost on top of them. They heard the snores of sleeping warriors, the muffled sounds of a couple copulating.

'Christ, I'd give my right arm for a drink,' a voice said, startlingly close. They pressed themselves against the wall of the hut where it had come from.

'Drink?' an older, deeper voice said gruffly. 'We'll be lucky. You know what Vortimer said.'

His companion laughed. 'King Vortimer,' he said, his voice heavy with cynicism. 'His father might be a cut-throat, but he understands the warriors.'

'Not like these pious arseholes,' the other man said, and yawned. 'That old abbot wears the crown, if you ask me. Or is it that Sarmatian? What's-his-name? Batraz?'

The other man snorted. 'The chief warrior,' he said grimly. Kerin peered round the corner. He glimpsed two black figures hunched over a flickering rush-light and lunged forward, one hand clamping over his victim's mouth as the dagger drove home. They rolled in the dust together and Kerin felt the body beneath him shudder and grow still. Vortigern got up, wiping blood from his hands. Kerin seized the light and they plunged into the hut. Macsen was lying on the earth floor, bound hand and foot with leather thongs. He started and shrank away from them. Kerin raised the light, illuminating their faces.

'Oh the gods!' Macsen exclaimed. Vortigern clamped a bloody hand over his mouth.

'Shut up or we're all dead,' he whispered. Macsen nodded feverishly. Kerin hacked at the tough thongs, nicking Macsen's wrists and ankles in his haste. Vortigern peered outside. 'Clear,' he said. Kerin extinguished the torch. Macsen staggered to his feet, gasping with pain as life returned to his numbed limbs. They walked quickly towards the river.

'Hey!' a drowsy voice said. 'Who's there?'

'Walk!' Vortigern hissed.

'Who's there?' the voice repeated, alert this time. They broke into a run. Shouts came from the village.

'The prisoner!' someone bellowed. Lights were swimming everywhere. They could hear the river. The bank fell sharply away, and the reluctant moon chose that moment to come out. Kerin dived headlong over the edge. In the moment before he hit the water, he heard the sound of horses careering out of the village. The current swept the three men downstream as they swam. It was impossible to tell if Oswi could see them. As they staggered out into the mud on the far bank, riders came plunging into the water behind them.

'Oswi!' Kerin bawled, floundering through the reeds. The bulk of a horseman rose above him. Kerin seized him by the foot and dragged him out of the saddle. Macsen, armed with nothing but his determination not to be recaptured, threw himself on the fallen warrior and they thrashed around in the mud. There was a blood-chilling scream and Oswi the Horseman came crashing out of the willows. Rufus's stunned warriors stopped short. Oswi tore into them, twin axes swinging. Four men were lying dead as he hoisted Macsen to his feet and hurled him up the bank.

'Come on, my friends!' he roared. 'Leave them for the fishes!' Kerin and Vortigern stumbled after him. Oswi had loosed the horses. 'Four men!' he shouted, shaking a fist above his head in triumph as they galloped into the dark.

The sky was lightening from the east as they sighted the Saxon village. A solitary figure on the rampart merged into the general darkness. A light beamed from the hall, then Hengist appeared, striding down the track towards them.

'Four men!' Oswi exulted. 'Four, by my hand alone!'

Hengist smiled and marched ahead of them, cupping his hands round his mouth. 'Lud! Out of your bed!'

Lud burst from his hut. Macsen leapt off his horse and they fell into each other's arms, laughing and weeping. Elir threw himself on top of them. Horsa and Aelle came running with jugs of ale and emptied them down Oswi's throat until he choked. Kerin and Vortigern watched them silently.

'Come,' Hengist said. 'Leave the children to their games.'

The two men slipped from their horses and followed Hengist towards the hall. Vortigern flung his arm round Kerin's shoulders and they supported each other, drunk with exhaustion and relief. Rowenna ran from the lit doorway. Vortigern's brow creased.

'Woman, do you never sleep?' he asked.

'My father told me,' Rowenna protested. 'How could I sleep?' Oswi and the Jutes came laughing and brawling out of the darkness, dripping with ale. Oswi swept Rowenna up in his arms.

'Four men, by my own hand!' he shouted. 'I swear these would be dead men, if Oswi the Horseman had not been there to save them.'

Rowenna freed herself. 'Is it true?' she asked.

'Yes,' Vortigern conceded. 'Every word of it, for once.'

Rowenna turned and clasped Oswi's hands, smiling radiantly. 'Thank you, Oswi. Tonight you have saved my life, too.' She stood on tiptoe and kissed him gently on the cheek. Oswi gave a despairing groan and trudged away into the darkness. Hengist watched him go. Rowenna turned to Vortigern.

'You must sleep,' she said. Vortigern grimaced.

'I hope you're not expecting anything else tonight, girl,' he said gruffly. Rowenna placed her hands on his shoulders.

'I told Kerin Brightspear that I did not want the goose down bed in my father's hall. But if you will share it with me, sleep will be enough.'

Vortigern shook his head and reached for her hands. 'Come on, then, Helen of the Hosts,' he sighed. 'I don't think even Gwyndaf would begrudge us that tonight.'

9

The sun went down in an angry blaze. The sea beyond the dried-up salt marsh glowed dull red.

'It's madness,' Hengist said, as Aelle replenished the six empty tankards.

'Then what do you want to do?' Vortigern asked. 'Sit here like a bunch of cripples and wait for my son to kill us?'

'Of course not,' Hengist said. 'But it would be madness to attack him from the front, in daylight, with this handful of men. It is not like the North, where you had an army waiting for the Picts. There must be another way.'

The six men regarded each other uneasily; Vortigern, Kerin and Lud on one side of the table, Hengist, Horsa and Oswi on the other. Any attempt at strategy had disintegrated earlier, when Hengist's tame Briton came to report that the young king intended to raze the Saxon village first thing in the morning. The Cambrian army was days away. There was no obvious escape route since Rufus would have every road and track covered, and no means of sending for help, even if there had been anyone who wished to provide it.

'We could cross the river higher up and take them from that side,' Lud said. 'It's the crossing they'll be watching.'

Vortigern drained his tankard. 'Yes,' he said. 'And the moment they see us, they'll turn round and slaughter us.

There's no advantage in it, Lud. We'll get wet before we die, that's the only difference.' He took a deep breath. 'Hengist, how many men do you have?'

'Fifty, lord. And a handful defending our women and children in the marshes, but I cannot call for them.'

'Of course not. We have a warband of twenty. And my son has –'

'Twelve to fourteen hundred, lord, according to the spy,' Hengist said. 'And men say that ships are coming soon with many more.'

Vortigern's fist pounded the table. 'Hengist, do you want to keep this land or not?'

Hengist stiffened. 'Of course I want to keep the land. The gods know we've shed enough blood for it. But it will be impossible to beat your son with the men we have. Even though each of ours is probably worth ten of his.'

'Then what?' Vortigern asked. 'What plan do you have, that's better than mine?'

Hengist spread his hands and walked slowly down to the doorway of his hall, where daylight was fading. Vortigern closed his eyes.

'Kerin, for the love of God what should I do?' he said quietly. Kerin reached for the jug of ale and refilled their tankards.

'It makes no difference now,' he said. 'We'll have to fight them somewhere, and Hefydd's not going to arrive in time to help us. Here or at the crossing, it makes no difference. If we don't go to them, they'll come to us, as sure as night follows day.'

'Yes,' Vortigern said resignedly. 'That's what I thought.' The others looked at them expectantly. In the silence Kerin could hear the men in the next hut sharpening their swords.

'We must do what we did against the Picts, then,'

Hengist said. 'You draw them out; we hide ourselves in the bushes on this bank and fall on them as they come out of the river. I still think it's madness, but at least there'll be some honour in it.'

*

Kerin sat on the rampart in the inky blackness of midnight, sharpening his spear by touch. Most attackers might have used the darkness to surprise their enemy, he thought, but Rufus had no need to think about strategy. He would already have decided to take the easy way; to surround the village in broad daylight and butcher its inhabitants like pigs in a pen. Kerin wondered what he was thinking about, just an hour's ride away on the other side of the river. It was hard to imagine an appropriate prayer for the occasion. He thought about Gael, and found that he hardly cared about the horse any more; then he thought about the carnyx, and wondered if Caradog would have kept it hidden, if he had known that there might never be a battle for it to grace.

'What are you thinking about?' Lucius asked. It was so dark that Kerin could barely see him, although if he had held out his spear, he could have touched him with it.

'Rufus,' Kerin said. 'And what might be going through his head. I can't imagine how it would feel to think about killing your father.'

'Well, I'd probably kill myself as soon as kill Marcus,' Lucius said, shuffling along to sit next to him.

'How's Publius Luca?' Kerin asked. 'So much has happened, I never thought to ask.'

'Much stronger. He should still be sitting around doing nothing, but he was never going to rest until he'd got rid of Severus Maximus. It was bad enough, the way Severus and

Alberius emptied the treasury into their own coffers, but betraying Vortigern was what Publius couldn't stomach. It gave all the other wealthy men the excuse they needed, not to help pay for the defences.'

'They didn't hang Severus, did they?'

'No. Publius just went round there with his son Titus and threatened him with – well, I'm not sure what, really, but it worked. Severus stepped down, and the day after that, the ordo elected a successor. A friend of Titus, a soldier originally, but he left the army to become governor of somewhere-or-other. His name's Valerius Dio and his mother's British. Severus fled the city with his wife and Alberius. He's got an estate near Verulamium, so I suppose that's where they went.'

'Do you know anything about the Sarmatians?' Kerin asked.

'They're an eastern people. Some of them came west and settled in Gallia, like the Goths. There was a Sarmatian cavalry unit supporting my father's troop. Fine horsemen, he said. Why do you ask?'

'Because I overheard some guards talking when we were getting Macsen out,' Kerin said. 'One of them mentioned a Sarmatian called Batraz. He called him the chief warrior, but as if there was no love lost.'

'I don't know,' Lucius said. 'I was only thinking about staying alive. But there is a man with Rufus most of the time. About thirty years old. Tall, with long fair hair. And the most piercing eyes I've ever seen in my life. It's like having a bird of prey stare you out. As if he'd kill you as good as look at you.' A distant roll of thunder came from the south-east and a sheet of lightning flickered briefly over the sea. 'I've got a girl,' Lucius said. Kerin chuckled.

'And about time.'

There was a silence. 'It's Garagon's sister,' Lucius said. 'You mean –'

'Yes, Livia, the girl who was raped by Macsen's brother. The bastard who did it to your girl in Londinium. And believe me, I think Vortigern did the right thing chopping his balls off, but I can't help thinking my manhood might go the same way, if Garagon ever finds out.' Kerin found that he was laughing. He knew that it was unseemly, but their situation was so preposterous that he couldn't help himself. 'She came to Londinium,' Lucius said. 'Not long after you left with Hengist's *annona*. She'd cut her hair off and dressed in a lad's clothes. Afraid to travel alone as a woman, probably. She turned up at Publius Luca's house and said that if there were two sides, she wanted to be on ours. I don't think Publius knew what on earth to do with her, so he sent her to us. My father found her some work in his warehouse. My sister, Paulina, took to her straight away. Have you noticed, the way girls seem to be able to get to know each other overnight? One minute they're complete strangers, and the next they know every detail of each other's life stories, down to the colour of their mothers' underclothes.'

'Yes,' Kerin said, with some chagrin. 'I had noticed.'

'I didn't know what to do,' Lucius said. 'She didn't want me near her, so I just made it clear that she could think of me as a friend. I don't know what changed her mind, unless Paulina put in a good word. I've told her that I'll wait. You can't hurry a girl after that, can you? Although if I'd known what I know now, I think I might have tried to move things along a bit.' He fell silent. Kerin saw the pale glint of metal as he drew his sword and tested the blade. 'Did you dream about all this?'

'No,' Kerin said. 'I don't dream, I just think. Too much, probably. But sometimes I can see what might be on the way. If we're still alive this time tomorrow, I'd just go and grab her, if I were you.'

Lucius laughed. Like Kerin, he possibly saw no alternative.

Sleep eluded Kerin. As the first streaks of grey began to thread across the sky he flung aside his blanket, picked up his tack and went out. A fine rain was falling. Shadows were moving in the horse-pens.

'Gods,' Lud muttered. 'This is high summer. Perhaps the powers are angry with us.'

Vortigern grimaced. 'The same rain falls on Rufus,' he said. Kerin saddled his mare and led her out of the pen. Hengist was waiting in the murky twilight, leaning on his spear.

'Lud told me that you and Vortimer were like brothers once,' he said. 'Will you kill your brother, when it comes to it?'

Kerin hesitated. The rain was sweeping in from the bleak marsh, soaking through his clothes. Hengist's cold eyes held his, and his heart filled with the desolation of the world. He mounted up and rode for the edge of the village. Vortigern was waiting for him.

'All those men in the wood,' he said. 'All those fathers and sons and brothers. And for what?'

Kerin did not reply. He could not bring himself to say that it might have been for the god of love. Hooves squelched in the mud and bridle-rings jingled as Lud brought up the warriors. Oswi and Lucius were riding together. Inevitably, they now shared a powerful bond. Gwyndaf and Elir were on two of the stolen Kentish horses, leading their lame warhorses on halters rather than abandoning them. The Jutes trudged behind, spears and axes on shoulders.

'Lord, there's a trick in this somewhere,' Kerin said. 'Hengist's deceiving us. I've no idea how.'

Vortigern stared up into the misting rain. 'How can he be? We're the only men left on his side, for God's sake.'

Horsa leapt onto the rampart, shook his spear and broke into a trot. 'Come on, lads!' he roared. 'To the slaughterhouse!'

By some rare stroke of providence, the rain became a thick, concealing mist. As they approached the river it was light, but the far bank was invisible. The smell of baking bread drifted from the camp.

'We'll taste that soon,' Horsa said.

'We'll taste blood first,' Oswi chuckled, smacking his lips. Hengist raised his hand for silence. Vortigern checked his mare and the horsemen reined in behind him.

'Now,' he said. Hengist looked up.

'Give us time to hide ourselves!' he complained.

'Now!' Vortigern bellowed. Whipping his sword out, he hurled the mare at the trees. Kerin hurriedly crossed himself, the first time he had thought of doing it since he married Gael at Padarn's makeshift altar. The bank sloped away and they were in the water. A cry of shock went up from the far bank. The horses plunged on. Oswi appeared at Kerin's shoulder, spear hanging from a leather strap around his neck and an axe in each hand. Horsemen were mustering on the far bank. Kerin let his reins fall and raised his spear to shoulder-height. He glimpsed a raw-boned white stallion in the front rank. Katigern. Kerin's eyes fixed on a dark lad at Kat's side. One of the leaders had to fall. Kerin's spear flew. He heard the familiar thump as the head buried itself in the lad's chest. The horse's rush carried it on into the river and the rider pitched down dead in the water. Kerin leaned from the saddle and jerked his spear free. He glimpsed the blood-stained tunic. One of Eldof's youngsters. The leading horsemen met with a crunch and a clash of metal. A terrified heron went screeching up from the reeds.

'Odin!' Oswi yelled as a pair of warriors bore down on him. The first axe flew and split the leading rider's head. The second man dived sideways, hit the bloody water and swung out with his sword, slashing Gwyndaf's mare across the hind legs. Her rear end collapsed and she crashed down, hurling Gwyndaf backwards. A flying spear grazed his head as he fell, and he disappeared beneath the foaming water. Kerin leapt down, seized him under the arms and hoisted him up. We *cannot* lose this man, he thought desperately. Blood was streaming from Gwyndaf's head. Kerin grabbed the reins of a riderless horse, heaved Gwyndaf onto its back and threw him a stray spear.

'Look out!' Macsen's voice bawled. Kerin ducked and a sword-blade whistled above his head. He whipped round and found himself an arm's length from Bertil Redknife. Bertil lunged, Kerin lost his footing on the slippery river bed and landed on his back in the water. A shower of water blinded him. He stumbled to his feet. Bertil had vanished, but Eryr was still beside him. He scrambled onto her back and swung round in time to see Bertil fleeing for the far bank with Elir after him.

'Don't let him get away!' Kerin yelled, but it was too late; Bertil had vanished into the clinging mist. Warriors were surging from the village, mounted and on foot. There was nothing left to do but run. Turn, Kerin thought, gritting his teeth as he fended off a heavy club. Turn, or we're dead men. Vortigern came out of the melee, his sword dripping blood.

'Where's Rufus?' he gasped. Kerin spun his mare. It was his call now.

'Turn!' he bellowed, above the clattering din of swords.

'Turn!' Lud took up his cry, and the warriors turned as one. Vortigern was swept with them, towards the willows where the Jutes were waiting.

'At them, boys!' someone roared from Rufus's ranks. 'We've got the bastards now!' Kerin drove his mare up the bank. She lost her footing in the reeking mud and Kerin pitched headlong over her ears. He landed running and threw himself flat as an axe flashed past his head. A powerful hand seized his scruff and hauled him behind a fallen tree. For a moment he lay quite still, recovering his breath. He looked up and found himself staring into Horsa's pale blue eyes.

'Where's Hengist?' he gasped. Horsa shook his head silently, his eyes sad and bitter. 'They've gone, haven't they,' Kerin said. 'They've gone to their boats.'

'Yes, Kerin Brightspear,' Horsa said. 'All except me and Oswi the Horseman. He was a dragon.'

'Why did you stay? Why didn't you save your skin?'

'I'm a warrior, Kerin Brightspear,' Horsa said. 'That's stronger than fear. Stronger than blood, even.'

'We may die here,' Kerin said shakily.

'Yes,' Horsa said, hoisting him to his feet. 'But it will be with honour.'

They clasped hands, drew their swords and rushed out into the open. A bay mare crashed down in front of them, speared through the heart. Kerin fell on her fallen rider. They rolled over and over in the mud, stabbing frantically at each other. Kerin drove his dagger home and crawled away. A warrior came out of the trees on a rangy white stallion. Horsa ran forward and hacked the horse to its knees. As it fell the rider leapt clear, sword drawn, and threw himself at Horsa.

'Kat!' Kerin gasped. Katigern turned at the sound of his voice, and Horsa's sword drove deep into his vitals. Katigern's eyes bulged and his lips framed Kerin's name. He sank to his knees, coughing blood. Horsa roared in triumph and turned his back. With his last shred of strength, Katigern drew a dagger and hurled it. Horsa's laughter ceased. He pitched forward, the dagger embedded deep below his shoulder-blades. Kerin caught him, staggering under the weight, and laid him down in the mud. Blood was trickling from his open mouth. A few paces away Katigern was sprawling on his face. Both were dead. Kerin crawled to Katigern's side and turned him onto his back. The blue eyes stared sightlessly at him.

'Oh God, Kat,' Kerin whispered. A spear thudded into the ground, bringing him brutally to his senses. He ran from the clearing, tears streaming. Rufus's horsemen were surging out of the river. Kerin glimpsed Gwyndaf with blood dripping from the head-wound, and then his own mare, galloping panic-stricken into the mist. There was no escape on foot. Horsemen were everywhere, slashing at the undergrowth. Kerin fled. Ahead of him a tangle of brambles and creepers screened a ditch. He dived headlong through them, tearing his face and hands on the prickles, and rolled panting into the filthy water at the bottom of the bank. After what seemed an age, the sounds of battle began to abate. Kerin scrambled up the side of the ditch and peered through the brambles. He could hear the sound of voices drawing nearer.

'Leave them to the crows,' snarled one, instantly recognisable as Bertil Redknife's.

'No,' said another, quieter but firm. 'You'll give them Christian burial. And bury the Saxon with his weapons. I think that would please him.' Kerin tensed. The familiar, long-loved voice. The two men came out of the trees. They were followed by Eldof and a handful of warriors. Bertil's thug Balin was amongst them; and, at Rufus's shoulder, a tall, broad-shouldered man with sleek yellow hair and pale eyes whose gaze could have bored through solid metal. He was wearing a white tunic emblazoned with a blue cross and spattered with someone else's blood. If you are not Batraz, Kerin thought, he doesn't walk the earth. Rufus looked around him.

'We'll search this copse before we ride. I don't want one Saxon left alive.'

Eldof leaned on his spear with a gratified smile. 'They won't escape. My lads will cut them off before they reach their boats.'

'The sea will run with blood,' Balin said, with relish. 'The sand –'

'For God's sake, be specific,' Batraz said curtly. 'You're sending a message, not killing vermin.'

'Bring up our horses,' Rufus said briskly. He and the others drew their swords and advanced through the trees. Kerin slithered into the bottom of the ditch and froze. He heard footsteps approach the ditch and stop just above his head. Heart thudding he peered upwards. Rufus was standing quite still, looking curiously at the tangle of bushes and briars. A few broken brambles; a slight but unexpected gap where the twigs had not quite sprung back into place. Cautiously Rufus parted the brambles with his sword and peered down into the ditch. His eyes met Kerin's. They stared silently at each other. Eldof came crashing out of the thicket.

'Anything?' he shouted.

'No,' Rufus said, turning abruptly and letting the brambles close up. 'There's nothing here. Let's ride.'

10

The footsteps receded. Kerin shivered in the bottom of the ditch as hooves clattered past above him. When the sound had faded into the distance he struggled to his knees. His teeth were chattering with nerves and cold, and his clothes were plastered with foul-smelling slime. His limbs were numb and he felt as weak as water, but he knew that he must move or die.

The ditch seemed to run away southwards. Kerin stumbled along through the reeking water until he was well clear of the river, then scrambled up the bank to level ground. He found himself on a well-worn track. The mist had closed in, obscuring landmarks, but he was almost certain that this was the track they had followed from Hengist's village. Clutching his sword, he set off. The mist grew steadily thicker. It was unnerving, but he knew that it favoured him. His enemies were sure to be on horseback, and he would hear them coming long before they could see him. He had been walking just long enough for the numbness to wear off when he came upon a horse lying dead on the track. It had been speared straight through the neck. He recognised the white legs and the battle-scars on the shoulders. Lud's roan mare. Kerin sank down beside the dead horse and leaned against her cold, stiff flank. He had no idea how long he had been there when he heard the soft pit-pat of horses' hooves over damp earth. He crouched low and waited.

There were two animals, travelling at a steady trot from a southerly direction. The last he saw of Rufus's horsemen, they were hurtling off down the road to the coast. It made no sense that two of them should be returning so soon and so slowly, unless they were convinced that they were about to discover something. Kerin put down his sword, drew his dagger and crouched, heart thumping, behind the dead mare. The horses loomed suddenly out of the fog above his head. One was riderless. Kerin seized the lone horseman by the foot and toppled him out of the saddle. The rider lashed out with his other foot as he fell, catching Kerin on the jaw and sending him staggering backwards. The horses bolted off into the fog. Kerin spun round, spitting blood, and saw that the other man was already up and going for his sword. If he gets to that it's the end of me, Kerin thought, cursing bitterly. He knew he should have hung onto his sword and brought the horse down. In desperation he hurled his dagger, striking his adversary in the shoulder, and dived headlong at the other man's legs. They crashed into the mud together and rolled down the bank, landing in a flailing heap in the stinking water at the bottom. Kerin's hands closed round his opponent's throat. A pair of dark eyes blazed at him out of the murk. Vortigern's. With a cry of astonishment, Kerin released his grip and rolled clear. Gasping for breath, the two men crawled back up the bank and sank down in the middle of the track beside the dead horse. Gritting his teeth, Vortigern wrenched Kerin's dagger from his shoulder and handed it back. Kerin gripped the weapon and slit the shoulder of Vortigern's tunic. To his relief, the wound was not deep; the folds of cloak and tunic had deadened the worst of the blow. He hacked a strip of cloth from the edge of his own tunic and rolled it up.

'God forgive me,' he said shakily, pressing it against the wound. Vortigern winced as the pain bit.

'You're an idiot,' he said. 'You should have dropped the horse.'

'I know,' Kerin said. He glanced at the dead mare. 'Lud's.'

'Yes, but Lud's alive, and his sons. Gwyndaf and Lucius too. Bened and Derfyn. I suppose we have half the men we came with.'

'Where are they?'

'At a Roman fort down the road. I told them not to leave it unless they're burned out. It's death in the open; Rufus's men are everywhere.'

'Then what in God's name are you doing up here on your own?'

'Looking for you,' Vortigern said. 'I didn't think I'd find you alive, though. When your horse came back, we all thought they'd finished you off.'

Kerin swallowed hard. An icy sweat was breaking out all over his body. He began to shake with cold and raw nerves as he realised what he had almost done.

'You thought I was dead,' he said, struggling to his feet 'And you came all the way back here?' Vortigern nodded. His silence broke the last brittle thread of Kerin's composure. 'You thought I was dead?' he bawled, voice rising to a howl of fury. 'You thought I was dead, and you came all the way back here? To look for a body? For God's sake, you can't help a dead man.'

He broke off and turned away, then looked apprehensively over his shoulder. Vortigern was still watching him silently, but with an amused little twitch at the corners of his lips.

'Go and look for the horses,' he said.

Kerin seized his sword and marched away up the track. As his thoughts began to clarify, he realised that it would have been quite possible to walk past a horse without seeing it. He stood quite still and whistled softly; a sweet, liquid note, like a curlew's call in a lower key. No sound except for the dull, monotonous trickle of water. He walked on for a while then whistled again. This time the unmistakable sound of hooves sucking in and out of liquid mud, coming slowly closer. Kerin crouched, sword braced, then sighed with relief as Eryr came stumbling up the bank. The mare nuzzled into him and he threw his arms around her mud-caked neck. Vortigern's mare was standing knee-deep in a boggy pool. She lunged forward, teeth snapping, and careered past Kerin in a shower of mud. 'Black bitch,' he gasped. When he caught up with her, she was standing beside the dead horse while Vortigern caressed her ears. 'The wind's getting up,' Kerin said. 'We can't be out here when this mist lifts.' They mounted and he reached for Annwn's rein. 'Lord,' he said. Vortigern frowned. 'Lord, Katigern's dead.'

Vortigern closed his eyes. 'Poor Kat!' he said softly.

'He died a warrior,' Kerin said. 'Horsa killed him, but he finished Horsa too.'

'Horsa!' Vortigern said sharply.

'Horsa stayed to fight. I wouldn't be here otherwise. Oswi too. We didn't see what happened to him.'

They rode quickly south into the lifting mist, towards the muffled sound of the sea. The track joined a Roman road, running due south along a high bank.

'Say it,' Vortigern said as they rode. Kerin did not respond. 'Say it!' Vortigern exclaimed. 'You were right about Hengist. Right, all this time.'

'I know,' Kerin said. 'But it gives me no pleasure. And anyway, it's Rufus we have to worry about now.' A distant movement had caught his eye. A little orange light flickered far down on the eastern horizon then flared upwards and outwards, flashing out across the thinning mist like dragons' tongues. Vortigern checked his mare.

'What's that?' he asked. Kerin hesitated. He could hardly believe that Vortigern did not know.

'It's Hengist's village,' he said. 'They're burning Hengist's village.' Vortigern let his reins fall and sat quite still, staring at the flames as they threw their flaring glow upwards, lighting the mist from beneath so that it rolled out across the sullen flat lands in a dull orange cloud.

'Rufus?' he said. 'Rufus, burning villages?'

Kerin glanced wildly around, his nerves jangling. Far ahead of them, down on the rim of the sea, the dark square block of the fort reared on its low headland. Kerin could see that it was served by a good, hard road. Probably the Romans used that road to send provisions and reinforcements down the coast, from their huge fortress and supply base at Rutupiae. The road passed within sight of Hengist's village, then ran as straight as an arrow's flight down to the fort; a mere canter for men on fresh horses.

'Come on,' he said, 'or those bastards will be there before us.' The stench of burning came drifting down on an easterly breeze with shouts and screams of panic. The two mares struggled up the incline to the fort. A dark head popped up over the battlements and disappeared again. There were shouts from within and the heavy gates groaned open. They were scorched dark and pock-marked with spear-holes, probably a legacy of the days when the Romans had to defend their gains. Inside was a paved courtyard and a roofless building, its sagging door hanging open. Lud and the other warriors came from the shadows, filthy and bloodstained. Vortigern tumbled from his horse and rushed past them towards the open doorway. Kerin slipped thankfully from Eryr's back and handed the reins to Macsen.

'Are you alright?' Lud asked anxiously.

'Yes,' Kerin sighed, glancing towards the doorway. 'He's wounded, though. It's not too deep, but get Rowenna to look at it. Macsen, rub Eryr down. Vortigern's mare too, if you can get near her.' He turned to Lud, who was cleaning the blood off his sword, spitting on it and wiping it with the corner of his torn cloak. 'How many men have we got?'

'Fourteen,' Lud said.

'Counting Vortigern and myself?'

'Yes,' Lud said, still polishing.

'Any wounded?'

'Nothing deadly,' Lud said, still not looking up. 'Derfyn's got a hole in his shoulder. Lucius was wounded in the arm and Gwyndaf caught a spear on the side of the head.'

'We'll need horses,' Kerin said. 'We'll have to walk these poor beasts home if we want to keep them alive.'

'Yes,' Lud said absently. He seemed oblivious to what Kerin was saying.

'Lud, for God's sake. What's going on here?'

Lud flung his sword down. 'The girl,' he said. 'She's gone.'

'Gone?' Kerin echoed.

'Yes. Back to her father, I suppose. One moment she was over there patching up Gwyndaf's head. The next, Elir was bawling his head off and she was running for it on one of those horses Hengist pinched.'

Kerin turned away. Here it was at last, then; the betrayal which he had been expecting ever since that night of insanity in Hengist's hall. Shivering in his sodden clothes, he followed Lud up the stone steps and leaned on the crumbling wall at the top. A desolate marsh was emerging into view as the eddying wind began to suck the mist up into the higher air. His eye followed the dead straight line of the Rutupiae road running between the marsh and the muddy beach fringing the sea.

'You're wasting your time, lad,' Lud said. 'She's gone, alright. Vortigern's with the wounded, I expect, but someone must tell him.' Before Kerin could move, a sound came from below, like the howl of an injured animal. Lud snorted. 'Sounds like Gwyndaf already had the pleasure.' Kerin pushed past him and dived towards the steps. Vortigern ran stumbling across the courtyard, hurled aside the cross beam and dragged the gates open.

'No!' Kerin bellowed. He leapt from the top of the steps, but Vortigern was already astride the nearest horse, galloping headlong through the gateway and out along the Roman road. Kerin landed awkwardly and pitched headfirst into a pile of filthy, stinking saddlery. A hand seized him by his belt, hoisted him to his feet and shoved him back against the wall.

'You should let him go,' Gwyndaf said. 'Any man who'll risk his neck out there for the sake of that faithless bitch is no good to himself or to us.'

Kerin closed his eyes, dizzy with fatigue and lack of food. 'I know,' he said. 'I know.' He blinked to clear his head. Gwyndaf was looking at him curiously. His deep-set grey eyes held none of their usual scorn. It was as if tiredness and desperation had burned the hostility out of him. The right side of his face was encrusted with dried blood below the frayed strip of cloth which Rowenna had used to bind his head.

'Look,' he said, 'we can't afford to lose one man, let alone two.'

'You're right,' Kerin said. Gwyndaf smiled briefly.

'I know I am,' he said. 'But I can't expect you to listen to me, can I? Come on, we'll go together. I owe you that much.'

'You owe me nothing,' Kerin said. 'And if you're talking about what happened at the river, forget it. I'd have done the same for any of the lads. For one of Hengist's, even.'

'I know you would,' Gwyndaf said. 'But I didn't expect you to do it for me. I haven't gone out of my way to make things easy for him, have I? And you breathe each other's breath; everyone knows that.'

Kerin frowned. 'Don't talk nonsense. I'm his warrior, that's all. I'm not even of his kindred. It's not the same. Ask Lud, or any of his blood-relations.'

'I don't have to,' Gwyndaf said. 'And you're right, it's not the same. He cares nothing for his blood-relations. He'd kill twenty of them to save your skin. Perhaps it takes an outsider like me to see it. Now. Are we going, or not?'

'Yes,' Kerin said abruptly. He had no wish to add to, or even to think about, what Gwyndaf had said. He loosed two horses which looked a little fresher than the others. Lud came down from the battlement as they mounted up.

'You're mad. I'd die for him myself, but you're both mad.' He handed Kerin a spear. 'Take this one. I've had a chance to sharpen it.'

'Whatever happens, don't come after us,' Kerin said. 'You can probably hold this place
against quite a lot of them until the gate burns through.'

Lud turned away, shaking his head. 'Go on,' he said. 'The gods protect you.'

Kerin followed Gwyndaf out. The gates closed behind them and the bar came down. They rode as fast as the tired horses would go, keeping to the soft ground beside the road to spare the animals' feet.

'Have you any idea where we're going?' Gwyndaf asked.

'Well,' Kerin said, 'Rowenna's gone to her father, so we must be looking for Hengist's boats. I know he beached them near his village, so I suppose that's where we're going.'

They struck inland away from the road, across ravaged cornfields whose scorched crops smouldered acridly under the rain. The tracks of two horses preceded them. Hengist's village was still burning, but deserted. Beyond it was a beach; not a beach as they knew it but a series of mud banks interspersed by tidal channels, and a gravel spit jutting out into the leaden sea. Two galleys were making for open water, their oars raking, sails hanging limp in the turgid air. A third was burning in the shallows. The mud banks were strewn with bloody corpses. It looked as if Rufus and his victorious army were long gone. Vortigern had left his horse on the gravel spit. He was standing knee-deep in the murky water, staring distractedly at the receding ships. Gwyndaf shook his head and stretched out his hand to take the reins of Kerin's horse. Kerin slipped to the ground, shouldered his spear and trudged along the gravel spit, which was still scarred by the deep furrows where the galleys had rested. He waded out into the sea. Vortigern turned, the wetness of the fog running in rivulets down his face.

'Lord, they've gone,' Kerin said. 'You can't stay here.'

'No,' Vortigern said absently, staring at the ships passing in and out of the drifts of mist. 'Not the girl.'

'Yes,' Kerin said. 'The girl too. We can't stay here. We've got to get back to the fort before they find us.'

Some note of fear or desperation in his voice made Vortigern turn. 'Get out of here,' he said. 'They'll be back soon. Get out now.'

Kerin folded his arms. 'Not without you, lord,' he said. Gwyndaf rode his horse into the sea. He looked white and rattled and the wound in his head had begun to bleed again.

'Look,' he snapped, 'that double-crossing bitch has gone, and I'm not making my wife a widow because you're too stupid to see it. Can we go, please, before your son comes back to slaughter us?'

Vortigern looked up at him, as if he were more surprised to see Gwyndaf there than by anything he had said. 'You shouldn't be here,' he said. 'Go back to the fort, for God's sake, and take this fool with you.'

'No!' Gwyndaf roared. 'Because I've got two fools to take with me, and I can't drag both of you with my head in half.'

'Be quiet,' Kerin said, raising his hand. They listened. Something had moved out on the mud banks. There had been some small, half-heard disturbance of mud and water.

'Perhaps one of those poor bastards is still alive,' Gwyndaf said, peering into the murk.

'Or perhaps Rufus is back,' Kerin said, raising his spear. Vortigern turned, and Rowenna came to him out of the drifting mist. She was trying to run, weighed down by her soaking clothes. Vortigern caught her in his arms. For a brief moment he looked like a drowning man clinging to a piece of driftwood.

'I had to see my father,' Rowenna stammered. She looked terrified, as anyone might have done. 'After this I may never see him again. Perhaps –'

'Later, later,' Vortigern said, pressing his hand over her mouth. 'Gwyndaf, the horses, quickly.'

'Oswi!' Rowenna wailed. 'Oswi lives! We can't leave him!'

'Where is he?' Kerin glanced desperately along the beach.

'Out there,' Rowenna said, flinging a hand towards the mud banks. 'He is badly wounded.'

'You mean they left him?' Vortigern said, in disgust.

'He has his horse,' Rowenna said. 'He would not leave the horse, and my father would not take it on his ship.'

'Show me where,' Kerin said, seizing her arm.

They waded out through the shallow water. Ahead of them the mist swirled and thinned, and Kerin saw Ghazal, standing with head drooped on a half-submerged mud bank. Oswi was lying on his back at the stallion's feet with the reins knotted in his fingers. Rowenna stumbled through the mud and dropped to her knees at his side. Oswi's eyes flickered and closed as her hand brushed his face. He was bleeding from wounds in his arm and shoulder, and his tunic was soaked with blood from the midriff down. Beyond them in the fog, two swaying mast-heads were the only visible trace of the Saxon ships. Oswi's blood formed a dark stain across the front of Rowenna's sodden tunic as she cradled his head, stroking back the wet strands of brown hair. Towards the land, the fires of the ravaged village spread a shifting yellow light across the drizzling mist as Hengist's galleys slipped noiselessly out to sea.

'You said I did my father's work,' Rowenna cried bitterly. 'You said I did not love Vortigern. Do you think I would be here now, if I did not love him to my soul?'

'No,' Kerin said. 'I was wrong. But for once, I'm glad of it.'

'I have lost my horse,' Rowenna sobbed. 'He ran away when I went to the ship.'

'It doesn't matter,' Kerin said. 'We'll manage.' Ghazal whinnied, stretched out his fine head and nibbled the sleeve of his tunic. Kerin smiled. 'You remember me, don't you,' he said, scratching the stallion's ears. It seemed years since that frosty night when he had liberated him. Perhaps horses did not measure time, only acts of kindness. Vortigern came up the bank with Gwyndaf and looked at Oswi in despair. 'I know,' Kerin said, 'but she's right, we can't leave him.' He and Gwyndaf heaved Oswi up onto the back of the mare which Vortigern had ridden from the fort. It left them with no illusions about the amount of strength they had left. Vortigern hauled himself onto Ghazal's back, swung Rowenna up behind him and turned for the beach.

'Well,' Gwyndaf said as he and Kerin followed them in, 'you were wrong about that.'

'Completely wrong,' Kerin said. 'Is that what you were trying to tell me in Henfelin?'

'Yes. But there's no point in telling a man something when he's determined not to believe it. I can see why you didn't, of course. Even I had my doubts at one point, particularly on his account. It was a relief to be proved wrong.'

'A relief?' Kerin said. 'Why do you say that?'

Gwyndaf watched Vortigern riding ahead of them, the girl's head pressed against his shoulder. 'Because it proves he's mortal,' he said, with a grudging smile. 'You see? He even had me doubting it in the end.'

11

The gates of the fort creaked open to let them in. The war-riors surrounded the sweating horses, greeting their riders with unspoken relief. Lud stared at Rowenna, his face set in a hostile glare.

'No,' Kerin said. 'I was wrong. She wasn't running away. Has anything happened?'

Lud raised his eyebrows, as if the change of heart were hard to credit. 'Nothing. We thought we heard horsemen galloping once, but we're probably going mad. What's it like out there?'

'Living hell,' Kerin said. 'They're bound to come soon. Hengist's gone, so they'll have no-one else to kill. What would you do?'

'Something quick,' Lud said. 'They're not going to wait for us to starve. I'd attack the fort from both sides and set fire to the gates. We'd be too busy fending them off to put the fire out. Where did you find the Saxon?'

'On the mud banks where Hengist beached his ships. He wouldn't leave his horse.'

Lud laughed out loud. 'They're as mad as we are. But I'm glad we've got the horse. The ones Hengist pinched aren't too bad, but our lot couldn't outrun a donkey.'

Kerin looked at the huddle of exhausted animals, heads drooping, some resting lame legs. Ghazal had sauntered over to join them. 'If we get out of here alive, I'm going to get a colt by that horse,' he said. Lud stared up at the sky.

'For the gods' sake, haven't you got anything more important to think about?'

'There's no point in thinking about getting killed,' Kerin said. He selected five serviceable spears and carried them up the steps to the battlement. Vortigern was leaning on the castellated wall, watching the coast road.

'What do you think?' he asked.

'Well,' Kerin said, 'if I were Rufus, I'd split my men in two. Then half of them could come this way, along the coast, and the other half down the road from the river. If he does that, we'll have two sides of the fort to defend, as well as worrying about the gates.'

'It's only a matter of time,' Vortigern said. 'We've hardly got a good spear each. Derfyn's had a dagger through his shoulder and Lucius can't use his sword-arm. It might almost be better to run for it. I know the horses are finished, but we're going to die here anyway.'

'You're right,' Kerin said. 'Shall I tell them to make ready?'

'Not yet. The less time they have to get frightened, the better. We'll ride bareback. Anything to lessen the weight.'

'Oswi,' Kerin said reluctantly.

'Well, we've got to take him or kill him,' Vortigern said, turning for the steps.

'Lord,' Kerin said. Vortigern looked round. 'I was wrong about Rowenna. I thought she was working something for Hengist. I'm sorry. She's probably told you that I've been a bastard to her.'

'She hasn't said a word about it, as it happens,' Vortigern said.

'He is not bleeding now,' Rowenna said, stroking Oswi's face. 'He has a wound here – ' she indicated a point below the ribcage. 'This is the worst. We cannot put him on a horse again.'

She straightened up, wiping her hands on her tunic, and screwed her muddy hair back. Macsen and Elir picked Oswi up and carried him gently to a rough-and-ready bed made from stinking horse blankets and a saddle. Vortigern drew Rowenna aside.

'We're leaving,' he said. 'We can't sit here, waiting for them to come and kill us.' Rowenna's eyebrows rose. 'You think we can run, on these tired beasts?'

'No,' Vortigern said. 'Perhaps we can escape them some-how. I don't see how, but we must try.'

Kerin stared up at the sky. Somewhere above the mist the sun was trying to come out, turning the dull grey shroud a glaring white. If it broke through the cloud-cover it would burn the mist off, leaving them cruelly visible. 'How late do you think it is? Mid-afternoon?'

'God knows,' Vortigern said, 'but we can't wait any longer. See if there's anything we can use to make a litter. I'll check the horses.'

Lud was sitting at the bottom of the steps, head propped wearily on his hands. 'We're leaving?' he asked.

'Yes,' Kerin said. 'We'll have to make a litter for Oswi. Is there anything here?'

'Nothing very good. We'll manage something.' He trudged off, calling to Elir. Kerin joined Vortigern amongst the horses.

'Any sound ones?'

'Not really,' Vortigern said. 'The stallion's fit, but even with him we're still short of a horse. Rowenna will have to ride double with Lucius; he's not too big, and he can't fight anyway, with his arm strapped up.'

The filthy, bloodstained crew assembled in the courtyard. Lud and Elir had cobbled together a litter out of wood, horse blankets and saddle-girths, which might hold together as long as the timber didn't break.

'Are we going to run for it, then?' Elir asked.

'Yes,' Vortigern said, 'although run isn't the word I'd use.'

'Hobble?' Macsen suggested. Vortigern gave him a scarifying look.

'Apart from the stallion, we've got four horses which aren't badly lame,' he said. 'Lucius, you and Rowenna will ride double on the stallion. This isn't your quarrel and you can't fight anyway, so if there's trouble, use the horse's speed to save your skin and hers. Lud, sort the rest out. The strongest men on the strongest horses, nothing else would make any sense.'

The warriors dispersed. Rowenna remained. 'You think I will run to save my skin?' she said defiantly.

'Yes,' Vortigern said. 'You will, if I have to knock you senseless and tie you to the horse. Now, go and see to Oswi before they put him on the litter.' He turned towards the horses, then stopped. He raised his hand for silence and stood quite still. Kerin had heard it already; the awful, rolling sound of a large number of galloping horsemen. He was halfway up the steps before anyone else had moved. Vortigern arrived beside him and they crouched behind the battlement. The wild, brawling mass was coming out of the mist along the coast road.

'How many, do you think?' Vortigern asked.

Kerin screwed his eyes up and peered into the thinning whiteness. He glimpsed Rufus, leading the charge on his dappled grey. Just behind came Batraz and other men in white tunics, then a formless, galloping chaos; banners streaming, a golden cross raised high like a battle standard. 'Five hundred? Six hundred? God knows. Too many.'

'Lord!' Lud bellowed. He had scaled the steps on the far side of the fort and was on the wall above the gateway, staring at the road which led to the river. Kerin closed his eyes. He could hear the second band of riders already.

'You were right,' Vortigern said, without looking. They ran along the battlement, ducking below the fortifications. Lud was standing quite still, gazing out over the wall.

'I hope everyone's made his peace with the gods, lord,' he said. The army bearing down on the fort from the north was easily twice the size of the band marauding along the coast road. Kerin watched them come, wondering how many he could take with him. Beyond the manifest threat of galloping death, there was something disturbing about them. They were not shouting or yelling or waving their swords like men on a murder-mission normally did; like Rufus's band were certainly doing, because Kerin could hear the clamour already. They were riding low in the saddle, straight as a line down the Roman road in ominous total silence. He shielded his eyes from the glaring whiteness as the dark, moving mass drew closer, swimming and separating in the shifting mist like blobs in a mirage. Vortigern's eyes narrowed.

'Who are they?' he asked.

'I don't know,' Kerin said. 'But give me Rufus's crew.' Rowenna came sprinting up the steps and grabbed a spear. Vortigern wrenched it from her hand.

'They are coming to kill us!' she protested. 'I learned to throw these things with my brothers.'

'Alright,' Vortigern said, tossing the spear back. 'Pick a man, and don't take your eyes off him. And don't throw it until they're almost up to the wall.'

Kerin brought a spear to his shoulder Soon they would be within his range. Every able-bodied man was on the battlement now. Vortigern raised a spear.

'Lord!' Kerin said sharply. 'Lord, wait!' There was a split second in which he had no idea why he had said it; then the dark, shifting fragments on which he had focussed his eyes coalesced into a single, hurtling shape. 'Loving God, it's Publius Luca!' he shouted.

'And Gorlois!' Lud roared, clenching his fists above his head. 'The Bear of Kernow!'

The commander was riding at the head of his troops in full uniform, the red legionary's cape which Kerin had never thought to see again billowing above his shoulders. On his heels came Gorlois and a young officer carrying the faded old banner of the Second Augusta. The horse-men streamed after them, three hundred or more of the cavalry Lucius had led against the Picts and a mob of Gorlois's Kernow men, coming out of the mist with their heads down and their spears braced. No-one would have taken their leader for a commander of legendary decency and compassion. Publius Luca was riding with the anger of hell on him. As his riders swept below the walls, half of them peeled off and surrounded the fort, spears raised in a bristling, impenetrable ring. The remainder galloped on, straight at Rufus's charging warriors. Gorlois rose in the saddle and hurled his spear. It sank itself in the chest of Rufus's warhorse. The mare gave a ghastly screech and crashed down under the hooves of the horses behind her, throwing her rider clear. Rufus seized an outstretched hand and was hauled up onto a horse's quarters. He yelled frantically to his warriors. They wheeled in the middle of the road and careered off up the coast the way they had come. Gorlois gave a howl of triumph and took off in pursuit. Kerin glimpsed Varro riding beside him; the man who was once chief warrior to Eldof of Glevum, proving his loyalty to Vortigern in the most crushing way possible, by leading the charge against Eldof's allies. Lud and Macsen raced down the steps and flung open the gates to admit Publius Luca. Kerin gave a crow of delight and leapt from the steps. He landed heavily, stumbled across the courtyard and arrived, almost weeping with joy, in front of the man who had saved their lives. Both the commander and his venerable cavalry horse looked as if they might have overdone things a little, but Publius Luca was smiling. He clasped Lud's hand and cuffed Kerin over the head. Vortigern came down the steps. Publius Luca stepped forward to meet him, and they embraced with transparent affection and relief.

'We were dead men,' Vortigern said, leaning on Publius's shoulder. 'How on earth did you find us?'

'I knew you'd come to Kent as soon as you learned about Hefin,' Publius said. 'We soon heard that you'd fought them at the river, and this was the most obvious place to hide out. Now, get your horses, we can't stay here. They've got more men ranging around somewhere, and they're expecting reinforcements by sea any day. We're quartered at Lemanis, the next fort west of here. Marcellus is there, and he'll see to your wounded. It'll give him something to do, other than telling me that I'm an old fool who should be sitting at home with his wife.' He broke off, with a look both surprised and intrigued. Rowenna was standing on the far side of the courtyard, watching him warily. Her face and clothes were still spattered with mud and Oswi's blood, and she was still holding the spear.

'My wife, Rowenna,' Vortigern said. 'Hengist's daughter. I would have told you. Put the spear down, girl, and come here.' Rowenna leaned the spear against the wall and approached cautiously. 'This is my great friend, Publius,' Vortigern said. 'I've told you enough about him. You should know that there's no need to look at him like that.'

Rowenna allowed herself a small smile. Two tears slid from the corners of her eyes, making white trails down her grimy cheeks. She stood on tiptoe and planted a kiss on Publius Luca's cheek. He looked astonished, but far from displeased. 'I am muddy,' Rowenna said gravely. 'I am sorry.'

'She'd have got on her father's boat if she had any sense,' Vortigern said. 'There's nothing but grief for her with me now.'

Publius shrugged. *Volenti non fit injuria,*' he said. Kerin looked at them both uncertainly.

'To one who is willing, no harm is done,' Vortigern said, brushing a hand over his wife's hair. 'But that belongs in the law courts with Titus, don't you think?'

'It belongs here,' Publius Luca said, drawing the three of them close.

12

The fort at Lemanis was much larger than the little outpost along the coast, with higher walls, big, projecting towers and a deep defensive ditch. There was a building which had once housed the garrison commander's headquarters, a barracks and stables, all in excellent repair despite a few years of abandonment. A bonfire of rotten timber and weeds was smouldering in the ditch outside. No-one who had made the forced march even noticed these things. Once messengers had been despatched to Henfelin, they simply handed their spent animals to Publius Luca's horse master and allowed themselves to be led to the barracks, where beds, blankets and oblivion were waiting.

On the morning of the second day – or was it the third or fourth, Kerin couldn't be sure – one of Publius Luca's men came to find him as he was taking breakfast. Marcellus had brought dried fruit and sheep's cheese, and they were sharing it in the sunlit courtyard.

'News from the Lord of Kernow, sir,' the legionary said. 'Your army's arrived from Cambria. They've joined forces and routed the band that was attacking your fort. They're just clearing up the stragglers, but they should be back by nightfall. No sign of Lord Vortimer and his chief warrior as yet. I've told the king, of course. Publius Imperator said I could leave the rest to you.'

Marcellus waited until the messenger had gone. 'I can't abide the Lord Vortimer nonsense,' he said. 'The boy doesn't deserve the honorific, and if Rufus is good enough in Cambria, it should be good enough here. Be that as it may. I imagine Publius means that if Rufus and his henchman surface, you should deal with it as you think fit. The commander isn't given to understatement, as a rule, but perhaps he fears that there are lines the king won't cross. Do you think so?'

'I don't know, yet,' Kerin said. 'Perhaps it'll depend on the circumstances. Vortigern could have killed Rufus in the North. He chose not to, but no-one else was going to die; not immediately, anyway.'

'Whereas you had a far more brutal choice to make,' Marcellus said. 'You could let Rufus kill his father, or throw Vortigern your sword, knowing that he might then kill your friend. It's those brutal choices that show where the truth lies. We shall come to it one day, I'm sure.' He smiled and offered Kerin the last of the dried figs. 'Now I must visit Oswi, your mad Saxon. He'll live now, not that he deserves to, in my view; any man who'd sooner die than be parted from a dumb animal has the brain of a filbert. What will you do with him?'

'Well, we can't abandon him,' Kerin said. 'He saved Lucius's life, probably mine and Vortigern's too.'

'Leave it with me,' Marcellus said. 'I am returning to Londinium shortly. It'll be weeks before the man's fit to ride, and he'll need medical supervision for a while. The worst part will be enduring his company on the journey. Now go, and attend to all those things which the king's right arm has to do.'

*

Gwyndaf was leaning on the battlement, looking out towards the east. Marcellus's medication might have eased the pain in his head, but there was surely no remedy for his grief at the loss of Leil and Cadfan. Once, in the North, the standard-bearer had described Derfyn as the son he never had; but he seemed to have developed something approaching a father's affection for all the rootless boys he had taken in after the slaughter of his first wife and their children. He turned and smiled as Kerin approached, then went back to his contemplation of the empty road.

'Oswi's going to live,' Kerin said, leaning beside him.

'Good,' Gwyndaf said. 'He deserves to. Do you think Hengist had it planned?'

'Yes. I knew something was wrong, but I didn't see it until too late. We were just the bait for Rufus's army; the distraction to keep them busy.'

'Is it true what they say about you?' Gwyndaf asked. 'That you can see what's to come?'

'No,' Kerin said. 'Not in the way you've probably been told. When I was a little sprat living in Lud's house, I had a dream about Lud's deerhound. It was lying dead in its bed. Anyone could see why; us lads used to play with the dog, and Lud was forever telling us that we'd wear it out and kill it. I was scared to death of Lud, so I worried about it and had a dream about the dog dying. I woke up crying, Mora dragged me outside and showed me the dog, large as life, and that was that. Except that a few days later, the dog did die. Lud – well, something happened to him. I was too young to understand any of it. Lud's superstitious, isn't he, he talks about the old gods as if they were living in his house. All I know is that someone dragged me off to live in the chieftains' hall. I was just a nipper, Gwyndaf, I didn't wonder why until one day Lud asked if I'd had any of those dreams lately.' He hesitated, but the other man's gaze was so open, so touched with concern, that the admission came easily. 'Then Lud told me that the only reason Vortigern had me was that men like him needed prophets. I couldn't see the future at all, so I started trying to work it out from what people said and did. Sometimes I was right. Lud began to take notice. He'd ask if I'd dreamed something, and sometimes I'd lie and say yes. Now we're here, and half of Cambria thinks I'm a prophet.'

Gwyndaf nodded, seeming to understand perfectly. His own preoccupations resurfaced and he looked away. 'Those boys were like family to me,' he said. 'Not as close as Derfyn. But all the same.'

Kerin laid a hand on his arm. 'I don't know if Rufus or Batraz got away,' he said. 'If they did, and I find out where they are, I'll tell you. No-one else.'

*

At dusk a cry went up from the lookout on the eastern tower. 'The Lord of Kernow! And the army of Cambria!'

Gorlois was first through the gate. His tunic was heavily stained with blood, not much of it his own, judging by the way he sprang from his horse. 'By the gods, we hammered the bastards!' he roared. A rowdy cheer went up. The Kernow warriors were hauled down from their horses and everyone embraced. Hefydd and the Cambrians poured in behind them, singing lustily. The leading men forged towards the doorway of the commandant's headquarters, where Vortigern and Kerin were waiting. 'It's done!' Gorlois exclaimed, above the sounds of rejoicing. Hefydd was fighting tears but seemed content that honour had been satisfied. Publius Luca came from within and calmly assessed the chaos in the courtyard.

'Go inside,' he said to Vortigern. 'They won't be so over-joyed to see me, so I'll get more sense out of them.'

Kerin followed Vortigern into the cool interior. There was a square oak table, where generations of garrison commanders must have sat to deal with their officers.

'I don't care if I never make another forced march,' Vortigern said, as he sat down.

'Nor me,' Kerin said, wincing and stretching his limbs.

'I'm sure. But you have over twenty years of stupidity ahead of you, before you start feeling it in the same way. And it saps your patience. I'm glad Publius is out there, trying to screw sense out of Gorlois and Hefydd. It's hard enough when they've been sitting at home doing nothing. Occasionally there's something to be said for the disciplined Roman mind.'

They waited, enjoying the peace and quiet, until Publius Luca came in. He had a sheet of papyrus in his hand, and he had brought Varro.

'Alright,' Publius said, as they sat. 'Here is what the other side have. Around two thousand men in all, as far as I can judge. But they're scattered. Disorganised. Most are Kentishmen, within the walls of their capital by now. There were around five hundred with Rufus, largely from Kent and Gallia, at least half of whom have been killed. Father Paulinus is riding for Venta Belgarum, with fifty armed fanatics. There are probably five hundred men of Glevum, last seen heading for home, and the same number of troops from Gallia. Your son is alive, as far as anyone knows, and probably has a handful of his best men with him. My guess is that the Gallians will head for Dubris, where their transports are anchored. All the talk has been of more ships, but they'll bide their time now, I expect. What do you have, to the best of your knowledge?'

'Probably five hundred with Hefydd and the same with his son, Mabon,' Vortigern said. 'They had next to no time to raise them. Then your men, and whatever Gorlois brought. How did he get here, anyway?'

'I went for him,' Varro said. 'The news about Hefin and Macsen was all over Glevum. I knew you'd ride to Kent, but I thought it would be more help to head for Kernow. I knew Gorlois wouldn't fail us.'

'You're a true friend,' Vortigern said. 'A true friend. How many did you bring?'

'Four hundred Kernow men and twenty of my own. And I believe Publius Imperator has about the same.'

'Indeed,' Publius said. 'Three hundred first-class cavalry, and a hundred rough lads on their own ponies who heard that the king needed them, and wouldn't take no for an answer.'

Vortigern grinned. 'There are still a few of us mad men left, then. Alright, Varro; go and get the commanders. Gorlois, Hefydd, Gwyndaf, Lucius, Lud and Mabon.'

Publius waited until Varro had gone. 'I'm truly sorry about Katigern,' he said. 'He was a nice, harmless lad who shouldn't have been where he was.'

'Poor Kat!' Vortigern said. 'The slowest mind of all my boys, and the biggest heart. And he was only there because Rufus frightened him witless. If he'd spent less time worrying about hell and damnation, he wouldn't have been stabbed in the guts. And the man he killed. Horsa, of all people.' He drew out his dagger and looked down at the blade, pitted by some recent collision with metal or bone. 'It's a filthy business, Publius. A filthy business.'

Publius Luca patted his arm. 'They're coming back,' he

said. Varro and his six companions sat down around the table. Vortigern greeted them with a warm smile, a look of gratitude and pure relief.

'My brave friends,' he said. 'Not one of you is here because I commanded it, or even requested it. You're here because you were needed, and would probably have come even if I'd forbidden it.' The other nine men nodded an acknowledgment. 'That's the best kind of loyalty. And God knows we'll need it in the days to come, because this is only the beginning. The first skirmish. Will you all stand with me, until it's settled?'

'I will,' Publius Luca said. He stretched out his arm and placed a clenched fist on the centre of the table. Murmured assents and eight more fists followed. Vortigern shook each man's hand in turn. No more was said, because no more was needed. The pledge was as solid as if it had been carved in granite.

'So, what now?' Varro asked.

'We have a choice,' Vortigern said. 'The old choice of horse warfare. You can't pursue a fleeing, disorganised enemy unless you scatter your own force. By doing that, you lay yourself open to any fresh, disciplined reinforcements they may bring. Do they have such a force? We don't know. If they have, it'll be at Dubris. How far is it from here, Publius? Twenty miles?'

'Thereabouts,' Publius Luca said. 'My spies should be back shortly. There's not much cover, so they'll lie low until it's dark.'

'And the choice?' Lud asked.

'We can pursue them and take the risk, or we can let them go,' Vortigern said. 'There's no point in chasing the Glevum men. They'll be halfway home by now. We could hang Abbot Paulinus, but that would just antagonise the ordinary Christians. And we'd have to burn the Kentishmen out of their capital. If we're going to fight, it should be against the Gallian mercenaries.'

Publius Luca took a steady breath. 'No disrespect, sir,' he said – and it was some time since Kerin had heard him use any form of polite address with Vortigern – 'no disrespect at all, but at the moment you and your warband aren't in a fit state to fight a nest of kittens.'

The warriors exchanged nervous glances. There was a portentous silence. Someone cleared his throat. Vortigern's face creased into a grin.

'Alright, Publius. We're not at our best. So, what would the commander of the Second Augusta like to do?'

'Sink all the Gallian transports,' Publius Luca said. 'We can't do that, of course, because Dubris is a deep water port, and they'll just run out to sea when they see us coming.'

'What, then?' Gorlois said indignantly. 'We didn't come here to sit on our arses. Are we going to fight Rufus again?'

'Without a doubt,' Vortigern said. 'But not now. As I said, this is only the beginning. We can't afford to lose men for no good reason. So at first light I want you, Varro, Hefydd and Mabon to go to Durovernum. Plant your banners, surround the city and frighten shit out of everyone in it, but don't fight them unless they attack you. I don't want a war with Kent if it can be avoided. Give it a week, then leave.'

'And if they do attack us?' Mabon asked, looking patently disappointed.

'Well, if they're stupid enough to do that, you can kill them all and flatten the place,' Vortigern said. 'But don't start it.'

'What do you want the rest of us to do, lord?' Lud asked.

'Nothing,' Vortigern said. 'You heard Publius Imperator's

verdict on our capabilities. There's food prepared. All the men who made the forced march should eat it and get some sleep.'

Kerin began to rise but found Marcellus beside him. The haruspex leaned across the table and caught Varro's arm. 'You have an affliction of the throat,' he said. Varro started as the claw-like fingers dug into his arm.

'Er – yes. An old battle wound. I couldn't speak at all for a year. I don't think there's much to be done.'

'And I suppose you think a warrior's the best judge of that,' Marcellus said acidly. 'It hurts you to speak, I take it?'

'Yes. Like daggers. That's why I don't say too much.'

Marcellus's bony finger traced the scar. 'Well,' he said, 'that problem at least I can remedy. I came to tell you all that I'm leaving at first light, and I'm taking your mad Saxon with me, so the rest of you might want to bid him farewell.'

The sickroom was dark, lit only by wavering candles. Kerin lifted one and illuminated Oswi's face. After a while Vortigern came in and felt the Saxon's forehead, which was filmed with sweat.

'Ah!' Oswi whispered. His eyes widened in fear as the unfamiliar surroundings and the odd, medicinal smell of Marcellus's remedies crowded in on him. 'You will not leave me here!' he exclaimed, seizing Vortigern's arm.

'No,' Vortigern said. 'I'm nothing like Hengist. You're safe with us.'

'Marcellus says we go to Londinium,' Oswi said apprehensively.

'Yes,' Kerin said. 'You'll be better off there until you get your strength back.'

Oswi reached for his hand. 'You take my Draca,' he said. Kerin smiled.

'No. He's your horse, Oswi.'

'You take him! You save my life, so you take the horse. One day he makes many colts, then I have the best ones. But now, he goes with you.'

Kerin could hardly believe his luck. 'Alright,' he said, clasping Oswi's hand. The door to the stairs creaked open and Gorlois came in, ducking his woolly head to avoid the lintel.

'Consider it done,' he mouthed. Vortigern gave him a look which discouraged any elaboration. Kerin wondered what plan they could possibly be hatching. For now, he was too overjoyed about the horse to worry about it.

'Eat and prepare your men, Gorlois,' Vortigern said. 'Garagon deserves a nice surprise when he gets up in the morning. And come to us for midwinter. You and all the commanders. I can never repay you, but a good feast might be a place to start.'

Gorlois beamed. 'If the gods are willing and the seas are open, let nothing prevent it,' he said. There was a clattering on the stairs. Hefydd and Mabon appeared at the door with a dripping leg of pork, some loaves and a pitcher.

'Come on, Bear!' Hefydd chortled, still wavering between laughter and tears. 'Help us fill our bellies and drown our sorrows!'

At the doorway, Gorlois turned. 'I married the girl,' he said. There was something almost apologetic about the way he said it. Kerin had no idea what he was talking about. There was no time to ask because Macsen was at the door.

'Publius's spies are coming up the road,' he said. 'And they've got prisoners.'

Kerin recognised the leading rider straight away; the young soldier who had knocked on Publius's door in the Castra, the day Titus Luca brought his dismaying news from Gallia. Shorn of his uniform, he looked like a nondescript horse boy; hair grown shaggy, threadbare brown clothes, knock-kneed pony. His companion was riding a raw-boned farm horse which was dragging a litter with two men in it. They had both been trussed like roasting fowl and had sacks over their heads, tied round the neck with twine.

'Antonius?' Publius Luca said.

'They've gone, sir. All those mercenaries from Gallia who were supposed to join up with the Lord Vortimer and his men. Looks like they left in a hurry. The port's full of injured horses and stuff they didn't have time to load. We caught one of them, a lad with an awful spear wound. He got left behind when the ships put out. We found him bleeding to death in a corn warehouse. A half-British lad who'd ended up in Gallia with his family. He told us a few things before he passed. The Sarmatian stayed here with Lord Vortimer, but they told everyone else to get out. Said they'd send for them when they were ready to have another go. The Sarmatian told them to wait near – what's the name of the Roman port across the channel? Bononia? – yes. Shame we couldn't have saved the lad, he might have told us some more.'

Some muffled cries were coming from the litter.

'Who are those two?' Kerin asked.

'Some scruffy bastards we found hiding in a rowing boat near the wharf, sir,' Antonius said. 'We thought if we brought them back and – well, gave them to some of you, sir, that you might be able to get some information out of them.'

Kerin heard a merciless chuckle just behind him. 'That's work for my standard-bearer,' Vortigern said. Gwyndaf shoved his way through the circle of warriors. Antonius and his companion dragged the captives from the litter, forced them to kneel and tore off the sacks. Kerin's heart lurched.

'Cadfan! Leil!' he exclaimed. The two young men burst into tears. Gwyndaf fell to his knees, cut them free and embraced them. Derfyn came stumbling forward, arm strapped across his chest, and joined in as best he could. Vortigern and Kerin linked arms and went back to the food and their beds. For now, the four men needed no-one else to share their joy.

*

They left at dawn; just Publius Luca's cavalry, Macsen, Gwyndaf's lads and the survivors of the forced march. Marcellus was on his way back to Londinium with Oswi the Horseman. Lucius was driving the carriage. 'I have business to see to,' he said as they left, giving Kerin a covert smile. Everyone else had gone to Durovernum to frighten Garagon and his citizens. The cavalrymen rode at the head and tail of the procession, sparing the king's warriors the need for vigilance.

'Where are we going?' Gwyndaf asked.

'To a villa north-west of here, about a day's march,' Vortigern said. 'It belongs to Publius Luca's brother-in-law. We're to be honoured by the presence of the new praetor, Valerius Dio. I hope he can drink and sleep, because it's all I have in mind for the next few days.'

'Human after all, then, lord,' Gwyndaf said mildly.

13

The villa was beautiful. There was a stately red-tiled house with ancillary buildings, arranged around a central courtyard where figs and vines flourished in the warm, windless air. There were hot baths and cold baths, a steam room, a small temple presided over by a statue of Apollo, an elegant library full of books and scrolls for those who knew how to read them, and a stable full of well-bred horses for those who preferred less cerebral pastimes. Orchards full of plums and apples skirted the walls on the western side. Alongside lay a secondary court composed of barns, grain stores, slaves' quarters and a large, airy room housing the winepress where the villa's own grapes were crushed to produce a dry, fragrant wine. The house overlooked a broad valley where a river meandered gently between fields of ripening corn and pastures full of the sleek, well-bred cattle for which their owner, Marcus Fulvius, was renowned.

The horses had been turned out to graze. As the late afternoon sun cast lengthening shadows across the cornfields, Kerin leaned on the window ledge of his guest chamber and watched with an affectionate smile as Eryr and Vortigern's mare chased each other along the riverbank, frolicking like fillies. The horses must have thought that they had found paradise, and he would probably have thought so himself, had his wife been there to share it. Their first days at the villa had slid lazily by in a pleasurable stream of sleep, good food and fragrant baths. Now all that remained was to await the arrival of the new praetor, Valerius Dio.

'Anyone turning up yet?' Macsen asked, helping himself from a basket of candied fruit.

'No,' Kerin said. 'If they don't hurry, we might have to eat all that food ourselves.'

The kitchens had been in full swing since dawn the day before. Kerin, wandering past, was astounded by the orgy of gutting, boning, feathering and stuffing going on inside. Marcus Fulvius himself was in there, checking that things were going according to plan; a tall, personable man of Publius Luca's age.

'Have you seen the girl?' Macsen asked. Kerin went on scanning the road, a pale ribbon across the undulating plains to the east.

'What girl?'

'Well, I don't know, exactly. She might be the owner's grand-daughter, I suppose. She was with Publius Luca's wife when we arrived, and I saw her this morning by the river. A vision of loveliness.'

Kerin looked round. 'Macsen, don't even think about it.'

Macsen chuckled. 'Don't worry, I know when I'm outclassed.'

They both jumped to attention as the door opened without warning and Vortigern came in. Like everyone else, he had been obliged to accept the offer of a change of clothes, to replace the stinking rags of the forced march. Marcus Fulvius had provided a selection of the smart tunics and breeches in which he and his people went hunting. Vortigern looked refreshed, and unreasonably alert for a man who had spent most of the previous day and night drinking.

'Please,' he said, 'continue your conversation.'

'It's alright, lord,' Macsen said amiably. 'Kerin was just warning me to keep my hands off the owner's grand-daughter.'

Vortigern sat down on the bed. 'I don't suppose you have any idea what it means to trifle with a Fulvius, have you.'

'Would it be like trifling with your daughter if you had one, lord?'

'Worse, in fact,' Vortigern said. 'The Fulvii are one of the oldest patrician families in the Empire, and they think they're the children of the gods. We're all barbarians as far as they're concerned, even me. Marcus's father fought tooth and nail to stop Gaia Fulvia marrying Publius Luca. He's no better than an educated peasant to a Fulvius, even though he's from a solid old Roman family. And all that aside, I need to keep the Fulvii as allies at the moment; so heed Kerin's advice, and remember what happened to your brother Custennin.'

There was a silence. Vortigern helped himself to a bunch of candied grapes.

'Lord,' Macsen said, 'do you know what's happened to him?'

'No,' Vortigern said.

'Not at all?'

'No. He survived, but as for where he's gone, you know as much as I do. It gave me no pleasure, Macsen, but it was necessary; and anyway, you saw what he'd done.'

'I know all that, lord,' Macsen said, 'but he's still my brother, and I'd like to know what's happened to him, even if I hate what he did to those girls.'

'You'll have to find out for yourself, then,' Vortigern said. 'I'm not wasting my time, and if he ever shows his face in Cambria again, I won't be the only man waiting to cut his throat.'

Kerin turned back to the window and looked out over the peaceful golden fields. He had not yet told Gael about Faria. There had been so much else to share which was more joyous, more urgent and less susceptible of misunderstanding. He thought about the night of his marriage, vaguely aware that Macsen and Vortigern were still speaking. He knew that he would never have married Faria, but that did not prevent an image of her from rising before him; the sinuous body and luminous green eyes. When he came back to the present Macsen had gone, and Vortigern had moved to his side.

'Let her sleep,' he said. 'There's no point.'

'I know,' Kerin said, turning away. He felt Vortigern's hand on his shoulder.

'You and I are going to meet Valerius Dio,' he said.

'Just you and I?'

'Yes. Anyone else would be a distraction, for us and for the praetor. I don't have to tell you how important this is. If this man turns against us, or even if he's useless, we have no ally in the east. You know what that means.'

'Yes. It means that we'll have to fight a war in the east from our bases in Cambria.'

'Yes,' Vortigern said. 'Not next year, perhaps. It'll take time for Hengist to build enough ships, and to replace lost warriors. But when he comes, it'll be worse than fighting the Picts.'

'I know,' Kerin said.

'Of course you do. I don't know why I'm telling you this.'

Kerin hesitated, reluctant to ask the question which had formed in his mind, but it was too late; Vortigern had detected the uncertainty.

'What?' he asked.

'Rowenna,' Kerin said. 'Does she realise –'

'No,' Vortigern said. Kerin shook his head.

'But surely –'

'No. She has no disguise where I'm concerned. She thinks her father's gone for good. That's why she was so desperate to see him in Kent. It hasn't occurred to her that he'd try to take the kingdom from me. At some point I'll have to tell her; but not yet. And not here.'

Kerin hardly knew what to say. 'I shan't mention it, lord. And no-one else will either, because I don't think they've really thought about it yet. Except possibly Gwyndaf, and he won't say anything.'

'No,' Vortigern said, looking out across the tranquil valley. 'Gwyndaf's change of heart is one of the better things to come out of this mess.'

A dog barked over in the stable yard, and they heard the sound of hoofbeats on the warm wind. Travellers were coming down the Roman road at a smart trot. The low sun winked on shining breastplates and helmets. There was no chariot. Kerin had never known Severus Maximus travel in any other way, and he had assumed that it was the universal custom of the praetors. But there were the praetorian guardsmen in their splendid uniforms, and there was Titus Luca on an elegant grey blood horse, so he supposed that one of the other riders must be Valerius Dio.

'That's him, I think,' Vortigern said, shading his eyes as the party turned into the villa's approach road. 'Next to Titus, on the chestnut horse.'

Kerin had seen the man before. He was small but well-made, with very broad, square shoulders and short-cropped brown hair. He was wearing a good cloak and dark felt breeches tucked into fine leather riding boots; a well-to-do gentleman's travelling clothes. After months with Severus Maximus, Kerin found it difficult to envisage a praetor without sandals and a snow-white toga, particularly a man whose father had been born in Rome.

'I've seen him before,' he said. 'In the curia, the day you crowned Constans. He was sitting with some of the military men. Lucius said he served in the army for a while before becoming governor of wherever-it-was.'

'Veronia,' Vortigern said, as the villa's gates swung open. 'A small province in Gaul, somewhere to the south-east of Armorica. Prior to that he was an officer in the Tenth Equestris, stationed on the Danube. His father was Silvius Dio, a member of the imperial secretariat, and his mother is the elder daughter of a landowning family from Corinium. His wife is related to the repulsive Alberius, and they have been blessed with a son and a daughter.'

Kerin smiled half-heartedly. And someday, I'll be one step ahead of you, he thought. Publius Luca appeared in the doorway.

'They're here,' he said. 'Will you meet them now?'

'Yes,' Vortigern said crisply. Publius Luca shook his head.

'Look,' he said, 'Valerius is honourable.'

Vortigern raised his eyebrows. 'I'll be the judge of that,' he said.

They waited for Valerius Dio in the grand library, watched over by a life-sized statue of one of the Caesars. A pitcher of wine and three goblets had been set in front of them. The table glowed, bright as a mirror, and as Kerin looked down at his reflection he realised that his hair needed trimming and that his face was paler and more tired-looking than he had expected.

'I don't look much like the king's right arm,' he said gloomily. Vortigern observed his own reflection.

'You look exactly like this king's right arm,' he said. On the opposite side of the table a single chair awaited the praetor. They heard footsteps coming along the passage from the reception room next to the courtyard.

'The library, sir,' a quiet voice said deferentially, in British. The door opened and Valerius Dio came in, still wearing his travelling clothes. He walked straight up to the table and bowed from the waist.

'Lord King,' he said respectfully. Vortigern rested his chin on his hands and looked up at him.

'You may sit, if you like,' he said.

'Thank you, Lord King,' said Valerius Dio. He sat down with a confident smile. Close to, the elbow-length sleeves of his tunic revealed an impressive collection of scars on his forearms. At least his time in the legion had not been spent behind an administrator's desk.

'This is my second-in-command, Kerin Brightspear,' Vortigern said. 'Whatever you've come to say can be said in front of him, so please, feel free to speak.'

'Lord Kerin,' Valerius Dio said. His handshake was firm and deliberate, reassuringly unlike Severus Maximus's limp clasp. 'I've seen you both in Londinium, of course. At the first meeting in the curia, as I recall.'

'How did you find time for that?' Vortigern asked. 'Isn't there much to do, being governor of Veronia?'

Valerius Dio smiled. 'If someone steals his neighbour's dog they talk about it for weeks. But I would have come to the meeting in any case. Publius Luca wrote to me several weeks beforehand, telling me that it was not to be missed.'

'Ah,' Vortigern said, with interest. 'Why would he have said that, do you suppose?'

'Because he thought I should see for myself the man who would soon be King of all the Britons,' the praetor said. Vortigern smiled faintly.

'It's a long way to come, to look at a poor sad wretch like Constans.'

'Oh no,' Valerius Dio said, folding his hands on the table. 'He didn't mean the monk.'

There was a brief silence.

'Well,' Vortigern said, 'if you are as prescient as Titus's father, perhaps you should tell me what you see as the greatest danger facing the kingdom.'

'The Saxons, of course,' Valerius Dio said, without a moment's hesitation.

'Not a civil war?' Vortigern asked.

'Against your son?' Valerius Dio said, with a degree of surprise, Kerin thought.

'Well,' Vortigern said, 'he does have an army of sorts.'

Valerius Dio leaned forward slightly. 'Lord,' he said, 'I saw you leave for the North. *That* was an army. Whatever your son has in Kent, it's not an army.' He cleared his throat. 'I may have spent the past few years in administration, but I'm a soldier, as you know. I'll grant you that the Lord of Glevum has some decent warriors, but what else do they have? A malicious old windbag of a priest and a bunch of makeweights who couldn't fight their way out of a sack.' He broke off, slightly breathless with excitement, as if realising that he was about to overstep his better judgment. His deep-set dark eyes gleamed indignantly. Vortigern leaned back in his chair and laughed.

'Well,' he said, 'you're nothing like Severus Maximus, are you?'

The praetor coughed politely. 'Please God, may no-one ever accuse me of that, Lord King.'

'What do you think should be done about my son, then?' Vortigern asked.

Valerius Dio looked steadily at him. 'That's not for me to say, lord.'

'If he tries to march into Londinium, it'll be for you to

say. What will you do then? Keel over and make him king, like Severus would have done?'

'No, lord,' Valerius Dio said. 'There'll be no keeling over on my part.'

'You haven't yet mentioned Garagon of Kent,' Vortigern said. 'Why not? He's your city's nearest neighbour.'

'I don't consider him a threat,' said the praetor. 'Everyone knows how he performed in the North. A man who'll run away from a battle and leave his men to fight alone isn't worth the time of day. Did you know what happened to his uncle Edlym, incidentally?'

Vortigern leaned forward on his elbows. 'The man who refused to garrison the shore forts of Kent? Let me guess. He was found strangled in his bed a few days ago, with an iris sprouting from his back passage.'

Valerius Dio looked back without a flicker. 'The flower was a lily, as I understand. But otherwise you are correct.'

Kerin closed his eyes, remembering the inexplicable acknowledgement which had passed between Vortigern and Gorlois in the fortress at Lemanis. Even at the time, it seemed too conspiratorial to be anything to do with a straightforward siege. Kerin doubted that he would ever have done it himself; but at the same time, he realised that he would never again have to worry about the statue of Ceres.

'Your father was quite highly placed in the administration, wasn't he?' Vortigern asked.

'Yes, lord. He was responsible for the upkeep of the public facilities – the baths and the drains, and so forth. He held the post until just before he died. I'm afraid things have gone downhill since then, but I've got it in hand.'

'Good,' Vortigern said. 'And I hope you have a few other things in hand, too, like ensuring that public monies aren't wasted on the private bathrooms of the elite.'

'Yes, lord,' Valerius Dio said, looking a little shamefaced on his predecessors' behalf. 'You can count on that.'

'I hope I can, Valerius Dio. Titus's father came within a hair's breadth of hanging Severus Maximus when we found out what happened to the fleet monies, and I can promise you, there will be blood on the floor of the curia if it happens again. Do we have enough money in the treasury to maintain an army?'

'Enough to pay the city garrisons and Publius Luca's cavalry units,' the praetor said. 'Not enough to organise the defence forces we need.'

'It won't be easy to raise taxes while half the country's being ruled by a bunch of disaffected incompetents,' Vortigern said.

'No. It was easy under the Empire, of course, you could –'

'I know what it was like under the occupation,' Vortigern said sharply. Valerius Dio gave an apprehensive smile. Kerin felt sorry for the praetor. It was impossible that he had intended any offence.

'Do you think we should fight Vortimer, then?' he asked. Valerius Dio looked pleased by his directness.

'No,' he said. 'Not unless he starts it. Both sides would lose a lot of men, leaving the kingdom wide open to the Saxons. But unfortunately, if Vortimer can't see reason, it's probably inevitable.'

'Our men have spent a year doing nothing but fighting, battle-training and riding on forced marches,' Kerin said. 'Most of them have been wounded, and most of our best warhorses are sick or lame. It would be good to have the winter for recovery, if we can. Could you hold things together in Londinium until the spring?'

'I'm sure of it,' Valerius Dio said, with an air of calm confidence. Kerin remembered, with some misgivings, that he had not yet had to hold anything more challenging than Veronia together for very long.

'Vortimer's alliance is fragile,' he said. 'He knows he'll never rule without dissent while the king lives. He knows that he'll need a big enough, strong enough force to cross the river and take us on in Cambria.'

Valerius Dio's eyes narrowed. 'But that's madness!' he exclaimed.

'Yes. Hengist would laugh all the way to the beaches of Kent. Now Vortimer's had a beating, and they've all gone home to their warm beds. But if he gets enough good reinforcements, or some new allies, things might change. We have to be prepared.'

'And beyond all that,' Vortigern said, 'whether next year or later, most of these men who are against me now will have to fight Hengist's Jutes. Or Saxons, Angles, what you will. I can resist them, but only if the others stand with me, as they did against the Picts. At the moment all they want to do is kill me. My son thinks that he can do what I did in the North, and hold them together. He's deluded.'

'But he's right about one thing,' Valerius Dio said. 'There can only be one King of All the Britons.'

'Yes. Everything falls apart otherwise. And I'm a battle commander, not a politician. I know it's insane to waste good men fighting my own people. But they may leave me no choice.'

'They're the mad ones, Lord King,' the praetor said. 'You'll have my unfailing support.'

'Then it's settled,' Vortigern said. 'We'll spend the winter in Cambria, events permitting. I expect a messenger from you every two weeks; more, if there's anything important to be said. And tell Publius Luca's successor, Magnus Julius, to go to every garrison commander in the country and demote anyone who can't come up with a hundred well-trained and equipped warriors. We need them ready, and we need them mobile, in case it's necessary to move them to Kent.'

'Yes, lord!' Valerius Dio said crisply. He had come briskly to attention, a soldier addressing his commanding officer. 'Shall I tell him to organise a cavalry unit to go out with the tax collectors?'

'Yes,' Vortigern said, 'but send men of experience, like the members of my warband, otherwise our good citizens will murder them on sight.' He reached for the pitcher, a clear sign that he had learned as much about the new praetor as he needed to know for the present. Valerius Dio raised his hand.

'I never drink wine, lord,' he said. 'No disrespect intended, of course; but I find it blunts the senses. Do I have leave to go now? I should at least wash the dust off before attending a Fulvius feast.'

'Yes, of course,' Vortigern said. He and Kerin both stretched out a hand for the praetor to shake. His footsteps faded away down the passage outside, the soft tread of his riding boots almost inaudible on the mosaic.

'Ah well,' Vortigern said, filling two of the goblets. 'Nobody's perfect.'

<h1 style="text-align:center">14</h1>

It was the most lavish feast Kerin had ever seen. The guests, around sixty in all, were seated around the perimeter of the hall facing a large central table, on which four well-drilled servants were piling food. There were countless roast fowl and whole kids, boned and stuffed with small birds. There was a spit-roasted deer, something which Kerin was assured was part of a bear, and a row of hares to which little pairs of white wings had been affixed, to make them look like Pegasus the flying horse. Most of the guests were already at table and plates of small delicacies were being presented; green and black olives, honey-cakes, tiny sausages and stuffed dormice rolled in poppy seeds. Kerin was honoured to be shown to a seat between Publius Luca and his brother-in-law. To Marcus Fulvius's right were two vacant seats, which Kerin supposed must be reserved for Vortigern and Rowenna. Beyond them, Gaia Fulvia and her sister-in-law, Flavia, were chatting whilst the younger women whispered and giggled and fluttered their eyelashes at the warriors on the side tables.

'How did it go with the praetor?' Publius Luca asked.

'Better than it ever went with Severus Maximus,' Kerin said. 'He seems very sensible and clear-headed, and on the whole, I'd say that Vortigern quite likes him.'

'I'm amazed,' Publius Luca said, and chuckled loudly. Kerin suspected that he might already have indulged in some of the villa's excellent wine, now appearing on the tables in huge jugs. Marcus Fulvius heard the sounds of merriment and leaned across to investigate.

'It's very good,' Kerin said, savouring the intense fragrance of the golden liquid in his goblet. 'Do you produce much of it?'

'Only enough for ourselves and a few friends,' Marcus Fulvius said. 'An indulgence, really. It resembles *spolentinum*, I'd say; even better than a good young *falernum*, according to Martial. We planted the vines when we came here, thirty years ago. The first thing we built was the house which has become the slaves' quarters. Publius and I dug the foundations with our own bare hands.'

'I didn't have much choice,' Publius Luca confided. 'I was trying to get into Marcus's father's good books, so that he'd let me marry his daughter.'

Marcus Fulvius tutted indignantly. 'Anybody'd think we were the spawn of Caligula, the way you talk,' he said. Kerin, his head spinning with information about wine and unfamiliar Romans, was thankful that the conversation had turned to something as straightforward as a trench. The doors at the far end of the room opened. Fingers were put to lips and the many different conversations ceased abruptly. The king and his wife were coming into the dining hall. One of the ladies of the house had lent Rowenna a dress, a fluid wisp of white silk which shimmered as she moved. A week of rest and Flavia's pampering had healed her blistered hands, smoothed her skin and restored the colour to her face. Her hair gleamed and her eyes shone as she smiled at some remark of Vortigern's; not coyly, like the daughters and granddaughters of the villa, but with a look which was regal, open and self-assured. The girl had become a woman, scorched by the midsummer fires and blooded on the hell-ride to Kent.

'A Saxon queen,' Marcus Fulvius mused. 'Who on earth would have thought it?'

'None of us,' Kerin said. 'Least of all the king.'

'It wasn't a stratagem, then?' Marcus Fulvius said, with some surprise. 'We all took it as a political move. A way of exercising a hold over the father.'

'No,' Kerin said. 'Not at all.'

'I'm intrigued,' Marcus Fulvius said, as Vortigern and Rowenna paused to talk to Lud and his sons. Macsen, worryingly, appeared more interested in making eyes at the granddaughter of the house, who was returning his gaze from behind a delicate fan of peacock feathers.

'If you knew the father, Marcus, you'd appreciate that he wouldn't let paternal affection stand in the way of ambition,' Publius Luca said.

'Why did he abandon Kent, then?' Marcus Fulvius asked.

'He hasn't abandoned Kent. He's gone away to rebuild his strength, and when he's ready he'll come back to reclaim what he thinks is his. And when that happens, I'll be looking to men like you to pay for the army we'll need to stop him. What do you say to that?'

Marcus Fulvius paused, the goblet halfway to his lips. 'I'll pay my share, if necessary,' he said. 'But aren't you being a little alarmist?'

'No,' Publius Luca said. 'And while you're calculating how many days' income it might cost, you should consider how many good natural defences there are between this place and the coast of Kent.'

Marcus Fulvius put down the goblet. He looked profoundly uneasy. 'We're talking about a few skirmishes on the beaches, surely.'

'No,' Kerin said. 'We're talking about a full-scale war against warriors who are worse enemies than the Picts, and may well outnumber us when they come back.'

Marcus Fulvius had no response. Perhaps, until now, it had been easy for him to ignore what went on outside his corner of paradise. His eyes moved to the conversation at the end of the table, now breaking up amidst laughter and well-wishing.

'What about his wife?' he asked. 'Will she be her father's daughter in all this?'

'Marcus, that's hardly a question for the dinner table,' Publius Luca said. Marcus Fulvius raised his eyebrows.

'I'll grant you that. But it'll rear its head at some point, won't it.' He turned with a sudden, welcoming smile as Vortigern and Rowenna took their seats.

'Thank you, Marcus Fulvius,' Vortigern said graciously, as the solicitous host produced a pair of wine goblets; one identical to his own, the other much smaller, like the ones from which the ladies were sipping with delicate restraint. 'And please, feel free to continue discussing us, if you would like to. There can be very little which has not already been said.'

Marcus Fulvius gave a small, disconcerted smile and filled the goblets with his golden wine.

'It smells very good,' Rowenna said, sniffing her goblet. She sipped it experimentally, smiled and knocked back the wine in one mouthful. Marcus Fulvius blinked. Rowenna laughed, her eyes sparkling. 'I am sorry,' she said. 'At home, we have tankards, like this –' she spread her hands. 'When I was a small girl, my mother died. I did not want to stay at home with the women, so I learned to sail ships with my two brothers. And when you sail with the boys, you must drink with the boys too. I may have some more?'

'But of course, my lady,' Marcus Fulvius said courteously. He smiled and replenished Rowenna's goblet. 'Please be advised that it's very strong, though.'

'Don't worry about her,' Vortigern said equably. 'She'll drink you senseless.'

Marcus Fulvius continued to smile, though with an unmistakable trace of offended propriety. For all that, Kerin noticed, he seemed unable to take his eyes off Rowenna. She looked arrestingly beautiful in the white dress, which gave her an air of fragility Kerin was unaccustomed to, after weeks of seeing her in riding clothes. She was wearing a fine silver necklace set with emeralds; a gift from Vortigern, Kerin supposed. He turned, hearing further greetings being exchanged; in breezy Latin this time. Valerius Dio had arrived and was shaking hands with Publius Luca. Gorlois hailed him cheerfully, despite having no idea who he was, and orchestrated a shuffle to the left. The praetor squeezed himself into the vacant space beside Publius Luca.

'A tight fit, but I'm sure I'll manage,' he said. Gorlois roared.

'By the gods,' he said, wiping his eyes, 'that's just what I said to my new wife.'

As fate would have it, the initial remark and the subsequent exclamation fell into a naturally occurring pool of silence amongst the several conversations. Marcus Fulvius looked deeply shocked. Publius Luca coughed into his sleeve. Valerius Dio grinned nervously. Kerin turned away, clamping his jaws, and resolutely avoiding the eyes of Vortigern, who seemed to have discovered something interesting on the ceiling of the dining hall. Macsen and Elir dissolved into hysterical guffaws. Marcus Fulvius sprang to his feet and clapped his hands; then, mercifully, the meat began to arrive.

Afterwards, there was a period between the serving of the main courses and the final clearance of which Kerin recalled very little. He remembered eating a stuffed quail and a duck breast wrapped in bacon fat, and he remembered Gorlois, who must have changed places with Publius Luca, explaining that his new wife's name was Ygraine, and that she was the most beautiful creature that ever walked. After this, everything dissolved into a warm yellow haze, very much like the colour of the wine which induced it. Even Marcus Fulvius must have consumed a fair quantity, because by the time Kerin came round he was singing some old soldiers' marching song with Publius Luca and Valerius Dio; unintelligible to anyone unfamiliar with Roman legionary slang, but amply explained by the obscene gestures which accompanied it. Kerin rubbed his eyes, drank some water and picked at a plate of figs. He felt as if he had eaten a large amount of food, and regretted not having been sober enough to know what it was. Almost all the guests had gone to bed. Hefydd was asleep under a table. Macsen and Gwyndaf were attempting a serious discussion, with Lud snoring noisily in between them. Next to Kerin, Vortigern was leaning back in his chair looking sleepily contented. Rowenna's head was resting on his shoulder and his right hand played idly with a few strands of her hair whilst the left investigated the figs.

'What was the food like?' Kerin asked. Vortigern grinned.

'You ate it, didn't you?'

'No,' Kerin said, scratching his head. 'I think that was someone else.'

'It was very good,' Vortigern said. 'But over-elaborate; not the sort of thing you'd want to eat every day.'

'There was a huge bird,' Rowenna said drowsily. Kerin smiled. He had thought she was sleeping.

'A swan,' Vortigern said.

'Oh dear,' Kerin said, remembering the feasts in Londinium.

'And inside it was a goose,' Rowenna said. 'And inside the goose was a duck. And inside the duck was a partridge, and inside the partridge a tiny, tiny *thrysce*.'

'Thrush,' Vortigern said, yawning.

'God,' Kerin said. 'Did you eat it?'

'A poor little songbird?' Rowenna said indignantly.

'I'd have eaten it,' Vortigern said. 'But I've got more meat on my little finger.'

They all looked up as Valerius Dio appeared on the opposite side of the table. The song over, Publius Luca and Marcus Fulvius were meandering off to bed, leaving him to his own devices. Kerin wondered about a man who could sing as loudly and raucously as that while stone-cold sober. Vortigern did not look as if he could be at all bothered with him, however much of an improvement on Severus Maximus the new praetor might be.

'A marvellous feast,' Valerius Dio said. 'I'll be hard put to equal it when you visit Londinium, Lord King.'

'Don't bother,' Vortigern said. 'A few roast lambs and some pitchers of mead will do very well.'

'The delicacies of Cambria,' the praetor said, smiling. 'You must have missed it all. When are you thinking of leaving?'

'In the next few days,' Vortigern said. 'The horses are fit enough to make the journey now, and the men will start to be a nuisance if I let them stay here much longer. Too much luxury is no good for warriors. Or for me, if the truth be told.'

'Well, as you said, they deserve a rest,' Valerius Dio said. 'But please, bear in mind what we discussed, and try to ensure that they save their strength for what matters.' He bowed courteously and marched off down the hall in a very straight line. Vortigern closed his eyes. Rowenna sat up sharply.

'What did he mean?' she asked.

'Nothing important,' Vortigern said. Rowenna sighed.

'How can you say this?' she asked, reaching for his hand. 'He tells you to save your warriors for something, and you say it is not important.'

'It isn't,' Vortigern said. His voice was quiet, but the threat was there, for anyone who knew how to recognise it. Rowenna withdrew her hand. She played with her silver goblet for a moment, then her eyes met Kerin's. She's not going to give up, he thought. Vortigern reached for a wine pitcher. Rowenna leaned across him.

'Is it Rufus you are saving your warriors for?' she asked.

'No,' Vortigern said.

'He deserves it,' Rowenna protested.

'I know,' Vortigern said. 'But that's a sideshow.'

Rowenna tossed her head impatiently. 'He has not been like a son. Why should you still be like his father?'

Vortigern looked away. 'It's not that,' he said. Rowenna looked at him anxiously, as if she knew that something terrible was coming. Vortigern's hand cupped the back of her head, gently, as if he had been holding a wounded bird.

'*Anwylyd*, I'll soon need every man I've got to fight your father,' he said. Rowenna froze. She backed away from him, shaking her head silently. 'Look,' Vortigern said, reaching for her arm, 'it's not my choice, it's –'

'No!' Rowenna breathed, twisting out of his grip. 'Do not touch me!' She threw her chair aside and ran from the dining hall. They heard the heavy outer door slam behind her and the sound of footsteps flying across the courtyard. There was an awful, protracted silence, broken only by the clatter of plates as the servants began to clear the tables; then an agonised cry, something in Saxon, came floating back through the open window. Macsen came ambling over, blinking and rubbing his eyes.

'What the hell was that?' he asked sleepily. 'What did she say?'

'I've no idea,' Kerin said sharply. 'Go to bed, Macsen, for God's sake, and take the others with you.' In fact, she had said 'murdering bastard'; but Kerin was not about to translate.

'Go after her,' Vortigern said, staring at the open doorway.

'I think that's your place, lord,' Kerin said.

'No,' Vortigern said. 'Find her, and tell her that if she wants to go back to her father, I'll arrange a ship.'

Kerin shook his head. 'She's your wife, lord. She can't just leave.'

Vortigern turned. 'Look, there can be no bargain between us other than the one we've had. It's that or nothing. I'd sooner let her go than keep her here against her will. Go and find her.'

Kerin raised his hands in resignation and walked slowly out of the hall.

She was sitting on the river bank, staring at nothing. The moon was hanging low in the sky and cast its golden trail across the gliding black water. Kerin sat down beside her and waited. She had stopped weeping now. Perhaps, in the time it had taken him to find her, she had exhausted her tears. She was sitting with arms wrapped around herself, clutching tight, as if she thought it might bring her some comfort.

'I should have known,' she said. Her voice sounded dull and defeated. 'I thought my father had gone for good, but I know him better than that. I know them both, so why did I not see it?'

'Perhaps because you couldn't bear to see it,' Kerin said.

'Yes,' Rowenna said. She had taken off her emerald necklace and was twisting it around her fingers.

'He said that if you want to go back to your father, he'll arrange a ship,' Kerin said. Rowenna looked up. She had not quite used up her tears after all, it seemed.

'Most men would beat their wives or lock them up,' she said shakily.

'Some would,' Kerin said. 'But he said that it could only be one way between you. That if he had to keep you against your will, there'd be no point. I know it's not the sort of thing that powerful men usually say. It's not what most people would expect from him, or from any King of all the Britons.'

'Ah,' Rowenna said wistfully. 'But I didn't marry the King of all the Britons. I married the brigand chief.' She looked down at the necklace. For a moment Kerin thought she might be about to throw it into the river.

'He says that you can see things sometimes,' she said. Kerin had hoped that this moment would never come.

'Yes,' he said reluctantly. 'Sometimes.'

She clutched his arm. 'Tell me what you see for us,' she said. Kerin avoided her eyes. He had no heart to tell her what he feared, but she was like a ferret when she was after the truth.

'There will be trouble, all kinds of trouble,' he said, 'and I don't know whether we'll all live to see the end of it. We'll have to fight your father sooner or later, because he's had a taste of this country, and you know he's not the man to turn his back if he thinks there's a chance of getting all that for his people. Naturally, we're determined to deny it to him; but I don't have to tell you how well your warriors can fight, so anything might happen. I don't think we'll ever lose Cambria, but apart from that, I don't know how it'll go. You know your father betrayed us, and that we can never trust him again, but it's worse than that. How would you feel if Vortigern killed him in battle? Would you hate Vortigern for doing it?'

Rowenna stared down at the gliding water. 'I will stop breathing first,' she said. 'But I love my father, too. I know he did wrong, and I told him so; but for me, he has always been a good father. Perhaps he thinks too much of the Jutes, and it makes him do wrong to other people.'

'You're probably right about that,' Kerin said. Rowenna shivered. Kerin took off his tunic and put it around her shoulders.

'Now you will be cold,' she said, looking at his thin undershirt.

'Warriors don't feel the cold,' Kerin said. Rowenna smiled reproachfully.

'Warriors are liars,' she said. She shuffled closer to Kerin and laid her head on his shoulder. He put his arm around her and they sat watching the river, listening to the tawny owls calling in the orchard and the peaceful sound of cattle munching grass in the water meadows on the far bank.

'Gael left her father for you, didn't she,' Rowenna said.

'Yes,' Kerin said. 'But that was different. He treated her worse than an animal. I've never liked your father at all, but I don't think that of him.'

'No,' Rowenna sighed. 'Hengist is a good father.' She looked up. 'You know, he was shocked when he saw that I was going to marry Vortigern. Many people think he planned it, to get Kent, but he didn't.'

'No,' Kerin said. 'I know he didn't.'

'Of course, when he saw that it would happen anyway, he started to think what he could get from it. Perhaps if Rufus had let him keep Kent in peace, this would not have happened.'

'Do you really think so?' Kerin asked. Rowenna hesitated.

'No,' she said reluctantly. 'Hengist is Hengist. He wants always what is on the other side of the river.'

'Yes,' Kerin said. 'And you must know that we can't let him have it.'

'I know,' Rowenna said bleakly. 'I know.' She got up and walked slowly away along the riverbank. Kerin let her go. In the end, no-one could help her decide. He rose stiffly to his feet and walked back towards the villa. One of Marcus Fulvius's chariot horses craned its head over the door of its box. Kerin stopped to talk to it. The horse was big and sleek and well-fed. It had a slightly supercilious air, and looked as if it had never done any serious work. Kerin wondered if the horse was a Fulvius too. He looked around him at the golden walls with their clothing of vines and the huge grain stores waiting for autumn's harvest, and thought how opulent it all looked, and how vulnerable. He felt a hand clutch his arm and looked down. Rowenna's face was white and her eyes were as distressed as before, but she had stopped weeping. She had tidied her hair and replaced the emerald necklace.

'Please, will you take me to him now?' she asked.

The dining hall was deserted except for a handful of slaves clearing the last of the debris from the tables.

'We'll leave the wine, lord,' one of them said. 'There should be plenty in those pitchers over there, if you're still thirsty.'

Rowenna's fingers tightened around Kerin's arm. 'Where has he gone?' she whispered.

'God knows,' Kerin said dispiritedly.

'If you're looking for the king, lord, I think he's gone to his bed,' the slave said cheerfully. 'He didn't look too happy, though. I'd let him sleep, if I were you.'

'Thank you,' Kerin said. 'And please, take a pitcher of wine for yourself, if you want one.'

The slave chuckled. 'More than my life's worth, lord. Things must be a bit different in the West.'

The corridors of the villa were deserted and echoed eerily. As they reached the top of the marble staircase, Rowenna hesitated.

'Does he think I will leave now, and go back to my father?' she asked.

'I don't know,' Kerin said. 'Possibly. Do you want me to come in with you?'

Rowenna smiled, blinking tears. 'To the door, please.'

Kerin put his arm around her shoulders and they walked slowly down the moonlit passage. The door at the end was barred. Kerin knocked lightly. There was no response. He knocked again, more insistently. 'Lord?' he said. After a while, they heard the sound of the bar being drawn. Kerin eased the door open. Rowenna clutched his hand. Vortigern was standing with his back to them.

'I am here,' Rowenna whispered. Kerin could feel her shaking. Moonlight flooded in through the window. Vortigern turned, a black cipher against its golden brightness.

'I'll order a ship,' he said. His voice was stiff and expressionless, like another man's. Whatever he was holding in check, he probably feared it himself.

'Why?' Rowenna asked tearfully. 'There is no water between here and Henfelin.'

Vortigern paused. In the brittle silence, they could hear him breathing. 'Look,' he said, 'you're mad if you stay. We'll have the winter; a year or two at the most, perhaps, and after that it'll be all hell and grief. If you think I'm lying, ask him.'

Rowenna looked beseechingly at Kerin. He had no idea what she hoped he might say.

'It's probably true,' he said. 'We're not talking about winning or losing, though. That's not what this is about.'

'No,' Rowenna said. 'I know what it is about. We have spoken of it just now, by the river.'

'Yes,' Kerin said. Rowenna had steadied herself.

'I will stay,' she said. Vortigern did not reply. Whatever his silence signified, she seemed to have decided that she could manage it. Kerin felt her fingers tighten around his. 'Please, leave us now,' she said. Kerin pressed her hand to his lips and let it fall. 'You are a better friend than either of us deserves,' she said. Kerin went out and closed the door behind him. There would be no ship to Jutland, and that was enough to send him straight to his bedchamber, not back to the dining hall and the remains of Marcus Fulvius's golden wine.

*

Kerin woke with a start. He could smell burning. He got up, flung on a robe and went to the window. A dull orange light tainted the misty dawn sky. It was nothing, really – some servants had got up early and lit a bonfire in the paddock beyond the stables – but in Kerin's imagination, the villa was burning. He remembered what Publius Luca had said to Marcus Fulvius about the lack of natural defences between the villa and the coast. He tried to stop visualising what that might mean, but he could not. In his head, the roof-timbers were already cracking above him. Flames were licking along the red-tiled roofs and flickering inside the windows of the bedchambers below. Beyond the paddock the cornfields were on fire and waves of armed warriors were coming over the eastern ridge. Something was happening in the temple of Apollo. Marcus Fulvius was lying dead in the doorway with his throat slit, his blood seeping out onto the exquisite mosaic. A pair of hands seized Kerin by the shoulders.

'What on earth?' Vortigern said. Kerin took a deep breath and calmed himself. The villa and its outbuildings were sleeping under a golden sunrise. Beyond them the cornfields rippled and gleamed, while smoke drifted from the bonfire and cattle grazed peacefully in the meadows along the river.

'Oh God,' Kerin said softly. 'Please can we leave this place?'

15

Kerin stood in the darkness and looked up at the house. He had never been inside it, although he had passed it many times on his way to and from the praetor's residence. The walls were white, clothed in ivy. A young servant answered his knock and led him inside.

'In here,' the boy said, halting in front of an ebony door. He rang a small silver bell hanging from an iron bracket above his head, bowed politely and withdrew. The door was opened by a slight young man in a white silk tunic.

'Please, come with me,' he said. The room beyond the outer court was bare except for a low table and a simple altar. A flame burned in a brazier with an eerie blue light. The room had been scrubbed, but underneath the scent of cleansing herbs and incense, Kerin could smell the blood.

'Marcellus *magister,* you have a visitor,' said the young man. Marcellus was facing the altar. He was wearing a bizarre red head-dress and a sleeveless white robe which exposed his thin arms.

'Thank you, Octavius,' he said. 'You may go now.' Kerin waited. Marcellus bowed to the altar. 'Kerin Brightspear,' he said, without looking round. 'I have been expecting you.'

Kerin felt suddenly cold. The chill of the bare room and its foul intimations of death froze him to the marrow. 'How did you know?' he asked. Marcellus turned round. He was still holding the knife.

'I knew you would come,' he said. 'You have come to tell me about the destruction of the Villa Fulvia.'

They sat beside a window overlooking a leafy courtyard, drinking a warm infusion of rosehips and mint; the same honey-sweetened liquid Kerin remembered from the little garden at the praetor's residence, with its fountain and amiable doves. Moths flittered in the pools of light cast by the oil lamps. The rosehip liquor was brought by Marcellus's wife, Elissa, a small, plump woman who looked several years younger than the haruspex. She greeted Kerin warmly and offered him a bed for the night, despite all her husband had implied about the hell she inflicted upon him. A fire of apple logs crackled on the hearth, scenting the air, and Kerin was grateful for its warmth, although the night was not cold.

'When did this come to you?' Marcellus asked.

'Yesterday,' Kerin said. 'But it wasn't any sort of a prophecy. Publius Luca had spoken about it at dinner. That place has no defences at all. I started wondering what the Saxons would do. It's not far from there to thinking about burning and killing. I should be on my way home with the others, but I couldn't go without talking to you.'

'And you haven't mentioned anything to Marcus Fulvius?'

'No, of course not. He wouldn't even listen to Publius, never mind some idiot from Cambria. I was going to ask you to make something up for him, but perhaps I don't have to.'

'No,' Marcellus said. 'But putting it to Marcus won't be easy. It would be an insult to suggest that the Fulvii couldn't defend their own villa. However, the whole point of omens is that a devout man should consult them before action; in much the same way that you might look out of the window and examine the sky before going out. I'm invited for the Saturnalia, so perhaps I can find the right time for a cautionary word.'

'Thank you,' Kerin said. For the moment, it was enough not to have to bear the burden alone.

'You're staying the night with Lucius Arrius, then,' Marcellus said.

'It was arranged this afternoon. He's training youngsters tomorrow, and he wants me to watch. I'd have accepted your wife's offer, otherwise. She's very kind.'

'So they tell me,' Marcellus said plaintively. 'She's a good woman in many ways, but we were never blessed with children, unfortunately. I already have two sons, from a marriage I made as a young man in Ravenna. Elissa's first marriage was childless too, as it happens; and when she found herself married to a man who had already fathered two boys, and still not with child, I think it was too much for her. She'll have nothing to do with my sons or their families.'

'Has she met them?' Kerin asked.

'No. It's my dearest wish to go home to Ravenna, but she'll have none of it.' Marcellus gave a shrug of resignation. 'You're pleased with that girl of yours, I take it?'

'Yes,' Kerin said, 'though she may not be pleased with me, when the others arrive home without me. I'll have to take her a gift; some jewellery, perhaps.'

'There's an excellent goldsmith in the lane behind Publius Luca's house,' Marcellus said. 'But in the meantime, come with me to the house of Gallus Mercator, to see your mad Saxon.'

Kerin grimaced. 'I'm not sure I can stomach it,' he said. Marcellus patted his arm.

'Don't be too harsh on the merchant,' he said. 'His fault was lack of foresight.'

'Yes,' Kerin conceded. 'But Marcellus *magister*, you were not in the curia after the triumph. Whatever you've heard, whatever you've been told, it absolutely cannot convey what it was like to be in that room on that night. Seven of us, sat round a table in the middle of that big, empty space. Vortigern and myself. Eldof and his brother, Eldadus the bishop. Severus Maximus, Gorlois of Kernow, and Gallus. And all Vortigern wanted – all he wanted, after all that pain and bloodshed in the North – was enough money to garrison the defences and maintain a small standing army. That's all. And one by one, all those men who had made him king denied it, and walked out. All except dear, loyal Gorlois. Severus Maximus and that scum Alberius gave them the excuse by emptying the treasury, and by God, they all grabbed it with both hands. Gallus at least had a reason because he hadn't been paid for his ships, but in a way it was worse, because he and Vortigern were friends. Or so we thought. And if Gallus feels guilty, I'm glad of it, he deserves to feel guilty, because I've never in my life seen a man as destroyed as Vortigern was that night, when the last of them had gone. And yes, he's dealt with it, he's the King of all the Britons, most people don't notice or give a damn, but there was damage done that night, Marcellus *magister*. Real harm.' He stopped and cleared his throat. A film of sweat glistened on his brow. He had been ranting, he supposed. Marcellus fetched a cool, perfumed cloth from somewhere, dabbed Kerin's brow and sat down again.

'And of course, there was also damage done to these islands,' the haruspex said. 'I know that's not what you meant, but it has to be your concern, because we all know what the consequences are going to be. A defenceless kingdom, an embittered enemy in Hengist, and a bunch of greedy cut-throats off to shed some blood in the name of religion. Some of whom have ships, as I recall; ships which Publius Imperator would have liked to sink, if he'd had the where-withal. So don't you think it's time to swallow your resentment, grit your teeth and speak to Gallus Mercator? You will find that being the wealthiest merchant in Londinium is not a cure for everything.'

*

It was a private room in the servants' quarters, usually reserved for a senior member of the merchant's household staff. Oswi the Horseman was sitting on the bed, looking ridiculous in one of the loose white robes which Marcellus provided for his wounded patients. Kerin had never seen him wearing anything other than the customary Jute dress; brown tunic and cross-gartered breeches, sometimes topped with a plain cloak. His long, sandy hair was pulled back from his face as usual, but the leather thong which normally secured it at the nape had been replaced by an inappropriate white ribbon. Kerin grinned. Oswi was a tall, powerful man, not someone he'd have chosen to take on in a wrestling match. It was oddly reassuring to see him like this.

'Look,' the Jute said mournfully. 'A girl's dress. Not for warriors.'

'Don't complain,' Kerin said. 'You're lucky to be alive.'

Oswi scowled and picked up a small blue beaker from the side table. 'You try. I don't give to my dog.'

'I'd soon drink it if I thought it was going to save my life,' Kerin said. Oswi patted his chest.

'My life is fine. Maybe tomorrow I go down to the river.'

He nodded towards the small window. A full moon, softened by a thin haze, cast its pale light across the city. There was a fine view of the green courtyard and the garden, where a number of well-dressed women had gathered to talk and drink wine, but the object of Oswi's interest lay beyond; the river shimmering under the moon, and the tall, rocking masts of Gallus's merchant ships. *After all you've done to help us,* Kerin thought, *you deserve a berth on a ship like that; even if I have to pay the price of talking to Gallus.*

'Would you like to sail on one of those?' he asked. Oswi's eyes gleamed.

'I give everything for a ship like that. You think one day there are British ships to fight Hengist?'

'Perhaps,' Kerin said. 'What will you do?'

Oswi looked affronted. 'I am British warrior now. You think I run away like Hengist?'

'No,' Kerin said. 'You could have done that at the river. And you risked your own life to save Lucius, when Rufus's people were going to hang him. No-one made you do that. You didn't have to help me and Vortigern when we went to free Macsen. But fighting your own people is something else.'

Oswi put down his beaker and leaned forward. 'Oswi the Horseman does not fight with traitors. I swear on Odin's head, I did not know what Hengist would do at that river. He did not even tell his brother Horsa, because Horsa was an honest man. Horsa would have stopped it. I would have stopped it. I tell you, I am British warrior now. Fight with you and the Lord.'

'Good,' Kerin said. 'I haven't seen many men fight as well as you can. There's something you should know, though. A British warrior wouldn't think twice about drinking that medicine.'

Oswi gave a resentful glare, seized the beaker and swallowed the contents in one gulp. 'Baby's milk,' he said scornfully.

Kerin found Gallus on the wharf, sitting on an empty olive-oil cask. He was dressed like a deckhand, and looked as if he might have been working on the galley tied up alongside. The cheerful, gossipy gathering in his garden seemed to hold no appeal for him.

'Kerin Brightspear,' he said, with palpable surprise. 'You're the last man I expected to see.'

'I hadn't planned to come,' Kerin said. 'But Marcellus *magister* told me that I should, and he's a wiser man than I'll ever be.'

'Does Vortigern know you're here?'

'No. Vortigern's on his way home to Cambria. Read nothing into that; I had private business here, and I'm as much his man as I ever was.'

Gallus stood up. 'I have no excuses,' he said. 'What happened in the curia that night was a disgrace to us all. To myself more than anyone. I had the gall to call myself Vortigern's friend. He expected better of me, and I failed him. It was selfish and mean-spirited, and I've regretted it every day since.'

'At least you're honest,' Kerin said. 'More than I can say for the others. What do you want to do about it?'

'To make amends in any way I can. What can I do?'

Kerin paused. The merchant's contrition was so patent, it was impossible not to feel a little sympathy. 'You've been working on the boats,' he said.

'Yes. The first time in twenty years. It'll always be my first love. Making money came afterwards. But at the moment I need something that can make me sleep.' A burst of female laughter came from the garden. A dark-haired young woman in a floating red dress clambered onto the balustrade and began to walk along it, wobbling precariously, while her tipsy companions shouted encouragement. 'The praetor's wife,' Gallus sighed.

'Good God,' Kerin said, thinking of the sober, well-mannered Valerius Dio.

'Your advice, then?'

'Do all you can to prevent the city from recognising Vortigern's son as king,' Kerin said. 'Keep telling people that the Saxons are the greatest threat, and that Vortigern's the only man who can protect the kingdom from them. And as a favour to me, when Oswi's strong enough, give him work on one of your ships. He'll go mad if he can't go to sea, and you never know; it could be useful to have a good sailor who hates Hengist and knows how a Saxon war fleet works.' He smiled. 'But first of all, if you have time, I'd like you to talk to me about boats.'

*

The torches cast a flickering light. Gallus's servant, Hani, had placed one in each of the brackets attached to the frescoed wall. Two more stood in tall earthenware jugs, one at each end of the polished table. Kerin and Gallus sat opposite each other. Oswi the Horseman was sitting in the corner. Spread on the table were writing materials familiar to Kerin from his lessons with Dimos; a pot of ink, two ready-sharpened quills and a roll of papyrus from which the merchant had excised a single sheet with his pocket knife. The sheet now bore an impressive likeness of the ship lying alongside the wharf, sketched with a few confident strokes of Gallus's pen.

'All my ships are like this one,' the merchant said.

'Traders, built in the Phoenician style. The ship out here is of medium size, like most of my fleet. Out on the river I also have a few smaller boats for short trips, and three monsters, which we use only for sailing to distant ports like Byzantium. As you can see, this ship here is wide in proportion to its length. It has a deep hull with plenty of room for cargo, and it's powered by wind alone. The ships we fitted out to deal with the Picts are like this one.' He paused and took a draught of his own strong wine. 'Now, true warships are quite different.' He picked up the pen and sketched a vessel wholly unlike anything Kerin had ever seen. 'A Roman bireme. As you can see, it has two banks of oars on each side, as well as a sail and – here at the front – a beak set with bronze blades, for ramming enemy ships. A little ambitious, and not even necessary. What we need is something like this.' A few more strokes of the pen.

'That's like Hengist's ship,' Kerin said. 'The one he had when he first landed in Kent.'

'Yes. The morning after that meeting, I went down to the beach to see what they had. Just because I'm interested in ships, and because I'd suggested that we might use the Saxons against the Picts at sea. It was obvious that Hengist's galleys would be more than a match for them; the boats we fought off Londinium were no more than glorified fishing boats, with a few oarsmen and a small sail. But Oswi tells me that Hengist now has a new galley, with fifteen oarsmen each side and a steering oar at both ends. If the Saxons can build enough ships like that, we'll have trouble.'

Oswi cleared his throat. 'Already we have trouble,' he said. 'I sail this ship myself. It is like no ship I sail before. One day, Hengist comes. And now you talk of ships and make plans, so now I speak.' He folded his arms. Kerin gave him a nod and turned to Gallus.

'Do you have a plan for Oswi, once his wound is healed?'

'I do,' the merchant said. 'Come here, Oswi. Sit down with us.' Oswi sat, looking a little surprised. Gallus fetched an extra goblet from a side table and filled it from an amphora set beside his chair. 'Here,' he said, shoving it towards the Jute. 'It probably won't go with your medication, but Lord Kerin and I are going to empty this amphora, so you can suffer too. Have you seen the ship tied up by my wharf, the one that's under repair?'

'Yes, Master Gallus,' Oswi said, looking taken aback. 'It is a fine ship. If I could work on a ship –'

'Don't get ahead of yourself,' Gallus said. 'There's a few weeks' work to do before she's seaworthy. I've built a new ship for her commander, Petrinus. He's off to Ostia in her tomorrow, with cowhides and wool. And you, my friend, are going to sit in your bed and heal your wounds, because when the *Audax* is ready she'll need a commander, and if you're still limping around like you've been kicked in the balls, I'm going to throw you in the river and find someone else.' He topped up Oswi's goblet. 'Now, take this with you and get some sleep. If Lord Kerin didn't trust you he'd have knifed you in Kent, but trusting you with a ship and ten crewmen is something else. Can I do it?'

Oswi stared at him, dumbstruck with joy. 'Yes!' he shouted. 'I do this thing, and if I do bad, you throw me in the sea for the fishes!'

'Oh, I will,' Gallus said mildly. 'Now get lost, before I change my mind.' He waited until Oswi had gone, singing his way down the passage to his sleeping quarters. 'There's talk about Rufus bringing in reinforcements by sea. Is that true, or just pissed sailors' talk?'

'It's true,' Kerin said. 'Do you ever sail to a port called Bononia, in Gallia?'

'Now and again. The Romans built it, but the wharves are still in good shape. Why do you ask?'

'Because when we were fighting in Kent, Rufus had some transports down in Dubris,' Kerin said. 'After our boys gave him a hiding they took off to Bononia, but Publius Luca said something that made me think. He said that if we'd had the boats, we could have trapped the transports in the harbour and destroyed them. Could that be done, with the ships we have now?'

Gallus's eyes shone with excitement. He looked as animated as a lad with a new toy when an idea gripped him.

'Yes. Pick your moment, and it would be easy. If we blockaded the harbour mouth – well, unarmed transports – ' he gave a ruthless grin.

'Perfect,' Kerin said. 'When Oswi's ready, send him to Bononia to see what's going on. Can you find an excuse to go there regularly, once a month, say?'

'Yes, of course. There are warehouses along the water-front. I'll rent one for a while and store some goods in it. No-one will think twice about it.'

'Alright,' Kerin said. 'In the morning, I'm going to see the praetor, Valerius Dio. Do you have a seat on the ordo yet?'

'No,' Gallus said. 'It's not easy for a slave's son, even if you're prepared to pay for it.'

'I'll get you one. And I'll ask the praetor to release funds, so that you can start building some ships like Hengist's galley. There'll be money enough in the treasury soon, if Valerius is doing his job.'

Gallus leaned forward. 'You're not telling Vortigern?' he asked.

'No,' Kerin said. 'After what happened in the curia, he doesn't trust you. He might forbid it. You can tell him yourself, when you've got a galley to show him. Until then it's between the two of us and the praetor. Is there something you can tell your shipwrights?'

Gallus chuckled. 'I'll tell them I've designed a new merchantman that can outrun everyone else. They're used to that sort of thing. And whatever you agree with Valerius Dio, I'll build the first ship at my own expense. I'll send word when it's done. This remains between ourselves?'

'Yes,' Kerin said. 'For now, at least. When you write, address the letter to my scribe, Dimos, and send it with Valerius Dio's messengers. Keep it simple, and I might even be able to read it myself.'

The torches had burned low in the courtyard, although the moon's soft golden light still filtered down through the swaying branches of the acacias. Kerin walked along the paved path, letting his fingers trail through the fragrant leaves of the rosemary bushes. Something moved along the colonnaded walkway beneath the wall. The girl in the red dress came out of the darkness. Her long black hair was coiled at the nape of her neck, fastened with a pin which was starting to come loose. It was far too late to escape from her. She weaved her way towards Kerin and planted her hands on his chest.

'You're a handsome one, aren't you,' she said, with a coy smile.

'And you're the praetor's wife, I understand,' he said, taking her hands lightly.

'Ah, the praetor!' the girl sighed, as if she had just remembered about him.

'Ariadna!' a shrill voice echoed. 'Come here, you stupid girl, and leave that man alone.'

'Come on,' Kerin said. He took her by the shoulders

and propelled her gently towards the lawns and the terrace. Four women rushed to meet them, although it seemed more, thanks to the noise they were making as they threw their bejewelled arms about and greeted Ariadna.

'I'm sorry,' one of them said, taking Kerin's arm. She looked a little older than the praetor's wife, and far less intoxicated.

'It's alright,' Kerin said. 'Just make sure she doesn't fall in the river.'

The woman regarded him curiously. Her pale face, crowned by fair curls and a silver band, seemed to consist almost entirely of a pair of large blue eyes and a wide, full mouth. 'You're one of the king's warriors, aren't you?'

'Yes,' Kerin said. For a moment he wondered whether he should ask her which king she meant, but it seemed that there was no need for that in Londinium, as yet.

'I thought you'd all gone back to the West,' she said. 'Publius Luca's daughter said so.'

'The king and his wife have gone,' Kerin said. 'And I shall be leaving tonight.' He felt it necessary to add the second remark because Ariadna and her friends had returned, looking like a flock of eager birds contemplating a tasty bowl of fruit. The fair-haired woman drew him aside, and the party flowed back towards the garden.

'We hear the king has taken a young Saxon wife,' she murmured. Her large eyes held both apprehension and a touch of salacious curiosity. Kerin knew what she was asking him.

'Don't worry,' he said. 'It won't dispose him towards her father. If the Jutes cause any trouble, they'll be dealt with just as the Picts were.'

The slender fingers tightened round his arm. 'That's not what some people say,' the woman whispered. 'Some people say that he's never out of her bed, and that he'd have given her father the kingdom for her, never mind Garagon's corn-fields. It's the talk of all the good dining-rooms, you know.'

Kerin looked down at the perfumed hand with distaste. 'The people who say it don't know much about the king,' he said. 'Who are they? The Lord Vortimer's servants?'

'No, indeed, sir!' the woman said indignantly. 'They are well-informed men and women.' The large eyes glanced towards the garden. 'Some of them from the finest old families, actually.'

'Ah,' Kerin said resignedly. That brief aside had told him more than he could ever have wished to know.

16

The overnight rain, though light and short-lived, had dampened down the dust on the Campus Martius, giving a bright, clean-washed quality to the willows beside the Roman road. The sunshine had drawn crowds from the city, and the fringes of the Campus were swarming with children chasing each other round the trees or playing cavalrymen with blunt sticks and a few reluctant dogs. The adults sat around enjoying the sun and wandering back and forth to a roadside stall for ale, mead and food.

Far out on the great bare field, thirty cavalrymen were practising spear-throwing and mounted sword-fights. A heavy wagon containing harness and weapons was standing nearby, and Publius Luca was watching from the driver's seat. Kerin walked slowly out across the Campus. It was hard to believe that this pleasant, peaceful scene was being enacted only a day's ride from the place where he would have been butchered or incinerated, if Publius and his warriors had been even two miles slower.

'I thought you'd all gone home,' the commander said, as Kerin climbed up to sit beside him.

'Everyone else has,' Kerin said. There was no future in being evasive, so he came straight to the point. 'I couldn't stop thinking about what you told Marcus Fulvius at dinner. About the villa having no defences. I know he didn't take you seriously, but I did. If the Saxons found the place, they'd burn it to the ground and slaughter everyone in it. But Marcus wasn't going to listen to me, so I came here to see Marcellus. I thought that anyone who has his own temple to Apollo might take notice of a haruspex. As it happened, Marcellus told me why I'd come before I said a word. Don't ask me whether he'd seen it in some beast's gut or worked it out for himself, but either way, he said he'd have a tactful word with Marcus. God knows if it'll do any good, but at least I've tried.'

A distracting shout went up from the field, followed by hearty cheers. Lucius had allowed himself to be unhorsed by one of his recruits. He picked himself up and came over to the wagon, beating the dust from his breeches.

'They're doing well,' Kerin said. 'Where did you get them?'

'The countryside,' Lucius said. 'Ordinary lads who never got near the fighting at the Wall. A bit green but brave as you like. They're fit, and they've got reasonable horses. We've decided that if Rufus moves against Cambria, we'll march to the West and oppose him.'

Kerin took a moment to absorb the information. Lucius's bluntness had caught him out, but it was the logical conclusion of the pact they had made in Kent. Publius Luca's commitment to Vortigern was unshakeable, and there was a harder edge to Lucius since he escaped hanging. Perhaps there was nothing like the treachery of one's own side for putting it there. In the end, Kerin simply felt sad and angry that it had come to this.

'Rufus was my friend for all those years,' he said. 'All those years. I should have been able to stop him.'

Publius's eyes met his. Compassion and frustration made uneasy companions. 'Give it up, Kerin,' he said. 'That boy thinks he's the messenger of God. His father can't compete, and neither can you. Lucius, take this man for a jar and something to eat. I'm going to give these lads of yours some real training.' He winked at Kerin, climbed down from the wagon and strode off across the Campus, barking a string of orders. The cavalrymen came to attention and formed a neat column.

'I've got no money,' Kerin said as they approached the roadside stall. 'Look, I spent my last sesterce on this.' From the pouch at his belt, he drew an exquisite necklace wrapped in muslin; a single golden leaf hung from a fine gold chain, its delicate veins and indentations worked by a hand as skilled as Cilydd's. In the centre of the leaf a tiny jewel gleamed like a silver dewdrop.

'Well,' Lucius said, 'it looks good to me, but I know as much about necklaces as I knew about horses until you made me sit on one.' He paid for two tankards of ale and two split loaves filled with salt pork and olives. They sat down on a bank under the willows and watched the cavalrymen, the children and the dogs, enjoying the mundane normality of it all.

'I had a jar with your fisherman Manius last night,' Lucius said. 'Do you remember, the old codger who used to give you all the river gossip, back when Constans the monk was king?'

'Yes, of course I do,' Kerin said. 'Vortigern's enemies were livid when Constans was crowned. There were rumours that they might try to bring the monk's younger brother over from Gallia and set him up as king instead. Ambrosius. It was worth keeping in with Manius, because nothing happens on the wharf without him knowing about it. He told me straight away when Maximian Galba hired a boat to bring Ambrosius to Londinium. And the next thing we knew, Maximian's head was in the river, and Constans had handed control of the armies to Vortigern. So yes, I do remember Manius, and he was worth every denarius I paid him. Did he have anything interesting to say last night?'

'I'm not sure,' Lucius said. 'He was prattling on as he always does, but I didn't know what to make of it, really. Constans used to talk about a bishop, didn't he. A powerful bishop from somewhere in the Empire, Germanicus, or some such.'

'Yes,' Kerin said, suddenly attentive. 'Germanus, not Germanicus. He came over here years ago, when Rufus and I were little lads. I don't remember much about it, but when Constans started bleating about him, I asked Vortigern for his opinion. I think he quite liked Germanus when they met. The bishop was an ex-soldier, a man's man. But by the time we spoke, Vortigern had lost patience with him and the Church, because religion was getting mixed up with politics. There's no doubt that Germanus and his associates have influence in Rome, probably access to the military, if they want it. And now Abbot Paulinus, Germanus's close friend, is pulling Rufus's strings. So what did Manius have to say about him?'

Lucius looked a little taken aback, perhaps realising that he might have missed a trick. 'He said that one of Germanus's disciples has been tutoring Ambrosius and Uther. Constans's brothers. Apparently he thinks the Saxons are something to do with the wrath of God.'

'What on earth do you mean?' Kerin asked. Lucius grimaced.

'This priest thinks the Saxons are God's revenge on Vortigern for killing Constans. Not that he actually killed him, of course; the Picts in the bodyguard did it. But everyone knows that Vortigern hired the Picts. I haven't met a single person who thinks that Constans was ever anything more than a puppet, and it's not much of a jump from there to saying that Vortigern killed him, is it? I don't care either way, to be truthful; I'm just glad that we've got the right king. But that's what this priest is telling the boys.'

Kerin saw it all, then; instantly, like the blinding flash of sheet lightning over a black night sky. The sudden illumination of the lowering clouds, the awful, pin-sharp detail of everything lying beneath. It didn't matter one jot if the priest believed his claptrap about the Saxons. All that mattered was the slow drip of poison into the minds of two indignant, fatherless young men; the fashioning of a depraved monster, and the patient digging of the deep, deep well of hatred.

'Kerin?' Lucius said fearfully, as if he too had glimpsed the revelation.

'They'll do nothing,' Kerin said. 'Ambrosius and his brother, and all the men who are driving them. They'll sit over there in Gallia and watch us spending all our strength. Fighting each other first, then fighting the Saxons. They'll sit there and let us do it. And then they'll come.'

'Is there anything I can do?' Lucius asked.

'Yes,' Kerin said. 'Did you see Garagon's sister?'

'I did. I proposed marriage. She didn't refuse me. She's thinking about it.'

'Well, ask her again. Marry her if she'll have you. Marry her, and then get out. No-one will be safe in this half of the country for much longer.' He fetched Eryr from under the trees, where she had gone to avoid the flies. 'We'll meet in the spring,' he said, mounting up.

'Not before, I hope,' Lucius said. 'That would only mean trouble.'

'There's one more thing,' Kerin said, leaning down from the saddle to clasp his hand. His eyes strayed out across the

Campus Martius to the distant figure of Publius Luca, still putting Lucius's youngsters through the mill. 'Please ask him not to build his villa in the east,' he said, and turned his horse towards the road.

<h1 style="text-align:center">17</h1>

The house was empty. The beds looked neat and undisturbed, and the cooking pots were cold. Kerin went back outside, walked briskly across to the chieftains' hall and hammered on the door. There was no response. The citadel was deserted, as if everyone had suddenly died of the plague. Anxious and deflated, he walked over to the horse pens. Vortigern's horses were there, and so was Gael's filly, the animal she had given away so that it could get half-killed on the ride to Kent. Kerin unlaced the leather pouch on his belt and took out the necklace. On the journey, over and over again, he had imagined his arrival. There would be time enough for explanations. She would be waiting at the door for him. He would take her in his arms and give her the beautiful necklace, and then she would lead him to the bedchamber, where all the agonies and uncertainties of the past weeks would be resolved. He had relived that moment time and again as he rode across mountains and through forests, through the heat of the day and the cool, starless nights, until his head spun and his body burned for her. And now he was here, and he was alone. Kerin slipped the necklace back into his pouch and began, despite his best intentions, to think about the horse.

'Kerin Brightspear!' a breathless voice gasped. Caradog the archdruid was hobbling up the track from the valley, leaning on his oak staff.

'Caradog,' Kerin said, trying not to sound too disappointed.

'Home at last, eh?' the old man panted, struggling to get his breath.

'Yes,' Kerin said. 'Caradog, why's it so quiet here? Where is everyone?'

The archdruid sniffed. 'Well, in case you'd forgotten, it's corn-harvest,' he said. 'All the men and women who do any work are in the fields. But of course, that doesn't apply to the *uchelwyr*, does it? The warriors are hunting. And most of the women have gone to the market in Leucarum.'

Kerin's eyes moved to the silent hall. 'Where's the King of all the Britons?' he asked. Caradog chuckled.

'If you mean that young lad who's been strolling about with his pretty wife, he's gone off up the valley with his dog. And the girl's with Morvid, collecting stuff to mend all the sore bellies and split heads.' The druid's thin hand clutched Kerin's wrist. 'What's Rufus up to, then? Him and those traitors? Elir said you gave them a bit of a trouncing.'

'We did, in the end,' Kerin said. 'Not without help from Publius Luca and Gorlois, though. I expect they'll be back. Perhaps you'd better light some fires for us, just in case.'

'Ha!' the druid said. 'I knew you weren't a monks' man underneath. You'll have your fires, Kerin Brightspear. And something to terrify your enemies, if you recall. Come and find me when you're ready.' He patted Kerin's arm and limped off towards the large house under the western wall where his cousin, Cynfawr, lived. Kerin fetched a saddle and bridle, flung them onto his young, untrained black stallion and rode off down the track towards the valley before anyone else had time to catch him.

The settlement was deserted too except for old people and housedogs enjoying the sun, and children swimming in the river. Kerin rode with a loose rein, letting the young horse set his own pace. He had expected a lively ride, but was surprised to find the animal as responsive and disciplined as if it had had a month's training in good manners. Someone had been riding it, alright. The horse trotted on up the valley and turned right at the water-mill. At the next fork in the track, a stream wound inland through woods of oak, birch and rowan. The valley floor was broad and grassy, with shallow pools full of watercress where herds of deer came down to drink at dusk. Hardly anyone passed through, except for shepherds bringing their sheep down from the moors at shearing time.

Kerin soon came upon Vortigern. He had lit a fire and was cooking a brown trout on the end of a sharpened stick, like any peasant might have done. His deerhound Fanw, stretched out nearby, opened one eye and thumped her tail. Kerin tied his horse to a bush and sat down on the warm grass. Clouds of gnats rose and fell above drifts of mint and meadow-sweet.

'Where have you been?' Vortigern asked, stirring the fire.

'In Londinium,' Kerin said. 'There were things I had to do.'

Vortigern looked up. 'You should have told me.'

'I know. But I didn't know how to put it.'

'I wouldn't have cared how you put it,' Vortigern said. 'But I'd have had something to tell your wife.'

Kerin stared up at the sky. 'Where is she?'

'Gone to the market with Mora and the children. Your Saxon took them in his wagon.'

Kerin grimaced. 'Did Macsen talk to her?'

'Yes. As soon as we got back. He gave her whatever message you'd given him, but it didn't satisfy her, so she came to me.'

'What did you tell her?' Kerin asked.

'That you were mad but would soon come back,' Vortigern said. 'There didn't seem to be much harm in that. I knew I was right on both counts.'

'I bought her this,' Kerin said, producing the necklace. 'I hope she'll forgive me when I give it to her.'

Vortigern raised his eyebrows. 'You don't know much, do you,' he said. Kerin gave him an uneasy look and put the necklace away. 'She's not Mabli. You won't buy her off with that.'

'I don't want to buy her off,' Kerin said indignantly. 'Just to apologise for not coming back with the rest of you.'

Vortigern shrugged. 'Please yourself,' he said. 'But it won't work.' He stripped the flesh from one side of the trout and held it out.

'I'm not hungry,' Kerin said, staring at the river.

'Why did you go to Londinium?'

'To see Marcellus. About the Saxons and the villa. I thought it might carry more weight, coming from him. But then, I don't suppose you believe in the entrails, do you.'

'The entrails?' Vortigern said, in disgust. 'You can't believe that nonsense, surely.'

'No, I don't,' Kerin said resentfully. 'But when Marcellus told me why I'd come, and before I so much as opened my mouth, it did make me think.'

Vortigern ate the trout and tossed the bones into the water. 'You should do less of that,' he said. Kerin was about to make an indignant retort when he saw that Vortigern was smiling, or perhaps even trying not to laugh.

'I don't see the joke, lord,' he sighed.

'There isn't one,' Vortigern said. He leaned on his elbow and closed his eyes. Perhaps he was simply too contented to pursue an argument of any kind. Around them the soft crooning of turtle doves hung in the warm air, and insects buzzed amongst the grass blades.

'How do things feel here?' Kerin asked.

Vortigern shrugged. 'Rufus has no support at all. Hanging Hefin was his biggest mistake. Even the Christians can't swallow that. And anyway, what does it matter to them as long as the corn grows, and the sun comes up in the morning? Caradog's celebrating, Cynfawr is composing a poem and the women haven't got a thought in their heads apart from Mabli's wedding. And Iustig's up in his chapel preaching forgiveness, so I'm told; although I really don't know who he thinks should be forgiving whom.' He looked up, and Kerin thought for a moment about what Brother Padarn said on the road to Glevum. The monk had seemed convinced that Iustig was responsible for the falling-out with Vortigern. Kerin still found this unthinkable, however astute Padarn normally was.

'What should I do, then?' he asked. 'You've spoken to Gael. You must have some idea.'

'I'm the last man to tell you,' Vortigern said. 'Ask someone like Lud or Hefydd, who's managed to keep a woman alive and happy for thirty years.'

Kerin shook his head. 'Lots of women die in childbirth, lord. Lud and Hefydd were lucky that their wives didn't, that's all.'

Vortigern raised his eyebrows, picked up a second trout and threaded it onto the stick. Kerin understood, as he always did, that beyond this point the door was closed to him. He scratched Fanw's ears and threw a twig for her. She yawned and looked up at him as if he might have been slightly deranged.

'Someone's been riding my horse,' he said. 'Do you know who it is?'

'No,' Vortigern said; untruthfully, Kerin suspected, from the smile on his face.

'Are you sure, lord?'

'Yes. What of it, anyway? The horse isn't spoiled, is he?'

'No,' Kerin said grudgingly. 'He's improved, actually.'

'Well, then,' Vortigern said. Kerin glanced up at the sun, hanging on the rim of the woods.

'I should go. They're bound to be back from the market soon. Will you come with me?'

'No,' Vortigern said. 'Not just yet.'

Kerin untied his horse. He could see why Vortigern was in no hurry to leave the place; there was probably as much healing in the peace of this valley as in an amphora of Marcellus's remedies.

'Perhaps you should tell Publius to avoid building his villa in the east,' he said. 'I did ask Lucius to mention it.'

'It's a good suggestion,' Vortigern said. 'But Marcus Fulvius has offered him land already. Fine, rich land with woods full of deer, and pastures watered by a stream. Marcus doesn't even want anything for it; I think he'd be happy enough to have his sister living close by. How many men would turn that down?'

'Not many,' Kerin said dispiritedly.

'Stop thinking about it,' Vortigern said. 'Go and find your wife.' The horse whinnied and fidgeted, impatient to be off. Vortigern held out the trout on the end of the stick. Kerin shook his head. 'Eat it,' Vortigern said. 'You'll need your strength.'

Kerin gave a wry smile. 'You think so? I'm not counting on it.'

'You're a fool,' Vortigern said. 'And you complicate things too much. Find the girl. Apologise. Abase yourself if you must, admit you're a worthless bastard who doesn't deserve a minute of her time. Ride her till you're both too weak to stand. And *then* give her the necklace.'

18

It was late. Men and women were trudging home from the cornfields through the warm evening. The sun was low in a rose-coloured sky, bathing the calm sea and the headlands in a soft golden light. Every one of Kerin's saddles, bridles and headcollars had been checked and, where necessary, repaired. He had sharpened his hunting spear, his battle spears and all the other assorted weapons until he could hardly put his finger to the edge of a blade. He had even sharpened Cheldric's kitchen knives. His body was beginning to tell him that he had ridden through the night to get home, but he could not go near the marriage bed without being reminded of what had happened there; and the more he tried not to think about that, the more it drove him mad.

The ox-cart was coming up the track from the valley. It would have been impossible not to hear it, or at least, not to hear Cheldric swearing in British. There was a creak and a rattle, then nothing. Kerin opened the door of his house just a crack and peered out. The cart was a few paces away, outside Lud's house. The oxen were standing with their heads between their knees, sweating and steaming. Mora was sitting high up on the driver's seat beside Cheldric, proud as an empress on a throne. Behind her were Marc, Catula and the horse boy Ashur. The cart was laden with casks, mysterious boxes, bales of cloth and a cage containing four large, vocal geese. Kerin went over to them. Mora smiled at him, but there was something guarded about it. It was not quite the greeting he had expected. Cheldric jumped down from his seat and slapped Kerin on the shoulder.

'Ah!' he cried. 'The wandering man is back!'

Kerin smiled half-heartedly, wishing that Cheldric had not put it quite like that. 'I wasn't wandering, Cheldric,' he said. 'I had to go to Londinium for something important, and I came back as soon as I could. Now, where's Gael?'

'She's talking,' Mora said, before Cheldric had time to open his mouth.

'Talking?' Kerin said vaguely. Cheldric seized the head of his lead ox and kissed its moist pink muzzle.

'Is nothing,' he said. 'She talks to the Lord, that is all.' He nodded back towards the track. Mora looked daggers at him and clambered down. The Saxon flung his hands in the air. 'Is nothing!' he protested. Kerin ran, between the houses, through the open gateway in the stockade and across the short, wiry grass to the head of the track. He stopped short, breathing hard. Vortigern and Gael were standing about halfway down the track. They had not seen him. They were talking, or rather, Vortigern was talking; about something quite important, judging by the way he used his hands for emphasis as he finished what he was saying. Kerin was too far away to hear, but close enough to see his wife smile as Vortigern took her hands, and quite close enough to see her stand on tiptoe and kiss him lightly on the cheek. Vortigern said something and laughed, and went back down towards the valley. Gael gathered her skirts and ran, still smiling to herself, up the hill. Kerin stood still and let her come. He had no idea what to make of what he had just seen. He realised that Mora was standing beside him.

'Be careful, lad,' she said, putting her fat, wrinkled hand on his arm. Kerin looked at her blankly. He was quite unprepared for the feeling of speechless dread which was rising inside him.

'What do you mean? What's happening?'

'Nothing,' Mora said calmly. 'Nothing at all. But be careful. You're a good, brave, honest man like my Lud. But good men have to work hard all their lives to keep their wives happy. Men like Vortigern have only to look at a woman, and she'll leave her father's house and walk the road to hell. Gael's a treasure, but she's flesh and blood like any other. And he's been breaking hearts since he was old enough to know what it was for. Be careful.' Kerin felt her hand slacken and fall. Her heavy footsteps stomped away towards her house. Gael almost ran into him before she realised that he was there.

'Kerin!' she exclaimed. Her face was transformed with joy. For a moment Kerin thought that she was going to hurl herself into his arms, but then she checked herself, as if she had remembered that she had a reason for not doing it. 'Where have you been?' she asked, her eyes anguished.

'In Londinium,' Kerin said. He hardly knew whether to touch her or not. 'There is a good reason, and I will tell you, but please, not now. Please, just come back to the house with me.'

'Alright,' Gael said. They walked slowly up the track and into the citadel, hand in hand, without speaking. Once inside the house, Kerin closed the door behind him and barred it. Gael stared at him reproachfully, hands folded in front of her. The golden light flooded in through the small window, glinting on her hair and turning the fine stuff of her dress to a translucent veil, through which the outline of her slender body was cruelly visible. Kerin shook his head, wanting her so badly that he could barely think.

'Look,' he said, 'I know I should have let you know somehow, and I'm sorry, but please, can't it wait? Can't we –'

'No,' Gael said, with a toss of the head. 'Tell me first.'

Kerin stared up at the roof. The stratagem on which he had pinned his hopes was not working at all. He wondered whether it would have worked for Vortigern, who had suggested it. Breathing deeply to steady himself, he walked across to the table and sat down.

'Come here, then,' he said, more sharply than he had intended. Gael sat down opposite him and folded her hands on the table. 'On the way back, we stayed at a villa belonging to relations of Vortigern's friend, Publius Luca. At dinner, Publius warned his brother-in-law that the villa had no defences. That if the Saxons came back, there was nothing to stop them destroying it. I couldn't sleep that night, but I'd had a skinful of wine, and I started imagining what might happen. Saxons burning the place down, kill-ing everyone – ' he flung his hands up. 'I couldn't possibly tell the owner of the villa because he'd have thought I was crazy, so I went to Londinium to tell my friend Marcellus, the soothsayer. If he tells the family, they might listen to him. And that's it. That's all. I told Marcellus and spent the night with Lucius Arrius, and then I came home as fast as my horse would go.'

'But why didn't you tell Macsen? All he said was that you had important things to see to in Londinium.'

'They were important,' Kerin protested. 'And if I'd told Macsen, he'd have laughed in my face. He'd probably have thought I was making it all up.'

'The perhaps you should have told someone else,' Gael said. Her eyes were bright, but she was not going to weep. Kerin remembered the touch of Mora's heavy hand on his arm.

'Perhaps I should have told Vortigern,' he said. If he had intended it to sound like an accusation, it had worked. Gael's face creased with anxiety.

'Why not?' she asked, reaching for his hands. Kerin freed his hands. He could barely think about the things Mora had implied, let alone articulate them, but there was another matter, of course; separate, and yet inextricably linked.

'Why did you give his wife the horse?' he asked.

'Because I had to,' Gael sighed.

'It was my gift to you!' Kerin exclaimed. 'My first gift. My love-gift. And you gave it away, so that it could get ridden to death on a forced march. For God's sake, didn't it mean anything to you?'

Gael's eyes were desperate, but she had controlled her tears. In Glevum, the only men she had been close to were her father, a dust-dry bishop and her brute of a husband. It had taught her self-mastery, and perhaps more besides.

'Of course it did,' she said. 'More than any other gift has ever done. But Rowenna is my friend, and she had no-one to help her. Her pony is lame, and she'd have killed herself trying to ride a warhorse. Can't you see? She'd have gone anyway, on her bare feet, if necessary. How could I not help her?'

'She shouldn't have come!' Kerin protested. 'A woman, on a forced march with a warband? It's madness. And you can't think that Vortigern wanted her there. He treated her like dog-dirt all the way to Kent. It's complete madness.'

'I know it is,' Gael said. 'But that's the point!'

Kerin drove a hand through his hair. 'Loving God!' he roared. Gael took his hands between her own and looked at him very directly.

'You were at Hengist's feast,' she said. 'You saw it happen. She could have had anyone, but oh, no. One look at Vortigern, and that was that. Surely you can see why.'

'So,' Kerin said coolly. 'You see something in him that you don't see in me.'

'No, no!' Gael exclaimed, pressing his fingers to her lips. 'You are my only love, and you always will be. But that doesn't prevent me from seeing what Rowenna sees. What any woman with blood in her veins would see.'

Kerin removed his hands from hers and sat, staring down at the table. However lovingly she looked at him, no matter how sincerely she protested the opposite, he could not help feeling that all this in some way diminished her love for him. He thought about what Mabli had said, long ago on a spring evening; about Mora's gloomy advice, and about foolish, beautiful Flora, watching the Roman road for a man who would never come. He remembered the girl on the deck of her father's galley, who had hardly even noticed that he was there.

'So, what has this got to do with the horse?' he said stiffly, knowing how cold and unresponsive his voice must sound. 'I know she's your friend, but giving her the horse just made it easier for her to leave. Couldn't you have talked some sense into her instead?'

Gael laughed out loud. 'How can you possibly say that? You, of all people?'

Kerin recoiled. 'What on earth does that mean?'

Gael threw herself across the table. 'You'd lie on hot coals if he asked you to,' she said, her face up against his. 'You'd give him your horse. You'd give him your life. You'd walk barefoot into hell after him. So don't blame that poor girl if she wants to do the same. And don't blame me, for understanding why.'

'I don't!' Kerin cried, seizing her by the shoulders.

'Good,' Gael shouted, her eyes flashing fire. 'Because you've got absolutely nothing else to blame me for, I promise you.'

'Nor you me,' Kerin said indignantly. 'Alright, I didn't

come back, and I should have told someone why, but – well, I'm a stupid, thoughtless bastard, and I didn't.'There was an explanation, but he had forgotten what it was, because by now Gael had scrambled across the table and was sitting astride him on the bench. 'Look, he said shakily, 'if you'd seen the place, if you knew how Saxons fight – ' His wife appeared not to have heard him. She was more concerned with throwing off her fragile dress, undoing the belt of his breeches and sliding her hand inside.

'Mother of God, do I have to wait any longer?' she asked.

19

The knock on the door was sharp and insistent. Kerin kept his eyes closed and hoped that it would stop. The sound came again, loud and repetitive, as if someone had been trying to hammer a nail into the door. Kerin opened his eyes. The first faint glow of dawn was beginning to filter in at the bedroom window. He was lying on his back with his arms around his wife. As far as he could remember, she was exactly where she had been when sleep overcame them at last, after an odyssey which had taken them from the bench beside the table, to the table itself, to the floor next to the hearth and then to the pile of blankets and saddlery in the corner of the store room, ending at last on the bed where they now lay. The knocking began again. Cursing quietly to himself, Kerin lifted Gael gently to one side, wrapped himself in a blanket and stumbled towards the door.

'Alright, alright!' he grumbled, flinging the bar aside and dragging the door open. Cheldric was standing outside in the dim half-light. Morvid and Marc were just behind him; not hiding, exactly, but looking as if they wouldn't have had the courage to knock on their own account.

'You lock us out!' Cheldric roared accusingly. 'We have no beds. We stay all night, all night in the straw, with Cenydd's stinking cattle. And now we wake, we are hungry, and the food it is here, inside the house!'

Kerin blinked the sleep from his eyes and stared at

Cheldric. If he had had the strength, he would have picked the Saxon up and hurled him into the drainage ditch. Something of the sort must have been apparent to Morvid and his grandson, who began to smile nervously and back away.

'We're sorry, lord,' Marc mouthed. Kerin raised his hand.

'It's alright,' he sighed. 'I'm awake now. But next time you're thinking of disturbing a man who's just come back to his wife after a battle, think again.' He seized Cheldric by his leather jerkin. 'And as for you, I'd throw you in the ditch if I had the energy, except I know that Mabli won't scrub you now she's got Derfyn to keep her busy. Get in the house and make me some gruel. And make it with milk. I need it.'

'Lord, I have no milk!' Cheldric squeaked.

'I'll get some, you fool,' Morvid said hastily, prodding Marc in the back. 'Come with me, boy. You can get the wood.'

Kerin leaned on the doorpost and watched them go. The sky above the dark hills to the east was clear and bright. Down in the valley, the wagons were setting off for the cornfields. The still air smelt of salt and wood-smoke and home. Cenydd came by, carrying a wooden pail in each hand. He waved cheerily to Kerin and trudged off towards the spring, whistling. Kerin smiled and waved back. In spite of everything, it was very good to be home. Footsteps approached. Dimos appeared, satchel slung on his shoulder, looking far healthier than he had done in Londinium. His face had filled out a little, and his complexion suggested that he spent most of his free time in the open air.

'Lord Kerin,' he said warmly. 'Are we to start work at last?'

'This afternoon, if nothing else gets in the way,' Kerin said. He grinned and adjusted his blanket. 'I'll put some clothes on first. How are things going with the youngsters?'

'Very well,' Dimos said. 'Even your lad Marc can read a few words, and he's not exactly a willing pupil. But the girls are the best. They don't always get the opportunity, so I think they're keen to outdo the boys. That little Catula, she's as sharp as a needle. The only one ahead of her is Ashur, and he could already read and write in Greek and Coptic, so he only has to catch up with Latin. He told me his father's a horse master in Egypt, quite keen on education. The slavers caught the boy, didn't they?'

'Yes,' Kerin said. 'We came across him in Londinium. Vortigern brought him along to look after his warhorses.'

'And to get him away from his master, according to Ashur,' Dimos said. 'He understands more British than you'd think. And he had a lucky escape. Alberius comes across as a foppish idiot, but there's a nasty streak underneath.' The scribe smiled. 'Forgive me. I had to keep my opinions to myself in Severus Maximus's house. It's like breathing different air here.'

'There's nothing to forgive,' Kerin said, 'but I have something to explain. I'm expecting a letter from a friend in Londinium. It's private business, so I asked him to address the letter to you, and send it with the praetor's messengers.'

'I'll look out for it,' Dimos said. 'But may I ask a favour in return? A friend of mine still works in the praetor's household, and he's a great communicator. A bit of a gossip, to be truthful, but very funny. Do you think the king would mind if we exchange letters now and again?'

'I don't think anyone could object to that,' Kerin said. 'And if there's any scandalous news, I hope you'll share it with us. There hasn't been nearly enough laughter around here lately.'

'It's a bargain,' Dimos said, smiling broadly. There was

a warmth to him which Kerin suspected he might have been hiding for years. Shouldering his satchel he set off to find the children, whistling as he went. Kerin went into the house, growled at Cheldric just fiercely enough to make the Saxon jump, and sauntered back to the bedroom. Gael was awake. She had opened the shutters and was sitting on the bed, arms wrapped around her knees.

'Wanton bitch,' Kerin said. 'Where are your clothes?'

'Out there with yours, I suppose,' Gael said, waving her hand vaguely. 'Who was knocking?'

'Cheldric,' Kerin said. 'I locked him out last night. He had to share a bed with Cenydd's cattle. Anyway, stay there. I've got something for you.'

Gael smiled demurely. 'What, again?' she said. Kerin raised his hand.

'God, no. Or at least, not until I've had some breakfast and a good sleep.' He ventured out of the bedroom. Cheldric had lit the fire and was standing beside it, chin on hand, gazing thoughtfully at Kerin's tunic and breeches, which were lying in a crumpled heap on the floor. His belt was to be found some distance away under the table, and Gael's dress was dangling, inexplicably, from a hook on one of the roof beams where Cheldric usually hung his joints of salt meat. The Saxon looked up and raised his eyebrows enquiringly. Kerin shrugged, gathered up the discarded garments and went back to the bedroom. Gael had wrapped herself in a blanket and was sitting on the edge of the bed, looking as eager as a child on her birthday.

'Here,' he said, handing her the leather pouch. 'I'm no good at this sort of thing, so you'd better open it yourself.'

Gael seized the pouch, then hesitated. 'No,' she said, handing it back. 'It's your gift.'

'Alright, then. Close your eyes, and put your hands out.'

Kerin laid the necklace across her outstretched palms. Gael felt the cool touch of the metal and opened her eyes.

'It's beautiful!' she whispered, running the tip of one finger over the delicate links.

'Put it on, then,' Kerin said impatiently.

'No,' Gael said, holding it out. 'You put it on for me.'

Kerin took the necklace. He was almost afraid of breaking the clasp. 'Please,' he said, kissing her as he fastened it around her neck, 'promise me that you will always wear this. That you will never give it away to anyone, for any reason.'

'Never as long as I live,' Gael said. She looked up at him gravely. 'I hope you have quite forgiven me, because I have two confessions to make.'

Kerin's brow creased. He had hoped that all that was behind them. 'Confessions?' he said. Gael lowered her eyes.

'The lesser of the two first,' she said.

'Well?' Kerin said apprehensively. Gael looked up, trying not to smile.

'I've been riding your horse.'

'My horse!' Kerin exclaimed. 'The black one!'

'Yes. He was looking so lonely and fretful on his own – rather like me, in fact; perhaps that's why we understand each other so well. I enjoyed it so much that I've ridden him almost every day since you left. I hope I haven't spoiled him.'

'No, no,' Kerin said. 'But wasn't he too much for you? I mean, girls don't usually ride stallions, all the women here ride fillies or mares, if anything.'

Gael kissed his cheek. 'I told you my father taught me as if I were a boy,' she said. Kerin raised his hands.

'You're right. And I've seen you ride often enough. I should have known better.'

'He's a lovely horse,' Gael said. 'I call him Seren, for the star on his face. You don't mind that, do you?'

Kerin grinned. 'No, I don't mind that,' he said, putting his arms round her neck. 'But he'll be no good to me, after your training. He's far too polite for a warhorse. I think you should keep him, and let Rowenna keep your filly. They seem to have got to like each other.' He paused, realising that he had a confession of his own to make. 'I was wrong about her, Gael. I misjudged her completely. I hate her father so much that I couldn't see past him. I've tried to mend things.'

Gael took his hands. 'There's nothing to mend. She understands. All is forgiven. And I have made friends with Tirion. She comes to visit us here. Her heart is broken for Hefin, but at least she speaks to us, and tries to smile now and again.' She looked up, her eyes anxious. 'Rowenna told me what happened at the villa. Not what you foresaw. Everything else.' Kerin blinked; a slight shake of the head. It was hard to think about it, let alone put it into words. As always, Gael understood. He knew that she bled for his distress, as if the wound had been her own. 'Rowenna is strong,' she said, pressing her lips to their clasped hands. 'She will manage this.'

Kerin stroked her hair. He hoped that she was right. He couldn't manage it. He wondered if, after all, to borrow Gorlois's words, he was just a horse warrior and a head-splitter who happened to see what was coming round the corner now and again.

'What?' Gael asked.

'I wanted to help her,' Kerin said. 'At the villa. She knows I'm good at guessing what might come. She wanted to be told about it. She's not a person you can lie to, but I tried to tell her the best of it, because there will be a way through for some of us. I don't know who, I don't know how, but there will be a way.'

'For us? For Rowenna and Vortigern?'

'I don't know,' Kerin said. 'Perhaps it's best that way. All I can say is that, for as long as I live, protecting the three of you will be all that matters to me. You above all.'

'Even though I stole your best young horse?' Gael asked sadly.

Kerin chuckled. 'Yes,' he said, then remembered what else she had said. 'But if that's the lesser of your confessions, I think you should tell me what the other one is.'

Gael lowered her eyes. A faint flush of colour rose up her neck, suffusing her face with a warm glow.

'Gael?' Kerin said curiously. She looked up at him and smiled, her eyes glistening with tears.

'I am with child,' she said

20

After that, any man would have been entitled to pause for a moment, give thanks for life's blessings and enjoy the remains of the summer. But a vision kept recurring in Kerin's mind, vivid and disturbing, of Rufus and his murdering band charging towards the Roman fort; except that this time they were charging across the moors towards Vortigern's citadel. The vision grew and niggled, infecting all the bright mornings and long golden evenings, reminding him that everything he loved was fragile and at risk; and the more deeply he grew to love his wife, the harder it drove him. Making peace with Gallus had been just the first step. Soon, with Dimos's help, he would write to as many men of honour and goodwill as he could name, to ask for a pledge of allegiance. But there was something else; more mysterious, more potent, within touching distance.

'Come and find me when you're ready,' Caradog had said. In the morning Kerin rode to the top of Penrhyn Fawr, where the archdruid usually went to watch the sun rise over the eastern headlands. 'Wait till dusk,' Caradog said. 'Come alone, and tell no-one. There'll be time enough for that.'

Kerin had no idea what to expect. He hoped that the sound the carnyx made was as impressive as Caradog had implied. It would be quite an anticlimax if something as ferocious-looking as that could only toot like a whistle. The morning was fine, so he rode over to visit Gwyndaf in his citadel. Leil and Cadfan came riding across the hillside to meet him.

'Did you see them on the road?' Cadfan asked.

'I came by the beaches,' Kerin said. 'I haven't seen a soul.'

'Derfyn's gone to Henfelin to see Mabli's father,' Leil said. 'And Gwyndaf's gone along to hold his hand. I've never seen Derfyn frightened of anything. It was wonderful to know he can get terrified just like the rest of us.' The two lads dissolved in laughter.

'Come on,' Kerin said, laughing with them. 'Let's go and throw some spears.' He would have said it anyway, just for fun, but as with most things he did now, there was another purpose. The young warriors were good spearmen, but not as good as they could be; not as good as they would need to be, to hold the River Hafren in the spring.

*

It was late afternoon when Kerin reached home. Sounds of music were drifting from his house. The lyre, unmistakably, and two women's voices singing a song he didn't recognise, the melody underscored by the soft notes of a reed pipe. The sounds stopped abruptly as he opened the door. Gael and Rowenna looked at him, then at each other. Tirion, who had been playing the pipe, gave a hesitant smile.

'I must go now,' she said, lowering her eyes.

'Not on my account, please,' Kerin said. 'I haven't heard that song before, Gael. Is it one of your mother's?'

'Yes, but I've put it into British so we can sing it together. And Tirion's pipe makes it sound even better.'

Tirion stood up. She was a pretty girl with wide green eyes and a cloud of soft brown hair, but grief had treated her cruelly, hollowing her cheeks and draining the colour from them. 'I must go,' she said. 'Not because of you, Lord Kerin, but Mabon's sitting around with the pony and cart, waiting to take me home. They'll be sending a search party if we're not back before dark. And don't look so worried. Mabon's the soul of caution. But I hate the cart. This child can't come soon enough. When it's here, I'll wrap it to my back in a shawl, and come visiting on my horse.'

The three women embraced and went outside. Kerin listened to the affectionate farewells, Mabon's laughter, the creak of harness as the pony moved off. Gael came back in, lightly humming the tune of the Irish song.

'Perhaps you'd like to sing that for everyone else,' Kerin said. 'I'm told that Derfyn has gone to ask for Mabli's hand, so there'll probably be a marriage feast before long.'

Gael clapped her hands with delight. 'A feast!' she said. 'We have two marriage feasts to make up for when you think about it, don't we.'

An appetising smell was drifting from the kitchen. 'That smells good,' Kerin said. 'What's Cheldric making?'

'The stew of two pigs. You know, the one with roast pig and smoked pig and all the roots and herbs. It's my absolute favourite, and I'm starving.'

'So you should be,' Kerin said, bending to kiss her cheek. 'There's something I must do, but I'll be back by the time it's ready. Has he made it in the big cauldron?'

'Yes. There's enough to feed a warband.'

'Good. Invite whoever you like, and ask Cheldric to tap a cask. We'll have our own little feast tonight.'

Gael stood up and slipped her arms around him. 'I love you more than ever,' she said. 'And I wouldn't trade this for anything. Do you remember, I told you that I could see what Rowenna sees? But I would never, in a million years, want what Rowenna wants. She's a wild girl, Kerin. And

that day in her father's village, she found her kindred spirit.
But I want this. A home. Children with the man I love. I
want this.'

Kerin drew her close. Whatever might come to them in
the months ahead, nothing could rob him of this moment.
He imagined himself back in Morvid's valley, in the little
shack she had made a home by filling it with love, warmth
and laughter; and now she had brought it all here, to this
house which had never been more than a place to sleep,
even though it stood on the ground he loved.

'Thank you, my singing bird,' he said softly.

*

Even beneath the trees it was still warm, as the sun moved
westwards; but within the druids' cave, the air was cold
enough to turn breath to smoke. Caradog had brought
torches, tightly-wrapped bundles of slow-burning twigs
dipped in olive oil. Rammed into crevices in the rockface,
they flooded the inner chamber of the cave with a dim,
wavering light. A Roman lamp of fine clay flickered on the
boulder where the carnyx stood. Kerin had tangled with
boars in the hunt. He knew that a strong one could outrun
a horse and take a man's arm off with one bite, leaving its
venomous saliva behind as a terrible gift. The draco was
startling enough, but dragons were creatures of the imagination, as far as he knew. The boar was real, and this boar
was here; and Kerin now realised that, wherever you stood
in the cave, it was looking at you.

'Aren't you going to do something, then?' he asked,
realising with a rush of shame that he sounded frightened.
The thing could not, by any stretch of the imagination, be
any more of a physical threat than Tirion's reed pipe, or

Gael's lyre; and yet his voice was strained, and his hands were sweating. The bard Cynfawr and his son looked at each other, and Cynan shrugged. Caradog had said that it was he who cared for the carnyx, visiting it, polishing it lovingly with salt, flour and crab apple juice, just in case; but Cynan was a gentle soul who would always defer to his father in matters of music. Cynfawr cleared his throat.

'Go on,' he said, patting his son's arm. 'You're a poor singer, but you're a mighty man in this.'

Cynan moved behind the carnyx, grasped its slender tube in both hands and raised the mouthpiece to his lips. Kerin was astounded by the height of the thing. Like his father, Cynan was a tall, well-made man, and in his hands the instrument towered towards the invisible roof of the cave, far higher than Kerin had expected when it was propped against the boulder, leaning towards him.

'First I shall play a little paean to the gods,' Cynan said gravely. 'We are in a holy place, after all.' A single, prolonged note came from between the gaping jaws of the carnyx, akin to the sound of the Roman military trumpets Kerin had heard in Londinium, but sweet and liquid, sliding downwards into a melodic warble. Cynan played it over and over until Kerin knew that it would be lodged in his brain forever, ending with an odd low note resembling the mournful sound a calf made when it called for its mother. That can't be all, Kerin thought. The sound was beautiful, but surely there must be more, after all Caradog had said. Cynan smiled, as if reading his thoughts.

'Don't worry,' he said. 'That was simply for reverence and respect. Now we'll begin.'

He raised the carnyx, filled his lungs with air and blew. Kerin was utterly unprepared for the sound which hit him; so loud, so forceful, that he stepped backwards and fell against the wall of the cave, as if he had been flung there by a storm surge. On and on it went, deeper than any beast's roar, more resonant than thunder, and so amplified by the cave's vast chamber that Kerin thought his head might burst.

'Stop!' he cried, covering his ears. The sound sank to a low rumble, punctuated by a liquid, high note like a curlew's night call, then stopped. With extreme care, Cynan replaced the carnyx in its cradle and looked up. The torchlight revealed a broad smile and a face beaded with sweat.

'What did you think of that, then?' Caradog asked.

'You were right,' Kerin said. 'About the gates of Annwn. If I heard that coming towards me out of darkness or a thick fog, I'd probably be too frightened to move. Or if I wasn't, I'd run. Are there others, or is this the only one ?'

'The only one we know of,' Caradog said. 'Once there were many, but most were destroyed when the enemy slaughtered our people.' He gave a bitter smile. 'Melted down and turned into Roman trinkets, perhaps. And who would make one now?'

'Why have you kept it hidden all these years?' Kerin asked. 'Why didn't you bring it out when we went to fight in the North?'

'Because I was sure in my heart that you could win without its help,' Caradog said. 'And because the men of the North used to have war horns of their own. Perhaps it lives in the memory up there. As we've just seen, its greatest power is in the horrible shock it can give to a man who doesn't expect it, or doesn't know what he's hearing. We conferred, Cynfawr, Cynan and I, and we decided that it should be saved for more dangerous times. We have them now, wouldn't you say?'

'Yes,' Kerin said. 'We have them now.' He paused. 'I believe you're right. If that sound can frighten me – and God knows, it did – then it can frighten anyone. Any warriors who haven't heard it before, never mind their horses. It could turn a battle.'

Caradog's eyes burned with the fervour of all the old passions; the indignities, the shed blood, the rage of the occupied. 'Then it's for you to convince the others,' he said. 'Unbelievers like your standard-bearer. Sceptical men like Publius the Roman, who need proof of everything. And above all, the Lord. Men say he's a madman in battle, but they don't know the half of it. Everything's measured against all those lives he holds in his hand. If he doesn't believe that our carnyx could save a few, it'll never get further than this cave.'

Kerin's hand slid up the slender neck and caressed the pricked ears. 'I'll choose my moment,' he said. 'And I'll do my best.'

21

There was little news. Valerius Dio's messengers arrived punctually every two weeks, as Vortigern had commanded, but their sealed scrolls contained nothing alarming. For a while it seemed as if summer would go on forever, and then one morning Kerin woke up and found, quite suddenly, that it was autumn. It always came upon Henfelin like that; no more than a subtle change in the light, as if some unseen hand had drawn a fine veil across the countryside. One clear, crisp morning, when he was out on the beach introducing Ghazal to the pleasures of trotting through the surf, he heard hooves clopping towards him across the firm sand. It was Dimos, on Padarn's brown mule.

'I'll have to find a horse for you,' he said. Dimos smiled.

'I'm no expert, but I can stay on.' He held out a leather bag. 'I thought you might want to see this. It arrived with the praetor's messengers just now. They'd been told that it was for me, but clearly it isn't.'

Kerin took the bag and drew out a slim scroll. The seal bore the impression of a cockerel, immediately recognisable as a copy of the golden image adorning the tabards of Gallus's guards. Beside it, the inscription: *Kerinus Hastaclara*. Kerin looked up. 'You'd better stay,' he said. 'I might need your help.' Dimos withdrew courteously as Kerin broke the seal and opened the letter. The words sprang out, immediately intelligible. *Factus est. Rex navem habet.* His face broke into a smile of utter delight.

'Good news, then?' Dimos enquired.

'It's done,' Kerin whispered. 'The king has a ship.' His smile broadened and became a crow of joy. 'It's done!' he shouted, jabbing the letter with his forefinger. 'The king has a ship!' Dimos smiled back, sharing his pleasure.

'I'm glad to hear it,' he said. 'Is there any more?'

'Yes,' Kerin said, frowning over the remaining lines. 'Something about me and you, and – oh God, here, read it for me. In British, please, I need to know now.'

Dimos took the scroll. *'It is done, the king has a ship,'* he read. *'The first of many, I hope. Please tell no-one, as we agreed. And don't come to me, I will come to you. Your loyal friend, Gallus Mercator.'* He smiled, rolled up the letter and held it out.

'Keep it, please,' Kerin said, passing him the leather bag. 'I know I can trust you. I can't tell the king because Gallus wants to do it himself. You probably know that they fell out; it's no secret in Londinium. I think Gallus hopes that the ship may put things right.'

Dimos stowed the scroll in its bag and they turned for the settlement. 'I know Gallus Mercator,' he said. 'Or at least, I've met him several times. When I was tutoring the children for Marcus Arrius. He used to visit the house quite often. I wouldn't say that he and Master Marcus are close, but as merchants, they're on good terms.'

'It's odd,' Kerin said. 'Lucius is one of my best friends – I've stayed at the house more than once – but I hardly know Marcus Arrius. Lucius introduced us, and I'm sure he supports the king, but that's as far as it goes.'

'Marcus is a quiet man,' Dimos said. 'And he doesn't move in the same circles as Gallus. A very devout Christian, prays three times a day and so forth. You shouldn't worry, though, he wouldn't have any time for the ones in the white tunics. The Sword of God, or whatever they are. He's a peace-loving Christian, like Brother Padarn. And a king's man heart and soul, I believe, but I'm told that Master Gallus went round to the house to make sure of it. Not a man I'd cross, to be truthful. I think he wields quite a lot of power in Londinium, in some quite startling ways.' Dimos paused. 'Is it true that he beheaded Maximian Galba?'

'Well,' Kerin said, with an equal degree of caution, 'I think he was probably glad to see the back of him. But men with that sort of power don't really need to do their own beheading, do they.'

'No, of course not,' Dimos said. 'You'll have seen Gallus's crewmen about the wharf, I expect. When he was a young man with just one ship, he used to captain it himself, and he wouldn't hire anyone who couldn't fight. The Mare Nostrum is full of pirates. Gallus got where he is because he wasn't afraid to take them on, and he had the men to do it. His ship got through when others didn't. They say he never lost a cargo. Then he captured a *liburna* – one of those fast, light ships the pirates use – worked out how to build another one, and sent them out with his cargo boats whenever they went somewhere risky. He still does it, I believe.' The scribe grinned. 'A bit of a pirate himself, perhaps.'

And that's probably why he gets on so well with the king, Kerin thought, but decided to keep to himself. 'Come to the water meadow with me,' he said. 'We'll choose a horse for you.'

Twenty or more horses were out on the grassland near the settlement; mares with foals at foot and a few of the spare animals which all warriors kept for pleasure and hunting when they were at home. 'Those are mine,' Kerin said, pointing. 'The two brown mares, the chestnut gelding and the black mare with the foal.' They dismounted and approached the animals. The black mare whickered and stamped a forefoot. Her foal, an iron-grey filly, watched them attentively. 'Have you seen Vortigern's grey warhorse, the Pike? That little one is his daughter. I hope she'll be fast and brave, like her father. And that by the time she's old enough for war, I'll never have to fight another one.'

'Do you believe that?' Dimos asked.

'No,' Kerin said reluctantly. His head was filled with the excitement of hearing the carnyx for the first time, and the news of Gallus's warship. It was easy to forget that both these things were merely a means to an end, and that the end was bloodshed. The chestnut gelding wandered over to inspect them. Dimos reached out to stroke his neck and the horse let him do it.

'Does he have a name?' the scribe asked.

'No. I only name the warhorses. It would get out of hand otherwise.' Kerin smiled as the horse shoved Dimos with his head and nibbled the shoulder of his tunic. 'It looks as if he's chosen you, so you can name him yourself. Go to the blacksmith's and ask if you can borrow a halter. Then bring him up to the stables and we'll find a saddle and bridle. You can ride him to Caerwenn and return Padarn's mule.'

'This is most generous of you, lord,' Dimos said. 'Anyone could see that he's a well-bred horse. I should work for nothing for a while, to repay you.'

'That won't be necessary,' Kerin said. 'I'm paying you to teach me and write the odd letter, not to educate half of Henfelin's children.'

'It's my pleasure,' the scribe said. 'I like it here, but it's quiet after the city. And sitting around doing nothing drives me mad. In Londinium I was allowed to use the praetor's library when there was no work to do. I don't think Severus Maximus read from one day to the next, but he kept a magnificent collection of manuscripts, just to impress his guests – all the great historians and poets.' He kissed his new horse on the nose and smiled. 'I miss the library far more than I miss the praetor, to be truthful.'

<h1 style="text-align:center">22</h1>

'You and your wife are invited to Derfyn's marriage feast,' Gwyndaf said, without preamble. He and three of his youngsters had turned up unannounced, just as the citadel was coming to life on another fine morning.

'Thank you, Gwyndaf,' Kerin said. 'We'll be honoured to accept.'

Gwyndaf frowned. 'From what I've been told, it sounds as if half of Henfelin is planning to descend upon us. Please make it clear that anyone who wants to come along is welcome, but that the feast is for my guests. They'll have to sit out on the hillside. There'll be ale and meat for them, though. This doesn't happen every day.' He glanced around him, twitching impatiently, as if he were eager to get something done and be off. 'Where's Vortigern, then?'

'In his hall, as far as I know,' Kerin said. 'The days when he got up before the first bird opened its beak seem to have gone.' Gwyndaf looked over his shoulder at his warriors, who appeared to have found something to amuse them.

'Be off with you,' he said. 'Go and find something to do until I've finished.' The three young men rode off towards the settlement, laughing amongst themselves.

'What was all that about?' Kerin asked.

'You'll see,' Gwyndaf said moodily. Cenydd was sitting outside the chieftains' hall in the morning sun, polishing a silver jug. As the shadow of Gwyndaf's horse fell across him, his eyebrows rose, conveying a degree of surprise which he was far too polite to articulate.

'Lord,' he said, bowing his head respectfully.

'Where is he, then?' Gwyndaf snapped.

'The Lord?' Cenydd said, as if Gwyndaf might have meant someone else. 'Inside, having breakfast. Shall I tell him you're here?'

'Yes. And tell him I haven't got all day.' The smell of hot bread was drifting enticingly from Kerin's house. Marc came out, clutching a half-eaten loaf. 'Here,' Gwyndaf said gruffly. 'Make yourself useful.' He got down from his mare and tossed her reins to the boy. Vortigern came out of his hall.

'Gwyndaf,' he said, extending his hand. Gwyndaf shook it firmly. Vortigern grinned, and Gwyndaf looked at him curiously. There was a lightness about him which Kerin had grown accustomed to after a whole summer of it, but it must have come as a surprise to Gwyndaf.

'You were looking for me?' Vortigern asked.

'Yes,' Gwyndaf said, avoiding his eyes.

'Well?' Vortigern enquired. Gwyndaf cleared his throat.

'Derfyn's wedding feast,' he said, frowning. 'His marriage to Mabli, that is.'

'It's in ten days' time,' Vortigern said. Gwyndaf stared up at the clouds.

'I know when it is, man,' he said. 'But the point is, Mabli's a Henfelin girl, and her father Cilydd is your loyal man. They wouldn't be happy if – well, it wouldn't seem right if –' Vortigern looked bemused. Gwyndaf growled and drove his fist into the doorpost. 'God's blood!' he roared. 'What I'm trying to say is that I'd be honoured if you and your wife would attend the marriage feast. I know I've left this rather late, but there it is.'

Vortigern inclined his head courteously. 'The honour is ours, Gwyndaf,' he said. Gwyndaf straightened his shoulders.

'Good,' he said briskly. 'That's that, then.'

'Bread?' Kerin asked.

'No, no, not now,' Gwyndaf said, looking around for his horse. It was as if, after the effort of making the invitation, he needed to go riding off on his own straight away just to cool his head. Mark came trotting back with the mare.

'She's a nice horse, lord,' he said. 'I'll bet she's as fast as anything. I don't suppose –'

'No!' Gwyndaf shouted, swinging into the saddle. 'If you want to ride a fast horse, ask this fool here. He's stupid enough to give you house room. Now, get out of the way before this nice, fast horse tramples you to death.'

Marc shrieked in mock terror and bolted off towards the headland. Vortigern caught Gwyndaf's rein. 'I'll send provisions,' he said. 'They're a Henfelin family, as you said, and if half my people are going to tag along as well –'

'No,' Gwyndaf said stiffly. 'I want nothing from you. Derfyn's as good as my son, and it's my feast.'

Vortigern let the rein fall. 'As you wish,' he said. Gwyndaf coughed slightly.

'I owe you some cattle, anyway,' he said. Vortigern looked up.

'I hadn't noticed,' he said. The sound of running footsteps made them turn. Marc was racing back from the headland, leaping anthills.

'Lords!' he panted. 'There's a ship in the bay.'

Gwyndaf whipped his sword out, spun his mare and galloped off down the track towards the valley. Vortigern and Kerin ran, through the gap in the rampart and out onto the clifftop. The tide was out and still receding. The ship had come in as close as she dared and was riding at anchor on the calm, shining sea beyond the waves. Two crewmen were lowering the mainsail and making it fast. A lighter had already put out for the beach.

'A merchantman, plain as day,' Vortigern said, with some relief. Kerin screwed his eyes up and peered down at the sea. His heart quickened.

'Lord,' he said. 'The carving on the prow, and the colour of the sail –'

'Gallus!' Vortigern said, shading his eyes from the pale sun.

They went back to the citadel and took a pair of riding horses from the pens. By the time they reached the shingle bar, the sailors were beaching the lighter. Gwyndaf had reined in on the riverbank and put his sword away. People were already venturing from the village to investigate. The three horsemen forded the river and rode out across the beach, scattering flocks of gulls and waders. A tall man detached himself from the little group around the boat and waved his arms above his head.

'It's Oswi!' Kerin exclaimed. He rose in the saddle and cupped his hands around his mouth. 'Oswi! Oswi the Horseman!' The Jute danced about and started running up the beach. He was wearing a gaudy red tunic, a belt with a huge gold buckle and a pair of loose trousers, startlingly patterned in black and gold. Kerin jumped down from his horse. Oswi seized him in a crushing bear-hug.

'Kerin Brightspear!' he crowed. 'I bring my ship all the way to Cambria to see you and my Draca.'

'He's fine,' Kerin gasped, freeing himself. 'There'll be colts for you next spring. What are you doing dressed like that, Oswi?'

'I am the captain of Master Gallus's ship,' Oswi said,

thumping his chest proudly. He bowed deeply to Vortigern. 'Now he sends gifts for you, lord.'

'Gifts from Gallus?' Vortigern said. 'You can take them back where you found them.'

Oswi gave a wary smile. 'Perhaps you tell him yourself, lord.' Down at the edge of the sea, Gallus was clambering out of the lighter. He started up the beach whilst his sailors waited with the boat at the water's edge. Vortigern sat on his horse, cool and aloof, and let him come. Kerin remembered the night when Gallus had welcomed them to his opulent house in Londinium, and thought how different he looked here; out of his element, and dwarfed by the great sweep of sand and sky.

'Lord King,' the merchant said. 'Do I have leave to anchor here, and bring my men ashore?'

'You do,' Vortigern said.

Gallus turned to Oswi. 'Leave two men with the *Audax*,' he said. 'Tell the others what will happen if they make trouble ashore. Then go and do as we agreed.'

Gwyndaf circled his mare. 'I'll see to all this, lord. You have matters to discuss, I imagine.'

'Thank you, Gwyndaf,' Vortigern said, watching Gallus attentively. 'Go to Cenydd, and tell him to feed the sailors and billet them in the village.'

Gwyndaf gave the merchant a venomous look as he rode away. Oswi trudged back to the lighter and the boat headed out over the gentle waves. Vortigern dismounted and handed his mare's reins to Kerin. He and Gallus faced each other in the middle of the empty beach. Gallus watched Gwyndaf go.

'He disapproves,' he said sadly. Vortigern had a hard, expressionless look about him which Kerin had not seen for some time.

'He's my standard-bearer,' he said. 'He values loyalty.'

Gallus looked down at the sand. 'And I too, though you might struggle to believe it at the moment.'

'I believe what I see,' Vortigern said. 'I believe in men who'll follow me when they're starving. Any man can be loyal when it doesn't cost him.'

Gallus looked pained. 'I've worked all my life to build my fleet. How could I pour my money into the treasury for scum like Severus Maximus to spend it on bathrooms and mangy beasts?'

'You couldn't,' Vortigern said. 'But we could have dealt with that together.'

'I know,' Gallus said, meeting his eyes. 'I failed you that night, and I'm not proud of it. In fact, it's the only thing I've ever done which is a source of abiding shame to me. No amount of regret will alter it. But I'll stand with you against Vortimer and his allies, and against the Saxons, when they come. I was wrong, and I know it, but I won't fail you again.'

Vortigern looked back at him without a flicker. 'No man alive has failed me twice,' he said. Gallus's large, dark gaze wavered and then held. He knew exactly what he had been told. Whatever his failings, cowardice was not one of them.

'I've brought goods from Ostia,' he said. 'Fine clothes and perfumed oils, bales of cloth and good wine. I'm not taking them home again. You can dump them in the sea if you like, but that's up to you.'

'A young man of my following is to be married,' Vortigern said. 'I'll accept my share on his behalf, as a marriage gift. I want nothing from you. But I won't turn away a man who wants to fight the Saxons. You'd do well to make Oswi your captain of defence. He knows how his kinsmen fight, and he's forgotten more about sailing ships than most men will ever learn.'

'It's already done,' Gallus said. 'I'll go back to the *Audax* now, if you want me out of your sight. But look out there first, then decide.'

They looked. A second ship was rounding the headland to the east of the bay; a long, slim ship, so like Hengist's that if Kerin had not known what it was, he would probably have gone for his weapons. The sail was reefed, and it was being driven simply by twenty oarsmen pulling in perfect unison. Oswi the Horseman was at the steering oar. Kerin supposed that the ship must have stayed anchored out of sight behind the headland as the *Audax* ventured into the bay.

'A Saxon ship?' Vortigern murmured, incredulous.

'No,' Gallus said. 'It's your ship. My gift, built to my design, by my own shipwrights.' He gave a wry smile. 'The good ship *Excusatio*. It's up to you, if you want to accept it or not. If you do, we can build some more. If you don't, I'll burn the bastard right here on your beach, and you can clean up the mess.'

Vortigern turned to Kerin. 'You're not surprised at all, are you,' he said accusingly. 'This is why you went to Londinium, after we left the villa.'

'No,' Kerin said. 'As I told you, I went to see Marcellus *magister*. But Marcellus told me that I should visit Gallus, and he's got more sense than I have, so I did. I visited Gallus. Then we got drunk, and decided to build a ship. And here it is.' He shrugged. Gallus, for all his usual nerve and confidence, was on tenterhooks.

'Well?' he snapped.

'Of course I'll accept it,' Vortigern said. 'And you've already apologised. More than once, as I recall. Let the ship be a pledge between us. No more of that nonsense.' He put out his hand and Gallus shook it, smiling. The two men embraced. 'As for you, however –' Kerin snorted with laughter and ducked as Vortigern took a swipe at him. The ship had reached the shallows. Oswi shouted to his men, who shipped their oars, jumped out and drove the vessel up onto the firm sand.

'We towed her here,' Gallus said. 'I didn't want to bring two full crews. Most of those are the *Audax* boys. Oswi has trained them on this ship, as you can see. They can do anything with it. But when Kerin was in Londinium, he told me about Rufus's transports. If I'd known what was going on, we could have blockaded them in Dubris and burned them out of the water.'

'I didn't know myself, until we got to Kent,' Vortigern said. 'Rufus has always prattled about reinforcements, but I wasn't convinced that it was true. Publius Luca's spies said that the ships had gone to Bononia.'

'Kerin told me,' Gallus said. 'I've rented a warehouse there, so my ships can come and go. But there's no guarantee that the Gallians won't use another port. It depends where Rufus makes his headquarters, I suppose. If I were one of his captains, I'd land as close to that place as I could, to spare the horses.'

'We'll speak of it tonight, after meat,' Vortigern said, and raised an eyebrow to Kerin. 'You'd better come too, since you seem to know more about all this than I do.'

Kerin smiled and passed his reins to Gallus. 'Take my horse,' he said. 'I want a word with Oswi.' He stood in the middle of the windy beach and watched the two riders heading for the citadel. *'Factus est,'* he said softly, as the next piece of his plan slid gently into place.

23

'Mabli should have got married in June,' Gael complained, surveying the clearing in the woods. Rowenna laughed.

'She will have a better marriage feast than you or I had, flowers or not,' she said.

Kerin sat beneath a spreading oak and watched while his wife and the Queen of all the Britons foraged around gathering decorations for the wedding carriage. He had been brought along to drive the ox-cart; and, he suspected, to climb into any bush which the women judged too high or too prickly to yield its bounty without a struggle. Cheldric's cart was already half full of hawthorn boughs, laden with shiny red fruit. There were bunches of bright yellow fleabane, pretty purple spikes of woundwort and great creamy-white heads of angelica. Morvid was grubbing around beneath the trees, adding handfuls of leaves to the basket of mushrooms he had gathered at the edge of the wood. He straightened up with a groan and eyed the contents of the cart.

'A waste of good plants,' he grumbled. 'Most of that stuff could be used for healing, instead of dressing up a cart for an afternoon.'

Kerin watched the women coming triumphantly back across the clearing with some sprays of tree mallow. 'You can tell them if you like, Morvid,' he said. Rowenna surveyed the contents of the ox-cart.

'It is enough,' she said. 'Now we go.'

Kerin picked up the reins and prodded the oxen into life. He was looking forward to this wedding. Once it was over, and everyone had recovered, he hoped that the men who mattered would still be in a mellow enough mood to give their blessing to the carnyx. Morvid and the women climbed into the back of the cart with the flowers. The sky was as clear and the wind as warm and light as any girl could have hoped for on her wedding day. In the village the cart was besieged by young women, all eager to help with the decoration and half of them drunk already. Cilydd came up to the cart and ran a desperate hand through his thinning hair.

'Oh gods, lad,' he said, as Kerin jumped down. 'Come and have a jar with me, and start praying that that woman of yours gives you a son.' There was a table outside Cilydd's house, laden with jugs of ale and mead. 'We're not allowed in,' he explained. 'The menfolk, that is. The women say that it's bad luck.' Cynfawr was sitting at the table with Elir, Gwynfi the weaver and a bunch of Hefydd's boys. His eyes were closed, and his hands were folded in front of him. 'He's giving a poem at the feast,' Gwynfi said, 'but I think he's been at that stuff of Hefydd's.'

Kerin leaned across the table and moved his hand up and down in front of the bard's eyes. Disturbed by the interruption of light, Cynfawr blinked and drew in his breath.

Soft blew the breeze across the cornfields of Henfelin,' he began.

'Swift skimmed the swallows above the singing stream –'
Elir chortled and handed him a small earthenware flask. Kerin sat down at the table and accepted a jar of ale from one of Hefydd's boys.

'I'd have made one for you, Kerin Brightspear,' Cynfawr

said accusingly. 'But was it my fault that you chose to wed your wife behind all our backs? It was not.' He shook his head, with the sorry air of a man denied his due. 'And as for the Lord, marrying that girl on the other side of the country – we were deprived, Kerin Brightspear. We were deprived. I had waited twenty long years for him to make a second marriage. I had composed the oration, for love of the gods. He could at least have held a feast, even if he couldn't wait for the marriage. We were all deprived.'

'Never mind, Cynfawr,' Kerin consoled him. 'You'll have to make up for it today.'

The bard sniffed and took another mouthful of Hefydd's brew.

'Fair was the bride in her marriage garments,
Pure and white as the seabird's breast – ' he began. Elir guffawed loudly. 'Pure and white?' he said. 'It's a bit late for that, old man.'

They sat at the table until the sun was high above the sea and the women, having finished with the cart, drifted off to make their own preparations. Some time after the third jug of ale, the sound of hoofbeats intruded. A horse was coming fast down the track from the citadel. Everyone, with the exception of Cynfawr, looked up to see what was happening. Macsen rode up to the house, scattering children and dogs.

'You'd better get up there,' he said, tossing Kerin his reins. 'Those messengers of Valerius Dio's have just arrived, and I don't know what news they've brought, but it doesn't look good.'

Today of all days, Kerin thought, as he rode for the citadel. He had anticipated a delightful occasion. His affection for Mabli and Derfyn, the forging of another link between Vortigern's people and Gwyndaf's, the celebration of a blessed interval of peace; everything had dictated it. And now this. The horses of the two praetorian envoys, with their distinctive red and gold browbands and cheek-pieces, were standing outside the chieftains' hall. Ashur was rubbing them down with handfuls of straw. The two men were sitting at the table which Cenydd kept outside in fine weather, attacking a heaped platter of bread and cheese. Kerin went into the hall. Vortigern was standing alone in the centre of the room where the feasts were held. The scroll was lying, unrolled, on the table. Vortigern looked up without speaking, his eyes desolate.

'Rufus and Garagon have left Kent,' he said. 'They're marching to join Eldof and Paulinus, somewhere near Sarum. Rufus plans to winter in Glevum and gather enough of an army to attack Cambria in the spring.'

'He's mad,' Kerin said. He looked at the scroll lying on the table. 'Is there anything else in that thing?'

'Yes. They may have five hundred Sarmatian cavalry, under that chief warrior of his.' Kerin walked to the open door and looked out over the valley. Gallus's ship was lying becalmed on the placid sea, and down in the settlement the wedding procession was beginning to take shape. 'If I had the men to do it, I'd crush Glevum,' Vortigern said. 'I'd leave half the warriors on this side of the river with Lud, then you and I would cross and take the city from the east.' He shrugged. 'We don't have half the men we'd need to do that, of course. If Rufus can count on having all of Eldof's warriors, and Garagon's, then a few hundred disaffected self-servers and a bunch of Christian hotheads – well, they'll outnumber us two to one, easily. Perhaps more. And who can we call on, outside Cambria? Good, brave Gorlois. Lucius and his cavalry. But not Publius, whatever he's told you; it's beyond his strength now, to fight so far from home.

And not Valerius Dio, because he has enough to think about, keeping his city safe.'

'We've got all the ordinary men,' Kerin said. 'Not just from Cambria; from Glevum and Londinium. From everywhere they till the ground and smelt metal. I know it. And we've got the best warriors. No-one can match them'

'I know,' Vortigern said. 'But because of that, we took the most casualties in the North. We've got more wounds to heal. The fighting horses, as well as the men.' He gave Kerin a wry look. 'You were wrong this time, weren't you.'

'What do you mean?' Kerin asked.

'What you told Valerius Dio,' Vortigern said. 'About Rufus's alliance not surviving the winter.' Kerin hesitated. There was, he knew, one eventuality which would upset things. 'What?' Vortigern asked.

'It's obvious,' Kerin said, avoiding his eyes. 'What would you do if you wanted to kill a snake?'

'Cut its head off,' Vortigern said. He stopped short as Kerin's meaning became clear to him. 'God,' he said softly, 'I can't believe that came from you.'

'No,' Kerin said. 'Nor can I.'

A faint sound made them turn. Rowenna had come from the bedchamber at the far end of the hall. She was dressed for the celebrations, in the sea-green dress Kerin remembered from her father's feast. The emerald necklace sparkled. She came to them smiling, preceded by a light cloud of perfume in which warm, subtle spices mingled with the gentle scents of lavender and roses. Vortigern sniffed curiously.

'What's that?' he asked.

'A gift from Gallus,' Rowenna said. 'He was very insistent. But it is good, don't you think?'

Vortigern raised his eyebrows. 'I think that you should

either save it for later or prepare to suffer the consequences,' he said. Rowenna giggled.

'I shall wear it every day now,' she said. 'And I shall give some to Gael, too. Although she tells me that she does not need to drag her husband into the bedchamber.' Kerin grinned and looked up at the roof.

'Go and see if she's ready,' he said. Vortigern watched his wife leave.

'We shan't tell any of them yet,' he said. Kerin looked down at the settlement. Branwen and Eleri, Mabli's attendants for the day, were threading flowers through the bridles of the two white oxen which had been harnessed to Cilydd's cart.

'It would be cruel to spoil things for Derfyn and Mabli,' he said.

'Yes,' Vortigern said. 'Let them have their day of grace. But there'll be no grace for us, until we've found a way to deal with this.' His eyes strayed to the draco, propped in the corner of the hall with the tattered banner furled around its pole. 'And I must tell the standard-bearer, before anyone else does. But not today.'

Cenydd came from the horse pens and made an exaggerated bow. 'Your horses await you, lords,' he said. 'In their best saddlery, naturally. And your wives await you too. I know which I'd prefer to keep waiting, I can tell you.'

As the two men went outside, Gael and Rowenna came from Kerin's house, arm in arm. Gael was wearing a dress of deep blue muslin, bought at the fair in Leucarum, with a cluster of red clover fastened just below the left shoulder by a jewelled pin. She leaned across and whispered something to Rowenna, and they glanced at their husbands and laughed. Kerin thought how beautiful they looked, and how fortunate he and Vortigern were to have chanced upon them, whatever complications had arisen from it all. He remembered standing on this spot as Vortigern weighed the choice forced on him by Rufus's ultimatum. No choice at all, really, when the fate of the kingdom was in the balance; but Kerin had known, in that moment, that the man would have chosen what the king could not. That Vortigern would have settled for this place, this life, this end to more than thirty years of blood and death and grief. And I cannot, Kerin thought. Not yet. For the future, he wanted nothing more than to ensure the prosperity of their home in Henfelin; he wanted his sons and daughters to look out over the valley, as he did now, and see nothing but ripe cornfields and fat cattle, and a peaceful sea where merchant ships could come and go in safety. But the only way to secure it was to fight, so he would fight. He would fight, he would lead, he would protect all he loved and give Vortigern the peace he longed for, and he would kill any man on earth to do it; even Rufus. Bring all you have, he thought. I am ready for you.

'Come on!' Gael cried, seizing his arm. 'Mabli's about to get in her carriage, and you're still in the same old clothes you wore to go to the woods.'

'And here is Cheldric for us!' Rowenna said. The cook was beaming proudly, and had an unnaturally bright pink look, as if he had scrubbed his face with a horse brush. His oxen were gleaming, and he had tied ribbons to their bridles and bunches of flowers to their harness. He jumped down from his seat and lifted Gael gently into the back of the cart.

'Why didn't you ask Cenydd for the carriage and horses?' Vortigern said. 'The Queen of all the Britons shouldn't ride to a marriage feast in a cook's ox-cart, for God's sake.'

Rowenna folded her arms calmly. 'And why not? I prefer

to go with Cheldric. And besides, if we go in a carriage, it will be better than Mabli's cart. We should not be better than the bride going to her marriage feast, should we?'

'She's a silversmith's daughter!' Vortigern protested.

'Today she is the queen of the world,' Rowenna said, and climbed into the cart with Gael. Vortigern raised his hands.

'Please yourself,' he said. Kerin suppressed a smile. He was not used to seeing anyone win an argument with Vortigern.

They caught up with the cart outside Cilydd's house, where the procession was waiting to leave; a formless mass of riders, wagons and people on foot. All the women were carrying bunches of flowers, and most of the men flasks of ale or wine. A rowdy cheer went up as Cilydd came out of his house, leading his daughter by the hand. The bodice of Mabli's white dress was embroidered with fine blue and silver thread, her hair was dressed with white ribbons and a silver necklace sparkled at her throat, each link a tiny flower joined to the next by a curling tendril. Cilydd lifted her into the back of his cart alongside her mother, sister and attendants, and climbed up onto the driver's seat. Gwynfi clicked his tongue and swirled his whip, and the procession moved off up the valley. Kerin and Vortigern fell in beside Cheldric's cart, which had acquired a few extra occupants. Padarn was sitting with Lud and Mora, whose startling yellow dress looked as if she had acquired it when she was younger, and a good deal thinner. Opposite them, Cynfawr was wedged between Gael and Rowenna with a glazed look on his face.

'He can hardly speak,' Padarn said. 'God knows how he's going to give his poem.'

Ahead of them, someone broke into song; an old tune

they all knew, about springtime and young love, and the comforts of marriage and fidelity in an uncertain world. Almost everyone joined in; even Cilydd, who was almost too nervous to speak, and Padarn, who should not really have cared too much about such things. The song echoed up through the valley; a light wind stirred the trees, and high above their heads buzzards wheeled, tiny dark specks against the huge luminous sky. Vortigern caught Kerin's eye.

'Oh God,' he said softly, 'we can't let this go.' He reached out and brushed his hand across Rowenna's hair, as if in some way that could blunt the agony of betrayal.

Gwyndaf met them in the valley below his citadel. He dismounted, shook Cilydd's hand and kissed Mabli, then marched back along the procession to meet Vortigern and Kerin.

'The marriage will take place on the hillside,' he said, looking stiff and awkward. 'There'll be a riot if they can't all watch. Then my cooks will feed the people, and my guests will withdraw to the hall for the feast.' He coughed and straightened his shoulders. 'There are twelve seats at the high table. Derfyn and Mabli will occupy two of them, naturally; then there'll be my wife and myself, Mabli's family and Brother Padarn. That leaves four seats; and I suppose that you two and your wives may as well have them, if it's all the same to you.'

Vortigern dismounted. 'It'll be a great honour, Gwyndaf,' he said. 'One offered by a man I respect. There is none greater.' Gwyndaf's lips tightened. He seized Vortigern's hand and shook it violently, then threw himself onto his horse and galloped away up the hill.

*

It was not the marriage ceremony itself which Kerin re-membered in the years afterwards, although it was joyous and memorable; Mabli beautiful and windblown, Cilydd almost paralysed with fright, Derfyn handsome and nervous, stumbling over his words as Padarn guided him through his vows with a steady, loving hand. Derfyn and Mabli were lifted shoulder-high and carried to the door of Gwyndaf's hall, leaving behind them a singing, dancing, cheering mob. Gwyndaf's cooks came out with food and drink. There could hardly have been a living soul left in Henfelin; and even Gallus, Oswi and the crew had found their way along. No-one there had ever witnessed a mar-riage like it, according to everyone who was sober enough to string the words together. But it was the feast which Kerin remembered, burned into his brain like the brand on a bullock's hide.

<h1 style="text-align:center">24</h1>

'What a day, lad,' Padarn said as Kerin sat beside him at Gwyndaf's high table. 'What a day. I've conducted a few marriages, but never anything like this.'

'Why didn't Iustig come?' Kerin asked. 'He wasn't offended because Derfyn asked for you, was he?'

'No, no,' Padarn said. 'Some travellers arrived looking for him. Iustig sent Brother Cadog, to say I should set out without him. Now then; how about some of that wine, as Paulinus isn't here to curse me?'

Kerin smiled and reached for the jug. 'You're quite a man, Padarn,' he said. 'Not at all like any other monk I've known.'

'That's probably because I was lots of other things first,' Padarn said. 'Farm worker, lover, swordsman and general drunkard. When God called me, I told him there were bits that it was too late to change.'

'All the better,' Kerin said, filling two large goblets. He looked around with a feeling of happy anticipation. Gwyndaf's hall was small enough to be homely, and the feast felt like a family gathering rather than a formal occasion. Most of the warriors were standing around, drinking and bragging and offering manly advice to Derfyn, while the women clustered round Mabli, speculating hilariously about what the night might have in store for her. Whatever it was, Kerin thought, it could hardly come as a surprise to Mabli.

'Kerin!' Gwyndaf hissed. 'For God's sake, help me get them seated.' Kerin laughed and waded into the crowd. He seized Macsen and Elir and threw them into their seats, shepherded Hefydd and his boys towards a table and hauled Lud away from the serving maid who was ladling out the mead. Gwyndaf seized Derfyn by the collar and marched him towards the high table to riotous applause. Kerin turned to look for Gael, and found himself face to face with Mabli. She smiled and flung her arms round his neck.

'You look beautiful,' Kerin said warmly, kissing her forehead. 'And very happy.'

'I am, I am!' Mabli cried ecstatically. 'And you see, I was right. You've found your girl, and I've found a good, brave man who makes me feel like the queen of Cambria.' She pulled Kerin's head down and pressed her mouth to his ear. 'He's also as well-equipped as that stallion of yours, I'm happy to say.' Kerin laughed out loud and propelled her towards the high table. Derfyn leaned across, grabbed her by the waist and hoisted her into her seat. To his right, Cilydd's wife was downing her wine, looking enchanted with her new son-in-law. Vortigern was sitting at the extreme end of the table. He must have chosen his place deliberately, Kerin supposed, since some of the more honoured places were still unoccupied.

'Wine, lord?' he asked.

'Yes,' Vortigern said absently. Kerin fetched an untouched amphora, sat down and poured. He recognised the smell of the wine and the clear, deep red of liquid rubies. Gallus's Phrygian hell-brew. Vortigern drained the goblet.

'Look,' Kerin said, 'there's nothing to be done today.'

'Nor tomorrow,' Vortigern said, reaching for the amphora. 'And if you have some idea of talking sense to Rufus, forget it.' He looked along the table at Padarn, who was sitting between Rowenna and Gwyndaf's wife Mari, relating some story which the women seemed to be enjoying. Gael came floating across the room, singing a snatch of the old love-song which accompanied the wedding procession. She squeezed into the space between Kerin and Rowenna and kissed her husband on the nose. Gwyndaf's servants brought platters of roast lamb and further brimming jugs.

'Ah, the food!' Rowenna said rapturously.

'Be careful, or you'll end up like Mora,' Vortigern said.

'No, no,' Rowenna said, carving herself a hunk of lamb. 'Our family, we are like hunting dogs. We eat and never get fat.'

'Eat like hunting dogs and drink like fishes,' Kerin said, filling the women's goblets.

'Not too much for me!' Gael protested. 'Our child will be born a drunkard like its father.'

'It's alright,' Rowenna said carelessly. 'You give it to me instead.'

Gael touched Kerin's arm. 'It pains her, to see me with child,' she whispered. 'And now Mabli is, too, although hardly anyone knows yet. And of course, Rowenna knows that Vortigern fathered children with his first wife, so she thinks she's at fault.'

'But that's mad,' Kerin said. He turned, sensing that Vortigern was looking at him.

'It's a wedding,' Vortigern said. 'An occasion for rejoicing, or so I'm told. You and your wife chose to do without a wedding feast, so you should make the most of it.'

'And you too, lord,' Gael said. Her voice held a particular grave note which Kerin had learned to recognise. Disconcertingly, Vortigern appeared to recognise it too.

'Your husband's fond of telling me what to do,' he said. 'I trust you don't plan to do the same.'

'No, lord,' Gael said. 'Not too often. But tonight, you should take your own advice. You have a beautiful wife who loves the ground you walk on, and she had no wedding feast either. Whatever's troubling you, why not leave it for another day? Tonight, Rowenna wants only what I want. To be with her lover, and to know that nothing else comes before her in his thoughts. Not even the troubles he must face tomorrow. Is that so much to ask?'

Vortigern reached for the amphora and filled his cup to the brim. 'No,' he said. 'Not that it was your business to tell me so.'

'No, lord,' Gael said, and smiled. 'But it's out now.'

Padarn finished his tale with an explosive shout and threw his hands in the air. The women laughed and hugged him. Rowenna turned and smiled lazily. It looked as if even her legendary capacity for holding her drink might have been challenged by Gallus's wine.

'Come here,' Vortigern said. Rowenna raised a roguish eyebrow. Vortigern leaned forward. 'Come here,' he said, with a look so blatantly lascivious that, if he had suggested a roll on the high table, it could scarcely have been more explicit. Rowenna wriggled past Kerin and Gael and climbed onto his lap. Gwyndaf observed them from his seat beyond Padarn and Mari.

'He has no shame, has he,' he said. Mari, looking prettier and more animated than Kerin had ever seen her, leaned across and whispered something in her husband's ear which made him blush to the roots of his hair.

'I'm going to send this devil's juice back to Gallus,' Gwyndaf said sternly; but there was a smile fighting to appear at the corners of his mouth. Kerin thought how much he had grown to like him, and how glad he was to have brought him to Henfelin. He turned as Gael's hand closed over his.

'Are you satisfied now?' he asked.

'Oh yes,' she said. 'Everyone looks quite happy. I know there's some sort of trouble, of course, and I'm sure you'll tell me about it tomorrow; but we all need a night's respite, don't you think?'

'It's the least we deserve,' Kerin said. Daylight was fading.

'The bard!' someone shouted. 'Where's the bard?'

'Cynfawr!' Hefydd bellowed. 'Give that poem, man!' Cynfawr sprang up as if someone had jabbed him in the rear with a pitchfork, fell back into his chair and passed out. The gathering dissolved in mirth. A band of musicians struck up, and Mabli came prancing out into the middle of the hall. The women laughed and cheered and ran to form a wheeling circle around her.

'Gael was right,' Vortigern said. 'We should treasure this night. The gods know when we'll get another like it.' Kerin smiled as his wife skipped past, arms linked with Rowenna and Branwen. Someone had brought another amphora. They drank, and the women danced, and Kerin found himself entering that pleasant country between tipsiness and oblivion, where even the frankly impossible seemed within his grasp. Most of the warriors were hammering on the tables with goblets or tankards in time to the thud of the drum. It was not surprising that hardly anyone heard the knock at the door. Kerin saw Leil and Cadfan look at each other and get up. Cadfan drew the bolt and opened the door a crack. There was a brief conversation with whoever was outside, then he slid the bolt back and said something to Leil, who nodded towards the high table. Gwyndaf had noticed. The two young warriors weaved their way to him through the dancing women. Kerin moved up the bench towards Gwyndaf and Padarn.

'Who's out there?' Gwyndaf asked.

'That old abbot from Henfelin,' Cadfan said. 'He's got one of his brothers with him, and another monk on a mule, and a couple of warriors.'

Gwyndaf scowled. 'What the hell do they want?'

'To see the Lord Vortigern,' Cadfan said, in a whisper. 'What shall I tell them?'

Gwyndaf clenched his fists. 'This is no time for a religious conference.'

'I'd have sent them away,' Cadfan said, 'but the abbot's very insistent.'

Padarn looked up. 'Let him in and you'll be sorry,' he said. Cadfan raised his hands.

'I don't think he'll take no for an answer, Brother. And surely, there's no harm in him, is there?'

'Not in the way you mean,' Padarn said. 'But that's not the point.' The knocking came again, this time loud and insistent enough for everyone to hear it. The music fizzled out and the dance came to a lame conclusion.

'Let them in,' Gwyndaf sighed. 'Whatever they want, I'd sooner hear it and get rid of them than have them battering on my door all night.' Cadfan shrugged and went towards the door. Padarn shook his head.

'What's happening?' Derfyn said sleepily.

'Nothing,' Gwyndaf said sharply 'Swallow your wine, and stay where you are.'

Kerin got up and worked his way to the end of the table. Gael, standing with Rowenna in the middle of the room, gave him an anxious glance as he passed. The music started up again in a half-hearted way. Vortigern, in conversation with Lud, seemed unaware of what was happening. Cadfan drew the bolt and swung the door open. Iustig came in first, looking flushed and breathless. His pale young acolyte

Cadog was with him. Two dark-haired warriors in travelling cloaks followed, flanking a well-built man in a monk's habit and a black hooded cape. Kerin had never seen the warriors before, but he recognised the monk at once, with a feeling of deep apprehension.

'Father Septimus!' Gael cried, and ran to him. Septimus embraced her affectionately. He looked anxious and tired. Rowenna, left alone in the middle of the hall, gave Iustig a nervous look. She had learned what to expect from monks.

'Oh, you poor child,' Iustig said softly. Vortigern came over the table like a beast after blood. Iustig backed away, raising a disclaiming hand. Vortigern seized Rowenna and pushed her behind him.

'Don't,' he breathed. 'Don't talk to her. Don't even look at her, you miserable, two-faced old hypocrite.'

Gwyndaf lunged in between them. 'Alright,' he said, grabbing Iustig by the shoulders. 'I don't know what this is about, and I don't care, but it's not going to ruin Derfyn's marriage feast. Get on your scabby donkey and go home before I cut your throat.'

'Have some respect, in God's name!' Cadog protested. Gwyndaf snorted.

'God didn't help my wife and children. And he isn't going to help you, either, so get out now, unless you want to feel my boot in your arse.'

Kerin drew Gwyndaf aside. 'Look, we've got to hear them,' he said. 'That monk's from Glevum. He hasn't come all this way for nothing.'

Gwyndaf glanced over his shoulder at Vortigern, who had withdrawn to the end of the table with his wife. 'Can't it wait? He'll kill the abbot, for God's sake.'

'No,' Kerin said. 'I'll see to this. Is there somewhere we can talk?'

'Down there,' Gwyndaf said reluctantly, indicating a door at the end of the hall. 'That's where I speak to the warriors. Get them in there, and find out what they want.' He waved to the musicians, who launched into a hectic jig, and clapped his hands to summon the servants. 'Come on. More wine, and plenty of it.'

Kerin turned to the monks and the two unfamiliar warriors, who looked as if they were wondering what they had let themselves in for. 'That door down there,' he said, pointing. 'Wait in there, and we'll come to you.'

'Thank you,' Iustig mouthed. Kerin gave him a grim smile.

'This had better be important, Iustig,' he said, finding that the incident had shocked him into sobriety. Vortigern had sent Rowenna to the women, and was waiting for him. Kerin sat down beside him. 'Lord, whatever it is with you and Iustig, it'll have to wait,' he said. 'I know that monk. He's close to Gael, and he knows everything that goes on in Glevum. He knew Iustig years ago, but they weren't even close. He wouldn't come all this way just to renew an acquaintance.'

Vortigern looked up. Kerin wondered whether he had heard a word of what had just been said. He looked vacant and adrift, as he had done after the death of Quintus Parvo. Kerin thought of the old man, dying on the floor of his stinking hut in the North. He had no regrets about killing him. It was done without thought, a mere reflex. Publius Luca had been forthright about the barbaric cruelty of Parvo's rule in Isca. The man deserved to die as he did. But if Kerin had hoped that his death would bring some form of resolution, he was wrong. He had not seen it then, but looking back, he could trace the slow unravelling which began in Padarn's frozen village and reached its brutal conclusion on a night of harrowing desolation in the curia. It was nothing to do with Iustig. The bitter rift between Vortigern and the abbot was another matter entirely; but perhaps, in the end, all these things got shoved into the same dark room. Iustig's was simply the foot that kicked the door open again. Kerin supposed that he had dealt with it, insofar as anyone could; but as Vortigern had said, there was probably no cure. Kerin realised that whatever happened next would be of his own making.

'It's you they've come to see, lord,' he said. 'But I can talk to them. It might be better, since I have no quarrel with any of them.'

'Do it,' Vortigern said, staring at the closed door. Kerin left him with a full amphora and went to the private room. The three monks were sitting at the bare table, the warriors standing behind them.

'Kerin Brightspear,' Father Septimus said. 'I'm sorry we have to meet under such circumstances. Gael tells me that you've brought great joy to her.'

'And she to me,' Kerin said, sitting down.

'I understand that Vortigern has received messengers from the new praetor of Londinium,' Septimus said.

'This afternoon. They said that Vortigern's son is joining forces with Eldof, and plans to attack Cambria next spring.'

'Indeed,' Septimus said, 'but it's worse than that. For a start, the son is in Glevum already with a part of his force. And Gael's father has decided that it's worth burying his differences with Eldof if it means getting rid of Vortigern and yourself, and the rest of your leaders. Word is that they've got a band of picked men for the work. I know no more, but I'll do anything I can to prevent it, for your sake and Gael's. And as for Vortigern, I'll admit he was the leader we needed when the Picts were on our doorstep. Bertil and the others are quick to forget that.'

'They'll remember soon enough when the Saxons are marching through Kent,' one of the warriors said. Kerin looked up at him; a dark-haired bull of a man around his own age.

'Who are you?' he asked.

'Warriors who served under Varro, before he changed sides. Ordinary Christians who pray in Father Septimus's chapel. We've kept our heads down lately, but when the Father told us he was coming here, we decided to make ourselves known. We'll fight for you if you'll take us.'

'I'm Kerin Brightspear,' Kerin said, and extended his hand.

'Oh yes. We know who you are, alright.'

Kerin smiled in a guarded way. He looked across the table at Iustig, sitting silently with his hands folded.

'What do you think, then?' he asked, in a brisker tone than he had ever used with the abbot. Iustig recognised it.

'I think that someone should tell Rufus. He may or may not intervene; as God's my witness, I don't know any more.'

Kerin turned to the two warriors. 'Please, leave us now,' he said. 'You too, Father Septimus, if you don't mind. I mean no disrespect, but there are things which Father Iustig and I must talk about. Brother Cadog, please take them to Lord Gwyndaf, and ask him to give them food and drink.' Cadog bowed his head meekly and led the three men out. Kerin bolted the door and sat down. 'Will he listen to either of us, do you think?' he asked.

'I don't know,' Iustig said. 'But how will we sleep in peace if we don't try?'

'You're right,' Kerin said. 'We'll go together. But tell no-one. We'll leave at first light tomorrow.' Iustig nodded his assent and got up. 'Sit down,' Kerin said. The abbot looked at him in disbelief.

'I have things to do. Preparations to make.'

'Sit down,' Kerin said. 'We're not going anywhere just yet.'

Iustig stared at him and sat. 'What on earth's happened to you?' he asked.

'Lots of things. Some of which I'd prefer not to remember. I've respected you all my life, Father, and I hope that won't change; but I've changed. I'm sick of secrets and half-truths, and you're not going anywhere until you tell me what all that was about just now.'

Iustig closed his eyes. 'Kerin, you have no right to ask me this,' he said. Kerin's fingers encircled his wrist.

'Oh, but I do,' he said. 'You're going to tell me, and you're going to tell me now, because when we're done, I'm the one who'll have to deal with the consequences.' He released Iustig's wrist and sat back. The abbot sat with hands clasped on his lap and eyes tightly closed. Kerin thought of all the odd, stray pieces which had come to him, and about what Padarn had said on the road beside the Hafren. 'What did you do, Iustig?' he asked. The abbot looked up, angry, distressed and close to tears.

'I did what any right-thinking man would have done!' he burst out. 'I saw someone I loved in need of comfort, and I gave it to her. And let's not mince words; I did love Sevira. In the way I love all the children of my church. But also a little more than a man in holy orders should have done. Please, don't imagine any impropriety. I have never, ever dishonoured my vows, and anyway, Sevira would have been the last woman to respond. She loved Vortigern without condition or criticism. But I did become her friend, as well as her spiritual counsellor, so I was there when she needed a friend's comfort.' He paused, breathing steadily. Outside the sounds of the feast continued, jarring on the silence of that small, stifling room. 'He was never faithful to her, of course,' Iustig said bitterly. 'Everyone knows that. He married her because she was Magnus Maximus's daughter, and he saw an advantage in it. Well, that's nothing new; men have done it since the beginning of time, and it doesn't have to be a bad thing. But decent men manage some consideration for their wives, even if they can't manage love. Sevira never spoke about it. I hoped that Vortigern might mend his ways when their son was born, but unfortunately I was wrong. He found you, and you became closer to him than his own child.' He raised his hand. 'No, don't ask. As God's my judge, I know no more. It's a measure of Sevira's goodness that she never resented you for it. Were you ever treated any differently from their own sons?'

'Never,' Kerin said. 'I have no bad memories of my childhood. None at all.'

'No,' Iustig said. 'It was a happy time, in some ways. You might remember the days we spent wandering around when Vortigern was away from Henfelin. You and Rufus on Sevira's pony and Kat in a little reed basket.'

Kerin could feel a film of sweat forming all over his body. 'Go on,' he said.

'Paschent was born the day before Eastertide,' Iustig said. 'His name comes from the Latin word for the festival. His mother's choice; she was probably more devout than I am. When her child was coming, and Vortigern couldn't be found, she wrote a letter and sealed it, and asked me to give it to him. Then she asked me to send riders to look for him. God forgive me, I didn't do it. I went outside, so that Sevira would think that I had done as she asked, but I did nothing. I suppose I felt that I was the one who deserved to be there. She asked me to call her servant. The girl came in, took one look and sent for the wise women. I knew then that I had done something terrible, but it was too late to remedy it. They sent me out, but soon they were calling me back, to give the last rites of the church. There was blood everywhere. I could hear the child crying, so I knew he must be alright, but Sevira died just before Vortigern came back. I gave him the letter. I have no idea what was in it. We buried Sevira the next day. The whole of Henfelin came. There's a point where the priest is expected to praise the departed. Vortigern gave me that look he has when he thinks you're being a complete imbecile. I denounced him there, in front of everyone. He never loved or cared for his wife, and I thought he deserved to hear it said. Was I cruel? I don't know. But it was richly deserved, and he has never been sorry. My only regret is that I didn't send those riders when Sevira asked me to. Of course, Vortigern never found out about that, thank God. I'm sure I wouldn't be sitting here now, if he'd known. But you have your explanation. I hope it satisfies you.'

Kerin looked at the abbot, hunched in his chair with his windburnt face drained of colour and arms wrapped around himself, as if the pain of recollection were almost too great to bear.

'Thank you, Father,' he said, trying to keep his voice steady. 'That explains a great deal.'

Iustig gave him a wry look. 'If you share our secret with Vortigern, I'm sure he won't think it's too late to kill me for it.'

'I shan't tell him. Hasn't everyone suffered enough?'

'Yes,' Iustig said dully. Kerin got up.

'You'd better go. Take the others with you, but say nothing to them. Meet me at dawn where the track from the valley joins the Roman road.'

Iustig stood up shakily. 'You can tolerate my company all the way to Glevum, then?'

'Yes. There's not much choice. We have to do it.'

Iustig went out, closing the door behind him. Kerin stood quite still, trying to collect his thoughts. He was not aware of Gwyndaf until he felt the hand grip his shoulder.

'They're leaving,' Gwyndaf said. 'What the hell did you say to the abbot? He looks close to death.'

'Less than the abbot said to me,' Kerin said. 'I'll tell you afterwards why they'd come. Where's Vortigern?'

'In my bedroom,' Gwyndaf said. 'I was afraid what might happen, so I knocked him senseless. It wasn't difficult after all that wine. But be careful. The girl's got a knife, and I promise you she'll use it.'

He led Kerin through the hall, where most of the guests were still singing heartily. Gael, at the fringe of a little knot of chattering girls, looked up with an anxious smile.

'In there,' Gwyndaf said, indicating a door leading off a dark passage. Kerin tapped the door. When there was no response he eased it open. Rowenna leapt to her feet. Kerin caught the glint of lamplight on a naked blade.

'No!' he exclaimed.

Rowenna sank back onto the bed. 'Ah,' she said forlornly. 'It is you.'

Kerin sat down beside her. A single rush lamp burned high on the wall, casting a small circle of wan light. As Kerin's eyes became accustomed to the darkness he saw a large bed strewn with sheepskins, and Vortigern's motionless figure sprawled face down across it.

'Put it away,' Kerin said. 'You're among friends here.'

'The abbot is not a friend,' Rowenna said, placing the knife on a side table.

'He's not an enemy,' Kerin said. 'He's a good man in many ways, but he and Vortigern fell out years ago. It's in the past now.'

'In the past?' Rowenna said. 'And that is why we have this thing tonight?'

Kerin raised his hands. 'What I mean is that there's not much to be done,' he said. Rowenna twisted a length of her hair between her fingers.

'Why did the abbot call me a poor child?' she asked. Kerin tried, without success, to think of a reply which was both truthful and painless. His silence seemed eloquent enough for Rowenna. 'He must hate Vortigern very much,' she sighed.

'No,' Kerin said. 'But he thinks that Vortigern has many faults. And probably that he won't care for you as a man should care for his wife.'

'But that is not true!' Rowenna protested. Kerin smiled at her indignation.

'Well,' he said, 'if it's not, then it doesn't really matter what the abbot thinks, does it?'

'No,' Rowenna said, and kissed him on the cheek. 'You should go to Gael now. She thinks something terrible will happen.'

'I'm trying to stop it,' Kerin said. 'I have to leave soon, to do that. I know you'll look after her for me. But I'll watch until dawn, if you want.'

'Alright,' Rowenna said, blinking back a tear. 'You watch, I sleep. You are right. Tomorrow I will need my strength.' And you are wiser than you know, Kerin thought. He kissed the top of her head and went out, taking the knife with him. Gwyndaf was waiting in the passage. They sat down together on the earth floor.

'I said I'd keep watch,' Kerin said.

'You'd better tell me before anything else happens,' Gwyndaf said. 'Start with Valerius Dio's messengers.'

'It's between us,' Kerin said. 'The praetor said that Rufus

had left Kent with Garagon, and was marching to join Eldof and Paulinus near Sarum. That he planned to winter in Glevum, and attack us in the spring, when he'd raised enough men. Vortigern intended to tell you this himself, as soon as the wedding was over. But what Septimus said was quite different.'

'Who is he?' Gwyndaf asked.

'An abbot from Bertil Redknife's country. He's known Gael all her life. Always tried to look after her. He thinks that Rufus is in Glevum already, with part of his army. But Eldof and Bertil make their own rules. They're planning to send a bunch of cut-throats into Cambria to kill Vortigern, and you and me, and anyone else worth the trouble.'

'They kill all the leaders, and Cambria falls into Rufus's lap,' Gwyndaf said. 'When are they coming?'

'Septimus didn't say. Rufus knows nothing about it, according to him. Of course, he might not stop it, even if he did; but there has to be a chance that he would. So Iustig and I are going to talk to him. We're meeting on the Roman road at dawn.'

There was a brief, pregnant silence. Gwyndaf stared up into the darkness. 'Let me be perfectly clear about this,' he said. 'You and that pea-brained abbot are going to ride into the den of wolves in Glevum. If you don't get killed straight away, you're hoping to talk sense into a lunatic like Rufus. And then you'll need to get out, dragging along a man who can hardly stay on a donkey. Am I right?'

'More or less,' Kerin said. It sounded even more ludicrous, put like that. 'Do you have a better idea?'

'No. But that doesn't make it any less mad. What makes you think that Rufus will listen to you, for God's sake?'

'He may not,' Kerin said. 'But I was his friend once. And if there's the smallest chance that I can stop all this, I have to try. We can't afford to lose a single man, when we might have to fight Hengist too. Can't you see that?'

'Yes,' Gwyndaf said reluctantly. 'I just don't like to see good men wasted.'

'I'll be alright,' Kerin said, more confidently than he felt. 'I know the country, and there are some places I can hide if I need to.'

Gwyndaf shrugged. 'You'll go whatever I say. Just watch your back. I'd come along and watch it for you, but some-one's got to see to things here. And remember you've got a child on the way, before you stick your head in the noose. Once it's here you'll know what I mean. Now go to bed with your wife. I'll keep watch. It's not necessary, but that's not why you're doing it, of course.'

'No,' Kerin said, handing him the knife. He rose stiffly to his feet, wishing fervently that he had no further to go than back to his bed.

'You're not going to tell me about the other business, I suppose.'

'One day,' Kerin said. 'But not tonight.'

25

The valley slept under a shroud of mist. Above the dark moors to the east, dawn shivered in the sky. Kerin sat on a boulder beside the Roman road and waited. No-one would have taken him for a warrior of distinction. He was wearing a set of shabby, ill-fitting brown clothes belonging to Cheldric, and had borrowed two sturdy black ponies from Cenydd. To complement the disguise, he had discarded his sword and spear and was carrying only a dagger concealed in his left riding boot. The truth was that once in Glevum he would be alone, and at the mercy of anyone who fancied killing him, weapons or not.

Kerin heard the trap of hooves long before anyone came into view. He shook his head and sighed. Anyone with the barest instinct for survival, travelling alone and unarmed, would have ridden on the grass to muffle the sound; but here came Iustig, riding blithely along the middle of the road as if he supposed that God had cast a protective shield around him and his donkey. Kerin stood up as he approached. The abbot had brought a large bundle.

'You should ride on the grass,' Kerin said. 'I heard you coming a mile off.'

'No-one's going to kill me here,' Iustig said, dismounting.

'Don't be so sure,' Kerin said. 'I nearly killed you last night.'

Iustig looked wounded. 'If you hadn't insisted, I'd never

have told you. Don't you think I would have preferred to let it sleep?'

'Sleep?' Kerin exclaimed. 'Do you think that's what it's been doing?'

Iustig looked away. 'No. Some things never do.' He began to untie the bundle from his saddle. Kerin sighed.

'Father, I'm trying not to be harsh. I know you did what you had to, and God knows Vortigern's no saint, but –'

'I know,' Iustig said quickly. 'But when I saw the look that poor young girl gave him –'

Kerin laughed out loud. 'Iustig, you know nothing whatsoever about that poor young girl. She and Vortigern are a pair well met.'

Iustig looked alarmed. 'But I thought you said –'

'That she was doing Hengist's work? Yes, that's what I thought. But I was wrong. Completely wrong. I hated her because I believed it, and because – if I'm honest – I was jealous of the time Vortigern gave to her. I shouldn't have been. She'd die for him. And you have no reason to pity her; at least, not because of anything Vortigern might or might not do.'

Iustig shook his head sadly, as if he didn't believe a word of it. Kerin, maddened though he was, realised that it was time to abandon the argument if they were ever to get to Glevum.

'What's this?' he said, prodding the bundle with his foot. Iustig squatted down, untied the string and pulled out a monk's habit. 'What's that for? You're not thinking of staying long enough to need a change of clothes, are you?'

'It's for you,' Iustig said. 'And before you say you wouldn't be seen dead in it, try and think of a better disguise. Two pilgrims, travelling to Glevum for an audience with the bishop? They'll let us in without a second thought.'

'You're right,' Kerin said grudgingly. 'I'm not shaving my head, though.'

'Then you'll have to wear the hood, won't you,' Iustig said testily.

'Whose is it?' Kerin asked.

'Cadog's,' Iustig said. 'He didn't mind.'

Kerin looked up. 'For God's sake, Iustig, you haven't told him, have you?'

The abbot looked uncomfortable. 'He came in when I was packing the thing away. But you shouldn't worry. Cadog's trustworthy; he won't tell a soul.'

Kerin looked up at the sky in despair. 'Come on,' he said. 'Let's ride while we can.'

'Why the spare horse?' Iustig asked.

'It's not spare. You're going to ride it, because I'm not waiting around while you tag along on that donkey. Come on; get on. The pony's quiet enough. And the donkey should have the sense to find its way home.' Iustig sighed, transferred his bundle to the pony's saddle and clambered onto its broad back. Kerin pulled off his tunic, stowed it in his saddle-bag and put on Cadog's robe. The material was coarse and prickled irritatingly. He wondered whether there was any getting used to it, or if it was one of the things monks were supposed to endure.

'Your breeches,' Iustig said.

'Oh no,' Kerin said. 'They're staying where they are.' It had never occurred to him to wonder what monks wore under their habits, but he suspected that it might be very little.

'Keep them covered, then,' Iustig said curtly. 'You're lucky Cadog's tall.' Kerin mounted up and arranged his skirts, feeling intensely foolish. Iustig chuckled. 'That'll do. Now, put the hood on. And if we meet anyone, keep your head down and your mouth shut.'

Kerin scowled and pulled the hood down to his forehead. He turned his pony's head towards the east and kicked her into a trot. He did not look behind. It was hard enough knowing that he might not come back, without reminding himself of all that he stood to lose.

Things began to get interesting on the evening of the second day. They had crossed the river above Glevum and made camp beside the road. Dusk was falling fast. Kerin had lit a small fire, and Iustig was settling down to cook a pair of pigeons bought from an old goatherd. The warriors came round the bend at a rattling trot. Kerin bent low towards the fire. In the split second before the hood flopped over his face, he realised that the outlines of the three riders were familiar. The leader dismounted, threw his reins to a companion and marched towards the fire. Even in the half-darkness, even in the narrow strip of vision afforded by Kerin's close-drawn hood, there was no mistaking the square shoulders and tiny pig-like eyes of Balin.

'Good evening, sirs,' Iustig said cordially.

'Brother,' Balin said non-committally. 'What are two monks doing wandering around at this time of night, then?'

'We're on our way to Glevum, sir,' Iustig said cheerfully. Balin sniffed as the grease from the pigeons began to drip onto the hot embers, sizzling and smoking.

'Two fine, fat pigeons,' he observed.

'Indeed,' Iustig said. 'They're all we have, but you're welcome to them. I never met a warrior who wasn't starving hungry.' Balin gave him a humourless smile, waved his companions away and sat down. The other two warriors waited beside the road and watched grudgingly. 'You must excuse my young friend here,' Iustig said, patting Kerin's shoulder. 'He's a novice, and we monks must observe a year's silence when we take our vows. You won't hear a word from Brother Magnus till next spring.'

Balin snorted. 'Christians. Mad as coots, the fucking lot of you.'

Iustig smiled. 'Even your holy bishop in Glevum?'

'Oh yes,' Balin said, prodding one of the pigeons. 'He's no exception.'

'Well, I hope he's mad enough to give us an audience. We've come far enough to see him.'

Balin seized the pigeon, tore off one of its little legs and began to munch. 'Cambrian, aren't you?'

'That's right, sir,' Iustig said. 'From a community dedicated to St Polonius, up in the mountains. Not far from Segontium. It's taken us days to get here, but we heard that your bishop is soon to receive the venerable Germanus.'

Balin chewed his pigeon and raised a sceptical eyebrow. 'What's Vortigern up to these days, then? Still got that pagan witch in his bed?'

'Yes,' Iustig said, with a stony glare. 'That's why we're here. If you want to cure an infection, you must first root out the cause, don't you think?'

Balin grinned. 'That's one way of putting it.'

'You're warriors of Eldof's following?' Iustig enquired. Balin chuckled.

'No chance. We're Bertil Redknife's men. I suppose you've heard of Bertil, even in your hovels in the mountains.'

'Oh yes,' Iustig said respectfully. 'A mighty man of arms.'

'And no friend of Vortigern's, or of that cheeky young bastard who pinched Bertil's daughter from under the bishop's nose.'

'We did hear a rumour,' Iustig said cautiously. 'But one hears many these days. We even heard that Vortigern's son was on his way to Glevum, to ally himself with Eldof.'

'He's there already,' Balin said, seizing the second pigeon. 'They want to burn Vortigern out of Cambria. Don't know what'll come of that, though. The man's a fighter, you've got to give him that. He pulled it off with the Picts, didn't he?'

'Yes,' Iustig said guardedly. 'Not that that's an excuse for some of what's going on.'

Balin grinned and spat out a mouthful of bones. 'I'll bet you don't say that too loudly in Cambria, Brother.'

'No, I don't,' Iustig conceded. Balin drew his dagger and began to pick his teeth with the tip of the blade.

'I suppose all this suits you, Vortimer being such a Christian,' he said.

'Well, yes,' Iustig said cautiously, 'although that's another thing I wouldn't say too loudly in Cambria. I haven't met the lad, of course.'

'Now's your chance,' Balin said, straightening up with a grunt. 'He's staying with the bishop. He'll probably be glad to meet a couple of Cambrians, even if one of them's as dumb as an ox.' He guffawed at his own joke and prodded Kerin with the toe of his boot. 'Fair play though, lad, you can cook a pigeon.' Kerin raised his hand and nodded a silent thank you. Balin kicked the carcasses into the fire and strode off to rejoin his companions. Kerin and Iustig watched them vanish into the twilight.

'Well done, Iustig,' Kerin said. 'I couldn't have managed that.'

'It's a shame about the pigeons,' the abbot said glumly. 'But at least we know where we're going.'

'Yes,' Kerin said, thinking of the huge house with its impenetrable pale yellow wall, where he had already escaped death by the narrowest of margins.

'What next?' the abbot asked. Kerin shrugged.

'Wait till the fire goes out, bury the ashes, hide the

ponies and get some sleep. We'll find food in the morning, and make for the city when it's getting dark. Once we get to the house, you'll have to talk your way in. If they recognise me, I'll say that I forced you to help me.' Iustig sighed and crossed himself. 'Are we still from Segontium?'

'It might be wise, if anyone asks,' Iustig said. 'The time for honesty will come when we're face to face with Rufus.'

'Who's St Polonius, anyway? I know about St Alban, but I've never heard of him.'

Iustig stared up at the darkening sky. 'God forgive me, neither have I,' he said.

*

The following evening, at the same time of uncertain, shifting light, they came to Eldof's western gates. Rain was falling in a thin, wetting mist. Four guards were standing around leaning on their spears. One of them strode across. He looked overweight for a trained warrior and reeked of ale.

'Evening, Brothers,' he said, looking the two riders up and down. 'Where have you sprung from, then?'

'All the way from Segontium, in the far north of Cambria,' Iustig said. 'I am Father Pacatus, and this is my young friend, Brother Magnus, who has taken the vow of silence.'

'Silence, eh?' the guard guffawed. 'I know a few wouldn't hurt for that. What brings you here, then? It's a long way for two monks on short-legged ponies.'

'We're hoping for an audience with the holy bishop,' Iustig said, in a tone of plausible veneration. 'Would you happen to know where he lives?'

The guard chuckled. 'Everyone knows that. His house

is damned near as big as his brother Eldof's. They say the bishop sleeps between silk sheets and drinks from silver goblets. Not what you're used to at home, Father, I don't suppose.'

Iustig smiled politely. 'No,' he said, 'but some directions would be useful.'

'Straight ahead through the gates, then follow the street to the crossroads,' the guard said. 'Go down the narrow lane to the left – you'll have to close your eyes there, Father, because that's where the whorehouses are – then you'll find yourself in a big square. In front of you is the church of the Holy Cross. If you go round the side, you'll find the bishop's house. But ask nicely, they've doubled the guard since that young thug of Vortigern's got away with the bishop's niece.'

'I have no truck with that sort of thing, young man,' Iustig said sternly. The guard grinned.

'No more than I'd expect, Father. And I expect they'll let you in, two holy men like yourselves.' Iustig gave a gracious smile and Kerin crossed himself for good measure. The guard clutched Iustig's sleeve. 'Pray for me, Father!' he said. 'I'm a God-fearing man at heart, and these are dangerous times.'

Iustig patted his hand. 'Of course I'll pray for you,' he said; genuinely, Kerin suspected. He wondered, with a sinking heart, what he was doing riding into his enemy's citadel with a man who felt easy about praying for his enemy's guards. He began to sweat inside his habit, and the rough wool irritated his clammy skin until he wanted to scratch like a flea-ridden dog. They passed down the narrow lane, where groups of girls and older women were hanging around outside their dingy houses. A thin, black-haired girl with alluring eyes smiled at Kerin from a dark doorway.

'What are you hiding under that robe, then, Brother?' she asked impishly.

'More than you think, you saucy piece,' Kerin said, before he had time to think. The girl and her companions shrieked with laughter. Iustig gave Kerin a scarifying look and they rode on, leaving the women falling about helplessly in the street behind them.

'Not another word, you numbskull,' Iustig hissed. Kerin retreated apologetically inside his hood; and so they came, in perfect silence, to the house of Eldadus the bishop. 'Well, you were right,' Iustig conceded. 'There's no getting in there without an invitation.' Kerin looked up at the towering golden wall and solid oak gates. Nothing had changed, except that there was a chip out of the wall where Balin's axe had struck it, and someone had nailed a board above the gates with a Latin motto inscribed upon it in large white letters. Kerin looked enquiringly at Iustig. '*Ne hic intrant malefici*,' Iustig said. 'Let not the sinners enter herein. They've left it a little late, haven't they.'

Kerin gave a half-hearted smile, slipped off his pony and banged on the gate. After a while it opened slightly and a guard's whiskered face peered out. He had a small gold crucifix attached to his leather helmet; a mark of seniority, probably.

'What's your business, Brothers?' he asked.

'We seek an audience with your master, the holy bishop,' Iustig said. 'Please will you tell him that two poor monks, Father Pacatus and Brother Magnus, have travelled all the way from Segontium to beg a little of his time.'

The guard looked perplexed. 'You'd better come in off the street, Father,' he said, opening the gate enough for the two travellers to pass through. Once they were inside, he swung it shut and slammed the heavy bar down. Six of his fellows, who were standing on the steps in front of the house, came to see what was going on. Kerin recognised one of them from his previous visit and huddled even more shyly inside his hood. A smartly-dressed servant took charge of the ponies. 'We have to be careful,' the chief guard apologised. 'His Grace has an important house guest, and he'll string us up if we let in any undesirables. Not that two men of the cloth are undesirables, of course, but you can see why I didn't want to stand there with the gate open.'

'Indeed,' Iustig said. 'We did hear about an unfortunate incident –'

'Please, Father,' the guard said. 'We don't even talk about that, if you don't mind.'

Iustig smiled politely. 'Please God we shall have no repetitions, now that the Lord Vortimer is here,' he said. The guard looked taken aback. 'I think everyone within two days' journey knows about that,' Iustig said, behind his hand. 'It's no secret, surely?'

'Well, no, not a secret, exactly,' the guard said. 'But perhaps not something you'd want the world and his wife to know, either. I think Lord Eldof was hoping – well, no matter. But you'd be doing all good Christians a kindness if you kept quiet about it.'

One of the new recruits, a lanky lad with a crooked nose, smiled broadly showing a row of broken teeth. 'Your friend doesn't say much, does he, Father,' he said, slapping Kerin's shoulder.

'As garrulous as a tipsy girl when it suits,' Iustig said dryly. 'But Brother Magnus is a novice. He may not speak or bare his head until his initiation is over.'

The young guard hooted with laughter. 'I'll bet he wasn't much of a travelling companion.'

'Enough!' the chief guard barked. 'Go and tell His Grace that there are two holy brothers here to see him. If he won't receive them until the morning, see they have food and a bed for the night. Now!' The young guard gave a hasty bow and hurried away into the house. The chief guard shook his head. 'I don't know, Father,' he said gloomily. 'I hope you don't have as much trouble finding new blood as I do.'

The bishop would see them, the crooked-nosed young guard said. No servant of God, however busy, could fail to find time for two weary pilgrims who had toiled all the way down from Segontium for comfort and advice. The bishop was taking his evening meal, however; so the two weary pilgrims would have to wait in the antechamber.

'He's got important company,' the young guard whispered, giving them a wink as he opened the door. 'Lord Eldof, Lord Garagon and the young king Vortimer. I don't think I should be calling him king, personally, but the bishop's very keen on it.'

He went out, closing the door behind him, and the two pilgrims found themselves alone in a small room with a high blue ceiling. A carved image of Christ crucified, startlingly lifelike, gazed mournfully down at them, wooden drops of blood frozen on his cheeks and pierced feet. Kerin peered out from beneath his hood and winced, then retreated as the door opened and a servant appeared, swinging an empty wine jug.

'Brothers,' he said politely.

'Is the meal over, lad?' Iustig asked.

'Very nearly. They're on the candied apples. But His Grace will receive you when the other lords leave. He says that if you're hungry, you can eat in the servants' quarters afterwards. There's always leftovers when he's had guests.'

Iustig gave a courteous smile. 'That's most generous,' he said. The servant strode off along the echoing corridor, whistling gaily.

'What are you going to say to the bishop?' Kerin whispered. 'I realise he'll understand the vow of silence, but what about the head-baring nonsense? And what about St Polonius?'

'I'll worry about that when the time comes,' Iustig said. 'And in the meantime, stop talking, before someone realises how elastic your vows are.'

Kerin fell silent and stared up at the sad-eyed figure of Christ, wondering what it felt like to have nails hammered through your hands, and whether it could possibly be worse than having your flesh melted to liquid. He thought of the brave Pict, who would have burned to death if his brother had not put love before duty. He wondered exactly what had happened all those years ago in Isca, and why Quintus Parvo had not cut the rope. It seemed no time at all before the whistling servant came back to announce that the three lords had withdrawn, and the bishop was waiting.

Kerin remembered the broad marble staircase which led to the room where Gael knelt praying by candlelight. They continued along a lamplit corridor, past the dark passage which led to the kitchens and into a colonnaded atrium where clipped bay laurels grew in huge earthenware pots. Kerin kept his eyes on the floor, storing every detail in his memory in case he needed to retrace his footsteps in a hurry.

'In here, Brothers,' the servant said, opening a huge door. Kerin and Iustig passed through and found themselves in a grand reception room. The big polished table was bare except for an ornate silver pitcher, a single goblet and a small silver bell, but the smell of candied apples and roast beef still hung in the air. Eldadus, in a snow-white robe and a purple cape with intricate gold embroidery, was sitting on a carved chair in the centre of the room with hands folded in his lap.

'Your Grace, the two pilgrims,' the servant said, with a reverence. The bishop nodded and gestured towards one of the backless wooden benches beside the table. The servant picked it up, struggling under the weight. Kerin resisted the urge to offer a helping hand. The bench was put down rather hard in front of the bishop's chair, and the two monks sat on it. Eldadus leaned forward and squinted myopically at them.

'What brings you to Glevum, then? It's a devil of a long way from Segontium, even for an audience with me.'

Iustig bowed his head. 'I am Father Pacatus, Your Grace. And this is my young friend, Brother Magnus. He has taken the vow of silence, so I must speak for both of us; but as Christ is my witness, his dedication to the cause is as strong as mine.'

'The cause,' Eldadus said with interest. 'What cause is that, then, Father Pacatus? There are all sorts of mad causes floating around these days.'

'Your Grace, there can only be one cause in these times,' Iustig said, so fervently that Kerin wondered whether he might believe it. 'We must rid the kingdom of the Pelagian heretics, and drive their pagan friends into the sea. A traveller from Kent told us that the holy Bishop Germanus is raising arms. We decided to come to you, the greatest churchman in the kingdom, to pledge the loyalty of our little community. Please tell us that the news is true, and that you will accept our poor support!' He looked up at Eldadus with the mute yearning of an adoring dog. The bishop smiled graciously and smoothed his robes.

'Well, Father Pacatus, it is true,' he said. 'We do expect the holy Germanus next year, and I hope that you and your devout young friend will be amongst the first to welcome him. You are right, of course. We must root out the heretics and all who cling to them, particularly those heathen devils that Vortigern brought in to fight his battles for him.' He gave a cautious cough. 'And speaking of Vortigern, he still has the woman with him, I take it?'

'Yes, Your Grace,' Iustig said. 'Why do you ask?'

Eldadus harrumphed. 'Because,' he said, 'I think it would sit a great deal easier with the Church, not to mention the young king, if he were to put her away and take a good Christian wife.'

'But he already has a wife, Your Grace,' Iustig said carefully. Eldadus snorted.

'By her own people's foul rites, so I'm told.'

'No, Your Grace,' Iustig said. 'By ours, as it happens.'

The bishop's watery eyes narrowed. 'You mean he found a priest who'd marry him to that pagan witch?'

'Yes, Your Grace. Probably she should have been made to take the faith. But it's done now, and it's more difficult telling a man to dispose of his wife than his whore.'

'Well, it's his prerogative,' Eldadus said, yawning slightly. 'And it'll give his son one more good reason to hang him in the spring.'

Kerin gritted his teeth under the concealing hood. He glanced at Iustig, and saw no more than mild surprise.

'We did here something about an invasion,' the abbot said cautiously. 'But news can be slow to reach Segontium. The young king intends to take Cambria, then?'

The bishop gave a thin-lipped smile. 'Indeed, Father. It's his dearest wish. It must be plain that until he burns out the wasps' nest, his power will be at risk.'

'Yes,' Iustig said, folding his arms. 'And if there's anything we poor disciples of Christ can do to help, he has only to ask.' He leaned towards Eldadus. 'There are times when men of the Church can wield more power than men of blood. You must know what I mean.'

Eldadus's face glowed. 'Oh yes, Father. A rousing address here, a threat of hellfire there.' He chuckled. 'I am master of the art. But I can see no reason why two brothers from Segontium should not spread the word amongst the poor benighted souls of Cambria.'

'To prepare the ground, as it were,' Iustig said gravely.

'Indeed,' Eldadus said, patently delighted with what he thought he had arranged. 'It might even be worth breaking the vow of silence, eh, Brother Magnus?' Kerin cringed and crossed himself hurriedly. The bishop laughed and patted his shoulder with a scrawny hand. Kerin could smell the wine on his breath. 'To your beds, now, my soldiers. We'll meet in my chapel at dawn, and lay all these things before God.' Eldadus swayed across to the dining table and rang the silver bell. The door creaked open at once, and his servant came trotting in. Kerin wondered how much he had overheard.

'Show them to their beds, Primus,' the bishop said, waving a vague hand. The food seemed to have been forgotten; even the leftovers.

'You're lucky, you know, Brothers,' the servant said, as he led them away. 'Usually he won't see anyone much, especially when he's just sunk a pitcher of wine.'

'Why do you think he agreed to see us, then, Primus?' Iustig asked.

'Probably because you're from Cambria,' the servant said, turning down the passage towards the kitchens. 'You know that the young king's planning to fight Vortigern there in the spring, I suppose? Lord Eldof and Lord Garagon too.'

'We had heard,' Iustig said, giving Kerin a dubious look as Primus opened a door, liberating a warm draught of foul-smelling air. The tiny room was no more than a cell. Two narrow beds spread with dirty blankets had been crammed in there, with an upturned crate on which a candle sputtered in a cracked bowl.

'Sorry it's not much,' the servant apologised. 'I'll see if there's anything to eat.'

'One moment,' Iustig said. 'You seem to know quite a lot about Lord Eldof's plans. Do you think anything will happen before the spring? I have relations in Glywysing – poor labourers, no friends of Vortigern – but I'd like to warn them, if there might be trouble.'

Primus hesitated. Kerin reached inside his robe, drew a couple of sesterces from his pocket and held them out. Primus cleared his throat. 'I did hear a rumour,' he said. 'Something about killing off the leaders. But that's all I know.' Kerin's fingers closed around the coins. Primus looked at him in dismay. 'That would feed my children for a week, Brother,' he protested. Kerin shook his hooded head.

'Perhaps if you could remember a little more, Primus?' Iustig suggested. Primus shoved the door closed.

'This is more than my life's worth,' he whispered. Kerin spread his fingers and the coins winked in the candlelight. 'Lord Bertil,' Primus mouthed. 'He's got a blood feud with Vortigern's chief warrior, or something. Lord Eldof's in it too. The bishop knows, but only in private, if you see what I mean; bishops can't really go putting their names to that sort of thing, can they?'

'And when will this happen?' Iustig asked.

'Christmastide, when everyone's busy feasting,' Primus said. 'And I swear on my father's grave, that's all I know.'

Kerin nodded a silent thanks and held out his hand. Primus grabbed the coins and retreated.

'Thank you, Primus,' Iustig said. 'We shall be here for a day or two, and if you find out anything more, there'll be money enough to feed your children for a month. But if you mention this to anyone, I shall personally ask God to bring the plague upon you and your entire household.'

Primus smiled nervously. 'My lips are sealed, Brother,' he said. Iustig sat gingerly on the edge of one of the beds as the servant's footsteps pattered away.

'I imagine that's all true,' he said.

'Probably,' Kerin said. 'It squares with what we've heard, and the servants usually know what's going on.'

Iustig clenched his fists. 'For God's sake! How can they be planning something like that, without Rufus knowing?'

'Very easily,' Kerin said. 'Who'd tell him? Not Eldof or Bertil, because he might put a stop to it. Not the warriors, even if they know, because he doesn't have a way with them like his father does.' He retreated under his hood as the door was kicked open and Primus came in, carrying a platter full of meat scraps and crusts.

'Here you are, Brothers,' he said. 'I've seen better, but it'll fill your bellies for now.'

'Thank you,' Iustig said cordially. 'A veritable feast.' Kerin grinned inanely and nodded his agreement. Iustig picked up a half-cleaned bone. 'It's as good as most monks are used to.' They ate in silence until the platter was empty. 'You should get some sleep,' Iustig said. 'You have to get up at dawn to lay everything before God.' He blew out the candle, pulled the hood of his robe over his head and curled up on the filthy bed. Kerin sat and waited; not for dawn and a conversation with God, but for the moment when Iustig would fall asleep. He had no idea whether the abbot could be trusted. All he knew for sure was that, when he met Rufus, he wanted to be alone.

26

The last time Kerin stood in this spot, Gael had grabbed a sword and slashed a guard's legs to the bone. Three months of marriage had not dulled the memory of their escape from the bishop's house, and his mind's eye could still see the blood spreading across the floor. The new guard had taken off his helmet and hung it from the point of his spear, which was leaning against the wall. Kerin stood in the shadows with his hood drawn tight. This passage must lead to the bishop's quarters, and to the chambers reserved for honoured guests. Everything dictated it; the faultless mosaics underfoot, the ornate lamps, the murals where shepherds tended their flocks in improbably green pastures, untroubled by thoughts of betrayal or Saxon invasions. Bowing his head, Kerin crept forward.

'Where are you off to, then, Brother?' the guard asked, amiably enough. Kerin smiled, shook his head and pressed his finger to his lips. The guard chuckled. 'What do you mean? I'm entitled to ask where you're going, you know.' Kerin shook his head again, pointed to his chest and covered his mouth with one hand. 'Ah!' the guard said knowingly. 'So it's you who can't talk. Struck dumb, then, or did someone cut your tongue out?' Kerin opened his mouth to demonstrate that his tongue was intact, clasped his hands and gazed piously towards heaven. 'I know,' the guard said, laughing. 'You're one of those mad ones who promises God he won't speak.' Kerin beamed delightedly and nodded his head. He pointed up the passage, and assumed an enquiring look. The guard looked perplexed. 'Well, I don't know why you'd want to go up there, Brother,' he said. 'There's only the bishop's chambers, and the guest rooms. And his private chapel, of course.' Kerin nodded furiously, closed his eyes and put his hands together in an attitude of supplication. There was a weighty silence. He could almost feel the levers creaking in the guard's brain. 'Let me guess,' came the response. 'You want to pray in the chapel.' Almost weeping with relief, Kerin smiled happily and clasped the guard's hands. 'I ought to ask His Grace, by rights,' the guard said dubiously. 'But then again, it's more than my life's worth, to wake him when he's had a skinful. Come on, Brother, follow me. He's hardly going to stop a holy man from praying, now, is he?'

The door of the chapel was arched and bore the sign of the cross. On the opposite side of the passage, a series of grand entrances was set in the frescoed wall.

'Here we are,' the guard whispered, easing it open. 'But you'd better pray quietly. It would take a thunderstorm to wake the bishop after wine, but Lord Eldof always sleeps in that room over there, and I'm not too sure about him.' He grinned. 'I'm a bit of a fool warning you to be quiet, all the same. Shut the door after you, and make sure you put in a good word for me.'

Kerin pressed the guard's hand, slipped inside and closed the door. The small high room was cold and smelled of damp. Two tall candles illuminated an altar spread with an embroidered cloth on which a gilded crucifix stood, with a silver communion chalice and a jewelled bowl. There was a small window in the wall above, which Kerin fancied that he might be able to reach if he climbed onto

the altar. He stood still and listened. The guard's footsteps
had faded, but he could hear something else; the steady,
muted surge and slap of running water on the other side
of the wall. He remembered Morwen speaking about a
terrace overlooking the river, where Eldadus took the sun
on fine days. Opening the door, he peered cautiously out. A
mouse scurried across the passage and disappeared behind
a statue of Julius Caesar. There were three doors, other than
the one behind which Eldof was sleeping. Probably one of
them concealed Rufus, and another Garagon of Kent; but
choosing the wrong door could mean instant death, even
for a brother of St Polonius. Studying the doors, Kerin
saw that the furthest one was more intricately carved
than the others and had once been inlaid with gold, now
flaking away. He supposed that, had he been Eldadus, this
might be the room he would choose for the young king.
He drew the dagger from his boot, slipped the blade up
his sleeve and crept along the passage. The door was barred
from within. Kerin pulled the hood down to his eyebrows
and knocked gently. There was no response. He knocked
again, as loudly as he dared. This time the slap of sandals
was followed by the sound of someone fiddling with a bolt.
The door opened fractionally and a boy's pale face peered
out. He was wearing the same white tunic and embroidered
green girdle as Primus.

'Yes, Brother?' he asked.

'I have come from Venta Belgarum,' Kerin whispered.
'I have a message from our abbot, Father Paulinus, for the
young king.'

The servant looked astounded. 'At this time of night,
Brother?' he asked. Kerin leaned forward.

'God does not measure time, my son,' he said gravely.
'When you stand at heaven's gate, will you expect him to

turn you away if it happens to be the middle of the night?'

The servant smiled apprehensively. 'Well, perhaps not, Brother,' he said. 'Come into the antechamber, and I'll ask the Lord King if he'll see you.' Kerin mouthed his thanks and went inside. The small room was cool and dim and smelt of incense. He stood with the hilt of the dagger in his palm and waited for the servant to come back. 'He'll see you, Brother,' the boy said, with some relief. 'The Lord King doesn't sleep much, luckily. Through that door there. I'll go back to my bed now, if you don't mind.'

'Sleep well, my son,' Kerin whispered. 'May God give you pleasant dreams.'

The servant smiled. 'You too, Brother,' he said. Amen to that, Kerin thought. He opened the door and found himself in a lamplit bedchamber whose large window overlooked the central courtyard. There was a bed with red drapes, a polished table and a huge bearskin rug. Rufus was sitting at the table, studying a plan of some sort, etched on a thin sheet of wood. Kerin had not seen him at close quarters since the night he married Gael. The change in his appearance was startling. His shoulders looked broader and his face fuller, with the trace of a beard. He looked like a man who, having had responsibility wished upon him, had grown physically to accommodate it. For the first time ever, Kerin saw the father in the son, and it made his heart bleed.

'Rufus,' he said, without stopping to wonder if it was wise. Rufus started and dropped the plan. He looked up and his brow creased with bewilderment as he saw the unknown cleric who had spoken with the most familiar of voices. Kerin flung back the hood.

'Jesus' blood!' Rufus said. He bounded across the room in two strides and flung his arms around Kerin. It happened so quickly, and was so unexpected, that Kerin forgot about the dagger. He slackened his grip as he returned Rufus's embrace, and it fell to the flagstones with a clatter. Rufus recoiled.

'No!' Kerin exclaimed. 'For God's sake, I didn't know who was in here.'

Without taking his eyes from him, Rufus picked up the dagger and placed it out of reach on the bed. His face was set and pale. 'What are you doing here?' he asked.

'Looking for you,' Kerin said. 'Look, the dagger was for my own protection. It could have been anyone in here. If you must know, I was frightened to death.'

Rufus sat down heavily on the edge of the bed. 'I thought you'd come to kill me, for a moment.'

'No,' Kerin said, sitting beside him. 'That's the last thing I want, whatever's happened. And before anyone else arrives, I'm Brother Magnus from Segontium, and I've taken the vow of silence. Iustig thought I'd give myself away if I opened my mouth.'

Rufus's eyebrows rose. 'Iustig? He's here too?'

'Yes. Snoring his head off in the slaves' quarters. He's Father Pacatus, in case anybody asks. We both came to look for you, but I wanted to see you alone. He can say his piece later, but I'm first.'

Rufus's eyes grew dark. 'You were always first.'

'For God's sake, Rufus,' Kerin said. 'Come home with me and make your peace. Why fight each other? We should be fighting Hengist.'

Rufus stared up at the painted ceiling. 'My father will never fight Hengist while he's got the man's daughter in his bed.'

'You're wrong,' Kerin said. 'Completely wrong. He will fight Hengist, and the girl knows it. She's made her choice.'

Rufus's eyes flashed. 'As you did,' he said. There was an angry silence.

'Yes,' Kerin said. 'As I did. As you knew I would. It's not a choice I should have had to make. But at least I've never lied to you.'

'What does that mean?' Rufus asked. Kerin's fists clenched.

'You said you'd never fight us in Cambria. And now everyone says you're going to attack us in the spring; not only you and whatever army you've got, but some horde of Sarmatians. Why, for God's sake? Why not fight Hengist together?'

'Because it'll never work unless we have one leader,' Rufus said. 'I learned that much fighting Picts with my father. We only won because everyone answered to him without question. And this is no different. We can't both lead the army. Half the men I've got want him dead. And I'm not stupid, I know some of them serve their own ends. But if I can keep them until we've beaten the Saxons, it'll be enough. I'm not like my father. I don't want power for its own sake.'

'And what about the men of the West? Do you really think they'll follow you, too?'

'Not at the moment,' Rufus said. 'But they idolise my father because they think he's invincible. Things might change, if we gave him a good beating.'

Kerin paused, breathing deeply, while common sense did battle with natural inclination. 'I think you're wrong, and in more than one way,' he said. 'But why waste good men? I still can't see why it's impossible to fight the Saxons together.' He paused. 'That is what this is about, isn't it?'

'For some of us, yes,' Rufus said. 'Certainly for Garagon, who has the most to lose. Eldof hates my father enough to fight him anyway. But for Paulinus and his allies, this isn't about land. It's about faith, about getting rid of the pagans.

If my father had taken a Christian wife, they might have been happy to leave him alone. But he didn't. And they won't.'

'They won't?' Kerin said sceptically. 'Who makes the decisions? You or them?'

'I do, of course,' Rufus said curtly. He was calm, but smarting in a way Kerin felt he might not have been, had he been sure that he was right.

'So,' he said. 'Crossing the river and butchering your own father is one of your better decisions, is it?'

'I don't want to butcher him,' Rufus said angrily. 'If he'd surrender the kingship and put the woman away, I'd leave him where he is and ride back to Kent.'

Kerin stood up, retrieved the dagger and slammed it into his belt. 'You don't ask for much, do you.'

'It's necessary,' Rufus said obdurately. 'I mean to beat Hengist, and nothing's going to stop me.'

'No,' Kerin said, seizing the collar of his tunic. 'Not even sending your murderers to kill me and your father to make things easier. Why wait for Christmastide? Why not call your bootlickers and kill me now?' Rufus's eyes widened. The most practised deceiver could not have feigned the dismay they held. Kerin let his hands fall. 'You ought to know that there's a plot. Bertil and Eldof are behind it. They're planning to send assassins to kill your father and all our leading men. You should thank them; it'll make things a lot easier for you in the spring.'

Rufus looked aghast. 'I want a surrender, not a slaughter,' he protested. Kerin laughed aloud.

'A surrender? How well do you know your father?'

Rufus grimaced. 'Hardly at all, I suspect,' he said. 'But that's not all my fault.' He looked desolate.

'No,' Kerin said. 'I'll grant you that.'

'Is this why you're here?' Rufus asked.

'Yes. I shan't mince words. I don't know how much control you have. But if you're able to stop this, I thought you might want to.'

Rufus shook his head. 'How on earth do you know all this?'

'I can't possibly tell you that without endangering quite a few people. But I had to ask. It's your choice now.'

Rufus went over to the window. He looked down on the courtyard where the bishop's guards were patrolling in silence. Beyond the walls the city whispered and hummed.

'Whose idea was it, to come to me?' he asked.

'Mine entirely. No-one knows I'm here except Gwyndaf, and he won't tell anyone unless I don't get back.'

'You're married, I hear,' Rufus said.

'Yes. I imagine it's common knowledge in Glevum.'

'Was she worth the trouble?' Rufus asked.

'Yes. Every bit. She's wonderful, and she's carrying our first child. What more could I want?'

'Not a great deal, by the look of you,' Rufus said. 'Perhaps I should have married Branwen while she was willing.' He looked utterly calm now, despite the shocks of the past hour. Kerin remembered his conversation with Publius Luca in Londinium, and felt more frightened than he had done at any time since he left Henfelin.

'Someone told me that you saw yourself as the messenger of God,' he said. 'Is it true?' Rufus paused and a barely visible smile crossed his face. He seemed to like that idea. 'I believe that God has given me a purpose. To call myself his messenger would be too much, but I do believe that he's given me a task to do. I'm sorry if that's hard to understand. When you're a young lad, and your life's been easy, you think you can have all that and the faith too. But in the end, you have to choose. Don't you think I'd like to come home with you, and meet your wife, and bed Branwen, and make peace with my father? But I can't, because I have to put everything else aside until I've finished what I'm doing. And by then, it'll probably be too late; but that's the price. It's less than some have paid.'

'You're more like your father than I ever thought,' Kerin said. Rufus snorted.

'Hardly.'

'Oh yes,' Kerin said. 'You're doing it for God, that's the only difference. At least now I know that there's no point in arguing with you.' He drew the monk's hood up over his head.

'Stay,' Rufus said. 'There's a pitcher full of wine over there, we could –'

'No,' Kerin said. 'I've got a wife and child to stay alive for now, and I'll need a clear head to get home. Drink it with Batraz. He's your chief warrior, isn't he?'

Rufus's eyes narrowed. 'What do you know about him?'

'Enough,' Kerin said. 'Where did you get him?'

'I didn't get him,' Rufus said, resenting the inference. 'We met in Gallia. His father was recruited by the Romans years ago. They fought all over the Empire, but Batraz is a free agent now, with his own cavalry troop.'

'A mercenary,' Kerin said, with a barbed smile.

'No!' Rufus exclaimed angrily.

'I don't care either way,' Kerin said. 'I'm going home. I can't wait for Iustig, I've done what I came to do.'

Rufus looked taken aback. 'Don't you owe him your protection? I'll give him safe conduct across the river, but an old man travelling alone –'

'I imagine God will protect him,' Kerin said. 'And if you don't believe that, I'm sorry for you.' He turned towards the door.

'Kerin, wait!' Rufus said sharply. There was a note of desperation in his voice. 'I'll stop this thing. It's dishonourable and underhand, and I want no part of it.'

'Thank you,' Kerin said, as steadily as he could manage.

'I'll come to the gate with you. They won't let you pass without an argument at this time of night.'

The chief guard was still on duty. He was looking bored out of his wits, but he came to attention as he recognised the man who accosted him.

'Lord King!' he said, with an exaggerated bow. 'I'm sorry, sir, you were the last man I was expecting at this time of night.'

'No matter, Junius,' Rufus said. 'I've been praying with Brother Magnus, here. His friend the abbot is staying the night, but Brother Magnus has received word of a sick relative, and has to leave. Can you bring his horse, please?'

'At once, Lord King,' the guard said hastily, and trotted off across the courtyard.

'He seems like a good man,' Kerin said. 'I'm glad I didn't have to kill him to get out.' Rufus made no reply. They stood, uncomfortably silent. 'You said you had weapons,' Kerin said. 'Weapons we'd never dreamed of.'

Rufus gave a thin smile; more a twitch of the lips. 'I'd be an idiot to tell you about those, wouldn't I.'

'You're an idiot anyway,' Kerin said. 'Come with me. It's not too late.'

'Stop asking me,' Rufus said, turning away. 'As you said, there's no point.' Junius came back leading the black pony. 'Cenydd's,' Rufus murmured. Kerin struggled onto the pony's back, trying to make it look difficult. Junius hauled back the bar and swung the gate open. Rufus caught the pony's rein. 'God speed, Brother Magnus,' he whispered. 'I'll hold you in my prayers.' Kerin jerked the rein free and drove the pony forward. The gate creaked shut behind him and he was alone in the hostile city, with the heat of tears on his face.

27

The oil lamp cast only a dim light, but the fire was cheerful and the stew in the pot smelt delicious to a man who hadn't eaten properly in days. Outside a thick drizzle was falling, but the roof didn't leak. It seemed as if Berget had got a few things done while her men were away in the North. Her father Malan leaned forward and warmed his hands over the flames, his wrinkled face creasing into a grin.

'You're off your head, boy,' he said. 'You shouldn't have gone anywhere near Glevum.' He cackled and spat into the fire. 'And after pinching Bertil's daughter from the bishop's house, by God. Off your head.'

'Ignore him, Lord Kerin,' Berget said, passing a bowl of stew. 'That's what I try to do.' Her eyes were troubled. She looked tired, Kerin thought, and thinner than when he first met her at Malan's makeshift camp outside the walls of Londinium. How long ago was that? The best part of a year. A year since this spindly old man with the voice of a roaring bull had helped him take Londinium and secure Vortigern's crown, without a drop of blood being spilt. 'You should have gone straight home, all the same,' Berget said. 'Not that it isn't good to see you, but if Bertil caught you –'

'I know,' Kerin said, spreading the folds of his habit out to dry. 'That's why I'm riding around on a pony, looking like Brother Idiot. But I had to go to Glevum. And I had to come here, too. Do you remember what I told you last time? About what you should do, if things got dangerous?'

Berget put down her ladle. 'You said we should leave here and cross the river.'

'Yes. You should prepare yourselves. There's going to be trouble before long.'

Berget's husband, Runo, put aside the scythe he was mending and came to the fireside. 'What sort of trouble? We heard that some of them set the son up as king, and you had to go to Kent to fight them.'

'Yes, we did,' Kerin said. 'And we gave them a beating. But it's not over. The son is here, staying in the bishop's house. When he's got enough men, he'll want to fight it out with his father. We don't know when or where. Vortigern receives messengers from the praetor of Londinium every two weeks, but so far there's no sign of armies mustering.'

'We'll know if they do,' Berget said. 'I've got a woman in every village between here and Corinium. Good girls who can ride. If it's an army, it'll come down the Roman road. And if it does, I'll send word. We've got one good horse, haven't we, Runo.'

Runo folded his long, gangling legs under him and sat down beside his wife. For a man who had spent a lifetime avoiding fights, he had done a solid turn in the North with his axe and butcher's knife. Someone's sword had sliced across the top of his head, and although the hair had grown back there was now a snow-white streak bisecting his dark crown, which he probably considered a mark of honour. 'One good horse, yes,' he said. 'I pinched it in the North, to be honest. It was wandering around after the battle, so I grabbed it. I'll come myself, if we hear anything.' He paused. 'Berget told me. About crossing the river. We'll go if needs be, of course. My place is with Berget and our girls.

But once I've seen them right, I'll fight if you need me. All us boys who went to the North, we'll fight for the king. The real one, that is.'

'Tell him the rest, Runo boy,' Malan said, eyes gleaming with excitement. 'Tell him what's going on in Glevum.'

'We go there once a week,' Runo said. 'Me and Berget. We go to the market with eggs and rabbits, and afterwards I drink with the other market boys and the smiths and the carpenters. I'm telling you now, if that Lord Vortimer goes after his father, there'll be trouble like there was in Londinium.'

'Like the night when we rose up,' Malan said, his fingers digging into Kerin's arm. 'We won't be doing with it, boy. We won't be doing with it. Tell him about Edryd, Runo. Edryd the smith who was in the rising.'

'He's in Glevum,' Runo said. 'I know he meant to keep away because of Flora, but I ran into him in the market last week, and he looked – well, like a man who was doing something big and exciting, but he'd been told to keep his mouth shut. I thought you might want to know.' He shrugged and helped himself to stew.

'Thank you,' Kerin said. 'And I do want to know. If you see him again, tell him to come and find me. He's probably never been to Cambria, but once you're across the rivers, it's an easy journey.' He caught Berget's eye. 'What's happened to Flora?'

'Gone missing,' Berget said. 'About a month ago. Someone spotted her on the wharf in Glevum, asking where the ships were going. We think she got on one of them.' She sighed. 'I shouldn't say it about my sister's daughter, but I hope she did. There's nothing for her here, poor child. Perhaps if she went away somewhere else, she'd find some good man who'd take care of her.'

'She could have had Edryd!' Runo protested.

'I know, I know,' Berget said. 'But she was never going to want him while the king was in the same country breathing the same air, was she? Out of sight out of mind, I hope.'

'Well, that goes for both of them,' Runo said sourly. 'That boy deserves better.'

Malan reared up. 'Shut the argument in front of Lord Kerin, here,' he bellowed. His voice had lost none of its power. Kerin recoiled. It was like sitting next to the carnyx. Malan cleared his throat and leaned close. 'It's like this all the time,' he said, quietly for once. 'Come on, we'll go to my house. You look all in, and I've got a cot in the corner where Runo sleeps when Berget throws him out. It doesn't happen often now, though. That battle put some metal in the boy, and she likes that.'

Kerin finished his stew and got up. 'Thank you for feeding me, Berget,' he said. 'I'll be gone at first light. If I don't see you before I leave, keep your ears open. You too, Runo. You were a strong man in the North, so stay like that. We'll need all of you, before this is done.'

Malan drew the door screen and led the way into his small house. Inside it was dark but warm. Embers were still smouldering on the hearth in the middle of the floor and a feeble little lamp glowed on the rough table.

'Do you really want us to run away from here?' the old man asked, sitting down beside Kerin on the truckle bed.

'Yes, if your lives are at risk,' Kerin said. 'That's why I've come, to make sure that you understand how dangerous it might get. Eldof was there on the night Constans was killed. He knows quite well that you and your boys are Vortigern's men. I saw what happened in Kent. Some of them crucified a Saxon boy, and then they hanged our warrior Hefin to draw Vortigern out of Cambria and make a fight of it. Vortimer does have scruples, but some of the men who ride with him have none. They'd think nothing of massacring a whole village. If trouble starts, cross the river in the dark, before anyone starts burning the bridges.'

Malan's brow furrowed. "But where would we go? I've got twenty families in this village. Over a hundred people, if you count all the little ones.'

Kerin smiled inwardly as he realised that Berget had kept her secret. 'Don't worry about that,' he said. 'The king wouldn't see you starve.'

Malan clutched his arm. 'Am I known in Cambria?' he asked. 'Do they know about Londinium? About the rising?'

'Yes,' Kerin said. 'Everyone knows about the rising. They talk about it in the alehouses, and around the cooking fires. They talk about the thousands who marched on the city, and about the man on the black mule who led them.'

Malan closed his eyes. 'Then my life is full, Kerin Brightspear,' he said, with a smile of profound happiness. 'My life is full.'

28

A sharp wind was gusting off the sea, driving banks of high cloud across the sun.

'You look ridiculous,' Vortigern said. He had appeared from the woodland near the water mill, riding a fine young bay horse which Kerin had not seen before.

'I know,' Kerin said. He stripped off the prickly habit, rolled it into a bundle and flung it as far as he could into the river. The early morning air was cool on his bare skin. 'That's a beautiful filly,' he said.

'A gift from Gwyndaf,' Vortigern said. 'Something to do with an old debt and some cattle. I told him there was no debt, but you can't argue with Gwyndaf.'

'First a ship, now a horse,' Kerin said. 'It's been a good week for gifts.'

'Well, I'm sure you haven't brought me one from Glevum,' Vortigern said. 'Did you see him?'

'How did you know?' Kerin asked. Vortigern raised his eyebrows.

'Iustig should have kept his mouth shut. Did you see him?'

'Yes,' Kerin said. 'For what good it did. You know about the assassination plot, I suppose?'

Vortigern gave him a pitying look. 'I know how many teeth Cadog's got in his head and what his mother had to eat on the day he was born.'

'Rufus knew nothing,' Kerin said. 'He told me he'd put a stop to it. Underhand was the word he used. He'd prefer to fight it out with us, although I think a nice clean, bloodless surrender would be his choice.'

Vortigern looked disgusted. 'On whose part?' he asked. Kerin smiled. Vortigern rode off down the track, turned his horse in a wide circle and came back. 'We've had all this before, haven't we. All the allegiance nonsense, all the pious claptrap about God's will. What does he really want?'

'He wants you to surrender the kingship and send Rowenna back to her father,' Kerin said. 'He wants a Christian kingdom, free of heretics and pagans, and he thinks that's the only way to get it.'

'How did you find him?' Vortigern asked.

'He's unhappy,' Kerin said. 'And he looks older. God has a lot to answer for.'

They had reached the point where the track forked, the left-hand branch leading steeply upwards towards the citadel. Vortigern drew rein. 'What did Iustig tell you at the wedding?' he asked.

'That he held Rufus's mother in great affection,' Kerin said. 'That he was there on the night she died, and that he probably said more than he should have done at her burial.'

'There was more to it than that, surely,' Vortigern said.

'Yes,' Kerin said. 'But I was a little child then, lord. It's not my place to judge how it stood between you and Rufus's mother, even if Iustig thinks it's his.'

Vortigern's fingers knotted in the horse's mane. 'It's not his place,' he said. 'And I'm a better judge of it than Iustig will ever be.' He whipped his horse's head around and rode away up the track. Kerin followed, as quickly as the weary pony would go. He knew that there were things to be settled, but for now all he wanted was the safe dark womb of his familiar house, and the uncritical warmth of his wife's arms.

*

The following morning Gael sat on the bench outside the house, hands folded on her swelling belly, and stared disconsolately at the horse pen. Seren arched his beautiful black neck and stared back, as if beseeching her to jump back in the saddle. Kerin came out of the house with two mugs full of Morvid's soothing lime-blossom brew and sat down beside his wife.

'You are not riding that horse,' he said. Gael grimaced.

'I'm not,' she said, then allowed herself a wistful smile. 'It's tempting, though.' She peered into Kerin's mug. 'Why are you drinking this stuff, anyway? You're not with child, are you?'

'If I am, you can take me to the market in Leucarum and exhibit me in a cage,' Kerin said. Gael snorted and dug him in the ribs; then her hand closed over his, her eyes grave.

'I went to the wise woman yesterday. Mora's sister, Anwen. She thinks the child could come before the turn of the year. So perhaps it was conceived in my father's house, not in our warm, comfortable marriage bed, as I thought. I knew I was late, but it happens sometimes, when a woman's worried to death and not eating much.'

'My god,' Kerin said. The possibility had not even occurred to him. Shock became consternation as he thought of the miles they had ridden together, galloping heedlessly over sand and mountain, and worse – far worse – the near frenzy of their lovemaking in those first abandoned days. 'Can we have damaged it?' he asked fearfully. Gael smiled and kissed his cheek.

'Very unlikely. And anyway, Anwen may not be as wise as Mora thinks, if she managed to bear a son like Dull Bened.' Kerin put his arm around her shoulders and she nestled into him. He sat, watching the horses pulling contentedly at their nets of hay, and thought about the plan which had been forming in his mind since the moment he understood, without question, that the man he had loved since they were both little children would be prepared to burn him and his wife out of their house if he needed to. 'What?' Gael asked.

'I didn't speak,' Kerin said.

'You didn't need to speak,' Gael said. She slipped from his embrace and sat up, facing him. Kerin wondered what silent, invisible current had flowed from him, enabling her to comprehend with such certainty the enormity of what he was contemplating.

'The things I told you yesterday,' he said. 'About Rufus and his intentions.'

'About attacking us as soon as he has the forces, unless Vortigern renounces the kingship and puts Rowenna away,' Gael said. 'And of course the assassination party which he says he will prevent. I don't believe that for a minute.'

'All that,' Kerin said, taking her hands in his. 'But I haven't told you about something Publius Luca said to me on our way back from the North. He told me that one day I might find myself in command of Vortigern's army, because if it ever had to face Rufus, Vortigern might not lead it. I find that hard to believe, but I have to prepare for it. Mending things with Gallus was just the first step. I'm going to write to a few good men who will support us. And the first will be Brianus, the owner of the villa in the North where Marc found Catula. He's sure to have warriors to call on, and to know other men who do. I'll tell Vortigern about the letters, but not the rest. What on earth would I say? That I'm a better leader? That I have more courage? I'll never be his equal in either of those things. But that's not what Publius meant. What can I call it? A failure of the will? I don't know. Even Publius didn't know what to call it.'

He felt Gael's fingers tighten around his. She had been staring down at their joined hands, but now she looked up, her eyes bright with unshed tears.

'Kerin, I love Vortigern as you have come to love Rowenna. As the dearest of true, brave friends. He is one of the strongest men I have known. But if that strength breaks, everything will fall to you.'

'I know,' Kerin said, drawing her close. 'I know.' He realised that, in the truest sense, her distress was for him. A latch clicked somewhere. Ashur came from the stables and gave them a smile. He had entirely lost the hunted look which he had worn like a badge of shame in Londinium.

'Come here, Ashur,' Gael said. 'I want you to ride my black horse.'

The boy's eyes widened. 'He is beautiful. You trust me with him?'

'Of course. The horses love you, and you're a wonderful rider. Lord Kerin will get you his saddle and bridle.'

Seren stood patiently while Ashur ran hands over each of his legs in turn, then picked up each foot, pausing to hook a stone out of one of the stallion's forefeet with a little metal pick which he kept fastened to his belt. Kerin had noticed that he did this every time he dealt with a horse, unlike Marc, who usually took off without a second thought unless reminded.

'You've been well taught,' he said.

'Yes, lord. My father trains horses for the big men and the soldiers. If he thinks I go out without looking first at the legs, there is much hell.'

Kerin grinned. 'And here?' he asked. 'Is there much hell here?'

Ashur straightened up. 'No, lord. This is a good place. I miss very much my family. But everything else is good. The Lord King is a good master. He lets me ride all of his horses except for the warhorses, I make friends here, and Dimos teaches me Latin. All is good.'

Kerin brought Seren's tack and slipped the bridle over his head while Ashur placed the saddle, speaking gently to the horse as he tightened the girth.

'How's the white one?' Kerin asked. 'Alberius's horse?'

'He is my horse now, lord. The horse loves me, he is quiet for me, even without the papaver. The Lord King sees this, and he says, Ashur, this is your horse now. The horse has decided, so it must be. Now you will train this horse as your father does, because I want to see what is different, and what is better or worse.' Ashur sprang lightly onto Seren's back. 'So now I begin to train the white horse. Already he will take the bridle and the saddle. Next I must find something for the *katàphraktos*. I am sorry, I know only the Greek, one day I will show.' He smiled, clicked to the horse and trotted off out of the citadel.

29

Kerin rarely went up to the platform which ran along the inside of the stockade; high enough for protection, low enough for a man of average height to lean on his arms and look out over the valley and the sea. It was a defensive position, and he had never had to consider defending Henfelin; but it was a good place to go for peace and quiet, where a man could think things through unobserved except by the lookout on the watchtower nearby. He closed his eyes and took a deep breath of the salty air. Gallus's ship. Brianus's letter. And then, he thought, I will send for Elir, and have him make a list of all the able horses we can call on. Horses, men – and weapons. He realised, with a sinking heart, that he had never had more than a friendly, light-hearted conversation with Gwydion the blacksmith, except when complimenting him on a fine sword or spearhead. It was the chief warrior's responsibility to deal with Gwydion, ordering him and his team to produce enough weapons to maintain the Cambrian army's stock. Kerin doubted if it had been done. Lud remained chief warrior in his eyes, but something had happened to Lud. The stairway creaked. Vortigern came and leaned beside him.

'Gallus has gone, then' Kerin said, looking down at the deserted beach.

'Not to Londinium,' Vortigern said. 'Over to Tintagel with goods for Gorlois. And he was picking up Kernow ore for a buyer in Bononia, so he might bring news from Gallia.'

'I haven't been up here in ages,' Kerin said. 'But I needed to think.'

'About what Rufus might do?'

'Yes. And about what we must do, to stop him. I'm going to write to Brianus. Later, to other good men who will probably support us. And we should count our horses. I'll send Elir north and west; you and I already know what's around here.' He paused. 'I'd begun to consider weapons. I know it's Lud's preserve, but Lud isn't himself. I don't think it's anything to do with Custennin.'

'I'd say that he's chosen not to think about Custennin,' Vortigern said. 'It's not something you'd want to dwell on as a man, let alone a father. He blames himself for it. For not spotting that bestial streak early enough. I've told him he's wasting his time. If a man has that in him, you can't eradicate it. And you were right about the weapons. He hasn't given it a thought. I spoke to Gwydion and his brother myself, weeks ago. They know what they have to do, but we'll need more good metal-workers. And I can't tell Lud that he's no longer chief warrior. He stuck by me through everything, all those years ago. It's your place, in all but name. But I can't take the title from Lud.'

'I wouldn't want you to,' Kerin said. 'But I might have some ideas about metal-workers. After meeting Rufus, I went to Malan's village. They started talking about Edryd, the smith from Calleva. He's in Glevum, working on something. And almost in the same breath, Berget's husband Runo said that if Rufus comes after you, the ordinary men in Glevum will rise up and fight him. I asked Runo to find Edryd and send him here. He's one of the best metal-workers I've come across. And Berget has set lookouts in every village back to Corinium.'

'Then we have to leave them there for as long as we can,'
Vortigern said. 'But they'll need to be vigilant. Ready to
move. Look what we're dealing with.'

'Yes,' Kerin said, and paused. 'There's something I should
tell you. Or ask you, rather. When we stopped at their village
on the way home from the North, I spoke to Berget. You
know that Eldof's men threatened to hang her if she let us
pass without sending word to Glevum. I told her – and I
know I had no right – that you'd set aside a place for the
whole village to settle, which was magnificently better than
the one they have now. As a reward for all they've done. I
told her not to tell her father or anyone else, because you
wanted to do it yourself. Of course, what I really needed
was the right moment to tell you. Or ask you. I'm not sure
which it is, to be truthful, and there'll probably never be a
right moment, but there it is.'

There was a silence. 'The whole village,' Vortigern said.

'Yes,' Kerin said. 'Around a hundred people, I believe.'

'Perhaps we should put them in your house with the
others,' Vortigern said. Kerin threw his hands up.

'Look – ' he began.

'The last time you made a decision on my behalf, I acquired a standard-bearer,' Vortigern said. 'That turned out
well enough. And I should have thought of this at the time.
It's easily done. But I was more concerned about getting
your woman out of Glevum.'

Kerin grinned as relief enveloped him. It felt like slip-
ping into a warm bath. 'That turned out well enough, too,'
he said. 'But I had to watch my step in the bishop's house.
They've nailed a big sign up over the gate. *Ne hic intrant
malefici.*'

Vortigern snorted with laughter, then turned, his face
anguished. 'It's a damning thing, raising arms against your
own son. I hope to God that Gael bears you a daughter.'

Kerin smiled. 'If she does, and she grows up like her mother, she'll be the one raising arms,' he said; lightly, to ease Vortigern's distress, but the levity couldn't last. 'Lord, it's a choice,' he said. 'It was forced on me in the North. You or Rufus. I didn't even have to think, it just happened. But I've thought about it since. I see a balance, like Marcellus has for measuring remedies. On one side Rufus, on the other side ourselves and our wives. When I think of it like that, there's no choice at all. It still breaks my heart. But that won't stop me doing whatever I have to do, to protect us and this place.'

Vortigern gripped him tightly by the shoulders, as if for once he needed to draw on the strength Kerin was finding in himself. 'We should send a man with Elir,' he said. 'We need to assess men as well as horses. I'll ask Gwyndaf. He commands respect in a rare way, and he's a good judge of warriors. Can your lad Marc write yet?'

'Hardly,' Kerin said. 'You want a written record?'

'Yes. I'll send Ashur. Send Marc along too. He's a decent lad, but he's getting above himself. And a few hundred miles in Gwyndaf's company is enough to adjust anyone's expectations.' He made for the stairway and Kerin followed. 'When they come back, we'll call a meeting of leading men. They all know what's coming, but they need to prepare.'

They had reached the door of the chieftains' hall. Kerin took a breath. It was astonishing to him – unnerving, even – that Vortigern was able to recover as quickly as he seemed to have done from the debacle at Mabli's wedding. In a way, he would have preferred the process to take a little longer. It would have seemed more natural. But since time was of the essence, and there was a long, wide river to defend, he decided to seize the moment.

'There's something you should see,' he said. 'Send for Caradog. We can't go into the Druids' Wood without him.'

Vortigern looked bemused. 'The Druids' Wood? There's nothing there but trees and holy ashes.'

'No,' Kerin said. 'There's something there you should see.' He looked round as Cenydd came out of the chieftains' hall. 'Cenydd, will you go to Cynfawr's house, and see if the archdruid is there? If he is, please ask, very politely, if he'll take me and the Lord to see the thing he keeps in his cave.'

Cenydd shrugged, looking blank, and went on his way.

'You're drunk,' Vortigern said. 'At this time of day.'

<h1 style="text-align:center">30</h1>

Kerin had covered his ears this time. He slowly removed his hands as the sound subsided, its echoes spreading away down the unlit passage into the dark heart of the hill. Cynan lowered the mouthpiece to the floor, slid it away from him and turned the head of the carnyx so that they were face to face. Smiling, he caressed the ears and replaced the instrument gently in its stone cradle. Vortigern, who had stood mesmerised, opened his eyes.

'Mother of God,' he said. 'How old is it?'

'As old as our ancestors, lord,' said Cynan. 'The last time it spoke outside these walls, they were fighting the Romans at the river.'

'Come,' Caradog said. 'You can't linger in here. Come outside, and we'll speak of it.'

They all followed him out and sat down around a fire at the foot of the crag with Cynan's father, Cynfawr. The young men and women who had laid the fire withdrew respectfully, leaving behind a cauldron and some mugs.

'I know of these things,' Vortigern said. 'But only in the way that a man knows of Julius Caesar, or Hector of Troy. The Roman historians wrote about them. And there was a sculpture on the wall of a house in Isca where I used to go with my father. Looted, probably. There were spearmen, and several – what are they called? Carnyces?'

'Yes, lord,' Cynfawr said. 'Some men say it's a Greek

name, but most agree that it's borrowed from some other tongue, too old or strange for us to bring to mind. It's the sound that counts, though, surely.'

'Yes. I've been fighting for my life since I was fourteen years old, and I've never heard anything like that.'

'Did it frighten the legions?' Kerin asked.

'Frightened the daylights out of them,' Caradog said thirstily.

'Until they understood what it was, of course,' Cynan said. 'Then they crossed the river with fire and slaughter and robbed us of our homeland. But bear in mind, Lord King, this carnyx has slept for more than three hundred years. Warriors hearing this sound today will have no idea what is making it. We of the priesthood have made studies, and as far as we can ascertain, the roar of these things has not been heard in our islands since then.'

Caradog took the mugs, dipped them one by one into the steaming cauldron and passed them round. 'There were carnyces in Gallia too. Silenced long ago, probably, but our knowledge does not stretch that far.'

'I could ask my friend, Publius Luca,' Vortigern said. 'He's fought all over the Empire, from his youth. And we've spent hours getting drunk and talking about battles. I can't believe that anyone who had heard or seen a carnyx wouldn't have mentioned it.'

'Write to him,' Kerin said. 'Send the letter with the praetor's messengers.' He turned to Cynfawr. 'This is the only one you have?'

'It is,' the bard said. 'Our family only ever possessed the one.'

'Would you know how to make one? You made the dragon shriek.'

Cynfawr smiled. 'I did. But that was simply a matter of

placing wind flutes beneath his head. The carnyx is quite different. If you go back and look closely – don't worry, it won't bite – you will see that it has a moving jaw, and a wooden tongue. The tongue and the mouthpiece, we musicians know about. But the head, and that great bell of a mouth – that's a different skill. We could direct, Cynan and I, but we can't work in bronze or brass.'

'I know a man of great skill,' Kerin said. 'Thirty years old, perhaps. If he's willing, I think he could do this, with your consent. I can swear for his honesty. His skills would have excused him from battle in the North, but he chose to fight.'

'Then bring him,' Caradog said. He stood, and everyone else followed. Caradog limped over to Vortigern and seized him by the arms. 'I've already told Kerin that we of the old faith will stand with you if war comes. Not because your son is a Christian, but because he's an idiot who doesn't understand the harm he's doing. Can you beat the Saxons?'

Vortigern closed his eyes. 'Yes. But only if all the Britons are with me. Not if we waste time killing each other until Hengist's strong enough to come back.'

Caradog reached up, took Vortigern's head between his hands and drew it down. 'The spirits will protect you,' he said gently, kissing his brow. Even if it was said in hope as much as expectation, Kerin could hear the warmth in the archdruid's voice and feel the bone-deep conviction in his blessing. He stood quietly and let it enfold him, knowing that in the days to come they would need to take strength from wherever they could find it. 'And you too,' Caradog said, smiling at him. His hands slipped to Vortigern's shoulders. 'You still listen to him, I hope.'

'Yes,' Vortigern said. 'Most of the time.'

'Good. Don't forget what I told you, all those years ago.

You have a long way to go with this.' Vortigern nodded but did not reply. Caradog turned to Cynan. 'Cast the circle,' he said. 'Bring the sacred wood, and the herbs of power. And when the moon rises, bring the carnyx to the watch fire. Tonight we will bind it to the forces of the earth and the otherworld.'

He turned, his face glowing, as if the power he hoped to call down was coursing through him already. 'Go now,' he said. 'You have your work and we have ours.'

The two men walked down through the wood without speaking. It was hard to know what to say, after what they had seen and heard. They untied their horses from the willows on the riverbank and stood for a while, watching the sun dip westwards over the headland.

'Do you think it'll work?' Kerin asked. Vortigern looked round.

'Did it frighten you?'

'Yes. Even when it was standing there doing nothing.'

'Then it's possible, I suppose,' Vortigern said. 'And even if our enemies knew what it was, it might frighten their horses. We'd have to train ours to it, as we train them for battle. But for God's sake, Kerin. We can't stake men's lives on it. It'll be a rallying point, like the draco. I can't count on more than that.'

Kerin was only half listening. 'What did Caradog mean? About having a long way to go?'

'He was there,' Vortigern said. 'On the night I brought you down from the mountain. He thought it was meant in some way. That if I'd gone somewhere I had no reason or desire to go, if a blizzard had come from nowhere and driven me into a wood where I'd never been, it must have been the work of some power. Of the spirits he calls on. That they'd put you there for a reason.'

'And do you believe that?' Kerin asked.

'I don't know,' Vortigern said. 'I don't believe in the spirits. But we're still here, aren't we.'

'Yes.' Kerin said. 'We're still here.'

31

The breaking dawn cast a wash of pale light over the hills to the east. Gwyndaf, Elir and the boys were long gone. Vortigern's messengers waited outside the chieftains' hall; hard men with hard horses, and years' experience of travelling to obscure places in the back of beyond. At the table beside his hearth, very slowly and very painstakingly, Kerin added his signature to the letter which Dimos had written for him.

'There,' he said, handing it over. 'Read it back to me, in British. I want to be sure.'

The scribe took the letter and read in his clear, expressive voice.

'Friend Brianus,

We have not met, but I must call you friend, because I know that you are a loyal supporter of Vortigern the High King, whose servant I am until death. I know that you consider yourself in his debt, for saving the North from bloodshed and destruction. I was told by another loyal man, who was there when Eldof of Glevum and his company abused your hospitality and announced their treachery. Know that the king's son, Vortimer, is raising arms against his father and threatens to attack Cambria in the spring. If we fight each other, we will once again leave ourselves defenceless against invasion. I call on you, and all loyal men of the North, to stand with us. If we can count on you, I ask two things. Firstly, that you send word by return with the king's messengers. Secondly, that you share this message with all men whose loyalty and honour are beyond doubt. We do not seek battle, but if it comes to us against our will, we must be prepared. I await your reply with confidence.'

Dimos smiled. 'That's a good signature. Your hand improves by the day. And you have quite the turn of phrase. If I were this Brianus, I think I'd be sharpening my sword and giving my men a pep talk.' He laid the papyrus down on the table, reached for his satchel and drew out a small object wrapped in fine brown cloth. 'I took a liberty the other day, lord. When you gave me the horse, and sent me to the blacksmith to borrow a headcollar, I asked him to make this. I hope you approve of my design.' He removed the cloth, revealing a small round object made of solid brass. 'A stamp, as you can see. I thought it was time you had your own seal, as we seem destined to write a few letters together.'

Kerin picked up the stamp and stared at it. Never in his life had he imagined that he would have his own seal. Until very recently, he would not even have predicted that he would be able to master reading or writing. Now, here in his hand, was the proof that his goal was within reach; but it was more than that. It felt like an affirmation of all he had achieved, of the power he now possessed, and – as touching as it was unexpected – of the affection and esteem in which Dimos now held him. Taken together, these things moved him so profoundly that his eyes filled with tears. Dimos smiled.

'It's just a seal, lord,' he said gently.

'No,' Kerin said, recovering himself. 'It's much more than that. You must let me repay whatever you paid Gwydion.'

'Don't even think about it,' Dimos said. 'You gave me a horse, in case you've forgotten. And the chance of a new life. I've no idea what will come of it, but I know quite well what would have happened if I'd stayed in Londinium. I'd have wasted the rest of my days sitting around writing letters for men with more money than sense, until I was an ancient with crippled hands and failing eyesight. Anything must be better than that.'

Kerin laughed. 'Even living on top of a cliff in Cambria.' He turned the seal around in his fingers, examining Dimos's design – it was back to front, of course, so that its reverse would appear when applied to the sealing wax. The initials K and H, and between them a slender spearhead. 'It's good,' he said. 'Very good. Now let's seal Brianus's letter, and send it on its way.'

Dimos rolled up the papyrus. He had the wax ready in a tiny pan with a bound handle, set over a squat candle. 'I'll do the first one,' he said. 'It's not difficult, but you might like to practise on something unimportant. Just apply a little pool of wax, like so, and press the seal down firmly. There. Nothing to it, really. Just wait until it's set, then you can slip it into the messengers' bag. I'll take the seal to your kitchen and clean it up. I can smell food, I think, so I expect your cook will have some hot water.'

'Come back this evening,' Kerin said.

'To write the other letters?' Dimos asked.

'No. They can wait. Come and eat with me and my wife, and the rest of our household. One Saxon cook, one aged healer and a child who isn't ours. A Greco-Roman scribe should fit in nicely.'

Now it was Dimos's turn to be moved. 'You're a good man, Kerin Brightspear,' he said. 'And your head's older than the rest of you. The king is lucky, and so am I.'

*

There was a knock at Kerin's door. 'You've got a visitor,' said Lud. 'Gwynfi found him wandering around up by the mill.'

Edryd flung off his dusty travelling cloak and stretched. 'Thank the gods that's over,' he said. 'Runo Whitestreak gave me good directions, but it's still a long way from Glevum.'

Kerin laughed. 'Whitestreak! Runo would like that.'

'Well!' Gael said, rising from the table by the fireside. 'You must be Edryd the smith. We've been expecting you.'

'I'm honoured, my lady,' Edryd said. 'But how did you know it was me?'

'Kerin told me that you had the mightiest arms he'd ever seen,' Gael said merrily. 'I've never seen arms like that in my life. And don't be honoured, just be welcome. Come on, sit down here, and I'll tell our cook to bring you something to eat.'

She went off to the kitchen. 'What a lovely girl,' Edryd said. 'You're lucky, lord. And to save you the trouble of telling me I'm an idiot, I've washed my hands of Flora. Even if she turns up here, I won't be running after her.'

'Malan told me she'd been seen on the wharf in Glevum,' Kerin said, sitting beside him.

'Yes, they think she got on one of the ships. We might never see her again.'

And that might be best for all concerned, Kerin thought, smiling as Gael came back carrying a split loaf packed with salt pork and a tankard of ale.

'There,' she said. 'Get that down you and you won't starve. And don't look at me like that, Kerin Brightspear. There's mutton stew coming later, as you know.' She winked and tripped off to the bedroom, still light on her feet despite her extra burden. The sound of her lyre came faintly through the closed door.

'How much did Runo tell you?' the smith asked.

'As much as you'd told him, I think. This work in Glevum. Is it anything to do with the smith you spoke about in the North?'

'He sent word to my father,' Edryd said. 'So that's where I've been since then. In his workshop, making swords and axes and spearheads, in case this Vortimer is mad enough to fight his father. Because if he is, I'm telling you now, us ordinary men will rise up like we did when Constans the monk was killed. Fuck the high-born. They can side with Eldof and Bertil, if they like, but they'll have to do it without the rest of us.'

Kerin stood up. 'Finish your food,' he said. 'Then come to the chieftains' hall. I want you to repeat everything you've just told me to the king.'

*

Rowenna's voice answered Kerin's knock. He opened the library door a crack and peered in. She was sitting on the couch by the fireside with Fanw, the deerhound.

'Kerin!' she said warmly. 'Come in, come in. He has gone to see your Dimos about something.'

'I have someone with me,' Kerin said. 'A friend who fought with us in the North. He's come to help us.'

'Then you'd better bring him in,' Vortigern's voice said at his shoulder. He could move as silently as a cat when he wanted to. The deerhound jumped off the couch, gave Vortigern a guilty look and slunk under the table.

'I will go now,' Rowenna said.

'Stay if you wish,' Vortigern said. 'There are no secrets from you in here.'

'I know that. But Gael expects me.' Rowenna smiled.

'We too have things to discuss.' She went out, closing the door behind her. The three men sat down at the table.

'Edryd the smith,' Vortigern said. 'Your eye is recovered, I hope.'

'It's fine now, Lord King. I'll probably always have this scar, but I can see straight. I'm surprised you even remembered about it, with all that bloodshed going on.'

'I have a good memory,' Vortigern said. 'I also remember that you chose to fight, when you could have stayed at the camp mending weapons. And now Kerin tells me that you're working something in Glevum.'

'Yes, Lord King. A friend sent to Calleva for me. His father's in the bishop's guards, so he gets to know what's going on. He and a bunch of other lads had already decided that if – ' Edryd hesitated, as if not sure how forthright he should be – 'that if Lord Vortimer makes war on you, they'll rise up like we did in Londinium. And you can't fight without weapons, so that's what we've been doing. Making swords and spears and axes. We've got a place where we bury them, wrapped up in waxed sheets against the rust. I'll make one for you if you like, Lord King. I'm sure you've got a trusty sword that you've used for years, but it's no bad thing to have a spare one.'

'No bad thing at all,' Vortigern said. 'And you're right. I've trusted the same sword for twenty years. But I trusted my oldest son, too, and we all know what happened there.' He went to the shelves where his books and manuscripts were stored and drew out a single slim sheet of papyrus. 'I had Cynfawr do this for me,' he said, passing the sheet to Kerin. The bard's drawing of the carnyx was remarkably clear and detailed.

'By all the gods,' Edryd said. 'What's that?'

'A carnyx,' Vortigern said. 'Have you heard of them?'

'Never. Does it do anything?'

'It makes a noise,' Kerin said. 'It can sing quite sweetly. The druids used it centuries ago to play music to their gods. But when it's played in anger, it's a war horn.'

Edryd ran a cautious finger up the slim neck and between the ears. 'I've never heard the name,' he said. 'But in Londinium, I once met a smith from Gallia. You'll find craftsmen there from all over the world. This lad came from a city the Romans called Lugdunum. We worked together on a bronze for one of the rich men. He was mad about hunting, and he wanted a plaque with a deer and a boar on it to decorate his dining room. Me and this lad, we didn't have much language in common, but he was trying to describe something the old men had told him about at home. A boar, like this one, but it had huge fancy ears like a butterfly's wings, and a big wide-open mouth with teeth in it.' He grinned. 'That's the Gallians for you, isn't it. The thing we made looked more like a normal boar, to be honest.' He studied the drawing closely. 'Bronze, I imagine. Do you have one?'

'Yes,' Vortigern said. 'Or at least, our druids and our chief bard have one, and they've been hiding it for years. Since their forefathers fought the Romans at the river, they tell me, so it must be three hundred years old if not more. But they've cared for it. The archdruid elect and his father, the bard, can both play it. But we have only the one.'

Edryd's eyes met Vortigern's. 'So, you want me to make one? Is that why I'm here?'

'Yes,' Kerin said. 'I've seen your brass work. Hefin showed me a beautiful belt buckle you made for him. Have you heard what happened in Kent?'

Edryd's jaw set hard. 'Hefin was a good man, doing his duty. They should have left him alone.'

'He rode with us for fifteen years,' Vortigern said. 'And now, probably, we must fight the men who hanged him.'

'Then show me this thing,' Edryd said. 'Once I've seen it, had it in my hands, I'll tell you if it's within my powers. Can we go now?'

'With the archdruid's permission,' Vortigern said. 'And we should take my silversmith, Cilydd. He's a craftsman of immense skill and imagination, but not a young man. I doubt if he has strength left in his hands to work a thing like the carnyx. All that said, he's served me faithfully since I was old enough to have a silversmith, and he must be asked.'

'Of course,' Edryd said. 'Nothing less would do. Can we go now?' He was on fire with impatience, as Kerin himself might have been if someone had offered to show him a well-bred warhorse. Perhaps it was necessary to be a metal-worker to get so excited over a lump of bronze, even if it was a carnyx. Vortigern went to the door and called Cenydd.

'Go to Cynfawr's house, and see if the archdruid is there,' he said. 'If he is, please ask if he'll be good enough to let us see the thing he keeps in his cave.'

Cenydd had heard this nonsensical request before. 'Of course, lord,' he said politely, and bowed, and went out.

32

Caradog and his acolytes had brought extra torches this time, to allow the metal-workers a better sight of the object they had come to see. He and Cynan, resigned to the fact that reverence must defer to the defence of the homeland, stood back with Cynfawr and allowed the two men to handle the carnyx and examine every detail of its construction.

'I think I can make one,' Edryd said. 'But I know nothing about instruments of music, so you three will have to guide me when it comes to shaping the parts which make the sound. And this wooden tongue, whatever that does.'

'I have woodworkers enough,' Vortigern said. 'Forge the metal, and the rest will come.'

Caradog leaned forward. 'Forty days with the hammer and the flame, master smith. Are you man enough for that?'

'I am. Must it be made here?'

'Yes,' Cynfawr said. 'If you make it in Cilydd's workshop, the world and his wife will know. That would rather defeat the object.'

'Very well. Will your smiths have the materials, Lord King? The copper and the calamine?'

'Yes,' Vortigern said. 'Gwydion can work in bronze and brass, but he's heavy-handed. Skilled, but not with this level of detail. That's the preserve of men like Cilydd.'

The silversmith bowed his head. The torchlight gleamed

on his balding crown, and in a pair of eyes wreathed in wrinkles from a lifetime's toiling over a bright flame. 'You're kind, lord,' he said. 'But it's beyond me now, to forge anything like this. When I get up in the morning, my hands are stiff as a corpse's. It's as much as I can do to clasp the bowl of gruel the girls bring me. I can still work pretty little things like Mabli's wedding necklace, but this great head –' he turned to Edryd. 'This work will fall to you. There's a bed in the lean-to next to my workshop. The lad I was training got killed in the North, so it's an empty bed now. You're welcome to it, and to any tools you need to borrow.'

'I'll see you right, Master Cilydd,' Edryd said, with delight. The silversmith patted his shoulder.

'I want nothing for it. Seeing the work come to life will be payment enough. But there's one thing you could do for me. I did make the head of the draco – it nearly killed me, but I did it – and if this new carnyx is to stand against our enemies, I want to play a part.' Cilydd's eyes shone. 'If it's all the same to you, then please, can I make the eyes, and some lovely ears?'

'Cilydd,' Edryd said, 'be my guest, as I am yours.'

*

Vortigern and Kerin loosed their horses and rode towards the citadel, leaving Edryd and Cilydd at the house beside the river. It seemed an eternity since the village had gathered there for Mabli's wedding. As they reached the citadel, a shout came from the watchtower.

'Riders, lord! Just passing the corn mill. The praetor's messengers.'

Mabon's cart was standing outside Kerin's house. Hitched to its tailboard was a dappled pony, Gwyndaf's wedding gift to Mabli. There was an ox cart Kerin didn't recognise, two thin bay hunting horses and a donkey with soft brown fur. Kerin could hear Gael's voice. She was speaking in the firm, no-nonsense tone he used himself when giving instructions to warriors. He strained his ears.

'God knows what they're doing,' Vortigern said. 'But whatever it is, I'd bet my warhorse that you won't be welcome, so come to the hall and see what the messengers have to say.'

The praetor's messengers sat at the table as Cenydd and his assistant brought bread, tankards of ale and platters of cold meat. The familiar senior man, a retired army officer, passed the leather bag to Vortigern.

'The usual missive from the praetor, Lord King,' he said. 'We'll bed down for the night, with your permission. We'd have been here hours ago, but when we got to Glevum we found that your son has men guarding the bridges.'

Vortigern looked nonplussed. 'Guarding the bridges? He has no right to guard the bridges.'

'Well, of course he hasn't, Lord King,' said the messenger, 'but that's what he's doing, and I didn't think it was any of his business to ask what we were carrying, so we rode north and crossed the river somewhere quieter.'

Vortigern got up, pale with anger, and grabbed the leather bag. 'Come on,' he said, nodding to Kerin. 'We need to see this.'

'There's a couple of other letters in there, lord,' the messenger said. 'One for you, from Publius Luca Imperator. And one for Lord Kerin's scribe, Dimos Bekuh.'

'My servant will see to your accommodation,' Vortigern said, tight-lipped, and marched out. Kerin followed him to the library. 'Guarding the bridges!' Vortigern said, and hurled the bag at the couch. 'Who the hell does he think he is?'

'Well, I suppose if enough people have told him he's king, then that's what he thinks he is,' Kerin said. He retrieved the bag and laid it on the polished table. Vortigern tore it open, steadied himself and drew out the three documents. He broke the seal on the praetor's letter and sat down to read it. Kerin waited.

'Garagon's army is camped at Sarum,' Vortigern said. 'Outside the walls, on the land running down towards the river. They must expect to be there for a while. They've built stables and dug latrines. Forges, grain storage, pens for beasts. A small contingent of Glevum warriors is there, training the Kentishmen and the new recruits. Bertil Redknife is in command. And the Sword of God has an encampment nearby. Idris and his idiot brother Aron are there.' He looked up. 'You probably don't know this, but Abbot Paulinus's order has a sister monastery at Ambrius, near the Giants' Ring. As you'd expect, Paulinus is at Sarum preaching hell and damnation. There are about three thousand men, well-armed, but not in a state of readiness. Everything we've heard about an attack in the spring is probably true. There's no sign of any reinforcements from Gallia.' He shrugged. 'Perhaps they'll never come. Perhaps Batraz doesn't have the capabilities Rufus gives him credit for.'

Kerin sat down. 'I can't believe that, lord,' he said. 'And don't discount what Rufus said about weapons we've never dreamed of. I brought it up when I went to Glevum, and he didn't deny it. He just gave me a funny look, and said he'd be a fool to tell me what they were.'

Vortigern pushed the letter away. 'Well, perhaps Gallus will be able to tell us when he comes back from Bononia.

Leave me now; I want to read Publius's letter in peace before I write to him and Valerius Dio. Here's your scribe's letter.' He held it out.

'Why were you looking for him earlier?' Kerin asked. Vortigern looked up with the suspicion of a smile.

'He's going to teach me Greek,' he said. 'I don't have enough to do, as you know.'

*

Darkness was gathering by the time Kerin returned to his house. Mabon's trap and the ox cart had gone, along with the rest of the animals. A pile of steaming dung remained, indicating a recent departure. Gael and Rowenna were sitting beside the fire. The table was littered with empty goblets. The place stank of wine and mulled cider. Kerin sat down beside the women.

'Have we opened an alehouse?' he asked.

'Women must drink when they talk,' Gael said.

'Women must drink when they please, as the men do,' Rowenna added.

'Is there any left?' Kerin asked.

'A bit of mulled cider,' Gael said, investigating her cauldron. Kerin fetched a goblet and helped himself.

'What's going in in here?' he asked.

'We're making something,' Gael said. 'When it's finished, you can see it.'

'Making something,' Kerin said. The first thing that came to his mind was the magnificent banner which the women of Henfelin had sewn for the draco, but somehow, that struck a false note. He had never seen his wife with a needle in her hand; she left the mending to Catula, and besides, the idea of intricate embroidery was something he

297

found impossible to associate with her. She rode horses. She sang and played the lyre. She could use a sword, and make good, hearty food from simple ingredients. Try as he might, Kerin couldn't imagine her, far less Rowenna, struggling with needlework. It had to be something else.

'I will go now,' Rowenna said, getting up without so much as a wobble.

'You'll probably find Vortigern in the library,' Kerin said. 'The praetor's messengers are here. He'll tell you what they said, I'm sure.' He reached for Gael's hand and drew her to him, and they sank down amongst the blankets on the hearth.

'Was there any terrible news?' Gael asked.

'Nothing unexpected,' Kerin said. 'Garagon's army has made a base at Sarum. Your father's there, training the Kentish warriors, and Abbot Paulinus has brought some of the religious. Vortigern was more upset to learn that Rufus is guarding the bridges at Glevum. He has no business to do it, of course, but the praetor's messengers decided to avoid the confrontation and cross the river further north.'

Gael turned to look at him. 'Why did Edryd come?' she asked. 'You haven't mentioned him since you told me about the rising. I'm sure he's come to help, but was there a particular reason?'

'Yes,' Kerin said. 'The smiths in Glevum are making weapons to arm themselves and their friends if there's an attack on Cambria. It must be kept quiet; there are men in Rufus's following who'd think nothing of murdering those boys if they found out. But for now, Edryd is staying here. Cilydd offered him a bed.' Kerin gave his wife a quizzical smile. 'He's making something, too.'

'Is it true that he's breaking his heart over some girl from Glevum?'

'Where did you hear that?' Kerin asked. Gael sighed.

'Do you think the women know nothing? One of Gwydion's lads got talking to Edryd in the North when they were mending weapons. It just spilled out, as these things do. And if Edryd is staying in Cilydd's house and they get drunk one night, everyone in the village will know the lot, because that house is the fount of all knowledge. I don't gossip myself, and I try not to listen to it, but Mabli and Macsen's Eleri can't keep quiet. They're good girls and I love them, but they could do with a stopper in the mouth sometimes. I know the girl is related to Malan, and that she spat in poor Edryd's face because she was in love with someone else.'

'With Vortigern, as it happens,' Kerin said. Gael sat up.

'Mother of Jesus,' she said. Kerin raised his hands.

'He has no idea,' he said. 'Before Constans became king, we went to Eldof's camp. Vortigern wanted to tell him about the monk before anyone else did. Malan and his people were there. Camp followers. The girl, Flora, is Malan's granddaughter. She was with him when we saved him from Brennan. She's a pretty girl, and Eldof took a fancy to her. It was obvious that she'd have to share his bed that night, whether she liked it or not. But Eldof got distracted, and Vortigern took the girl off somewhere. I didn't see them leave, and I don't know what happened. Very little, I suspect. I think he just wanted to get her out of Eldof's way, or even to spite Eldof – I don't know. But the girl couldn't let it go. She was there on the night Constans was killed. She had some mad plan to get him away from the city. Partly because she's a soft-hearted girl and was sorry for him, but more because she thought it would help Vortigern get the crown. Which it did, but it also came near to getting us all killed. I've never told Vortigern because

I couldn't see the point, but if the girl ever turns up here looking for him, at least you'll know what's going on. I'm glad you raised it. She's gone missing, according to Malan's family. Someone saw her on the wharf in Glevum, so she could be anywhere by now.'

Gael took Kerin's goblet and her own, and ladled into them the remains of the mulled cider. 'There's no reason why you should have mentioned it,' she said. 'We've had more than enough to talk about without this poor mad girl. But there is another thing we should get out of the way.' Kerin paused, the goblet halfway to his mouth. 'I know what Vortigern did to Macsen's brother,' Gael said. 'Macsen told Eleri after you got him out of Kent, and he might as well have shouted it from the watchtower. But he'd done it before, hadn't he. The brother had done it before.'

'Yes,' Kerin said, and swallowed the cider at one gulp. 'Twice before. To the same woman, in Londinium. A Phoenician slave called Faria. When we first arrived in the city with Constans, Severus Maximus let us stay in his house. That night, he sent slave girls to all of us. It's what these men do. Vortigern called it hospitality. Faria was sent to me. I was a young man. I didn't have anyone special. And here was this girl, offering herself to me. I accepted, of course. I don't know how these things work – no-one had ever sent a slave to me before. Whether it's commonplace for the same girl to go on serving the same man. I really don't know. But she did serve me, and no-one else, until I got hurt fighting the praetor's guards. I was in the slaves' quarters because I was looking for her. I hadn't seen her for a while, and it seemed odd. When I found her, she was cut and bruised from her face downwards. I don't want to describe it. Then the guards came, and I had to run for it. They'd have killed me if Cheldric hadn't thrown a pot of stew over them. You know the rest – Vortigern sent me home to get over the injury, and on the way back to Londinium, I met you in Morvid's valley. I knew that I couldn't look at another woman after that, so when I got back to the praetor's house, I sent for Faria to tell her so. She didn't come. She didn't come because the same animal had raped and beaten her again, and she'd killed herself with some medicine Marcellus *magister* gave to Severus Maximus. And then, when Garagon's sister was attacked in his own house in Durovernum, the moment I saw the girl, I knew that the same man had done it, because the injuries were the same. Just the same. God, do these bastards have a plan? I'd have killed Custennin there and then, but Eldof, Gwyndaf and Derfyn had hold of me. And then Vortigern did what he did. Partly because he had to stop our boys and the Kentishmen killing each other, but I think he'd have done it anyway. I should probably have told you, but I didn't know where to start.' He turned away. It had all been festering inside him for so long that he felt as if some dam had broken to let it out. Gael sighed and prised the goblet from his fingers. She took the corner of her shawl and dabbed his eyes.

'What difference would it have made? You didn't even know me when you were with that poor girl. And I'm glad you cared for her. Do you think I would have preferred you to treat her like most rich men treat their slaves? I'm glad it was like it was. And I expect she cared for you, too. She was probably expecting a man who'd use her like a dumb animal, but she got you. And you got her, when you were on your own in a big city. There was only going to be one result, wasn't there?'

'Yes,' Kerin said. 'And I don't deserve you.'

'I'll be the judge of that,' Gael said, reaching for his hands. 'Now take me to bed, and I'll show you what I mean.'

33

The *Audax* rode at anchor in the calm bay, low in the water, her hold loaded with whatever Gallus had come to tell them about.

'Ore!' he said, with a wide smile. 'A gift from Gorlois. I know you have your own, but Kernow's renowned for it, and Gorlois insisted. His smelters are working day and night. "We can't make weapons without metal, master merchant," he said, "and whoever we're fighting, we'll need a sword to stick them with." So here I am, with a ship full of ore. Where can we unload?'

'That depends,' Vortigern said. 'We ship from Isca and unload at the Roman wharf in Leucarum, but the ships are half the size of yours.'

'Isca's deep enough, though?' Gallus asked. 'I'm told it's the finest port in these islands, apart from Londinium.'

'Yes. Isca's deep enough.'

'You should see it,' Lud chimed in. 'I'm not the man to give the Romans credit for much, but they could build a port, alright. Big, solid wharves where transports can line up alongside the ships. I used to go down there to watch when I was a lad.' He dug Vortigern in the arm. 'Just a stone's throw from your father's house, wasn't it.'

'Yes,' Vortigern said. 'It was. Or is. I don't suppose the house has moved.'

Kerin, sitting across the table from Vortigern, met his

eyes. Gallus could not possibly have known what sensitive ground he was treading, but Lud should have known; must have known. He had been there, seen it all, lived through the aftermath. Or perhaps he had simply found a way not to think about those times, as he had with the maiming of his second son. Perhaps the consequences had washed over him unnoticed, even though they were sitting here at the table in the chieftains' hall, staring Kerin in the face. Lud helped himself from the pitcher of ale, as relaxed as if they had been discussing the price of cattle.

'What of Bononia?' Kerin asked. 'Is anything happening there?'

'Nothing of interest,' Gallus said. 'Just the usual merchant vessels, carrying harmless things like wool and corn. You were right about Rufus's allies, they did disembark there, but they didn't hang around. The men and horses marched off, the ships left and that was that.' He shrugged. 'We delivered Gorlois's ore – not to an arms dealer, I'd have dumped it in the sea – just an old acquaintance of his who makes pots and pans. Then we picked up a pretty horse Gorlois had bought, took it back to Tintagel and here we are. I should go home, but I want to explore your channel first. I've never sailed these waters. And I had a thought, when I was in Bononia. If you need to send forces to Kent, I could ship them from Isca. You can't drink anywhere in Londinium without hearing about the fucking miracle of the forced march, but I don't suppose you want another one, do you?'

'My arse took a month to recover from the last one,' Kerin said. 'Could you put us ashore somewhere east of Dubris?'

'Lemanis,' Gallus said. 'It's a magnificent harbour.'

'Of course. Publius Luca took us there after he saved our necks.'

Gallus's eyes glowed as he warmed to his plan. 'Most of my ships are the same size as the *Audax*, and she can carry two thousand amphorae,' he said. 'Two hundred horses and saddlery in terms of weight, but you can't pack them in like you could grain or olive oil. I have bigger ships, but they're slower. We could still load a strike force on the smaller ships, though. Fifty mounted warriors and their weapons, turning up where the enemy wouldn't expect them. It could be a killer blow!' He broke off, breathless with excitement. Vortigern smiled.

'Slow down,' he said. 'I have to think about this. All the possible configurations of mounted warriors and foot soldiers. And none of our horses has ever set foot on a ship.'

'They'd never stick it,' Lud said. 'Loading them would be hard enough, never mind what might happen if the sea got rough.'

'Well, don't discount it,' Gallus said. He looked beseechingly at Vortigern. 'Please, give it some thought. At least sail to Isca with me, when we go to unload the ore. I can assess the landing stages, and the overseers will fall over themselves to give you whatever you want.'

There was a brief pause. 'As I told you,' Vortigern said. 'I have to think about it.' Gallus was silent, as if he had detected some vague undercurrent which he couldn't understand.

'There's one other thing,' he said. 'As well as the ore, Gorlois has sent a big ingot of his finest bronze, ready for working. I've seen it, and the quality is exceptional. We could bring that ashore here, if you have a use for it.'

Kerin and Vortigern shared a complicit smile. 'Bring it in,' Vortigern said. 'Then come back here and scrub the sea off before we eat.' He turned to his chief warrior as Gallus went out. 'Go down to Cilydd's workshop and see if he and Edryd are there. If they are, tell them to meet Gallus's lighter on the beach. If they're not, get a wagon and bring the ingot back here. The other smiths aren't to touch it.'

'Why not?' Lud said blankly. 'It's an ingot.'

'Because I said not,' Vortigern said, his eyes gleaming dangerously. Lud shrugged.

'Horses on a boat,' he muttered under his breath, as he went out. Kerin poured the remainder of the ale.

'You do not have to do this,' he said.

'Yes, I do,' Vortigern said. 'After all Gallus has done, there's no possible excuse I can make for not going to Isca with him. And perhaps it's overdue. What's going to happen? Is the ghost of Quintus Parvo going to leap from the ruins and chain me to the floor?'

'Nothing's going to happen,' Kerin said. 'Ever again. I'll see to that.'

Vortigern looked up. 'Go and fetch Gael,' he said. 'The women can eat with us. They're the one saving grace to have come to us out of this mess.'

*

It was the song they had first heard on a sunlit evening in Hengist's village, before Rowenna was even a name, when she was just one of a crowd of girls laughing beside the lagoon where her father's fleet lay. Kerin remembered it vaguely, but Vortigern knew it note for note. And now here it was in British, sung by two voices, with a lilting lyre accompaniment which rose and fell like gentle waves.

Hear this my prayer, god of sky and sea,
Watch over him, till he comes home to me;
Stretch out your hands of power if his courage fails,
And bless the wind, oh bless the wind,
Lord bless the wind that fills his sails.

A final falling cadence of the lyre, then silence, broken only by the crackling of the fire. Gael and Rowenna smiled and hugged each other. Gallus, who had listened entranced, broke into applause. He raised a goblet to the women. 'That was a thing of surpassing beauty,' he said. And then, to Kerin and Vortigern, 'Where on earth did you find them?'

Vortigern shrugged. 'They found us,' he said.

'Drawn by our irresistible charms,' Kerin said, then burst out laughing. 'No. To be truthful, it was dumb luck, at least on my part. She just happened to be there when I was having a fight.'

'And I was the cup bearer at my father's feast,' Rowenna said. 'But then I saw this man here, and I thought, Ha! The King of all the Britons! If I can trap him, I will live for the rest of my life in a beautiful house with fountains and peacocks and heating under the floor.'

The women fell around laughing. Vortigern sighed, smiling, and replenished the goblets. Kerin thought that Gallus, if anything, looked a little envious. There was a knock at the door. Cenydd opened it a crack and peered in. 'Lord, Mora is here for the ladies,' he said. 'I believe they've brought Tirion to the wise women.'

'Oh, God!' Gael exclaimed. She and Rowenna got up hurriedly and followed Cenydd out. Mora's voice could be heard in the dining hall. Kerin thought that she sounded excited rather than concerned. He hoped that he was right, for everyone's sake.

'A warrior's wife?' Gallus asked.

'Yes,' Vortigern said. 'The widow of Hefin, who was hanged in Kent. She fell pregnant before we left for the North. She lost her first child years ago, and they didn't expect to be blessed with another. Hefin had been in my personal warband for fifteen years. It was obvious that he might get killed in battle, but warriors and their wives are used to that possibility, they accept it. I suppose it's the same for you, if men die at sea for some reason.'

'Of course,' Gallus said. 'The sea is dangerous. Everyone who signs on knows that he might not come back.'

'This was different, though,' Vortigern said. 'It wasn't a battle. I sent Hefin and Macsen to Kent with Oswi, to prove that the Jutes' land had been granted in good faith. I chose them because they were two of my best, and Hefin did the most good, because he was more level-headed than Macsen. But if I hadn't married Hengist's daughter, there wouldn't have been a land grant, and I wouldn't have had to send them. So it's entirely my doing that Hefin got hanged, and that Tirion is about to give birth to a fatherless child.'

'For God's sake!' Kerin exclaimed. 'If it's anyone's fault, apart from the bastards who did it, it's Rufus's for not being able to stop them. Or for standing back and letting them do it. But either way, capturing Macsen and Hefin was a ploy to get us out of Cambria and kill us. And don't forget for one moment that they only caught our boys because they deceived them. They'd have hanged Lucius too, if Oswi hadn't saved him.' He broke off, feeling a hand grip his arm.

'Save your rage,' Gallus said. 'Rage is like wine. Store it for a while, and it gets stronger. You'll have a use for it soon enough.' He reached into a leather bag he had stowed under the table and brought out an ornate little amphora. Three small silver cups followed.

'What's that?' Kerin asked. He was learning to harness his temper, but it could still catch him off guard now and again.

'Strong medicine for stupid men with consciences,' Gallus said. He filled up the cups and handed one to Vortigern. 'Go on, get it down. It's stronger than normal wine. I picked it up in Lusitania a few years ago. Made by monks, I'm told. I thought they were supposed to live in purity and deprivation, but not in Lusitania, apparently.'

The liquor was deep red and sweet, not quite a syrup, but heavier than a *fundanum*. Even after a great platter of roast beef, Kerin could feel its subtle influence begin to tiptoe towards his brain as the slow warmth spread from mouth to throat to belly. Two cups and it'll start to undermine my better judgment, he thought. Four cups and I'm a dead man. 'What's it called?' he asked.

'No idea,' Gallus said, 'but I bought it in a beautiful little port called Lacobriga, right down on the southern coast. Two cups and even my wife's ready to go to bed with me.'

They all laughed, then the door opened and Rowenna came in. There was blood on her sleeve, but her face was joyous.

'Tirion has a son,' she said. 'She is crying, but they are both well. Gael has stayed, but I will go to your house, Kerin, and fetch them some of Morvid's lime blossom drink. I don't think Tirion will want the men just now, but she asked me to tell you that all is well.' She blew them a kiss and went out.

'Thank God for that,' Kerin said. Gallus topped up the cups.

'Tirion,' Vortigern said, as they raised them in a toast. 'And may the child grow up in a time of peace.' The three men exchanged wry smiles. Not one of them had a shred of faith in that possibility; but it was good to know that, for Tirion at least, a small candle had been lit in the darkness. After they had sat for a while, savouring the liquor and enjoying the relief which Rowenna's news brought, Kerin noticed that Gallus was looking unusually pensive.

'Is something troubling you?' he asked. Gallus shook his head.

'It's probably nothing.'

'All the same?' Vortigern said. Gallus poured the last of the liquor.

'When I was in Bononia, I met up with the owner of the warehouse I've rented,' he said. 'We've known each other since we were youngsters. We had a jar together and talked about old times, ships and trade – the usual things. And then, just in passing, he mentioned that he'd seen an *oneraria*. Do you know what that is?'

'A ship of some sort?' Vortigern asked.

'Yes. The largest freighter the Romans ever built. I've only ever seen two, years ago in Ostia, unloading grain from Alexandria. I thought I was the big man with my own ship and crew, but next to one of those, the *Audax* looks like a rowing boat. They can carry up to forty thousand amphorae – around ten times more than any of the ships sailing out of Londinium. And just a few weeks ago, there was one in Bononia. Or outside Bononia, rather. It didn't try to dock, it just lay off the harbour mouth and sent a couple of lighters in for supplies. Nothing unusual – just some salt meat and fresh drinking water, enough to provision the ship's crew. They paid in denarii and off they went.' Gallus shrugged. 'And that's all, really. My friend was curious because you simply don't see those ships around there, but he didn't think it was anything to worry about. And it was empty, anyway. He could tell that from the way it was sitting in the water.'

'Do you know where it went?' Kerin asked.

'No idea,' Gallus said. 'Not Kent; I've got a man in Dubris. As I said, it's probably nothing.' He knocked back the rest of his liquor and got up. 'I'm for my bed, anyway. I have to sail a ship in the morning. You two can sleep all the way to Isca if you want to.'

Kerin pushed his cup away as Gallus tramped off along

the passage, humming the insidious melody of the women's song. He knew that there was often choppy water out in the channel, and he wasn't at all sure of his sea legs.

'Do you think it's nothing?' Vortigern asked.

'I don't know,' Kerin said. 'I'm ignorant about shipping. Gallus ought to know, I suppose. Although when people say, "it's probably nothing", it usually isn't.'

Vortigern took Kerin's cup and drained it. 'Leave me now,' he said. 'And get some sleep. I want you awake in Isca.'

34

The morning sky was clear, but the wind was keen; a chilly north-westerly. Kerin supposed that that was a good thing. Flinging on a heavy cloak, he walked out to the open hillside for a good view of the beach. Oswi the Horseman could be seen on the deck of the *Audax*, calmly directing his crew as they prepared to leave. A lighter had come in on the rising tide to await its passengers. Rowenna was standing at the edge of the drop to the valley. Hearing Kerin approach, she went to him and placed her hands on his shoulders.

'I know everything,' she said. 'But he will not take me. Do not leave him.'

'I won't,' Kerin said. 'But you needn't worry. Nothing will happen. I'll be there, and anyway, all the men who caused the trouble are dead and buried.'

'I know,' Rowenna said. 'But that is not where the trouble is.'

'No,' Kerin conceded, and gently kissed her brow. 'How is Tirion this morning?'

'She is well,' Rowenna said, smiling. 'Mother and child are both well. And the boy has a loud voice! I think he will be strong and brave, like his mother and father. Tirion has called him Hedd.'

'That means 'peace' in our language,' Kerin said, in Saxon.

'Then she lives in hope,' Rowenna said. 'Is Gael sleeping?

She looked tired last night, but she would not leave until Tirion and the child were settled.'

'She's sleeping,' Kerin said. 'I'll have to wake her to say goodbye, but with any luck she'll go back to sleep. And whatever this thing is that you're doing together, don't let her wear herself out with it.'

'I will not,' Rowenna said, and kissed his cheek. 'And you should not worry too much. As she will tell you, she is with child, not with some great sickness. I know that things can go wrong, as they did with poor Sevira. But most of the time they do not. You should try to think of other things, as women have to do when men go off to do dangerous things.'

*

The ship moved slowly upriver, the rising tide and keen wind more than a match for the sluggish current. Vortigern was standing at the prow, immaculate, regal. Kerin had not seen these clothes before. Black, as always, but this time the cloak had a crimson lining, visible when the breeze caught it. And here too was the simple silver crown, making one of its few appearances since the night Father Giraldus placed it on Vortigern's head in the chapel of St Alban. Plainly, having decided to make the journey, the king wished his presence to be noticed. Ahead and to the left Kerin could see the buildings of the Roman city, their stark outlines softened by a sunlit haze.

'The last time I came here was the day I married Rufus's mother,' Vortigern said. 'It was a transaction, as you know. There was no coercion; I was free to take it or leave it. But having decided to take it, I had no say in the arrangements. When Maximus was killed, his children became wards of the Empire. Rome still had a toehold in Isca, and everything was arranged by the governorate. Sevira had no choice in the matter. She was shipped over from Hispania like a commodity. Someone in her household had told her that I was a monster, so she was terrified of me.'

'How did you deal with that?' Kerin asked.

'By leaving her alone. When we got home, I had the servants take her belongings to my bedchamber. A chest full of clothes – she'd been warned that it would be freezing – and a little olive-wood box with some personal items and bits of jewellery. It's the one I use now for my writing materials. I told her that this was where she should sleep. She stood there like a statue, afraid to take off her travelling clothes. I told her not to worry, that as she clearly thought I was an animal, I was going to sleep in the library with my dogs. And that's what I did. That's how it was, for over two months. We ate together in the dining hall. I made conversation in Latin; she knew no British at all. She didn't have much to say.'

Kerin didn't have much to say either. He couldn't think of a single question which would not have felt intrusive or inappropriate. He had not expected this subject to be raised. Perhaps Vortigern found it easier to talk about something – anything – than to contemplate the outline of Isca, which was gradually revealing itself as the most arresting collection of Roman buildings Kerin had seen outside Londinium. First came the port, with its wharves and jetties – easily the equal of anything the capital could offer – backed by an enormous warehouse and a slew of smaller sheds, offices and ships' chandlers. To the landward side there were houses; huge houses like Gallus's and the praetor's, smaller dwellings, a basilica, an open square which might be a marketplace. An amphitheatre. And then, just upriver, the wall. A high, solid wall of dressed stone enclosing a vast square space. There was a towering gateway with no gates on it. Gallus left Oswi to steer the ship in, and joined the two men at the prow.

'Gods,' he said, watching the city emerge from the haze. 'I wasn't expecting this.'

'Why?' Vortigern said. 'Do you think we let things fall to pieces in the West, then?'

'No!' Gallus protested. 'I just didn't realise –'

'I'm sorry,' Vortigern cut him short. 'When we dock, I'll introduce you to Claudius Custos, the harbourmaster. He'll show you everything you need to see.'

Kerin withdrew and walked away towards the stern, hoping that Gallus would follow. Sure enough, the merchant was soon beside him.

'What the hell is it with this place?' he asked.

'Vortigern hasn't been here for twenty-five years,' Kerin said. 'I didn't really know what it was all about until Publius Luca told me. He was based here for years with the Second Augusta. Vortigern was around fourteen years old when they first met. The father was high up in the administration, but Vortigern couldn't stand for it. He and his lads caused endless trouble for the Romans. A man called Quintus Parvo was the garrison commander. If he managed to catch Vortigern, he'd beat him senseless and dump him outside his father's house. A few years later, when all those lads were young men, they kidnapped the governor, Marcus Decimus. Vortigern said he'd let him go if Parvo released everyone in his prison block. Ordinary, harmless youngsters were being rounded up, terrible things were happening in there. But someone betrayed Vortigern – some poor woman whose boy was being tortured – so he got locked up too. For weeks, according to Publius. Vortigern wouldn't say where Decimus was, Parvo couldn't break him. I don't know exactly what went on, even Publius won't say, and I'm not sure I want to know if a Roman general can't talk about it. All I know is that in the end Publius wrote to the governor in Londinium and got it stopped. Parvo was dismissed and the prisoners were freed. Vortigern was half-dead by all accounts, he probably owes Publius his life. And he hasn't been back here since, except for the day when he married his first wife, which couldn't be avoided. So I've no idea what will happen today, none at all. One night you two may get drunk and talk about it, but I'd leave it well alone for today, if I were you.'

Gallus stood in silence for a while, watching the bow wave running beneath him. 'Men are bastards,' he said. 'Absolute fucking bastards. What happened to Parvo?'

'I killed him,' Kerin said. 'We came across him in the North. It was a complete shock. We all thought he'd been dead for years. But we found him in a village where our priest Padarn used to live. I'd gone there with Padarn. Everyone had been slaughtered by the Picts except for this woman and her children, and their old grandfather. The woman was a widow, her husband was in the Victrix and the family got left there when he died. I had no idea who the old man was until Vortigern walked in and recognised him. I speared Parvo on the spot. I knew everything I've just told you, so I just did it. Afterwards I hoped it would help, but it didn't. It just stirred things up, like what happens when you stir the water in a filthy pond. And now we're here.' He shrugged. 'I thought you ought to know.'

Gallus sighed and gripped his shoulder. 'Thank you. And don't worry. Out here I'm commanding a ship, and I sound like every rough kind of arsehole. But I can tread as lightly as a dancing girl when I want to. I'll keep my counsel.'

A tall, thin balding man with a trim grey beard was standing on the quayside as the ship came alongside. Kerin recognised Claudius immediately. He was invariably with the contingent from Isca who visited Henfelin to discuss the city's business. Calm, authoritative, well-spoken; Kerin had taken him for a highly-placed estate manager. Until now he had supposed that Isca's port was no busier than the little harbour at Leucarum. Claudius was not looking calm at the moment. He was staring at the men on deck as if they had three heads. Oswi and his deckhands threw ropes to the wharfmen, securing the gangplank.

'Lord!' Claudius shouted. 'You should have sent word!'

Kerin and Gallus followed Vortigern down the gangplank.

'Claudius, this is my friend Gallus Mercator,' Vortigern said. 'The leading merchant in Londinium, as I'm sure you know.'

'Of course, of course,' Claudius said, recovering himself and shaking Gallus's hand. 'Master Gallus, your name is known wherever men sail ships and trade goods.'

'You have a fine port here, Claudius,' Gallus said, looking about him. 'Well placed, well furnished and well maintained. A credit to you, in fact. I'll see the ship secured, then I'll have a look around, if it's all the same to you.'

'Show him anything he wants to see,' Vortigern said, as Gallus spoke to his crew. 'You can answer any questions he has; he sails for me now, as well as for profit. When you're done, feed him and his crew and give them somewhere to rest.'

'Of course, lord,' Claudius said. 'But what of you and Lord Kerin? We'd have prepared a banquet, if we'd known to expect you. Should I summon the ordo? Do you wish to address them?'

'No,' Vortigern said. 'I don't want to address the ordo,

and I don't want a banquet. Just deal with Master Gallus and send someone for two good horses. Lord Kerin has never been here. There are things he should see.'

'At once,' Claudius said. He strode off briskly, hailing a youngster who was coiling rope on the quayside. As they waited for the horses to come, Kerin became aware of voices murmuring. People were starting to gather in the gaps between the buildings.

'We won't be able to avoid them, lord,' he said.

'If I wanted to avoid them, I'd have dressed like a deck-hand,' Vortigern said. 'There's no point. There was never any point. In avoiding this place, or in trying to bury what happened here. I should have faced it down years ago.'

Claudius was coming back, leading two grey riding horses. Like the buildings beyond the waterfront, the animals looked clean and well cared for. Never worked to death, never caught in a fight. There had probably not been a proper fight in Isca for over twenty-five years.

'There's a lot of people in the square, lord,' Claudius said. 'There wasn't much to be done, once the word got around. I've told the garrison commander to keep an eye on things.'

'Do people go into the fortress these days?' Vortigern asked.

'All the time. They've knocked down some of the bar-racks and pinched the stone to build walls. We didn't think you'd have any objection. And the storehouses are used by tradesmen. Carpenters and weavers and so forth. I'd have a ride around the town first, if I were you. By the time you're done, I'll have kicked everybody out of the fort so you and Lord Kerin can look around in peace.'

In many ways the town was like a smaller Londinium, Kerin thought. The buildings were not as massive, the place had a limit, instead of rolling away as far as the eye could see; but here were the Roman houses and the cobbled streets worn smooth by tramping feet, including those of six thousand Second Augustan legionaries. Kerin had lost his bearings entirely, but the walls of the amphitheatre were visible above the roofs to his right, so he supposed that the people from the wharf might have headed for the basilica he had glimpsed from the ship.

'Where are we going?' he asked.

'To the square,' Vortigern said. 'That's where the people are, Claudius said.' Kerin rode half a horse length behind, hand on sword, eyes on every alleyway, window and half-open door. Vortigern's tension was infectious, and besides, vigilance was burned into him now. He'd have preferred the city to be like Londinium, packed with cheering people, overflowing with excitement and euphoria. Crowds could conceal threats, but they were less unnerving than this desertion, this dead, perplexing silence. Ahead of them the street widened out, and there they were forced to stop, because the square in which it terminated was full. Not merely full, but crammed to the walls, as if the late arrivals might have been stuffed in by some unseen force, like salt fish into a barrel. People were hanging out of windows and standing ten deep under the portico of the basilica. No-one spoke. Some of the younger people looked confused. Most of the older people were weeping. Kerin had no idea what to say or do. Vortigern took a deep, steadying breath. There was a movement of bodies. An ancient man, easily Morvid's age, was spewed out by the crowd and stumbled against the shoulder of Vortigern's horse.

'Linus!' Vortigern exclaimed. He slipped from the horse, caught the old man under the arms and embraced him.

'You have not changed,' the old man said, rubbing away a tear.

'No, for my sins,' Vortigern said. He glanced over his shoulder. 'Kerin, Linus is a physician. Attached to Decimus, the governor we kidnapped. They sent him to care for me when I was freed. He stayed here when the occupiers left.'

Kerin would have liked to dismount and speak to the physician, but the crowd was pressing closer. 'Lord, say something to them, for God's sake,' he said, trying to calm his fretting horse. There was a plinth nearby, its statue destroyed. A truncated leg remained, a pathetic memorial to whatever petty official it had once glorified. Vortigern passed the silver crown to Kerin, seized the leg and hauled himself up. The crowd roared and murmured and fell silent.

'Some of you will remember me,' Vortigern said. You, Linus, my life-saver. You over there, Brychan. I hope your father's forgiven me.' A wave of merriment rippled out and faded. 'If you are younger than Kerin Brightspear, here, you won't have set eyes on me. I have blamed this place for the things which were done here. Things done by men who were a disgrace even to the rotten cause they served. Some of you fought with us. Some of you fed us when we were starving. Some of you hid us from the soldiers, some of you simply kept your mouths shut for us. And I have rewarded you by turning my back. Well, no more. No more. I am here now. And I am King of all the Britons, as you must know. But I'm not king in Isca, unless by your will.'

Kerin stood back, holding the horses, as people milled around the plinth, some shouting Vortigern's name, some cheering, some simply smiling and weeping. They hauled Vortigern down and embraced him; the crowd enveloped him. There was no threat. Kerin simply watched it happen. This was not Londinium. There was no excitement bordering on hysteria; no passion edging towards violence. It felt more like a blanket of love.

Claudius was waiting at the fort's gatehouse with four members of the city garrison.

'There's nobody in there now, lords,' he said. 'Most of the tradesmen had already gone to wherever you've been. No trouble, I'm sure.'

'None at all,' Kerin said. 'And I took the liberty of telling all the alehouses near the square to feed and water anyone who wants it. Just settle up with them and bring the account next time you come to Henfelin.'

'My pleasure,' Claudius said. 'These men will stay here until you're done.'

Vortigern straightened his clothes and handed the crown to Claudius. 'Give it to Gallus,' he said. 'He's not going to lose a lump of precious metal.' He pushed his horse forward and Kerin followed. Beyond the gatehouse they faced a vast square space and row after row of low buildings. 'I will take you exactly the way they used to take me,' Vortigern said. Kerin rode behind him, eyes flicking from side to side. Most of the structures alongside the broad entrance road were intact. 'Officials' houses. Barracks. More barracks. Over there the military hospital, and the bath house. Yet more barracks. And here –' Vortigern turned left under an archway, into an empty quadrangle enclosed by buildings – 'to our right, the commander's residence. To our left, the officers' dining hall. And here, straight ahead of us, the military headquarters and the prison. You'd think they'd have it somewhere else, wouldn't you. Somewhere separate. Or perhaps they enjoyed listening when they were eating their dinner.' He stopped. Kerin reined in beside him. They sat quite still in the deserted square, a few horse-lengths from the big closed door. Something fell over and banged within. Vortigern flinched and jerked his horse backwards. Kerin sprang to the ground, drew his sword, ran to the door and kicked it open. A boy was standing there, holding a piece of wood. Immediately Kerin thought of Marc, blazing with indignation, confronting him outside Morvid's hut. This boy looked half-starved but equally defiant. He couldn't have been more than twelve years old.

'Put that down,' Kerin said, sheathing his sword. 'No-one's going to hurt you. We were told that there was nobody here.'

'I'm not supposed to be here,' the boy said, and dropped the wood. 'I fell out with my uncle. I heard your horses, and I thought it might be him, come to look for me. I come in here because I'm friends with the carpenter's sons. They've got a workshop over the other side.'

'Why did you fall out with your uncle?' Kerin asked.

'We're always falling out,' the boy said. 'I never knew my father. My mother's lovely, but her brother's a bastard. He's a horse dealer down by the wharf. I work for him, but he beats me, any excuse. This time I tripped over something and spilled a bucket of water in the straw. That was enough for him.'

Vortigern dismounted. 'So, what were you going to do?' he asked. 'Split his head with that piece of wood?'

'Don't know,' the boy said. 'Just stop him splitting mine, I suppose. I grabbed the wood, then I fell over a table in the dark, and that's what you heard. Master Claudius said we all had to get out because the king was coming, so I hid in there.'

'Do you know anything about this place?' Vortigern asked.

'A bit. It was all empty by the time I was born, but my grandfather used to be with Vortigern. He's told me a few stories.'

'What's his name?' Vortigern asked.

'Celyn, lord. Why do you ask?'

'Has he got two fingers missing on his right hand?'

The boy looked astounded. 'Yes. How on earth do you know that?'

Vortigern ignored the question. 'What do you think about his stories, then? About what the Romans did in here?'

'I'll show you what I think about that, lord,' said the boy. He turned to face the door and dropped his breeches. A steady stream of piss hit the door and trickled down onto the flagstones.

'What's your uncle's name, boy?' Vortigern asked.

'Celyn, lord. After his father. You're not going to tell him, are you?'

'No,' Vortigern said. 'When I leave here, I'm going to tell Master Claudius to visit his house, and tell him that if he beats you again for no good reason, the king will personally come round and behead him. That should put him right.'

The two men mounted up. Kerin winked at the boy and tossed him a denarius. 'Buy yourself a good feed,' he said. 'And spend the rest on your mother.'

*

Gallus was pacing up and down the quayside. As the two riders dismounted he came striding over. Nothing was said, but for a brief moment, Kerin thought that he looked at Vortigern with different eyes.

'How do you find the port?' Vortigern asked.

'It's fine,' Gallus said. 'Every bit as good as Londinium. And your Claudius is a man of genius. There's nothing he doesn't know about draft and tides. Have you seen those records he has? They tell you exactly what the Romans used to bring in, what the river could and couldn't take. My only fear was that the river bed might have silted up, so Oswi and I went out to check. I should have trusted Claudius. It's fine.'

'His father married a Roman girl and worked the port before him,' Vortigern said. 'When the Romans left, the old man purloined all the documents. It's all there, going back hundreds of years, to the days when the Romans were in their pomp. Everything that happened in my lifetime was a footnote, really, however it seemed at the time.'

'I doubt that,' Gallus said. 'But it's done, so come and eat with us. Claudius has laid on a spread. Nothing fancy, good, honest sailors' fare, but it'll set us up for the trip home.'

Vortigern smiled. 'Come on, then,' he said, clapping Kerin's shoulder. 'Let's go and eat with the real men.'

'I'll follow you,' Kerin said. He stood for a moment, looking at the gleaming river, the ships pulling gently at their moorings as the tide receded, the wharves with the heavy gangplanks where they might soon load their horses for the long voyage to Kent. And beyond them, the great square block of the fortress, a place of darkness still, although briefly illuminated by a few slender shafts of light. Kerin thought of the evening when he had dined at Publius Luca's house, after discovering the King of all the Britons labouring in the commander's cornfield. The fragility of it all; the feeling, irrational but impossible to ignore, that there was something coming which he had not yet fully measured or understood. Sounds of merriment were starting to echo from the warehouse where the trestles had been set up. It's probably nothing, Kerin told himself, and went off to eat with the real men.

35

'How often does this happen in these waters?' Gallus asked. He was leaning on the deck rail of his becalmed ship, staring at the fog which had descended like a suffocating blanket. Behind him the mainsail hung limply in the windless air. Invisible gulls circled up above, their cries falling like dead weights.

'We get fog at home now and again,' Kerin said. 'Usually it only lasts for a day or so, then the wind gets up and blows it away.'

'If this was Saxon ship, we would have oars,' Oswi said darkly.

'If this was Saxon ship I wouldn't be able to load a cargo on it, and you wouldn't have a job,' Gallus said, aiming a kick at Oswi's arse. 'Go and find something useful to do, and tell those lazy bastards over there to scrub the deck. We've got no choice but to sit here until we get a wind.' Oswi grinned and sloped off to carry out his orders. He and Gallus seemed to have an understanding beyond the brutal banter they exchanged on board. A degree of affection, probably. Kerin was glad of it. He found it impossible to imagine what it would feel like to abandon your own people and fight for the other side, even though Oswi's choice was motivated by Hengist's treachery. 'He does have a point,' Gallus conceded. 'I've got better ships than this for coastal waters. Based on the old Roman ship, the *actuaria*.

They carry less weight, but they can take thirty rowers apiece and they're flatter-bottomed. Ideal for river ports like Isca. And for times like this, when there's no fucking wind.' He sighed and went off below deck. One of the sailors emerged offering tots of some dark liquor in metal cups. Vortigern was sitting on a pile of rope in the stern. Kerin took two cups and went to join him.

'I should have brought something to read,' Vortigern said.

'How far from land do you think we are?' Kerin asked.

'I don't know. Gallus dropped an anchor, so he must think there's something down there.'

Kerin sat down and passed one of the cups. 'We didn't go to see the house,' he said. Vortigern looked round.

'No. I didn't want to see it, particularly. You can see it some other time. Two of my estate managers live there with their families. It's not unlike Eldof's house in Glevum. Baths, mosaics and so forth. And – it shames me to admit – fountains, and heating under the floor.'

Kerin sighed. 'Rowenna was joking, lord. She doesn't give a damn about that sort of thing.'

'I know she doesn't,' Vortigern said. 'But I give a damn about not giving it to her. Worse, about having it to give, and deciding not to.'

Kerin swallowed his liquor. 'She doesn't care, lord,' he said. 'Just give yourself some peace. We may not have it for long.'

Vortigern met his eyes. He nodded, drank the liquor and set the cup down as the fog thickened and the gulls cried high above them in the still, cold air.

It was probably early afternoon, Kerin thought. The fog remained, but a vague brightening to the west suggested that the invisible sun had gone round. At first he thought he was imagining it, but then he heard the sound again; a slow, rhythmic thud. No-one else had noticed a thing, though, and the sound soon faded away, so Kerin supposed that he was mistaken. The sailors were playing knucklebones. Gallus was teaching Oswi to play backgammon. Vortigern was reading something he had found in the merchant's cubby hole below deck. And now here it was again, a little louder this time. *Boom. Boom. Boom.* Deeper than the note of a skin drum. Louder and far more resonant than a mallet hitting wood. Vortigern looked up.

'What's that?'

'I don't know,' Kerin said. 'But it's coming closer.' Vortigern and Gallus joined him at the prow. The sailors congregated behind them, eyeing each other uneasily. The sound intensified. Too loud for a drumbeat. Too loud and too ponderous, rolling towards them through the clinging fog like a slow, monotonous death march.

'Oh Jesus,' one of the sailors whispered. 'It's the crack of doomsday.'

'Shut up, you stupid bastard,' Gallus said. 'Whatever's making that noise is out on the water, and if we can't see it, it can't see us. Lower the lighter.'

'I'm not going out there!' yelped the man who had spoken.

'I'd sooner take my mother,' Gallus said. 'Master Oswi and I are going, and these two men here if they want to. Tie a long line to the lighter so we can find our way back.' The lighter splashed into the water. The sailors cast a net over the side, and the four men scrambled down into the rocking boat. Oswi grabbed the oars and propelled it out into the fog. 'That way,' Gallus said. 'Steering side.' Oswi pulled hard. The lighter began to encounter a rolling swell.

'Bow waves. It has to be. The sea's as calm as a lake. Stop. Stop.' Oswi shipped the oars. They sat completely still.

'Look!' Kerin whispered, pointing. 'There, look!'

It was a ship, or rather, two ships moving abreast. Sails reefed, oars raking. Two bald, thick-set men were standing in the stern of the nearer vessel. One was holding a bull-whip. The other was swinging a padded mallet, hammering out the slow, ear-splitting rhythm on a massive brass gong. Driven by the sound, the oarsmen were rowing in perfect time, fifteen to each side of each ship. The men in the lighter could hear the grunts and gasps of effort from where they were. One of the rowers missed a stroke. The bullwhip curled out and cut his shoulder. A choking cry, and the rhythm resumed.

'There's something wrong here,' Gallus murmured. 'Those are *actuariae*. They usually just follow each other. And look how they're sitting in the water. They're half empty. So why are the rowers killing themselves?'

The lighter rose on a great wave and fell back. The four men grabbed the sides and hung on tight. Kerin slapped the salt water and fog moisture from his face and rubbed his eyes. The splash of the oars and slow thudding of the gong had been overlaid by another sound; the surge of displaced water. Something was coming. A monstrous dark shadow slowly materialising out of the thick whiteness; and then, stretching away from the sterns of the labouring galleys, four taut, dripping ropes.

'There!' Kerin shouted, flinging an arm out, unable to keep his voice low as the thing rose and grew. Oswi grabbed the oars and fought to steady the lighter as another wave picked it up and carried it sideways.

'Oh gods,' Gallus breathed. 'It's the *oneraria*.' The four men sat quite still as the vast ship glided past, towering above them. Soon it became invisible again. The sounds diminished. 'It's loaded,' Gallus said. 'However big you think it looks from down here, believe me, when those things are empty it's like sitting at the bottom of a mountain.'

'Master Gallus, where does that ship go?' Oswi asked. 'This channel, if you go on, it is soon a river, no?'

'Yes,' Gallus said. He turned to Vortigern. 'They'll never get that thing to Glevum, will they?'

'No,' Vortigern said. 'The river's treacherous further on. I don't think you'd even get one of those *actuariae* up it. But there's another port on the southern bank. Abona. It's a river port like Isca, close to a city called Aquae Sulis. A big place, with lots of grand Roman buildings and bath houses. I haven't been there since I was a lad, but I'm sure the Romans used to land troops and supplies there.'

'Look,' Kerin said, 'wherever it's going, we have to find out what's on that ship.'

Vortigern gripped Gallus's arm. 'Get us back to Isca,' he said. 'Then find something small and fast, and a man who knows the channel.'

*

Claudius decided to come himself. No-one knew the banks and submerged rocks like he did, he said; and anyway, he was quite keen to have a look at the *oneraria*. 'I haven't seen one since my father took me to Alexandria for porphyry,' he said. 'I was just a skinny lad then, lord; no bigger than that little bag of bones you found hiding in the prison block. We won't be having any more trouble from that house, I can tell you.' Claudius had put on some rough seamen's clothes and a black woollen hat which concealed his balding crown. 'I'm well known on these waters,' he said, leading the way to the boat he had chosen. 'Usually it's a good thing, but not if we don't want to be noticed.'

The boat was a skiff with six oars and a simple sail which might be of some use now that a light breeze was blowing from the west, dispersing the fog and revealing a pale grey sky. Oswi and Claudius's five youngsters made short work of the river. Once in open water, Claudius raised his hand. The skiff drifted gently on the current.

'Where would you go if you wanted to unload an *oneraria*?' Vortigern asked.

'I wouldn't even bring it up here,' Claudius said.

'But suppose you had no choice?' Kerin said. 'Suppose it belonged to someone who'd hang a good friend to get his hands on the crown?'

Claudius gave Vortigern an uneasy look. 'Abona is the only possibility. I know the port well – boats like this skiff go back and forth from Isca all the time, to save travellers the long trudge around Glevum. An *actuaria* could dock there if the steersman knew the channel, but there are mud banks in the estuary. The *oneraria* would ground on the way in, and once it got stuck on a bank, you'd probably never get it off.'

Vortigern turned to Gallus. 'You're the merchant. Which would you rather lose, the ship or the cargo?'

'That would depend,' Gallus said. 'The cargo would have to be worth more to me than the ship. Ninety-nine times out of a hundred, I'd save the ship. But then, I sail for myself. If I had a paymaster, and he was an idiot like your son, I'd run the ship into Abona and get it stuck. Whatever's on that ship, Rufus must want it more than he'd want a bed full of randy virgins. There'll be a way to get the cargo ashore. Then, if the *oneraria* was blocking the river mouth, I'd break it up or set fire to it, I suppose.'

Claudius sighed. 'Spoken like a true man of commerce, Master Gallus,' he said. 'Alright, then, boys; let's see how fast you can row.'

Six strong oarsmen and a light following breeze brought the skiff to the river mouth in the deep blue of twilight. Oswi, at stroke, slackened his pace.

'Keep going,' Gallus said. 'No-one's going to take any notice unless they recognise one of us.' Vortigern pulled the hood of his cloak over his head. The *oneraria* was exactly where Claudius had predicted it would be, sitting forlornly in the middle of the river.

'It's stuck, alright,' Gallus said. 'Look, no anchor chains, nothing.' The two galleys which had towed the ship up the channel were already alongside the wharf. Voices were coming from the deck of the *oneraria*, the language unintelligible to Kerin. As the skiff cleared the bows, a rowing boat put out from the other side of the ship, heading for the wharf. Two men were sitting on the cross bench.

'The man in the blue cloak is the harbourmaster,' Claudius said quietly. 'More than likely the other one is the captain, and they're off to have an argument. If it were my port, I'd be sending some men out to inspect the cargo.'

'Then that's what we'll do,' Kerin said. 'Does anyone know what language those men were using?'

'Syriac,' Gallus said.

'Do you speak it?'

'Not properly, but enough to get us on the ship.'

Vortigern and Claudius exchanged looks which conveyed, all too clearly, that although the proposition was mad and risky, they had no better ideas.

'Take Oswi,' Vortigern said. Claudius and the oarsmen manoeuvred the skiff alongside the huge ship. Gallus cupped his hands round his mouth. 'Harbourmaster's orders,' he shouted, in British. 'We've come to inspect the cargo.'

Two men appeared by the deck rail high above. One of them waved his arms about and shouted something back. Gallus replied in the man's own language. The two seamen had a brief argument, shrugged and disappeared. A rope ladder came skittering down the side of the ship. Kerin, Gallus and Oswi shinned up it and heaved themselves over the deck rail. The men Gallus had spoken to were standing beside a big hatch cover, just forward of the main mast. Glancing up and down the vast deck, Kerin counted six other seamen.

'There aren't many of them,' he murmured. 'How many crew does a thing like this have?'

'Fewer than you'd think,' Gallus said. 'Twelve at the most.' He spoke to the two men and pointed at the hatch. With some reluctance, they dragged it open. An overpowering stench of horse and dung belched out. One of the seamen beckoned them and pointed to a steep wooden steps.

'Stay here, Oswi,' Kerin said. 'Watch the crew, and that boat with the harbourmaster on it. Call us if anything happens.' He followed Gallus and the seaman down the steps. There were a few oil lamps, set on high ledges behind protective metal grilles. The dim yellow light revealed rows of horses, tied by the headcollar in stalls so narrow that they could barely move. On a rack above each stall the tack was stowed, the saddles resembling the familiar Roman cavalry saddle with its high front and back. As Kerin got closer he saw that the horses were also hobbled to the floor beneath. They were big, strong animals, built like chariot horses. There must be well over two hundred of them, Kerin thought, glancing from end to end of the vast hold. Gallus was talking to the man who had led them down the steps.

'Two hundred and fifty,' he said. 'That big bin down the end is feed, and the amphorae are water.' He leaned closer to Kerin. 'There's something else going on here, though. We're not nearly at the bottom of the hull. There has to be another deck below this. Go and see if you can find the hatch, I'll keep this bastard occupied.'

Kerin walked amongst the horses, trying to look casual, pausing now and again as one of the captive animals vainly tried to stretch out its head to him. I'd have you out of here if I could, he thought. He noticed a gap, twice the width of the stalls. There was a trapdoor with an iron ring pull. Easing it open, he peered downwards into blackness. Gallus had lured the seaman to the far end of the hold and was examining the corn bin. With extreme care, Kerin prised away one of the metal grilles with his dagger, took the oil lamp and shone it down the hatch. There was a vertical ladder. The lamp illuminated only the area directly below, but as Kerin's eyes adjusted to the darkness, he was able to distinguish sacks; large robust ones, the sort used for storing grain, except that grain sacks had a smooth, round-ed outline and these did not. Heart hammering, clutching the lamp, he slithered down the ladder. The sacks, whatever they contained, were stacked in neat rows, covering as much of the bottom deck as Kerin was able to see. He set the lamp down and grabbed the nearest one. It was tied tightly at the neck with whipcord. One heave was enough to tell him that he would be unable to get it up the ladder without help. The sacks must have been lowered into the hold with a pulley, and stowed with a fair amount of manpower. He was on the point of drawing his dagger to cut the thing open when Gallus's head appeared in the hatch above him.

'Get up here now,' the merchant hissed. Kerin dropped the sack, blew out the lamp and clambered up the ladder.

Gallus closed the trap door behind him. 'Now walk out of here as if nothing had happened. A hundred armed warriors have arrived on the wharf, and that rowing boat's coming back with two extra men on it.'

'Where's the one you were talking to?' Kerin asked, as they climbed the wooden steps.

'At the bottom of the corn bin with a broken neck,' Gallus said. Oswi was waiting for them on deck. The rope ladder was still in place, the skiff still waiting below. The men aboard it could not have been aware of what was happening. The bulk of the *oneraria* blocked their view of the wharves and the water between. Oswi and Gallus swarmed down the ladder. Kerin was about to swing himself over the deck rail when shouting broke out behind him. The crewmen had gathered on the other side of the ship, pointing at something and jabbering hysterically. A commotion had broken out on the rowing boat. A tall, broad-shouldered man grabbed the harbourmaster, calmly cut his throat and tipped the body over the side. He turned, laughing, and waved to the crewmen. Batraz. Kerin dived for the ladder, threw himself down it and landed on his back in the skiff.

'Go!' he gasped. 'And keep that thing between us and them.' Oswi seized his oar, Claudius got the sail up and took the tiller, and the skiff sped away from Abona under the darkening sky. Kerin dropped his head between his knees, recovering his breath.

'It's full of horses,' Gallus said. 'Two hundred and fifty big, strong ones. And some other stuff down below in sacks, but we didn't have time to find out what it was. Around a hundred armed men have turned up, and the rowing boat was coming back.'

'It's worse,' Kerin said. 'You must have heard the shouting. As I was going for the ladder. Someone cut the harbourmaster's throat and threw him in the water. Lord, it was Batraz.' Claudius gave a little gasp. 'I'm sorry, Master Claudius. I know you knew that man.'

'I've known him for twenty years,' Claudius said. 'A good, honest, hardworking gentleman who didn't deserve a death like that.' He turned to Vortigern. 'What now?'

'Get us back to Isca,' Vortigern said. 'Do you have fast horses?'

'I can get them.'

'Two, then. Kerin and I will make better time on horseback. Gallus, get your ship back to Londinium. Leave the new galley where it is. I'll send word as soon as I know what we're dealing with.'

A sound came then; first a series of dull bangs, then the sharp creak of rending timber, followed by the crash of heavy bodies plunging into water. Everyone looked behind. Half of the great ship's upper planking had been hacked away, and the terrified horses were being driven out through the hole. A thin lad was astride the first one, and all the others followed it, as horses did; a mass of dark, bobbing heads making for the muddy beach beyond the wharves.

'We should have burned the thing when we could,' Gallus said. Oswi dropped his oar.

'You would burn all those living horses?'

'Yes,' Gallus said. 'Without a second thought. You might have to fight them soon.'

Oswi picked up his oar and shook his head. Even the thought seemed too much for him. 'You are a hard man, Master Gallus,' he said. 'And a horse has never saved your life. As Odin is my lord, I know that must be true.'

36

The horses were fast, but lacked the endurance which their riders took for granted in a warhorse.

'Slow down,' Vortigern said, as the Roman road took its long curve through the fertile coastal lands between Isca and the old fortress of Nidum. 'We're more than halfway home, and these beasts will drop dead soon if we don't rest them.'

'I suppose those were the Sarmatian cavalry horses,' Kerin said, as they slowed to a walk. 'The saddlery looked more like Roman tack than ours. Perhaps the men were on the other ships.'

'Perhaps,' Vortigern said. 'Do you have any idea what was in those sacks?'

'No,' Kerin said. 'It was too heavy for one man to lift, but that's all I know.'

Catula was sitting outside the house, mending a wicker basket, as the two riders came in. She gave a little squeak of excitement and ran back inside. Gael came out of the house and into Kerin's arms.

'I'll leave you to it,' Vortigern said, handing the horses to one of the stable lads. Gael led Kerin inside, all impatience.

'What happened, what happened?' she asked.

'Let me catch my breath and hold you for a moment,' Kerin said, sitting her down on the couch beside the fire.

'A drink, lord?' Catula asked.

'Please,' Kerin said. 'Nothing strong. Something hot, if you can, it's chilly on the road. And send Cheldric out, I want to see him.'

It was the cook who brought the drinks, two steaming mugs of something hot and fragrant. 'Blackberries and honey,' he said, and winked. 'Good for the cold, good for tired bodies. But if you do not drink soon, by next year it makes silly behaviour.'

The concoction was sweet and soothing. 'I don't think it'll be here next year,' Kerin said. 'You'll have to make some more. But first go down to the village and find Edryd the smith. Try Cilydd's workshop. When you find him, come straight back.'

Gael leaned close to Kerin as the cook trotted away. 'What happened in Isca?' she asked.

'I have to begin at the end,' Kerin said, and told her everything about their aborted voyage home; the becalmed ship, the hideous spectacle of the *oneraria* emerging from the fog, his risky inspection of the cargo – only in retrospect did he understand how mad it was – and finally the gratuitous murder of the harbourmaster, and the freeing of the horses. Gael listened, her fingers tightening around his whenever the account reached a point of extreme peril. 'I'd sooner fight a battle,' he said, 'and that's mad, because you can get killed anytime. But there was something horrible about all that. Stuck there with no wind, and then the noise, and that thing coming out of the fog, and finding that it was full of horses, and that Rufus had commanded all this – all this – so that he can come storming across the river and burn us out of our houses. Well, over my body. But there's something else. Something more, something I've missed. I'd sooner Rufus didn't have two hundred and fifty heavy cavalry, but at least you know where you are. I still don't understand what he meant when he talked about weapons we didn't have.' He paused. 'That's not really what you were asking me about.'

'No,' Gael said. 'As long as I've known you, Isca has simply been the place where Vortigern grew up. The place he was so determined to avoid, that all his overseers had to come here to discuss their business. I'm sure that terrible things happened there, but for now all I need to know is how you both survived it this time. That there was no more harm.'

'There wasn't,' Kerin said. 'It went better than I expected. Perhaps better than Vortigern expected, even. And I will tell you. But later, please. Later.' It wasn't even that he thought it would be difficult, but now that she was here, her head pressed to his shoulder and the rest of her as close as their unborn child would allow, his body was beginning to make demands which his brain could not counter. Gael looked up at him and raised an eyebrow.

'Master Brightspear, I don't know how close you'll be able to get, even with that famous spear of yours,' she said. Kerin pulled her to her feet.

'I'll find a way,' he said, propelling her gently towards the bedroom. Gael fell onto the bed, laughing, and burrowed under the blanket. Kerin threw off his breeches and underwear and slid in beside her. 'Turn your back, turn your back,' he murmured, pulling up her ample dress. She was naked beneath it. Trembling with excitement, Kerin pulled her close and slipped between her thighs. Outside, the door of the house banged open and something thudded onto the table.

'Lord!' Cheldric's voice shouted. 'Lady Gael! I am back, and I have the smith!'

'Oh, God in heaven,' Kerin groaned and rolled away. He grabbed his breeches and pulled them on. Gael rearranged her dress. Kerin flung the bedroom door open. Cheldric and Edryd stared at Kerin, and at each other. The Saxon looked petrified. The smith's face was the colour of a ripe apple.

'We're sorry,' Edryd mouthed. Kerin breathed out hard.

'You I can forgive, but he's done this before,' he said, seizing Cheldric by the collar. 'Do you remember, the day after I came home from Kent? Do you remember what I said I'd do if it happened again?'

'Yes, lord,' Cheldric mouthed. 'You said you would throw me in the drainage ditch.'

'Yes,' Kerin said, frogmarching him towards the door.

'Lord, it is frozen!' Cheldric protested.

'It is,' Edryd said. 'Up to you, lord, but he's right about the ice.'

Kerin sighed and released his cook. Gael ventured out of the bedroom and eyed the object on the table. It was wrapped in an old bedsheet.

'What's this?' she asked.

'It is from Brwyn,' Cheldric said. 'He comes from his house and says, bring it for Lord Kerin and his lady.'

Gael removed the sheet. Beneath was a cradle, newly made, redolent of fresh timber and rubbing oils. The panels at each side were exquisitely carved with lambs and small birds.

'Oh!' Gael exclaimed, 'Well, isn't that just beautiful!'

'I didn't know that Brwyn was so skilled,' Kerin said. 'Edryd, go and fetch the man.' The smith was soon back with Brwyn. Kerin had barely seen him since the night of the midsummer fire. He was a big, bulky man, around Vortigern's age, with curly hair and a brindled grey beard which might once have been the colour of a chestnut horse.

'Brwyn!' Gael exclaimed, seizing his hands. 'What a beautiful gift!'

'I had no idea,' Kerin said. 'This is better work than some of the carpenters do.'

'I used to dabble,' Brwyn said, looking down at the floor. 'When I was a lad back in Isca. But I thought you deserved something. My sons have caused you and the Lord no end of trouble, and there's been no complaint from either of you. I wish you luck of your child, and I hope it brings more joy than mine have done lately.'

Gael stood on tiptoe and kissed Brwyn's cheek. 'You're a good man, Brwyn,' she said. 'We can't always control what our children do, can we? I'm sure my father would chop my head off if he could catch me.'

'God forbid,' Brwyn said. 'And when I say that, I mean the God I serve, not what Vortimer and my boys make him out to be.' He patted Kerin's shoulder. 'I'll pray for you all. Tell the Lord I'm sorry.'

When Brwyn had gone, Kerin carried the cradle into the bedroom and covered it with a blanket. He didn't hold with Mora's mutterings about not bringing a cradle to the house until the baby was safely born, but for all that, he didn't want it staring him in the face just yet. Gael sat Cheldric and Edryd at the table and brought more mugs of the warming blackberry drink.

'You sent for me, lord?' Edryd asked.

'Yes,' Kerin said. 'How is the work going?'

'Almost done,' Edryd said. 'It's with the bard and his son.' He stopped. 'I'm sorry, Lady Gael. I'd love to explain, but I've sworn.'

'It doesn't matter,' Gael said. 'We all have our secrets.'

'You sent for me, though, lord?' Edryd said.

'Yes. I need you to go to Glevum. Or perhaps Aquae Sulis, the city of the baths. Vortimer's allies landed two hundred and fifty cavalry horses near there yesterday. The port's called Abona. I managed to get aboard their ship, and I saw the horses, but I had to leave in a hurry. There was something else on the ship. The hold was full of big sacks. I didn't have time to get one open, but it was heavy. I couldn't have carried it on my own. So I need to know what was in those sacks, because it may be something they'll use against us. Vortimer has been bragging about weapons we don't have. The ship was enormous, they had to ground it and smash the side to get the horses off. I want you to find out where the sacks are, and what's in them.'

Edryd sat and digested the information. 'Alright. I'll take my cart, with a few old tools in it. Not as obvious as a man on a good horse. And if I can get my hands on one of those sacks, I'll bring it back.'

'Lord, I will go too,' Cheldric said. 'For one man, it is hard. And maybe we need a boat. This man is good smith, but the Britons are no good with boats, and I know all.'

'Why not?' Edryd said. 'He looks like a strong lad, and if you didn't trust him, he wouldn't be cooking for you.'

'Alright,' Kerin said, 'but now, get the food on the table. I want you away at first light.'

When the two men had gone, Kerin drew Gael into his arms. 'We'll eat,' he said. 'Then I'm going to carry you into the bedroom, barricade the door and finish what I started. And tomorrow morning, I'll find Brwyn the master car-penter and tell him to make a nice strong bar for the inside of the door. Are we agreed?'

'We are agreed,' Gael said, and smiled, feeling him swell against her belly. 'Now, release me, Master Brightspear, or it's going to be finished here and now.'

37

'There was a letter waiting for me,' Vortigern said, closing the library door. 'From Publius. It came with Valerius Dio's messengers. They had no particular news, but this letter was odd. It said that he'd prefer to discuss the carnyx in person. And that there might be soon be an opportunity, as he had business in Venta Silurum. I can't imagine what business Publius might have in Venta, particularly business that I don't know about.' He shrugged. 'Where was Edryd off to with Cheldric this morning?'

'Glevum,' Kerin said. 'Or Abona, or Aquae Sulis. I hope they're going to find out what was in those sacks. Even better, that they might bring one back. I know it's risky, but at least a smith can find a reason for being around a wharf or a warehouse. And Cheldric can handle a boat. It's probably mad, but not as mad as going to search the *oneraria*.'

'What about the carnyx?' Vortigern asked. 'Are they done with it?'

'It's with Cynfawr and Cynan. They're doing whatever they have to do.'

'Good,' Vortigern said. 'I have a bad feeling about all this.' He turned. 'Am I right? Or have I just let that place poison me all over again?'

'No,' Kerin said. 'You're right. And you didn't look poisoned. You looked relieved.'

'I was,' Vortigern said. 'Next time will be easier.'

'We won't be shipping horses from there now, though,' Kerin said. 'We were expecting Rufus's reinforcements to land at Dubris, and now they're here, just across the river.'

'They could come now, if they wanted to,' Vortigern said. 'And we're not ready. When do you expect Elir and Gwyndaf?'

'Any day. And your messengers, too. But I think I may have got sidetracked. The main attack will come next spring, but if I were Rufus, I'd strike now. I wouldn't even care if I won or lost. He doesn't need to depose you. He just needs to weaken us, ready for the spring.'

There was a tap at the door. Rowenna came in. She was wearing breeches and a warm tunic, her usual riding clothes.

'Please come, both of you,' she said. 'There is something we wish to explain.'

They followed Rowenna to Kerin's house. A faint smell of horse and mule was hanging in the air outside, but the animals were not to be seen. Gael and Tirion were sitting at the table in the main room with Mabli, Mora, Branwen and Eleri. With them, to Kerin's surprise, was Gwyndaf's wife Mari, hardly ever seen outside her home on the Cribin. A crowd of other women, completely unfamiliar to him, filled the space between the table and the doors of the private rooms. He and Vortigern exchanged a mystified glance. Gael stood, and stepped forward to address them.

'Soon you will lead our men to battle,' she said. 'Whether in the spring or sooner, the result will be the same. The husbands, the fathers, the sons, all the heads of families, will be gone. For sure, some of the good, solid men who work the fields and man the workshops will still be with us, but the ones they look to for direction will be far away. Kerin, I've heard you speak of Berget, daughter of Malan, the old man who led the rising in Londinium. An ordinary woman from an ordinary village, but she took it on herself to lead that village when her men followed you to the North. And Mother of God, it shamed me that we, the wives and daughters of warriors, sat on our hands and did nothing. So know this. When you are away, nothing will stop. No-one will go cold or hungry. The hearth fires will burn, the beasts will feed, the children will learn, the houses will stand, what's broken will be mended. Each one of us has her own responsibility. And here beside me are women from as far away as Moridunum and Nidum, good, strong girls with strong horses. We will have each other to call on if trouble comes to any or all of us. So when you go off to fight, go with free hearts. All will be well. We, the women, will lead the families. And when you bring home the victory – as we know you will – a heroes' welcome will be waiting for you.'

Gael tossed her head back, planted her hands on her hips and waited for a reaction from the two men. There was a silence. Kerin looked at the woman he had married; so small, physically, weighed down by her unborn child, yet radiating the authority of a battle commander. Everything she had said shone with warmth and love, but beneath all that was a ferocity so patent that he could almost envisage a protective wall surrounding the people she had sworn to care for. Kerin held out his hand. It was for Gael to take it or not. This moment was hers, and he would not attempt to steal one sliver of her light. She took his hand, of course, her clasp as warm and steady as ever.

'Gael,' Vortigern said, 'you would grace any man's warband. It will never come to that while Kerin and I draw breath, but for this, you have the thanks of my heart. I have only one thing to add. If the women intend to act like men, they should drink like men. Here, in the house of their leader. Rowenna, go to Cenydd and tell him to bring trestles and food and drink.'

The women cheered and laughed and hugged each other. Gael kissed Kerin's cheek and hurried to the kitchen to alert Catula.

'I wasn't bargaining for this when I married my wife,' Kerin said.

'I wasn't bargaining for anything,' Vortigern said. 'But luck smiled on me that night, as it has on you. Now, go and find the bard and the druids, and ask them if the new carnyx is ready. If it is, tell them to bring it to my hall tonight.'

Amidst the chattering and laughter, and the banging of tables being set up, no-one heard the approaching carriage until it stopped outside the chieftains' hall. A handsome chestnut horse was hitched to the back.

'Lucius!' Kerin exclaimed, as the driver hailed him. Publius Luca emerged from the carriage, looking cheerful and healthy. Both men had exchanged their uniforms for warm travelling clothes. Publius embraced Vortigern and shook Kerin's hand.

'A moment before you bombard me with questions,' he said. 'I have company.' A small, bent figure alighted from the carriage, declining his offer of help.

'I am old, commander, not entirely shorn of my faculties,' said a familiar voice. 'But my travelling chest is inside, Lucius Arrius, if you'd be so kind.' The heavy, fur-lined hood was thrown back to reveal the smiling face of Marcellus. 'I fear that senility may be creeping in, however. Why else would I visit this benighted outpost?'

'Because you didn't have the balls to say no to my wife,'

Publius Luca said dryly.

'Come,' Kerin said, throwing an affectionate arm around Marcellus's shoulders as the door of the chieftains' hall swung open. He had never done it before – there was something self-contained about the old physician – but seeing him here was such an unexpected pleasure that the gesture came naturally. Most of the time, Kerin chose not to dwell on the fact that this man of profound wisdom and medical skill was also a haruspex, who sought the future amongst the innards of a barely-dead beast. At the threshold Kerin paused. 'Did Publius really need a physician to travel with him?'

Marcellus chuckled. 'What do you think? He's in fine form, as you can see. That little expedition to Kent rather taxed him, but there was no lasting damage. The wound has healed better than I expected. And he's right in saying that I accompanied him to prevent domestic carnage, but there was another reason. Unfortunately I'm not at liberty to discuss it, but I'm sure the commander will tell you in his own good time.'

'Look,' Kerin said, 'I don't mean to pry. But however well Publius has recovered, he shouldn't go marching into battle. Is this anything to do with Rufus's intentions?'

Marcellus gave a non-committal smile. 'It is and it isn't,' he said. 'And that's all I'm going to say.'

*

They talked about carnyces. Publius Luca had never seen one, but he had heard the old generals speak of them as something like a folk memory, handed down from antiquity. They talked about their wives, and Kerin had to make a conscious effort to remember that these three men, so well known to him, had yet to meet his beloved Gael. They talked about Rufus's two hundred and fifty cavalry horses, and whatever else had driven him to sacrifice a ship like the *oneraria* on the treacherous banks of the channel. By then daylight was fading, the large amphora of Gallus's wine was empty, and Marcellus was dozing beside the fire in the library, chin on chest.

'See him to bed, Lucius,' Vortigern said. 'Cenydd will show you where to go. Take the next chamber along. And tell Cenydd to fetch us another of these.'

When the two men were safely in bed, and Cenydd had brought the amphora, Vortigern turned to Publius.

'I have been to Isca,' he said. The commander's eyes narrowed.

'*Why?*'

'Because I couldn't avoid it. Gallus Mercator came to make amends. He has some scheme about shipping our horses to Kent. He wanted me to show him the port. I couldn't deny him without explaining or looking unreasonable. So I went.' He shrugged. 'It didn't kill me, as you can see.'

Kerin stood up. 'I can leave if you wish,' he said.

'No,' Vortigern said. 'I thought Publius should know, but I have nothing to add. Now, go and do what you were going to do. Find Cynfawr and the druids, and ask them to bring the carnyces. Quietly, wrapped in some way; no-one else can see them yet. Except our wives. Bring them, if they can still stand.'

Morvid was sitting on the bench outside Kerin's house. 'I felt like a fish out of water in there,' he said mournfully.

'Well, I have a task for you,' Kerin said. 'Go to Cynfawr's house, and ask if he and the druids can bring everything to the chieftains' hall. They'll understand. Then come back here and see if you can mix a remedy for too much wine and mead.'

The revelry had died down. Most of the women had gone home. Mabli, whose pregnancy was just beginning to show, was sleeping flat on her back beside the fire. Mora was slumped on the couch snoring with Lud's cousin Anwen. Not much of a wise woman tonight, then. Tirion was suckling her child, who would surely enjoy the sleep of the dead. Gael and Rowenna, the last women standing, were sipping Cheldric's blackberry concoction.

'Ah!' Gael said. 'The King's Right Arm! Is that arm feeling strong tonight, Master Brightspear?'

'Strong enough to carry you to bed, you drunken hussy,' Kerin said. 'But first of all, we have guests for you to meet. Can you both walk?'

'Of course we can!' Rowenna exclaimed, executing an unsteady pirouette. Kerin caught her, chuckling.

'Publius Luca and Marcellus *magister* are here,' he said. 'Well known to you, of course, but not to Gael. And Lucius Arrius, too. He and Marcellus have gone to bed, but Publius is waiting to see you.'

'Lucius!' Gael exclaimed. 'Your friend, who brought the news –' she broke off, giving Tirion an anxious glance.

'Your friend, who rode for days and nights to tell us about Hefin,' Tirion said, her voice steady. 'And then for days and nights again, to help you free Macsen. If you have friends like that, you are blessed.'

Kerin bent to kiss the baby's soft head. 'Sleep here,' he said. 'Take our bed. There's room enough for us in the chieftains' hall. I don't have to ask.'

'Thank you,' Tirion mouthed. She bent her head and a tear fell on the baby's shawl.

'Come on,' Kerin said, linking arms with Gael and Rowenna. 'They're waiting for us.'

The sound of voices and muted laughter could be heard coming from the library. Rowenna smiled to herself and led the others in.

'We are here!' she said.

'So you are,' Publius Luca said, rising to his feet and kissing Rowenna on both cheeks. Vortigern took Gael's hand and placed it in his.

'Gael, my dear friend Publius Luca Imperator,' he said. 'Publius, here is Gael, Kerin's wife and the leader of this *cohors muliebris* we have told you about.'

Publius Luca touched Gael's hand to his lips and sighed. 'What is it about us three men, that we chose women who are so hard to live up to?' he asked. Gael smiled radiantly.

'Oh, Commander Publius,' she said, 'I think the women chose you, because nothing less would do for us.'

Publius laughed. 'Long may you think so, and long may we deserve it,' he said. 'Now, I'm told that you've had your share of strong drink, but please, both of you, join us in a cup of Gallus's excellent wine. Your husbands, not to be outdone, have something to show you.' He filled the silver cups. 'To love and friendship,' he said, as they all shared a toast; and where better to celebrate it, Kerin thought, than in this place which had held his heart for his whole conscious life; this warm, dark place with its bright fire and glowing torches, its brilliant tapestries and treasured manuscripts and all its sacred memories. There was a tap at the door.

'Lord, the bard and the druids,' Cenydd said. 'They're waiting in the dining hall.'

Cynfawr, in a plain grey robe and black cloak, had abandoned the finery he usually chose for significant occasions. Caradog and Cynan were wearing their simplest robes. All three seemed to have decided that the light should shine elsewhere tonight. They had brought Cilydd the silversmith, who looked too overcome with emotion to speak. Two long, slender objects, wrapped in red blankets, were lying on the high table.

'It's time to show your work,' Vortigern said. 'To us and our chosen only.'

Cynfawr smiled gravely. 'The old one first,' he said. 'That's right and honourable.' He unrolled the blanket, grasped the ancient carnyx in both hands and held it out, tilted forward, its mouthpiece resting on the floor. Whether because of the flaring lamps, or because Cynan had polished it even more diligently than usual, Kerin had never seen it shine as brightly as it did now.

'By Mithras,' Publius Luca murmured.

'Oh!' Gael exclaimed, reaching up to caress the bowed head. 'Is it a battle standard? Or a druids' emblem, a sacred thing?'

Caradog smiled. 'It is neither and it is both,' he said. 'Look where it rests. Now can you see? You should; you're a fine musician, so I'm told.'

Gael's eyes widened. 'It's an instrument,' she said.

'Yes. Its name is carnyx; an ancient name for an ancient thing. And it can sing gently for our pleasure, and in praise of the gods. But when angered, it's a bringer of terror, and a harbinger of death.' He nodded to Cilydd. 'Come, silversmith. Show them what you and Edryd have worked.'

Cilydd went to the table. Hands shaking, he undid the blanket and brought the masterpiece out into the light. 'Take it, Cynan,' he whispered. 'In case I drop it.' Smiling,

Cynan raised it up, the new standing beside the old. The burnished metal glowed with the dazzling brightness of flame. Gorlois would be proud of his Kernow bronze. The new head was more intricately worked than the old, each great ear flared and bearing a central vein, the crest bristling fiercely, the jaws gaping, the irises set with deep red carnelians. 'Only the eyes are mine,' Cilydd said, staring at the floor. 'And the lovely ears.'

'Please, may we hear it sing?' Rowenna asked. Cynfawr cleared his throat.

'We have spoken,' he said, 'and we are agreed that the new carnyx shall be silent until Edryd its maker is here to hear its voice. Except in the cave, of course, where we find it to be just as loud as its older brother. Does that go well with you, Lord?'

'Perfectly well,' Vortigern said. 'Now, Cynan, please take the old one, and give us the tune you played last time.'

Cynan smiled an acknowledgment, took the ancient instrument and played the sweet melody which had haunted Kerin since he first heard it; softly, so that no-one passing by outside would feel anything but joy at the wondrous music coming from the Lord's hall that night.

'There,' Cynan said gently, when he had done. 'Now we will wrap them and take them home. And when Master Edryd comes back, bring him to the sacred wood, and you can all hear what our enemies have coming to them.'

Publius went happily to bed, leaving Kerin, Vortigern and their wives in the silent hall. Rowenna and Gael, dizzy with excitement and drink, laughed and hugged each other.

'We're homeless,' Kerin said. 'Tirion and her baby are sleeping in our bed.'

'Go to your old bedchamber, then,' Vortigern said. 'It's

just as it was. And neither of you will ever be homeless while I live.'

The four of them embraced, holding on tight, as if they already knew that this night was a jewel to be treasured. Hold it and keep it safe, Kerin thought, as he led Gael to the bed where he had slept for so many years. He wondered what Edryd and Cheldric were doing at this moment, and what he would have done, in Rufus's place. A vision reared up then; of the doomed *oneraria* burning on the banks, of the blameless harbourmaster being buried by a grieving family, and of Batraz, flogging gangs of oarsmen with a bullwhip as they laboured towards the shore with sacks full of something terrible.

38

'The messengers are coming across the moors, lord,' Dimos said, ducking inside out of the rain. The scribe had finally admitted defeat to the weather and accepted a warm woollen tunic and breeches, far more appropriate for the West than the Roman dress he had worn in Londinium. 'They've probably ridden through the night,' he said. 'The horses look all in.'

Kerin flung on his cloak and went outside as the men arrived. Cenydd came out of the chieftains' hall. The stench of soaking wet horse mingled with the sweet scent of oat bran and straw as Vortigern's stable lads led the exhausted animals away.

'Here you go, lord,' the senior man said, handing over his leather bag. 'A letter from Lord Brianus up in the North. The king's man through and through, I'd say; he couldn't stop talking about the way you thrashed the Picts. And if you think this weather is bad, you should go where we've been. Sleet and freezing rain. Gets in your bones, it does.'

Kerin took the bag. 'Cenydd, take them inside and give them food and a change of clothes. And tell Vortigern they're back. Dimos, come with me.'

Morvid had built the fire up to a blaze. Kerin opened the bag and carefully removed the papyrus, wrapped in an oiled cloth for protection. He unrolled it on the table. The writing was bold, if less refined than Dimos's.

'*Friend Kerin Brightspear,*' he began. That was a good beginning. *I received your letter with joy, but also with –* ' he hesitated. His scribe smiled.

'Shall I read it aloud, just for speed? If that's permitted, of course. Afterwards we can read it together, and I can explain.' He sat at the table and studied the papyrus.

'I received your letter with joy, but also with anger and disgust. As you rightly judge, I am a loyal ally of Vortigern, the High King. How could I be otherwise? Only he had courage and resolve enough to confront and defeat the invaders. Even the Romans could not do this. Whether unable or unwilling, I cannot say, but the result is the same. At last, we are delivered from slaughter and destruction, and can go about our lives in peace. And now you tell me that the king's son is raising arms against his father. I am outraged. It appals me that even some churchmen subscribe to this nonsense. I count myself a Christian, but sometimes I find it hard to believe that we serve the same God. Of course you may depend on me, and on all men of honour amongst my acquaintance. As you know, the roads will soon become impassable for armies. But we are preparing ourselves, and unless I hear otherwise from you, we will march as soon as the weather permits. Send word of your plans and disposals, and assure the King of my steadfast support.'

Dimos shrugged. 'That's it, apart from the signature. You couldn't ask for more, really, could you?'

'No,' Kerin said. 'And from a man I've never even met.' He looked up as Vortigern came in, shaking the rain from his hair. 'From Brianus, in the North,' he said, handing him the letter. 'I knew we could count on him.' Vortigern read it and smiled.

'A few more like him would be useful. Any sign of Elir and Gwyndaf?'

'No, but I hope they're close to home. If it's raining like this over the mountains, all the rivers are going to flood.'

Behind him the kitchen door creaked open and Catula peeked out. Seeing Vortigern, she hurriedly drew back. 'Sorry, Lord King,' she mouthed and closed the door. Kerin opened it.

'It's alright,' he said. 'Come out. What do you want?'

'Lord, I heard you speak of my old master, Lord Brianus,' Catula stammered.

'I've had my breakfast, child,' Vortigern said. 'I won't eat you.'

Catula gave a nervous smile. 'Lord Kerin, if you write to Lord Brianus again, please tell him that I wasn't running away from him. Just from all those high-born, and the one who did all that to my friend Alba.' She bit her lip.

'Of course I'll tell him,' Kerin said. 'Would you want to go back?'

Catula's eyes widened. 'Oh, gods, no! I never want to leave here. But Lord Brianus was a lovely master, and I just wanted him to know – well, all that.'

'Good,' Kerin said. 'We won't send you back, then. Now go and make a big pot of gruel with milk. I haven't had my breakfast, so I might eat you, even if the king doesn't want to.'

Catula giggled and fled into the kitchen.

'Poor girl,' Gael said. 'However good a master Brianus was, she must think she's landed in heaven here. And she's useful, anyway. She can cook when Cheldric's not here, and she does everything that Morwen used to do for me in my father's house. Poor Morwen! I wonder what's become of her?'

Vortigern raised his hand. 'You're not bringing any more lame ducks into this house to live on our charity,' he said.

'Well,' Gael said, 'the thing is with lame ducks, after they've been in this house for a while, they all learn how to fly.' She gave Vortigern an enquiring look. He snorted and threw his hands up and went out. 'Dimos Bekuh, come with me,' his voice echoed back. 'Before this madhouse turns your brain to soup.'

*

It rained solidly for ten days. Roofs leaked. Tracks became impassable. Publius Luca, Lucius and Marcellus postponed their travelling plans. The river, usually clear and benign, became a raging brown torrent spewing broken branches and drowned animals out onto the shingle bar and the beach beyond. On the eleventh day, as a watery evening sun swam in the sea mist over the bay, a shout came from the watch tower.

'Elir, Gwyndaf and the boys!' Bened bawled. 'And they've got the cook and the smith with them.'

'Thank God,' Kerin said. He would have sent a search party, if he had had any idea where to look. The riders were coming down the old track, avoiding the flood in the upper valley. Edryd's cart was close behind. The horse Ashur had been riding was hitched to the tailboard, and the boy was sitting in the back, hunched under a blanket.

'Stoke the fires up, man, we're all drenched to the bone,' Gwyndaf said. 'And get someone to look at that boy. I don't think they have this filthy weather in Alexandria.'

Kerin went to the cart. Ashur was shaking, teeth chattering. Kerin gathered him up, sodden blanket and all. 'Go to the chieftains' hall, Marc,' he said. 'Tell the Lord you're back, and ask Marcellus *magister* to come to our house.' He carried Ashur inside and laid him down on the hearth.

Gael threw logs onto the fire and ran to the kitchen. Kerin stripped Ashur naked and started chafing the boy's frozen limbs. Morvid brought blankets and wrapped him from head to foot.

'Here, boy, get this down,' he said. 'Just some blackberry stuff, but it'll warm you up.'

Gwyndaf came in with Elir, Edryd and Cheldric following. They flung off their wet cloaks and squatted beside the fire, rubbing their hands.

'There's broth,' Gael said. 'Nothing special, but good and hot.'

Catula came from the kitchen with a steaming cauldron and set it at the edge of the fire. Morvid ladled the broth into bowls and handed them round. The men drank thankfully.

'We have everything you asked for,' Gwyndaf said. 'The records are a bit damp but you can read them. It was lucky we ran into these two on the road. We sheltered in some-one's barn and piled everything into the cart, including that poor lad there. Are you alright, boy?'

'Better now,' Ashur whispered, with a shaky smile. Marc came in carrying a bundle of clothes and sat down beside him.

'I've taken all your papyrus and stuff to the hall,' he said. 'And the old man's coming with some medicine. Marcellus, who used to look after Severus Maximus.'

Ashur glanced up. 'I know him,' was all he said. Marcellus came in and knelt beside him. Ashur flinched as the thin hand of the haruspex felt his brow.

'No need of that,' Marcellus said, listening to the boy's chest. 'Just because I was sometimes compelled to treat that worthless fop Alberius, it doesn't mean that I'm a friend of his. He's a forgotten man now, even if he is related by mar-riage to the new praetor.' He drew a phial of powder from within his robe. 'Make a paste of this, please, Morvid. Yes, I was asked to treat the wretch last month, but I respectfully declined. I'm sure you'll all be delighted to know that he has recently contracted gonorrhoea.' He smiled brilliantly as a wave of snorts and sniggers rippled around the fire. 'The disease probably won't kill him,' he said, patting Ashur's shoulder. 'But give it time, and the king might. You don't have a fever, I'm happy to say, you're merely frozen. Your breathing's a little laboured, but when Morvid comes back with the paste, I'll rub it on your chest and that should ease things.'

The door opened and Vortigern came in with Publius Luca and Lucius.

'Good news, all in all,' Gwyndaf said. 'Around a thousand good men and horses fit to fight now, and three times that by the spring. Some of them need arming, but they're keen.'

'You've done well,' Vortigern said. 'You youngsters, too. We'll meet in the morning to examine the records.' He turned to Edryd and Cheldric. 'Well?'

'We've got one,' the smith said. 'Three, in fact. I opened one of the sacks and had a look. I've never seen anything like it to be honest, Lord King.'

'Get them, then,' Vortigern said. 'Bring everything to the hall.'

The three sacks were concealed beneath a waxed sheet and filled the cart. As Kerin had anticipated, it took two men to move them. Edryd and Cheldric heaved them down and hoisted the first between them. Gwyndaf and Elir took the second, Kerin and Lucius the third. Vortigern and Publius were waiting inside. The servants had cleared the floor of the dining hall. Edryd and Cheldric seized the bottom corners of their sack and upended it. The contents slithered out, a huge heap of gleaming bronze, tiny overlapping plates flowing down to the floor like liquid.

'*Lorica hamata!*' Publius Luca said. 'Scale armour. I've worn it myself. But there must be enough for a number of men here.'

Edryd looked up. 'No,' he said. 'This is something else.' He and Cheldric felt around amongst the slippery folds of metal, found two corners and drew them out. As they moved backwards, the heap spread and flattened. Kerin found himself looking down at the outline of a huge, shining horse.

'Cataphracts,' Vortigern said softly. 'Merciful God.'

'*Katàphraktos!*' Kerin exclaimed. Vortigern looked round. 'How do you know that word?'

'Ashur said it to me,' Kerin said. 'When I asked him about training the white horse. He said the horse would take the saddle and bridle, but he had to find something for the *katàphraktos*. He didn't know it in British, and nothing happened, so I forgot all about it.' He turned to Edryd. 'How did you get hold of these?'

'Pitifully simple,' Edryd said. 'We got to Abona when they were unloading. They had a string of wagons lined up on the wharf, so we just joined them. No-one asked us who we were. The slaves threw the sacks into the wagons. If I hadn't had such a poxy cart, we could have had even more of them. But there's more bad news, lord. The greybeard driving the next cart told us that they're expecting another big ship full of horses any day. He was all fired up because it meant more work for the carters, but it's not much good for us, is it.'

'Alright,' Vortigern said. 'Now we know. Publius, have you fought these?'

'Yes,' Publius Luca said. 'Years ago, on the eastern borders.

I think they originated with the Assyrians, centuries ago, but in my day it was the Sarmatians. Both men and horses were covered in this stuff, the men all over apart from eye-slits, the horses down to the knees. You can't possibly resist a charge with unarmoured cavalry. You have to find another way. We were lucky, it was the height of summer and it was baking hot. I just told my men to run, and they wore themselves out chasing us. There were light cavalry coming behind them, so we still lost a lot of men and horses, but it wasn't a complete defeat.'

'You were right, Kerin,' Vortigern said. 'Exactly right. They'll throw these at us now, soon, and try to decimate our best mounted warriors. They'll expect us to lose the spearhead, then in the spring –'

'But there'll be a way,' Kerin said. 'Frightening the horses, for a start. Edryd, go to Cynfawr's house and tell him to go to the cave with the druids. Then find Cilydd and meet us at the bottom of the Druids' Wood.'

*

Cynfawr was right. The new carnyx had as loud a voice as its older brother. Cynan, who had made it speak, set it carefully in the iron bracket Edryd had forged for it. He smiled hopefully at the cluster of stunned white faces. Edryd, speechless with pride, took the great bowed head between his hands and kissed its nose.

'I haven't heard one in a lifetime's military service,' Publius Luca said.

Caradog stepped forward. 'Enough!' he barked. 'Go elsewhere to make your plans. You are in a sacred space, and you have breathed enough of its air.' All the murmured conversations died.

'Your pardon, Archdruid,' Publius Luca said. 'I know my history. You had every right to forbid entry to a Roman.'

'And I know my history too, Publius Luca,' Caradog said. 'I know what you did for the Lord in Isca. You'd be outside in the cold otherwise. Now go, all of you, and prepare. But do your work quickly, because soon will come the night of Calan Gaeaf. The great fire will burn on the height of Penrhyn Fawr. We will feed it with the rage of our forefathers, and take the carnyces to drink of its power.'

No-one had words to add. The interlopers trooped silently out, leaving Cynfawr and the druids to douse the lamps. At the cave entrance Kerin paused, hearing someone sobbing quietly in the darkness. Cilydd was there, sitting on a boulder. A stray shaft of moonlight illuminated a face ribboned with tears and a glowing smile. 'Kerin Brightspear, if I never make another thing, my work is complete,' he said.

Kerin walked down through the wood. Gwyndaf was waiting for him on the riverbank below.

'You're mad,' he said. 'You and the druids. Yes, it's a horrible noise in a cave, but in the middle of a battle? With a few thousand men and horses shouting and screaming?' He sensed Kerin's disappointment and shook his head. 'Look, I hope I'm wrong, because god knows we'll need all the help we can get. But I can't see it. If I'm wrong, I'll eat my own stinking underwear.' He slapped Kerin's shoulder, unhitched his horse from the whitethorns and rode away.

39

It was the valley where Kerin had encountered Vortigern, on returning from Londinium with a guilty conscience and a necklace in his pocket. He had chosen it for the same reason Vortigern did, on that pleasant, sunlit day; no-one ever came here, except in late spring, when the shepherds drove their flocks to the shearing pens beside the watermill. The white horse stood patiently while Ashur removed his rope headcollar, replacing it with a simple bridle.

'Does he have a name now?' Kerin asked.

'Yes, lord,' Ashur said. 'He is Astra. I wanted a Latin name, because now Dimos teaches it to me. And that is one of the words for the stars.' He smiled and kissed the horse's nose. Cynfawr looked on, holding the old carnyx. A few paces away, Edryd and Cheldric were sitting on the cook's ox-cart. The members of Vortigern's warband, all on their warhorses, were ranged along the edge of the wood on the valley's eastern flank. Gwyndaf and Derfyn accompanied them.

'Alright,' Kerin said. 'How do you do this?'

'First the thing for the head,' Ashur said. 'Please to bring it.'

Kerin fetched the mail headpiece from the cart. Ashur drew the horse's head down and blindfolded him with a length of fabric. Moving as quietly as he could, Kerin placed the headpiece. The horse rumbled threateningly. Ashur spoke softly to him and eased his ears through the openings in the scale armour, rolled the protective sleeve down his muscular neck, then slid his hand inside the headpiece and slowly removed the blindfold. Astra's head jerked up and he backed away, snapping and snorting and shaking his head vigorously. Ashur hung on tight to the bridle. The horse calmed and stood still as the boy's hand closed gently over his muzzle.

'There,' he said. 'He is good with it. Now please to put the blanket, then the saddle, and then the *katàphraktos* cloak. This has –' he hesitated and gestured with his free hand.

'A hole?' Kerin queried. 'An opening, so that it can fit around the saddle?'

'Yes, yes. You put, and then I make the hooks.'

Kerin fetched the blanket and the Roman saddle. The smith and the cook heaved the armoured coat out of the cart and fed it over Astra's back. He flinched as the weight settled, but stood without complaint as Kerin arranged the scale armour around the saddle and rolled it back over his rump.

'Good!' Ashur said. 'That is good.' Reins looped on his arm, he hooked the neckpiece to the body armour, deftly closed the fastenings on the horse's chest and ran a hand over his quarters. 'There is no place for the tail. Sometimes here is a hole, and the tail comes through.'

He led the horse alongside the cart, jumped aboard and stepped gently over the side into the saddle. 'Now we try.' He chirruped to the horse and they set off at a sedate walk. The animal seemed more puzzled than resentful at the extra weight and clinking mail. Cynfawr watched as they made a wide circuit of the open ground beside the stream.

'You're not going to make that boy fight, are you?' he asked.

'I hope not,' Kerin said. 'But in case I ever have to kill a horse that's wearing armour like that, I want to know where the weak points are.'

He heard hoofbeats approaching. Vortigern was on his black mare with Publius Luca close behind, riding one of the hunting horses. Ashur came trotting over and jumped off. 'Lord King, in my father's house the *katàphraktos* is better,' he said, pointing to the fastenings on chest and neck. 'Here, nothing. One piece only, over the head and to the tail. A hole for the saddle is all. With this, if the enemies have bows –' he shrugged and drew a finger across his throat. 'Can you shoot the arrow, lord?'

Vortigern grinned. 'Not to save my life. Can you?'

'Oh yes, lord. In my family, all must learn. I shoot good, on the feet and on the horse. To front and to back.'

Vortigern waved to Elir. 'Come over here,' he said. 'Give him your bow.' He took the bow and quiver and handed them to the Parthian boy. 'Is your bow like this?'

'More light,' Ashur said, drawing the string back. 'And – I don't know the word.' He grasped the bow in both hands and bent it as far as he could.

'More flexible,' Vortigern said. 'Can you use this one?'

'Yes, lord. Maybe I shoot not so good.'

'Show us anyway. Can you shoot that tree over there?' Vortigern pointed to a young ash at the edge of the stream.

'Of course,' Ashur said. He fitted an arrow to the bow and loosed it. The head thudded into the slender trunk.

'You're good.' Elir said. 'I couldn't have done that at your age. Do it from the horse. Is the horse still, or moving?'

'Moving,' Ashur said. 'I show. But first, we take off all this. The *katàphraktos* does not carry the bow.' Edryd and Cheldric removed the armour and stowed it in the cart. Slinging bow and quiver onto his shoulder, Ashur sprang onto Astra's back and rode away towards the valley mouth until almost out of sight. The men glimpsed him bend forward and speak to the horse before launching into a brisk canter which was soon a gallop. As he flashed past, Ashur dropped the reins, raised the bow and let the arrow fly. It found its mark above the first one. Ashur rode to the tree, jerked both arrows free and came back. 'Now the other way, lords,' he said. 'Please to stay here.' He rode away past the ash tree, to the point where the valley narrowed and the wood closed in. The horse came galloping back with no apparent direction from his rider. As he drew level with the watching men, Ashur turned in the saddle, took aim and loosed both arrows in quick succession. They smacked into the tree and clung. The warriors of the warband roared and cheered. After a moment one arrow dropped to the ground. The boy came trotting back, looking aggrieved. 'That was not good,' he said. 'I have my own bow, the arrow does not fall.'

'Look,' Elir said, 'I've never seen anyone even try it. I don't know if I could turn in the saddle like that. How do you guide the horse?'

'Legs only,' Ashur said. 'I practise all on the beach with Marc. He is very good.'

'I've seen this,' Publius said. 'Years ago, when I was a young recruit. They turn tail – or you think they have – then they whip round in the saddle and shoot at the riders pur-suing them. My commander fell for it, and we lost scores of men.' He took the bow from Ashur and examined it. 'Their bows are different, though, aren't they, lad.'

'Yes, lord. Not all wood.'

'We copied them,' Publius said, handing the weapon back to Elir. 'The wood's layered with horn and sinew, that's why they're so flexible. I could lay my hands on some, probably.'

'Do it, if you can,' Vortigern said. 'But first, what we came here for. Cynfawr, get on the cart with that thing. Publius, dismount, your horse isn't trained for anything except chasing deer.'

Publius Luca tied the hunting horse to the cart and climbed in beside the bard. Ashur and Astra retreated towards the trees. Lud and Macsen led the warband to the centre of the open ground. Cynfawr, who had waited years for this moment of glory, looked suddenly apprehensive.

'Behold the carnyx,' Vortigern said. 'Cynfawr will speak.'

The bard stood up and cleared his throat. 'Lords, this is the war horn of our forefathers. You have never heard one, and neither have your horses. I have watched you train them for battle with shouting and banging and rackety drums, but believe me, they will not like this. I would advise you all to keep a tight rein.' He raised the instrument and blew gently. The horses' ears went up. Some of them stamped their forefeet as the sound intensified. Kerin felt Eryr stiffen and brace for battle. Macsen's grey reared and bucked. Vortigern's mare flattened her ears and bared her teeth.

'Keep going, Cynfawr,' Vortigern shouted. The horses jostled around, rearing, snorting and lashing out. No-one had given a thought to the effect the noise might have on Cheldric's oxen. With roaring bellows, they lurched forward and began to canter. The sound of the carnyx ceased abruptly as Cynfawr lost his balance and fell over in the back of the cart, taking Publius Luca with him. Edryd made a grab for the terrified hunting horse, missed, and went headfirst over the tailboard.

'Odin!' Cheldric howled, hauling on the reins. The hunting horse broke free and bolted. The cart bumped off down the valley with the oxen bellowing frantically, Publius and the bard rolling about in the scale armour and Edryd clinging to the tailboard. The warhorses all calmed down and stood around, chewing at their bits. Kerin closed his eyes. He knew that this was no time for levity, but sometimes it couldn't be helped.

'What the hell was that?' Derfyn asked.

'The mouthpiece of the gods,' Vortigern said, tight-lipped. In the middle distance, the ox-cart shuddered to a halt and people started to right themselves. Derfyn grimaced.

'They had a bad day, then,' he said. The king and his right arm exchanged wry glances, then began to laugh. The world is mad, Kerin thought, and we are adrift in it; about to confront five hundred cataphracts with no armour and a war horn that has been asleep for three hundred years. He watched the ox-cart lumbering back with Edryd driving, Cheldric throwing his arms about and Cynfawr hugging the carnyx to his breast as if it had been his wife. Tomorrow will be a better day, he thought. And at least it frightened the horses.

<h1 style="text-align:center">40</h1>

The council of war convened in the room where Vortigern met his estate managers. A handful of men sat at the table with the king. Edryd had been sent to Glevum on a fast horse, to learn how things lay. No solid strategy could be formulated until he came back, but everyone wanted to hear Publius Luca's account of cataphract warfare. A week had passed since the warhorses encountered the carnyx. Now, after days of solid training, they no longer feared it at all; they greeted its appearance with the quivering intensity which always gripped them in the moments before battle. Perhaps, in some obscure way, they already knew what it was for.

'Cataphracts are shock troops,' Publius said. 'The horses don't have to be fast or agile. The riders don't have to be skilled, although some of them are. You simply throw them at your enemy's front line like a battering ram, hoping that they'll flatten enough of his best men to leave the rest defenceless against the forces coming behind. More often than not, it works. Your horse warriors are the best I've ever seen, but even they couldn't withstand a cataphract charge. It's like being hit by a moving wall.'

'What weapons do they carry?' Vortigern asked.

'Lances. Like a spear with a much longer, heavier shaft. And swords. The lances aren't throwing weapons, the rider will try to impale you or stab your horse in the chest, or simply knock over everything in his path and trample it to death. I've seen you do that yourselves, of course, but this is different. Your horses fight. Cataphract horses don't fight, they just go where they're directed, and because they're big and strong and covered in armour, they're very hard to stop.'

'We could outrun them, though,' Kerin said.

'And outmanoeuvre them,' Gwyndaf said. 'That white horse was a different animal with the scale armour on.'

There was a knock at the door. Cenydd came in, looking agitated. 'Lord,' he said, 'Gallus Mercator is here, and that mad Saxon who sails with him. They look as if they've been in a fight.'

'Gallus!' Vortigern exclaimed. 'Bring them in here.' His eyes met Kerin's. Cenydd ushered the two men in and withdrew. Oswi had a black eye, and his right arm was bandaged from wrist to elbow. Gallus, who was limping slightly, was cut over his right eyebrow. An ugly bruise, probably inflicted by the same blow, ran from his cheekbone to the collar of his tunic. The men at the table shuffled along the benches and they sat down. 'Are you alright?' Vortigern asked. Gallus exhaled.

'Yes. But it's years since I had a proper fight. Not like you mighty warriors. These days I usually have someone to do it for me.'

'He fights good, lord,' Oswi said. 'You should put him in your warband, yes?'

'No, God forbid,' Vortigern said. 'What happened? I thought you were going back to Londinium.'

'I was,' Gallus said. 'But after you and Kerin left, Claudius came to find me. One of his ferries had just come in from Abona. The boys on the wharf there had told the captain that they were expecting another *oneraria*. Well, what could I do? We painted over the *Audax*'s nameboards and went over there. They've got a new man in charge of the port, one of Rufus's lackeys. I spoke British to him with an Anatolian accent and told him I was from Byzantium. Welcome to Abona, Master Kamani, he said, may we do a fortune's worth of business. Then he brought us a jug of wine and said we were welcome to stay, but if we wanted to leave we should do it soon, because he was expecting a big ship, and it might block the harbour mouth. Sure enough, when we got out into the channel there was the *oneraria* with the same two escorts, sitting around waiting for the high tide. We sailed back to Isca as fast as we could. There was an old shallow draft galley there, with sixteen oars. I asked Claudius if I could borrow it.'

'Ha,' said Oswi, 'you did not tell him that he would never see it again.'

'Well,' Gallus said, 'what should I have said? Lend me your galley, Claudius, so that I can set it on fire and ram it into the *oneraria?*'

'Is that what you did?' Lud asked blankly.

'Well, that was the intention. We loaded the galley with anything that would burn and went straight back out. The ships weren't far from Cambria, and the boys can row like demons, so it didn't take long. It was beginning to get dark. One of the *actuariae* had gone, probably to Abona, to check the depth of the water. I looked at the other one sitting there and thought, it's got a beak on it, it would make a better ram than this galley. We rowed round the far side. There was no sign of anyone, so we grabbed the grappling hooks – we always carry them, you never know, do you – and up we went. The crewmen were all down below, playing knucklebones. We just went down the hatch and jumped on them.'

'Was easy,' Oswi said. 'But then others come. Big men,

shouting words even Master Gallus does not know. Now we have a bad fight. But his boys are bastards, good with the knife. We lose only one man. The other side, fish food. Then we fetch all from the galley.'

'Pitch and oil,' Gallus said. 'And there were bales of clothing and horse blankets in the hold so we knew it would catch.' He took a deep breath; some unseen damage seemed to be troubling him. 'And then this stupid arsehole said he wouldn't burn the horses. I told him if he wanted to try freeing them, it was up to him, but he was on his own. He jumped straight in the water and started climbing up the anchor chain. And you think I'm mad. The boys got on the oars, and we rowed a bit closer to the *oneraria* to give them something to look at. A couple of the crew started shouting at us. Syriac again. They asked where the captain was. I told them he was sick down below – truer than they'd ever know – and we had to get him ashore. I just wanted a good run at them. There wasn't a breath of wind, it was all on the oarsmen. So there we were, rowing towards Abona, wondering how long it would take to cut through the tethers of two hundred odd horses. Then someone got thrown into the sea from the *oneraria*. Whoever it was, we had to go back. I was on the steering oar. I brought her about, then I went down below and set fire to everything in the hold. It went up like a bonfire. The boys gave me all they had. I told them to jump when I gave the command. Then the flames started coming up through the deck. I shouted, the boys jumped, I hung on the oar for a bit and we hit the thing broadside.'

'And then the ship tips over,' Oswi said. 'I pray to Odin for this! Now the side of the ship is the floor, the hatch is open, so horses can climb out and jump in the sea. Some will drown, but most will live. Everything starts to burn.

This is terror for the horses. They kick, break the wood. I grab one and go out with him. Here is the sea, full of horses, and here is our galley. We put a long rope on the horse, he swims, all follow. We all row, and we come to land somewhere.'

'Mother of God,' Vortigern said. 'Where?'

'No idea,' Gallus said. 'Somewhere east of Isca with mudbanks and a marsh. Us and about two hundred wasted horses. There was a man there with a flock of sheep. I told him he could have a horse if he could get word to Claudius in Isca. And that's what happened. They came to get us. I don't remember much more, to be truthful.'

'I remember all,' Oswi said. 'But first, please, Kerin, you send your old man for Master Gallus. He will not say, but he is hurt, here.'

'I've cracked some ribs, man, that's all,' Gallus said irritably. Kerin went out. There was only one man for this task, however confident he was in Morvid's skill.

The haruspex was in his guest chamber, poring over a manuscript borrowed from Vortigern's library.

'What ails you, my young friend?' he asked. 'Something does, evidently.'

'It's not me, it's Gallus Mercator,' Kerin said. 'He's just – well, he can tell you himself.'

Marcellus raised his eyebrows. 'Bring him here, then,' he said. 'I never travel without my remedies and my instruments, particularly when I'm likely to be in the company of mad men. Not that I was expecting this one.'

Gallus sat on the edge of Marcellus's bed and reluctantly removed his tunic. One side of his torso was blackened with bruises, the other covered by a makeshift dressing. Kerin filled a goblet of wine from the jug on Marcellus's side table and handed it to him.

'Sit still,' Marcellus said. 'You won't enjoy this, but I have to get it off.' Gallus downed the wine, clenched his jaw and cursed under his breath as Marcellus picked away. The dressing dangled from the forceps, covered in dried blood and pus and dead skin. The area beneath looked like raw meat. 'A burn,' Marcellus said, tossing the dressing into the fire. 'And quite an extensive one, but not too deep, I'm pleased to say. What have you been up to, Master Gallus?'

'Burning a ship,' Gallus said, wincing as Marcellus explored the other side of his chest.

'And yourself, evidently,' Marcellus said. 'You've cracked some ribs here, but they will heal on their own, as will these injuries to your face, which look like the result of an everyday brawl in the alehouse. Now, sit still while I mix something.' He took a small bowl from his medicine chest, poured in a measure of the red wine and added a spoonful of thick, viscous liquid from one of his many stoppered jars. 'Myrrh,' he said, stirring vigorously. 'A fine thing for preventing infection. Now, this will hurt like the devil, but be assured, you will thank me tomorrow. Kerin, perhaps you could ask the Lord King if he can spare a nightshirt or a lightweight undergarment. I'm sure Master Gallus isn't planning to leave tonight, and we don't want too much pressure. No, keep still! That's better. I'm not going to ask why you were burning a ship, but I imagine it had something to do with the coming conflict between Vortigern and his son. May I offer you some advice?'

'No, you meddling old goat,' Gallus said angrily.

'Well, I shall offer it anyway. I am one of the few men who know what really happened in the curia, that night after the triumph. You came out of it badly, but not as badly as most of the others. And you've made amends, so don't spend the rest of your life crucifying yourself over it. There's already enough of that going on in this house. Kerin, perhaps you could ask Cenydd to provide a bed. Now drink this, Master Gallus; something to ward off the infection, you understand. But sleep is the thing, you know; sleep is the thing.'

Kerin found Cenydd. 'Gallus needs a bed,' he said. 'And an undershirt of Vortigern's, something light. He's got a nasty burn, and Marcellus doesn't want anything weighing on it. There's no need to ask, just take one.'

'I'm past being surprised, lad,' Cenydd said. 'And at least I don't have to go to the bard's house and ask him to get one from the Druids' Wood.'

Kerin went back to the meeting. Vortigern raised his hand for silence.

'He's alright,' Kerin said. 'He's got a burn here the size of a meat platter, but Marcellus has dressed it and given him something – well, he said it was against infection, but I think it was a sleeping draught.'

'He would not leave the steering oar,' Oswi said. 'Afterwards he said to me, the beak has to hit the big ship just right. And it did. And now we have two hundred strong horses in Isca, and all the horse armour is at the bottom of the sea. We have done a good thing, yes?'

'Yes,' Vortigern said. 'You're a pair of raving lunatics, but yes. You've done a good thing.'

41

The *Audax* was lying in the bay. Gallus and Oswi had arrived in a carriage loaned by Claudius, but now the crew had come to fetch them, and to retrieve the new war galley from its hiding place in the sand dunes. Oswi was with them, directing operations. Another, smaller ship had followed the *Audax* in on the high tide and was anchored alongside. As Kerin dismounted on the beach, he saw that it was flying the bright blue banner of Kernow. Gorlois had come ashore in a rowing boat and was talking to the crewmen.

'Kerin Brightspear!' he hollered.

'The Bear of Kernow!' Kerin shouted back. Gorlois came striding over and pumped his hand.

'Put me out of my misery, boy! Those lads have been telling me a tale. It's so outlandish I can hardly believe it, but I don't think they've got the wits to make it up, either.'

'Well,' Kerin said, 'if it's about setting fire to an enormous ship full of armoured horses, it's the truth.'

'By the gods,' Gorlois said. 'Master Gallus came good in the end, then.'

'Yes, at great risk to his own life. And there's more to come, I'm sure.'

'Here he is now,' Gorlois said, waving enthusiastically. Gallus and Vortigern were walking across the beach. 'Master merchant!' Gorlois boomed. 'The hero of the hour!'

'I set fire to a ship, Lord Gorlois,' Gallus said dryly. 'It's quite easy, to be truthful.'

'The trick is not setting fire to yourself,' Vortigern said. 'He hasn't quite mastered that yet, unfortunately, so keep your arms to yourself.'

Gorlois, on the point of delivering one of his crushing hugs, looked cheated. 'I merely wished to offer my compliments,' he said.

'It has halved the odds against us,' Vortigern said.

'And we've also gained two hundred big strong cavalry horses,' Kerin added.

'Thanks to Oswi the Horseman,' Gallus said. 'I'd probably have burned the lot, so you'd better go and hug him instead. I'm sure he'll love it.' He turned to Vortigern as Gorlois strode away. 'The fight's imminent. I shouldn't be leaving.'

'You should by all means be leaving,' Vortigern said. 'Go back to Londinium, heal yourself and start building galleys. I've got hundreds of good horse warriors, but only two good sea captains. It would be the height of stupidity to get yourself killed in a cavalry charge, wouldn't it.'

'Yes,' Gallus conceded. 'Lord King,' he added meekly. The three men laughed and shook hands. It was a parting, but it didn't feel like one. It simply felt like the prelude to another mad, hair-raising enterprise.

*

The men who had gathered outside the chieftains' hall listened for the tell-tale clink of mail. Kerin and Ashur came to meet them with Astra, fully armoured. Gorlois stared, silenced for once.

'This is Lord Gorlois of Kernow,' Vortigern said. 'He's on our side, and he's going to help us against the *katàphraktos*. Show him the weak points in the armour.'

The rest of the strategists left them to it and went back inside.

'You can't stop a cataphract charge with unarmoured horses,' Publius Luca said. 'But you can wear them out, or outrun them, or encircle them and force them into close combat –'

'Or you could drown them,' Vortigern said. Everyone came to attention. 'You could drown them,' he repeated. 'We have a river. A deep, wide river with bridges which we can destroy or defend. And they're on the other side of it. If we cross the river, and make them chase us, we can ford it, but –'

'Stop!' Publius Luca raised his hand. For a moment, Kerin imagined himself back in a stifling tent, listening to Vortigern explain how he intended to lure the Picts from their mountain stronghold. 'This is different,' Publius said. 'This isn't the North. And Rufus isn't stupid. He won't let his cataphracts go into the water. If anyone chases you, it'll be Eldof's warriors and the Sword of God.'

'Then we should let the cataphracts cross,' Kerin said. 'We should let them cross on the big bridge at Glevum, then burn it behind them. They'll be caught between us and the river. If they charge us, we can run them ragged.'

'And if Eldof and Rufus are coming behind them with a thousand light cavalry who can ford the river?' Publius enquired.

'Then it'll be time to frighten the horses,' Kerin said. Publius sighed.

'Look, Kerin,' he said, 'I know you're excited about the carnyces. I applaud the smiths' skill for making the new one, and I don't want to upset the druids. But please, don't get carried away. Take your carnyces to the battlefront, by all means, but don't expect them to stop a cavalry charge. They didn't save the Gauls from Julius Caesar, and they're not going to save you.'

Gorlois came back in and frowned, sensing some development to which he wasn't party.

'Do you have any horse archers?' Vortigern asked.

'Well, I've got about twenty boys who can shoot,' Gorlois said. 'Not all of them could hit that sort of a target, though.'

'Send me the ten best' Vortigern said. 'Lucius, how many cavalry can you raise?'

'Around the same as we had in Kent,' Lucius said.

'Take your time,' Publius Luca said sharply. 'This is fraught with risk. And if you let them all cross the Hafren, you're sacrificing your one great natural line of defence.'

'Publius, you are the voice of wisdom, as always,' Vortigern said. 'But wisdom didn't beat the Picts, did it? It didn't get us two hundred fresh cavalry horses.'

Publius Luca threw his hands up. 'I simply don't want to see you lose your best men.'

Lud stood up. 'Publius Imperator,' he said, 'we owe you more than most of these men will ever know. But the day I stand back because my enemy has the advantage is far off. We didn't stand aside in Isca, did we.' He gave Vortigern a nod. 'I'm going to the archdruid, to ask him for a blessing. It's the night of Calan Gaeaf in ten days' time, in case you'd forgotten, and we should call on the strength of the true powers.'

Publius Luca stared at the ceiling as the sound of Lud's trotting horse faded away.

'Don't take offence,' Kerin said. 'None was meant.'

'I know,' Publius said. 'But I don't want to see any of you

killed because your incomparable leader has some hare-brained scheme –'

Vortigern began to laugh. 'It's not hare-brained, Publius,' he said. 'It's going to work. You have to trust me.'

'Look,' Gorlois said uneasily, 'there's something going on here that I haven't been told about.'

'Forgive me, Gorlois,' Vortigern said. 'There's something you need to see. Lucius, please take Lord Gorlois to the archdruid. Gwyndaf, go and alert your boys.' The three men went out. Publius Luca's hand closed over Vortigern's.

'Look,' he said, 'I know you're confident. But for the gods' sake, think, because if this goes wrong, you could all die at that river. You should not let your enemy cross it. And don't view your carnyces as anything more than glorified war trumpets. If you're wrong about either of these things, there'll be catastrophe.'

Vortigern leaned forward. 'I know,' he said. 'But I'm not wrong. You have to trust me, and my infallible instincts.'

Lucius came back. 'What now, lord?' he asked. 'Do you want me to go for my lads?'

'Yes. Go by way of Blestium. I'll give you letters for Varro, and for Claudius Custos in Isca. He can accommodate your men in the fortress. And find me a chariot. There'll be one there somewhere. It would be demeaning to take the carnyces to the battlefront in a cart.'

'I'll at least see to that,' Publius Luca said. 'If I can't drive a carriage from here to Isca and find a chariot, then I really am as fit for the funeral pyre as you seem to think.'

'I didn't say that,' Vortigern protested. 'I merely don't want to see you taking unnecessary risks.'

Publius Luca smiled gravely. 'I'll lay that one at your door, Lord King,' he said.

42

'The women will go to the fire,' Gael said. 'As much as Tirion and I are Christians, some of the others are not. Most of them can't make up their minds, to be truthful, but there are a few like Mora and Anwen who keep the old gods in their hearts.' She flung a blanket around her shoulders and fed the flames under the cauldron. 'I love the fires. Unless they're like the last one, of course, where all those things happened. They're exciting, whatever you believe. And I don't think God would be angry with us for enjoying them, do you, Brother?'

Brother Padarn, who had come to share the breakfast gruel, smiled broadly. 'No I do not,' he said. 'We Christians are quite happy to borrow from the old faith when it suits us. I'm sure it can't be coincidence that Jesus was born at the time of the midwinter feast, when people are hanging up bunches of berries and eating too much, just like they've always done.'

'I'll bet you wouldn't say that in front of Father Paulinus,' Kerin said, through a mouthful of warm bread.

'No, lad, I wouldn't,' Padarn said. 'Or at least, I wouldn't have done when I was living under his roof. I really don't care what the man thinks now. Even Iustig doesn't seem to mind his flock disporting themselves a bit, and if Father Septimus was here at midwinter, I think he'd be sitting down and having a jar with the rest of us.'

'What do the Saxons think about it?' Kerin asked his cook. 'Do you have fires?'

'We take out the old fire in the house, and make a new one,' Cheldric said. 'But not the big fire of the druids. I will go to see it. Midsummer's Eve was a bad night. There was trouble, so I stayed in the house. This time, I hope, no trouble.'

'There's no reason for trouble,' Kerin said. 'And the druids will make sure that it's a good fire, because they know there's a battle coming, and everyone will want to ask for the gods' favour.'

'Even the Christians,' Gael said, with a sly wink at Brother Padarn. 'Will you come with us, Brother? I expect I'll go with Cheldric in his cart, because this man here will play the devil if I try to walk up the headland.' She groaned and clasped her belly.

'And so he should,' Padarn said. 'I'll come with you, but I'll keep out of the way. If Father Iustig wants to argue with the druids, that's his business.'

'Quite so,' Gael said. She got up and kissed Kerin on the cheek. 'We'll leave when the sun's setting. I'm going to see Rowenna, to ask if she wants to come with us.'

'The Queen of all the Britons can't go to the fire in a cook's ox cart,' Kerin said sternly. Gael snorted with laughter.

'You can sound quite like him when you try,' she said. Catula came in to clear the breakfast bowls.

'May I go to the fire, lord?' she asked. 'I won't get in the way.'

'Of course,' Kerin said. 'Go to Lud's house, and ask Mora if she wants to go too. She's struggling to walk far these days.' He turned to Padarn as the girl went out. 'There's something you could do for me. Go to see Brwyn. He's a Christian in your mould, and he's breaking his heart because his sons have joined the Sword of God. He asked if I'd apologise to Vortigern. He'd feel better if he did it himself, but he can't face it. Could you just pray with him, or comfort him in some way?'

Padarn sighed. 'Thank God I'm a monk with no children to worry about. I'll ask him to make me a nice staff for walking around the cliffs. It's always best to have a reason for turning up at a man's door, instead of coming straight out with it.' He paused. 'These armoured horses. If you can see them off, will that be the end of it?'

'No. They've got enough men in reserve to fight us in the spring anyway. But if we can destroy the cataphracts, it'll be a fair fight.' Kerin flung some wood onto the fire, buckled on his sword belt and headed for the stables. He had not mentioned the other thing which had been niggling away at him, although he suspected that Vortigern must already have worked it out for himself. It was a costly business, fighting a war. He knew how much he had had to sequestrate, in gold and corn, simply to pay Hengist. He knew what it had taken to compensate Gallus for converting enough cargo boats to keep the Picts out of Londinium's river. He had no idea what it must have cost to pay for two enormous *onerariae*, the two accompanying ships and their crews, five hundred cataphracts and however many other Sarmatian mercenaries Batraz could call on; let alone the army which was about to spend the winter encamped at Sarum with its hundreds of hungry horses and hangers-on. And yet, to the best of his knowledge, Rufus had no money. Like most wealthy men's sons, he had been entirely dependent on his father for the food he ate, the roof over his head, the horses he rode, the clothes he wore, the weapons he used. All gone forever now, sacrificed on the altar of a pitiless god. And yet here was this massive, threatening force, gathering like a storm cloud on the far side of the Hafren, paid for by – whom? By frugal Abbot Paulinus? By Eldof and Garagon, fellow-travellers serving their own ends, who couldn't even loosen their purse strings to pay for the defence of the kingdom? Marc and Ashur came out of the stables, smiling, as if they'd just shared a joke.

'Marc, saddle Blaidd for me,' Kerin said. 'And Ashur, tell the Lord I'm going for a ride. I'd like him to come along, if he has time.'

*

The sky was clear, but the sea was leaden grey. Kerin felt cold just looking at it. Far above on the height of Penrhyn Fawr the fire of Calan Gaeaf was beginning to take shape as morning slid into afternoon.

'I've told them not to play the carnyces,' Vortigern said. 'Not loudly, anyway. They can bring them, but the people can't hear the battle roar. The whole of Henfelin isn't going to keep its collective mouth shut.'

'Wait until we come back from the river,' Kerin said. 'You've already promised a midwinter feast. If all goes well, they can play them there.'

'If all goes well,' Vortigern said. 'It's a gamble, whatever I told Publius. If the cataphracts have heard a carnyx before, if the bridge won't burn, if Rufus has more men in Glevum than we think –'

'The bridge not catching fire is a risk,' Kerin said. 'We'll need oil, lots of it. Pitch stinks, they'd know what was coming. At least the rain's stopped, and there's been a wind, so the timbers should be dry. And we'll need something that'll catch easily, like the horse blankets did on the *actuaria*.'

'Send Edryd and Cheldric to set the fire,' Vortigern said. 'If anyone can get a fire to light, it ought to be a smith and a cook.' He stopped in the middle of the windy beach. 'What is it? Something's troubling you.'

'I want to know who's paying for all this,' Kerin said. 'I know what it cost to pay Hengist and compensate Gallus, and it's a horse-fly's bite on the hide of this thing that's coming for us. Rufus hasn't got any money, and none of the others are going to pay for ships and cataphracts and armies.'

'I've spent days and nights thinking about this,' Vortigern said. 'If I sold everything I have, I couldn't finance Rufus's offensive. The money's coming from somewhere outside, probably from the Ambrosius family or their supporters. They're one of the richest families in the Empire. And this has happened since we went to Kent for Macsen. Anyone with modest wealth and the right message could have raised the forces Rufus had there.'

Kerin looked out at the sea. Its bleakness reflected his thoughts. 'Lucius told me something. He said that one of Bishop Germanus's associates has been tutoring Ambrosius and his brother. The boys have been told that the Saxons are God's revenge on you for killing Constans. I don't know if this priest believes it, or if it's just a tool. I haven't mentioned it before because there was no point.'

Vortigern looked up at the sky. 'Well,' he said, 'I shan't bother to say my prayers when Hengist comes back.' He reached out and caressed the pricked ears of the bay filly Gwyndaf had given him. Perhaps there was some comfort in simple gestures like that. 'You know what this means.'

'If that family are Rufus's paymasters? Yes. Even if we can destroy the cataphracts and hold off Eldof and the Sword of God, there'll be something just as bad coming next time. Unless the paymasters lose patience. Rufus has probably promised that he's going to trounce us. But he's already lost half the cataphracts, and if we give him another beating, they may decide that the price is too high. That they may as well dispense with him and look for another way to grab power. Or perhaps they'll just wait.'

'Until we've taken the edge off the Saxons for them,' Vortigern said. 'Yes. I'd thought of that. But we can't be distracted by it now. If we do nothing, they'll come roaring over the bridges and burn everything from Blestium to the coasts of Dyfed.'

Kerin smiled wryly. 'You don't need a prophet, lord.'

'No,' Vortigern said. 'But I need a right arm. Now more than ever.' He reached out and gripped Kerin's shoulder. Kerin returned the gesture and they sat like that in the middle of the windswept beach while the shouts of the fire-builders mingled with the harsh laughter of circling gulls.

'When I married Gael, I thought my life was complete,' Kerin said. 'Then she made a home for me, and conceived our child. And now these bastards – these crazy, deluded, bloodletting bastards – want to take all that away. I swear on everything I love that if it's the last thing I do in this life, I'll stop them at the river.' His hand fell away and stroked Blaidd's arched neck. You will carry me this time, he thought. You're ready, and so am I.

'Good,' Vortigern said. 'The right kind of anger. It's as Gallus said. Store it for a while, and it gets stronger. And it's stronger because you can control it, and use it with a clear head. It's the one thing you've lacked. But not any more. You're ready to lead in your own right.'

'Then let me do it,' Kerin said. 'No man should have to lead an army against his own son. For God's sake, you've spent your life drowning in blood. Longer than my lifetime. Let me lead.'

'I can't' Vortigern said. 'They'll say that the king's a has-been, who can't fight his own battles. It may be nonsense, but so is saying that the Saxons are the wrath of God.'

The sound of drumming hooves cut through the rush of wind and waves.

'Edryd,' Kerin said. 'He told me he'd be back for Calan Gaeaf.' The smith, a competent horseman now, came splashing across the river where its shallows met the sea. He and his mare were both blowing and looked as if they'd come a long way fast.

'Lords,' he gasped. 'It's all happening in Glevum.'

'Slow down,' Kerin said. Edryd took a few deep, steadying breaths.

'It's happening,' he said. 'They're gathering, for sure.'

Kerin's house was the one with the best fire. Gael and Rowenna were sitting beside it. Catula was walking around cradling Tirion's baby.

'We're looking after him,' Gael said. 'She's gone to put some wood on the fire for Hefin. He was for the old gods, if anything. Take him to the kitchen, sweetheart, and ask Cheldric to bring us some of that blackberry stuff.' Catula gave the three men a shy smile and went out. They sat down with the women amidst the blankets and cushions.

'So, Edryd the smith,' Rowenna said, 'have you come to bring us terrible news from Glevum?'

'Speak freely,' Vortigern said. 'There's nothing they can't know.'

'Well, the cataphracts are there,' Edryd said. 'It's the only place they can cross the river. They're training on that flat plain near the veteran soldiers' houses. Eldof's got about five hundred horse warriors inside the city, plus his foot soldiers, and some of the Sword of God have just arrived. Under that lad from Henfelin, I'm sorry to say, Lord King. Bertil Redknife's stayed at the training camp in Sarum, thank goodness, but that Sarmatian – Batraz, is it? The one who killed the harbourmaster? – he's got hundreds of other cavalry, normal ones. The bishop's boys said he's frothing at the mouth about losing the other ship. They managed to swim all the horses ashore from the first one, but when Batraz found out that he was missing three sets of horse armour, he beheaded the poor sod who was in charge of unloading. I felt a bit guilty for a moment. It's quite a thing, isn't it, to behead someone over that.'

'Don't worry,' Vortigern said, accepting a mug of steaming brew from Cheldric. 'He'll be dead before long.' The cook passed the drinks around.

'Sit down, Cheldric,' Kerin said. 'How do you feel about going back to Glevum?'

'With him?' Cheldric asked.

'Yes. There's work for you both. Lord, it's for you to explain.'

Everyone took notice; the two men, wondering what their mission might be, and the women, waiting for Vortigern to add detail to the prospect of horror which their minds had already fashioned.

'It's simple,' he said. 'The only way the cataphracts can cross the river is by the main bridge at Glevum. We let them cross, burn the bridge behind them and trap them against the river. We're hoping that they'll never have heard a carnyx before, and if they haven't, the horses may panic. But we can't count on that, so the most important thing is to burn the bridge. Edryd and Cheldric, that's your task. Tell no-one. Kerin will give you instructions in the morning. Now, go to the stables and tell Ashur to prepare two good, strong horses that can pull a grain wagon. Then collect whatever you need, eat, and sleep. Go to the fire if you wish, but I want you away at first light.'

The smith and the cook hurried out, chatting eagerly. Kerin had nothing to add to what Vortigern had said; it would have been cruel to embellish what the two women already knew. Gael reached for his hand.

'We know,' she said. 'But we have faith.'

Rowenna's hand joined theirs. 'And we did not choose for peace and quiet.'

Vortigern's hand closed over the three others. 'Good,' he said. 'We're not likely to see it in my lifetime.' The silence lasted for a few blessed moments. The latch clicked and Tirion came in.

'Oh!' she exclaimed. 'Forgive me, I didn't know –'

'Come in, girl,' Vortigern said. 'You've been to lay wood on the fire for Hefin, I'm told.'

'Yes, lord,' Tirion said. 'Even though I'm a Christian, it felt like the right thing to do. I didn't even have a body to bury. I expect they just threw him in a ditch in Kent. But once the wood is burned, I'll feel as if Hefin's spirit is free. As if I can take that with me, instead of thinking about a dead body all the time. Does that make sense?'

'Perfect sense,' Vortigern said. A shrill wail came from the kitchen.

'Oh, Mother of God, hark at that,' Gael said. 'Come on, feed the brat, then wrap him up warm and come to the fire with us. Better that than sit here fretting.' She took Tirion's arm and the three women went off to the kitchen.

'A moment with you alone,' Vortigern said, and went out into the twilight. Kerin stood beside him. It was quiet out here, just the crying of gulls high above and the contented munching of horses in the stables. 'At the river, you will lead your own warband,' Vortigern said. 'I'll lead the spearhead, as always. We'll draw the cataphracts, outrun them or confront them, depending on how it falls out. But you will lead a band of thirty, the horse archers and the finest spearmen. You alone will have the power to kill a fully-armoured man or horse from a distance, and at speed. And you're at liberty to take anyone you need from my own warband. Elir, obviously.'

Kerin took a deep, calming breath as the initial shock gave way to a steady glow of pride, mingled with a good dose of fear. 'I'll have to take the boys,' he said. 'I know they're young, but Ashur's skill is matchless, and Marc is the closest to him. Elir, obviously. Gwyndaf's lad, Leil. The best of Gorlois's archers.'

'The boys are the same age as you were, when you first rode with me,' Vortigern said. 'You shouldn't think twice about taking them. Take Macsen and Cadfan, too. They're the best spearmen by far, after you.'

'But your own protection –' Kerin began.

'That'll be up to your lads, if I'm on the wrong end of a cataphract lance,' Vortigern said. Kerin's eyes met his. It all sounded more immediate, and more frightening, put like that. His hand moved involuntarily to the crucifix Sevira had given him. Vortigern grinned. 'Do you think he's going to protect you?'

'I don't know,' Kerin said. 'But I'm not above asking.'

'Come on,' Vortigern said. 'It'll be dark before long. We should ask the spirits of Calan Gaeaf, for good measure.'

43

It was beginning. Down on the killing grounds beside the river, fires were already burning as the butchers prepared to slaughter the animals whose carcasses would pack the smokehouses, the salting sheds and the drying barns. Cynan had strewn the sacred herbs and blessed the fires. A thickset man with long, tousled hair was feeding the flames with ash branches. Gwydion the smith, who kept a few pigs, had brought them to the holding pens.

'I have a task for you,' Vortigern said. 'Have you seen the scale armour from Glevum?'

'Yes, lord. A fine bit of work. There's two lots in Cilydd's workshop.'

'And another in my stable,' Vortigern said. 'Can you cut it up and make it into tunics?'

Gwydion blinked. 'I dare say I can. When do you want them, lord?'

'The day after tomorrow. Two to fit young lads the size of your boy, and the rest to fit grown men. As many as you can make from what you have.'

'It'll be done,' Gwydion said. 'Even if we have to work through the night.' He cleared his throat. 'I had that horse boy of yours round the other day, lord, pestering me for arrows. Told me exactly what he wanted, as if he was some warlord. To be honest, it's a handy way to use up bits and pieces of metal, so I went ahead. Did I do right?'

'Yes,' Vortigern said. 'Make as many as you can, and bring them to the citadel with the tunics. Now go and kill your pigs. You don't have much time.'

'That was enterprising of Ashur,' Kerin said, as they rode away. 'Terrified little mouse that he was.'

'He's found his feet,' Vortigern said. 'Alberius had knocked them from under him. He proved himself with the horses, then we discovered something that he could do better than anyone else. Now he thinks he's Mithridates. I hope it doesn't get him killed, that's all.'

A rider was approaching, so familiar in outline that he was instantly recognisable, even in the half light.

'Gwyndaf,' Kerin said. 'You haven't come for the fire, have you?'

'Yes,' Gwyndaf said grudgingly. 'I know I never have done.' He sighed and shook his head. 'I've come for the blessing of the carnyces. I know, I know, I think they're probably a waste of time. But even if I don't believe in any god at all, the men who made them do. And everyone will be there. Men, women, children, priests, believers, unbelievers – everyone. And all that fire, all that hope – it makes a power of its own, even if you leave the gods out of it.' He looked up at the darkening sky. A chill wind had risen, driving ragged clouds across the face of a bright half moon. 'I might take the draco. They may as well bless him, while they're about it.'

'Why not?' Vortigern said. 'Go to the hall and get him. Is Derfyn coming?'

'All my warriors are coming,' Gwyndaf said. 'Our women and children and old ones are already there.'

'Good. Know this now, then. At the river, you and I will lead the spearhead, as before. But Kerin will lead his own band of horse archers and spearmen. He'll take Ashur and Marc, Elir and your lad Leil as bowmen. Macsen and Cadfan as spearmen, amongst others. Varro and Derfyn will replace Kerin and Macsen, insofar as it's possible. I still need my standard- bearer. But come fully armed. Pick someone who can carry the draco if you need to fight.'

'Done,' Gwyndaf said, and trotted off into the deepening darkness.

There was an old fortress on the headland, deserted for centuries. Nothing remained now except for the defensive banks and ditch and some faint humps and hollows within, showing where houses had once stood. A thicket of stunted, windbent trees protected the eastern flank, spilling over into the ditch. It was a good place to leave the horses. But the ditch was not empty. A donkey was picking at the dry grass. Its owner was sitting up on the bank. Kerin had not seen Father Iustig since he left him snoring in a rank little room in the bishop's house.

'What are you doing here, Iustig?' Vortigern asked. 'Why don't you just keep out of it? The druids don't go poking their noses into your church at Christmastide.'

'I'm not poking my nose anywhere,' Iustig said. 'They can light their fires, for all the good it will do.' He looked thinner and older. Whatever he had said or done in Glevum, it had not dissuaded Rufus from raising the most powerful force Vortigern had faced since he confronted the Picts at the Wall.

'Have you heard what's waiting for us across the river?' Kerin asked.

'Padarn told me,' Iustig said. 'It's madness. You can't fight armoured cavalry.'

'What do you want me to do, then?' Vortigern asked.

'Let them come? Let them burn this place to the ground and kill half the people in it, and pretend they're doing it all for God?'

'Talk to him!' Iustig exclaimed.

'Talk to him?' Kerin said. 'Talk to him, like our boys did in Kent, so we can get tricked and hanged like Hefin? Like I tried to do in Glevum? And I'll bet you tried too, didn't you. What did you tell him? That all this can't possibly be God's will?'

'Yes, for what it's worth,' Iustig said. He gave Vortigern a wan smile. 'I told him he should make peace with you. That you should fight the Saxons together.'

Vortigern began to laugh. 'That's the most sensible thing you've said in years, Iustig. But don't waste your breath. Rufus would have killed me in the North, if Kerin hadn't been standing there. And we'd both have been butchered in Kent, if Publius Luca – my friend, Publius Luca – hadn't risked his life to save us. How does that sit with you? Do monks have friends? Or is that one of the things you're supposed to give up, like luxury and women?'

Iustig blenched. They all turned as footsteps came crunching through the dead bracken. Caradog stood at the edge of the ditch, leaning on his oak staff.

'Ha,' he said. 'I thought I heard voices. Come to the fire, lords. We're almost ready. And I've never seen so many people here. What about you, Iustig? This is the night when the door between the worlds swings on its hinges. Will you join us, to ask the spirits to look kindly on the king and his warriors?'

'I'll pray in my own way, thank you,' Iustig said. Caradog grinned, looking up at the vast black dome of the sky and the racing clouds.

'Please yourself,' he said. 'There are more things abroad on this night than you can trap within the walls of your little church.'

Caradog led the way. Cynan had set his torch to the kindling and the fire was beginning to build. No-one could see beyond that blinding light, but the archdruid knew the path so well that the two men had only to follow his bent shoulders. Suddenly, when they were close enough to feel the heat, everything was revealed; a sea of pale faces illuminated by the flames, spilling away over the rough grass to the headland's edge, and upwards across the pasture to the slopes of Crib Garw. Not only the men and women of Henfelin, who came every year, but Hefydd's people, and Gwyndaf's, and beyond them hundreds of others, their limit beyond the reach of the dancing light. Caradog stopped and raised his staff. In the same moment, he and his companions became visible. 'It's the Lord,' someone said, close by. The murmur rippled out and became a roar.

'My God,' Vortigern said. 'Half of Glywysing is here.'

'And they're still with us,' Kerin said. Not that he had doubted it in his heart, but something had been eating away at him, undefined, only half-noticed. He realised that he had been waiting for another ghastly intervention like the arrival of Lucius on Midsummer's Eve. The crushing news of Hefin; the frenzy at the fire; the knowledge that, far away in Kent, a die had been cast forever. There was none of that horror tonight.

'You see?' a voice said at his side. 'I was right. All this has a power of its own.' Gwyndaf had brought the draco. The firelight's dazzling reflection beamed from the dragon's head.

'Yes,' Kerin said. 'Gods or no gods, you were right.' Whatever was waiting beyond the river, he knew that every man who faced it would carry a little of this light in his heart.

'Come,' Caradog said. They followed him to the great flat stone at the fire's edge, where he had stood and defied Iustig on Midsummer's Eve. A small cone of twigs and dried leaves had been built at its centre. The carnyces were lying before it, shrouded in their blankets. People pushed forward, struggling for a closer look, as Cynfawr and Cynan threw back the coverings and raised them up. Gasps and whispered questions followed.

'Are they battle standards?' someone asked.

'No,' Caradog said, drawing Gwyndaf forward. 'Here is the battle standard. These are the mouthpiece of the gods.' The crowd pressed closer. Gael and Rowenna were there, surrounded by the women they had fired with their own resolve. Edryd stood beside them, arm around Cilydd's shoulders. Cynfawr leaned towards Vortigern.

'Lord, may we play the paean to the gods?'

'Yes,' Vortigern said. 'But no more. Is that understood?'

'Completely, lord. Let everyone think that we are merely requesting a blessing upon your endeavours. Which, of course, we are.'

Silence fell over the vast, whispering crowd as Cynfawr began to play. It was the melody Kerin had first heard in the druids' cave, and then in the chieftains' hall; except that this time the new carnyx was singing in harmony with the old, Cynan's matchless skill weaving a kindred melody so lovely, so unforced, that anyone hearing it would think that he had been playing it for years. As the paean ended, there was a moment of stillness so profound that the night seemed to be holding its breath. Caradog raised his hands.

'Now to bless the carnyces and the dragon,' he said, and looked towards the women. 'Where is she? Where is Hefin's wife?'

'She's here,' Gael said, ushering Tirion forward.

'Ah,' the archdruid said gently. 'Come here, girl. This is for you to do.' He gathered the blankets and passed them to Edryd for safekeeping. 'Now, Tirion, bring a brand from the fire.' Tirion did as he had asked. Caradog took the brand and passed the flame lightly over the bowed heads of the carnyces and the draco, murmuring a blessing as old as the fire itself. 'Now,' he said, giving it back to Tirion, 'set light to the sacred things. I'm sure you'll find that when the smoke rises, Hefin's spirit will rise with it.'

Proud and defiant, tears welling, Tirion set the brand to the cone of twigs and leaves. Everyone watched as the fire caught and the smoke rose, higher and higher, vanishing into the upper air with the sweet scent of herbs and the swirling sparks of Calan Gaeaf. Tirion threw the brand into the fire and ran to Cheldric's cart, where Catula was sitting beside Padarn, Marc, Ashur and Dimos, cradling the baby. Cheldric leaned down to take her hands and hoisted her up beside them. She grabbed her child and held him tightly, burying her face in his shawl.

'Good,' Caradog said. 'Hefin's spirit is free now. And so is hers, I expect.' He turned to Vortigern and Kerin. 'There has never been such a fire gathering in my lifetime. Now the carnyces are filled with its power. Carry that power with you, and don't waste it.'

'We won't,' Kerin said.

'I wasn't talking to you,' Caradog said. He looked up at Vortigern. 'It's a cruel thing for a man, making war on his own son. But every one of these has come here for you. Promise me that you'll keep faith with them.'

Vortigern looked towards the towering pillar of smoke and flame. 'I swear by the gods by whom my people swear,' he said. Caradog raised his eyebrows.

'The old oath,' he said. 'Not quite a Christian after all, then.'

'No,' Vortigern said. 'Just a fool who'd die for this land and everyone in it. If anyone's listening tonight, perhaps it won't be this time.' He touched his fingers to Caradog's wild hair and walked away, shaking the smiths by the hand, kissing Gael's brow, catching Rowenna's hand and vanishing into the darkness with her. Caradog watched them go.

'Every year, since he was a lad no older than those two on the cart, every time he's gone off to take some mad risk, I've begged the powers to defend him. Their strength is infinite. But even I don't know how far their patience can be stretched. Whether one day they may tire of hearing the same old priest make the same request, time after time. If they do, will you be standing beside him?'

'I swear by the gods by whom my people swear,' Kerin said, then clasped his crucifix and pressed it to his lips, just in case.

44

The grain wagon was standing outside the chieftain's hall, horses harnessed, tools and scant food supplies stowed under the drivers' seat. Kerin handed the leather bag to Edryd. Inside was a letter, bearing his signature and secured with his personal seal. 'The letter is for Claudius Custos, the harbourmaster at Isca. I've asked him to give you as many amphorae of olive oil as your cart can hold. The other document is something you can produce if anyone asks what you're up to. The guards on the city gates, for example. It says that the oil belongs to a Byzantine merchant called Master Kamani, who's making his base at Abona.'

'Does he exist?' Edryd asked. 'This Master Kamani?'

'The new harbourmaster at Abona believes he does, and that's all that matters. To be truthful, you're not likely to be stopped by anyone who can read. But you can wave the thing at them and say that you've been told to take the oil to the market. Once you're inside the city, hide the oil somewhere safe, then go straight to Malan's village and tell them to get out.'

Edryd raised his eyebrows. 'I'll tell them,' he said. 'But can you see Malan listening to reason?'

'No,' Kerin admitted. 'But Runo and Berget might. Tell them to follow the river north. There's a decent bridge about a day from Glevum, and a good track going west. It passes a town with a few Roman buildings – Ariconium, I think. They can cross the Gwy there and follow the Roman road down to Isca.'

'I've heard of it,' Edryd said. 'It was a big iron-working place years ago. Not any more, but they should be able to get provisions there.'

'Do you have a plan?' Kerin asked.

'Yes. As soon as we've hidden the oil and seen Malan, we'll get hold of a boat and some tackle. There's always fishermen around that bridge. We'll be able to keep an eye on things without looking obvious. There's a shack on the bank just upstream where the river boys drink, you can see the boats pulled out on the bank. If we start having a jar there every evening, they'll get used to seeing us and you'll know where to find us.'

Kerin took a pouch from his belt and handed it to Edryd. 'This should pay for all you need. Buy a boat, don't steal one.'

'We'll be in that shack on the bank every night,' Edryd said. 'When you're close, send somebody that we know.'

'We are there,' Cheldric said fiercely. 'This smith, and his friend who does not speak.'

Edryd grinned. 'I tell them he's a deaf mute,' he said, cuffing Cheldric over the head. 'It saves explaining. And it shuts him up, so I don't have to listen to him.' He ducked, laughing, as Cheldric roared and swung at him.

'Get lost,' Kerin said, laughing too. 'It's a long way to Glevum.'

Gael came from the house as the wagon rattled away. 'They're brave men,' she said. 'I hope no harm comes to them. Or to your band. The boys are so young!'

'I know. But they're the best we have. Vortigern's left it to me, to tell them. Come with me, if you like.'

They went to the stables. Marc, who had picked up some good habits, was examining his horse's feet. Like its rider, the horse had filled out and matured since it set off for the North as a green colt. It had a name now. Hebog, the hawk. Not a bad name, Kerin thought; the horse was fast, agile and nasty with strangers, just as might be expected from a warhorse, or indeed from a bird of prey.

'Where's Ashur?' Kerin asked. Marc straightened up, surprised to see both Kerin and his wife.

'Gone to the grain store for feed. Why? Have we done something wrong?'

'Not as far as I know,' Kerin said. 'Go and find him. The feed can wait.'

The boys were soon back. They looked at Kerin and Gael, and at each other, as if expecting something unpleasant.

'You'll be fighting at the river,' Kerin said. 'The Lord has told me to form a warband of horse archers and spearmen, to attack the cataphracts. You two and Elir are the best archers by far. Your age doesn't matter. I was your age, the first time I rode with Vortigern. You can refuse if you wish. No-one enters the warbands without understanding that he might lose his life. Are you with us?'

'Lord,' Ashur whispered, 'it is the greatest honour.'

Marc stared down at his feet, reddening. 'I wasn't expecting this when I stuck a pig spear in Bertil Redknife.'

'Good,' Kerin said. 'Our strength will be in our speed, so no armour for Astra and Hebog. But Gwydion is making tunics from the scale armour for all you archers, enough to cover chest and arms to the elbow, so a little protection for you. Aside from that, you'll have the triple-layered leather jerkins and gauntlets which the rest of us wear. Exactly the same as Vortigern's, if that makes you feel better. Now get up to the mill, and ask Gwynfi for twenty new quivers, good strong ones, made of canvas. You'll answer to Elir, so find him and go out to practise shooting from the saddle. Feed the horses when you come back, and they've cooled down.'The boys rushed to their horses. 'Gael, I'm going for Leil and Cadfan,' Kerin said. 'Will you do something for me, while I'm gone? Because I think you'll do it better than I can. Tell Morvid what I've just told his grandson.'

He went to fetch Eryr's saddle and bridle. As he took them down, there was a tap at the tack room door.

'The Lord's asking for you,' Cenydd said. 'Cynan is here, in the council room.'

The druid was sitting at the table, hands folded in front of him. Cynan was the calmest of men, but today there was a glow in his eyes, an intensity which his steady demeanour usually hid. Vortigern and Kerin sat.

'Lord,' Cynan said, 'it's common knowledge that your son is supported by armoured horsemen, as well as the usual combatants that one might expect. I'm not a military man, so it's not for me to talk about strategy. But I believe with my heart and soul that our carnyces will be mighty. When the war horns sound, any men or horses who haven't heard one before will be frightened to death. But what would you say if I suggested that there was something else we could use, to make that sound more terrifying still? To make men believe that they were truly in the presence of a supernatural power?'

Vortigern sighed. 'Cynan, I have no idea what you're talking about.'

The druid smiled gravely. 'Lord, are you familiar with the great wave of the Hafren?'

'I've never seen it,' Vortigern said. 'But I've heard of it. Years ago in Glevum, when I was a lad. My father used to spend time there sucking up to the Roman administration. He wanted me out of his sight, so I was sent to a tutor, to improve my Latin. One of the other boys mentioned the wave. He said a wall of water came up the river from the sea. I thought he was talking rubbish, to see if the ignorant Cambrian peasant would fall for it and give them all something to laugh about. But years later, I heard of it again. After one of our usual scraps with Eldof at the river. We'd beaten them hollow and captured a few Glevum warriors. I had no intention of harming them, I was just making a point, but before we let them go, I spoke with one of them. There was timber strewn along the riverbank, big logs and whole uprooted trees, and a rowing boat sitting on top of them. A dead calf, and a few dead sheep. I said it must have been a bad flood. He said no, it wasn't a flood, it was a wave, coming up the river instead of going down. I remembered what I'd been told in Latin class, and thought that perhaps I shouldn't have thrown that boy in the fountain after all. So what are you saying?'

'That perhaps it's something we could use, lord,' Cynan said. 'I have witnessed this wave, years ago, when we attended a solstice gathering near Glevum. The first thing to come is the sound; a roar, like the sound of galloping warriors. Frightening enough of itself. Then comes the wall of water, travelling at the speed of a cantering horse. We're agreed that the carnyx can make a terrifying sound. But suppose that the sound preceded the wave? Like a herald, as it were. Men who were ignorant of both might believe that the one summoned the other, don't you think?'

Vortigern leaned back in his chair and regarded the druid with a mixture of amusement and respect. 'It's an ingenious idea, Cynan,' he said. 'But for love of the gods. What are the chances of getting the carnyces, never mind a large army, to the banks of the Hafren at the precise time when the wave is about to appear?'

'Better than you might think, lord,' Cynan said equably. 'The presence and size of the wave are ruled by the moon. We of the priesthood make a study of its phases, as you know. I am confident that I could predict, to the day, when a powerful wave was due to occur. And if one of the carnyces were stationed a little downstream – the sound carries over a distance, I assure you – then it could roar as soon as the wave appeared. By the time the wave reached the bridge, with the second carnyx blowing like fury, I think the enemy would be somewhat disturbed.' He smiled benignly and waited. Vortigern looked as if head and heart were doing battle within him.

'Cynan, I'd love to think it could work. But I'm a battle commander, not a priest or an astronomer. I can't stake men's lives on it. And anyway, most of the Glevum men will already know about the wave.'

'But the cataphracts won't,' Kerin said, too fired by excitement to keep quiet. 'And who'd warn them? Eldof and Rufus are no astronomers. And once the cataphracts are on the move, it'll be too late. What would you do? Grab two hundred and fifty men with scale armour all over their heads, sit them down and explain that the wave coming the wrong way up the river is nothing to do with the gods or the carnyx?'

Vortigern raised his hands. 'You're right,' he said. 'And of course, if the bridge does burn, and anyone attempts to cross the river from either side – ' he leaned forward on the table and clasped Cynan's hand. 'I'm not discounting this. I can't depend upon it, but I'm not discounting it either. What happens if it's cloudy, and you can't see the moon?'

'I don't depend upon seeing it, lord,' Cynan said kindly.

'I attune myself to its force. And just to please others, I also keep a record. A calendar, if you will. The greatest waves occur on the days after the new moon and the full moon. As we journey to the river, I shall mark the days off on my papyrus. And we could be in luck. After the rain we've had, there'll be a lot of water in the river. The more water, the bigger the wave, as they struggle against each other. And of course the wave comes with the rising tide, so I shall observe that too. As we approach the river, can I take it that you'll delay the march by a day or two if necessary, to give us the best chance?'

'Yes,' Vortigern said. 'I'll grant you that much, unless something unexpected happens. Has anyone else thought of this?'

'No, lord,' Cynan said. 'My father's not an expert when it comes to the moon, and I don't think it's entered the archdruid's mind.'

'Keep it to yourself for now, then,' Vortigern said. 'But you can tell your father that he'll be going to battle in a chariot. That should please him.'

Cynan chuckled. 'Indeed,' he said. 'I don't suppose many men wear their best clothes to war, but I'm sure he won't waste the opportunity.' He smiled, rose and went out. Vortigern stared up at the ceiling.

'I can't believe I listened to that, never mind entertaining it,' he said. Kerin grinned.

'We've done madder things. And anyway, if the wave doesn't appear, or it's just a little ripple, what difference will it make? No-one will be any the wiser.'

'No,' Vortigern conceded. 'No-one will be any the wiser.' His eyes sparkled with a mischievous light which Kerin hadn't seen for some time. 'By God, it would be fun, though.'

There was a tap at the door, and Cenydd appeared. 'I'm sorry, lord,' he said. 'It's Brwyn for you now.'

Brwyn was limping. The wetter the weather, the worse his painful back. Kerin had not seen him since he came to install the bar on the bedroom door. He looked close to tears.

'Brwyn,' Vortigern said. 'What's the matter, man?'

'Lord, I will fight with you,' Brwyn blurted. 'I fought in Isca. I fought the Irish. I fought in the North. And now I'll fight with you at the river.'

Vortigern sighed. 'You're not coming, Brwyn,' he said. 'You can't fight. And before you tell me that I'll be fighting my own sons, it's not the same. You have a choice. I don't.'

'Neither do I,' Brwyn said, beginning to weep. 'We're bound by oath, you and I. By blood. And my sons have caused you nothing but grief.'

'I release you from all of it,' Vortigern said. 'You still have a wife and a daughter to care for. Two grandchildren. And two sons who may come back to you one day, if the god they worship is ever good enough to open their eyes.'

'Then what should I do? Sit in the house? Even the women are doing more than that.'

'Do my work while I'm gone,' Vortigern said. 'Care for my people. Listen to their concerns. Be a strong man for them. We're not short of strong women, but most of the strong men are coming with me. And not everyone wants to lay their griefs upon a priest. Some will want a warrior's comfort. And you've been a warrior since you were old enough to fight. Be that man for me. And don't ask me this again.'

'I won't, lord,' Brwyn whispered. 'And I'm sorry in my heart for what my boys are doing.' He bowed as far as his back would allow and went out. Vortigern sighed.

'It's easier dealing with a bunch of bastards,' he said. They went out into the bright afternoon, blinking after the darkness of the council room. Morvid was sitting on the bench outside Kerin's house, pounding away with a pestle and mortar.

'Gael has told you?' Kerin asked.

'Yes,' Morvid said, concentrating on his work. 'Nothing I wasn't expecting. And naturally I'd sooner you didn't take him. But it was never going to be any different, was it? It's been Lord Kerin this, Lord Kerin that, ever since you gave him the horse and a little sword. You take a boy in, you teach him to fight, then one day he's not a boy any more. He's a young man, and you can't keep him shut up in the house.' He looked up and gave Vortigern a nod. 'A bit like you two, really. So I'm not complaining. But don't try to stop me coming with you. And if you get him killed, remember that I'm the man who knows what to put in the stew of two pigs, to send you both to the afterlife.' He went on pounding furiously. A single tear dripped down into the stone bowl on his lap.

45

It was almost time. The king's army was at full alert, its tight column encircling the transports and baggage trains. Casual observers might have imagined themselves back on a breezy, sunlit day in early spring; the last time Henfelin had seen a muster like this. But to men like Kerin, who had lived through the hell of the interim, it was the differences which caught the eye and chilled the blood. Of the warriors who had formed the front rank, only Macsen remained. The rest were either dead, on the other side, or – in one man's case – skulking around somewhere, ruing the day when he had raped Garagon's sister. Now Elir sat proudly at his brother's side, accompanied by Hefydd and Derfyn. Behind them were Leil and Cadfan, and two lads who seemed suddenly to have become young men; one sturdy and broad-shouldered, the other lithe and elegant. It was hard to imagine that Marc was once a swineherd's boy, or that Ashur was ever a slave.

Kerin sat his horse, exactly where he was before the march to the North; at the foot of the hillock where Vortigern addressed the priests, received the draco from the women and chose his new standard-bearer. Lud sat beside him, as he had done then, but the balance had shifted. As Kerin looked out over the mass of men and horses, he knew that it was to him they would turn in the moment of crisis.

He barely recognised the young man who had ridden out on that wild spring morning.

'Look,' Lud said, nodding towards the citadel. The women were coming. Gael, despite her husband's warnings, was riding beautiful Seren. She and Kerin had said their farewells privately, as the first grey light of dawn leaked into their bedroom. Once more, after they had made love, she had removed her ring, kissed it and threaded it onto the chain of Kerin's crucifix. Dimos was walking beside the horse. Rowenna was on her beloved brown filly. Tirion was riding Gwalch, the osprey, Hefin's dappled warhorse. The rest of the women followed behind. Kerin saluted them as he would have done an approaching band of allied warriors.

'What do you want me to do, lord?' Dimos asked. 'I can stay here and carry on with my work, or I can accompany you and record the events. I doubt if the king will have much time for writing.'

'You'd be surprised,' Kerin said. 'He wrote on the march to the North. Julius Caesar wrote on campaign, didn't he? And I need you here. The children like you and respect you. You can carry on with their lessons, and keep them out of their mothers' hair. They'll thank you, even if the children don't.'

The warriors came to attention. Vortigern was on his way down from the citadel with Gwyndaf. The draco's banner, repaired by its makers, curled in the light wind. Vortigern rode up onto his hillock. The women and Dimos had been joined by Brwyn and the archdruid. 'Gael,' Vortigern said. 'Rowenna and Tirion. Caradog. Dimos and Brwyn. Come forward.' He looked towards the edge of the gathering, where the monks and druids had assembled. 'Iustig. Come here. Yes, you. Over here.' The abbot walked slowly to the foot of the hillock.

'Why?' he asked, looking profoundly suspicious. Vortigern's face was hard, impossible to read.

'At least half of these people are Christians,' he said. 'They've never needed a sensible, compassionate priest as much as they do now. And since I'm taking that sensible, compassionate priest with me, I need you to put everything else aside and care for them as you did when we went to the North. As if we were fighting some enemy that we can all agree about. Can you do that?'

'Yes,' Iustig said, closing his eyes. 'With God's help, I can.' He went to stand beside Caradog. Tirion rode forward, holding something. It was the torn fragment of the draco's banner which Vortigern had used to bind his head in the North, washed clean of blood and gleaming in green and gold.

'Lord, please take this,' she said, holding it out. 'The women have mended the banner with new cloth. We ask that you wear it in the next battle, because it must surely have brought you luck in the North. And now it carries all our prayers, too.'

Vortigern kissed Tirion's hand, took the fragment of the banner and tied it around his head. There was a deep, swelling murmur of approval. He faced his people and flung an arm towards the group of men and women standing beside him. 'These are the ones you must look to while we are away. Look to them for courage. For guidance and comfort. But look to yourselves, too. Keep your hearth fires lit. Be strong. But sleep at night. Do not fear. We *will* hold the Hafren.'

Silence followed. No fierce exhortation today; no call to arms. And yet, in that moment, the bond between Vortigern and his people was so real, so palpable that Kerin felt he could have plucked it from the air and held it to his heart.

Out of the silence came the sound of two voices, raised in unison. Cynfawr and Cynan, standing beside the carriage which held the carnyces, were singing the simple tune they had played in the cave and beside the fire of Calan Gaeaf; an intonation merely, a song without words. Everyone sang, as if the melody had leeched into their bloodstream and become one with them and their dearest hopes. It was still hanging in the air as Gwyndaf raised the dragon, and the army marched.

46

'I gave them the olive oil,' Claudius said, and shrugged. 'Your man said it didn't matter about the quality, as long as there was plenty of it.'

Kerin smiled. He had offered no explanation in his letter. Claudius was trustworthy, undoubtedly, but letters could go astray. 'Is Publius Luca here?' he asked.

'Yes. Staying in my house, with his old physician. Or is he a priest? I'm not sure. And Commander Arrius's men are billeted in the fortress with the horses. Their own, and the ones that got shipwrecked. Trust me, Lord Kerin, if I hadn't seen the evidence, I wouldn't believe that any of that could have happened.' Claudius led the way to the private room where he dealt with ships' captains and merchants. A simple meal of bread and smoked meat had been laid out on the table. 'How far behind are the others?' he asked, inviting Kerin to sit.

'No more than half a day.'

'Why were you sent ahead?'

'I wasn't sent. I decided to come. There are people I need to see before the town gets flooded by our army. Before the noise begins. And don't be concerned. Vortigern knows what I'm doing, and why.'

Claudius poured two beakers of cool water. 'Preparing the way,' he said. 'Smoothing the path, if you can. Perhaps making this choice he must face a little more palatable.'

'No-one can do that,' Kerin said. 'But the rest is true. A good man once told me that the kingship would be a crown of thorns. Perhaps you see more than most.'

'I was here from the beginning,' Claudius said. 'A young married man with two little boys when Vortigern was giving hell to the Romans with his bunch of outlaws. My father used to say that they should let it go, but my mother was a centurion's daughter, so he had to keep the peace. Personally I admired their nerve. And your friend was right about the crown of thorns. It's complex enough at times, simply being a harbourmaster. Two hundred half-drowned horses, burning transports, complaints from Abona –'

'Complaints?' Kerin said. 'They complained to you?'

'Oh yes. Rufus's new man came over in person. Someone had recognised my old galley. I told them it had been stolen, and we'd found it drifting in the channel. There was no point in implicating myself when I was trying to hide two hundred horses. I said my piece, showed the man the door and told him to get out before he suffered the same fate as his predecessor. He looked shocked, as if he'd been expecting me to roll over and apologise. Just an ordinary fellow brought in to fill a gap, I suspect.'

'Will there be consequences for you?' Kerin asked.

'I doubt it. What would they do? Kill me? Burn Isca? They have more urgent concerns, surely. And they'd have to pass you to get here. If they managed to do that, we'd have more to worry about than another dead harbourmaster.'

The sound of voices came from the next room. Kerin recognised one of them instantly. 'Commander!' he said, as Publius Luca was shown in.

'The Lord Kerin Brightspear,' Publius said, smiling as he shook Kerin's hand. 'There are no secrets in this place. Someone spotted you and sent for me. How do things stand?'

'The army's half a day behind me,' Kerin said. 'Two thousand men, all our best mounted warriors and foot. Gorlois is heading towards Corinium with another thousand, and I have a band of archers and spearmen on fast horses to attack the cataphracts.'

'Capital,' Publius Luca said. 'Now, Master Claudius, I'm going to drag this man away; I have things to show him.'

The gates of the old legionary fortress had been reinstated. Two members of the city garrison were on guard outside. They saluted Publius Luca and shouted to someone up on the gatehouse. The gates swung open.

'Last time we came there were no gates,' Kerin said.

'I think the tradespeople removed them years ago,' Publius said. 'Claudius found them in one of the barns. You can see why he had them reinstalled when the horses and cavalrymen arrived.'

'They're not that old though, surely,' Kerin said, running a hand over the smooth-planed oak. There were a few pockmarks which could only have been inflicted by spears, but the gates were not scarred like those of the fortress in Kent.

'No,' Publius said. 'Vortigern and Lud burned the original gates thirty years ago. The legion commissioned these to replace them. I told you what happened when Quintus Parvo was dismissed. We opened these gates to release the prisoners. Vortigern was the last to come out. He could hardly stand, but of course, he wouldn't accept any assistance. There was a crowd waiting for him here. Someone handed him a brand from a fire. They probably expected him to burn these gates too, but he didn't. He did that, there.' Kerin looked where Publius was pointing. The letters were shaky, not at all like Vortigern's usual clear, elegant hand, but the inscription was clearly legible. *V. Rex.*

'And no-one removed it,' Kerin said, tracing the letters with his forefinger.

'No. I don't think anyone had the nerve. Everyone had had enough.' Publius shook his head. 'Come on. Let's inspect the cavalry.'

The horses which had escaped from the *oneraria* were concealed inside the quadrangle containing the military headquarters and the prison. Fences had been erected to hold them within the area fronting the officers' dining hall.

'Our own cavalry horses are in the stables,' Publius Luca said. 'We didn't want to confine these poor creatures too closely, but they seem to have recovered well. And they're friendly enough.' Kerin tried to concentrate as Publius explained how Claudius had gone about obtaining saddlery for the horses – some new, some donated by well-wishers, he thought vaguely – but the words washed over him and were lost. He could think of nothing but the inscription burned into the fortress gate. 'Kerin!' Publius said sharply.

'I'm sorry,' Kerin said. 'But that thing on the gate –'

'I know,' Publius Luca said. 'Half of me wishes they'd left the gates in the barn. But the other half thinks, by Mithras, that was something, from a man on the edge of death. Do you suppose he'll mind seeing it there?'

'I don't know,' Kerin said. 'I really don't know.' He shook himself back into action. 'For now I have to think about the cavalry. Is Lucius here?'

'No. He's gone to fetch his youngsters. He took a few good men with him in case of trouble, but the rest are here. By the time he gets back you'll be camped somewhere near Glevum, so I'll tell him to march straight away. Come and meet his deputy. You might be surprised.'

Kerin followed Publius past the stable blocks to an open

square where a cavalry troop was practising manoeuvres under the critical eye of a slight, dark-haired young man on a solid chestnut horse. He turned in the saddle. A familiar face, a cautious smile. For a moment Kerin struggled to place him, then memory jolted and transported him to a cool room next to Marcellus's garden in Londinium. 'Livius Gaius! The last time we met, you were half dead.'

'I don't remember it at all,' Livius said. 'I recall seeing you outside the guard room when we locked the Picts in, but that's all.' He hailed the leader of his troop, told them to carry on practising, and dismounted.

'I'll leave you two to renew your acquaintance,' Publius Luca said. 'Come to Claudius's house when you're done, Kerin. One of the guards will show you the way.'

Kerin looked Livius up and down. 'I'm surprised you didn't die of fright outside the guard room.'

'I wasn't much help, was I,' Livius said. 'But something happens when you come that close to death. It's nothing to do with religion. I just felt furious that someone had almost ended my life. Is the king here yet?'

'Not yet. By midday, I'd say. Ready your men, and tell the other troop commanders to do the same. When the army's approaching the city, form up below the walls either side of the fortress gatehouse. Give the king something to lift his spirits.'

'I will,' Livius said, eyes alight with pride and excitement. Kerin smiled, shook his hand and walked away. He had high hopes for Livius, but it was impossible to tell whether all that fervour and confidence would hold up when men and horses were spilling their blood and guts into the stinking mire of yet another killing ground. Kerin stopped at the gatehouse and stared at the inscription, burned into the pristine wood years before he existed. *V. Rex.* The ultimate, brazen insult. How was it even possible, after all that had happened here? One of the guards was watching him. It felt like an intrusion.

'Publius Imperator said you could direct me to Master Claudius's house,' he said.

'Of course, lord,' the man said courteously. 'Follow me.'

The house was close to the wharf; a pleasant, unpretentious building with a small forecourt where a bunch of men, probably merchants, were in conversation. Rather to Kerin's surprise, they recognised him, offered their greetings and stood aside to let him pass. A servant showed him into a spacious entrance hall, empty apart from an urn containing a small tree with glossy dark leaves.

'Kerin Brightspear!' Marcellus appeared in an unobtrusive doorway next to the tree. 'Come. I have tisane, and you have a little time before your company arrives.'

Kerin followed him into a small room with red walls and couches set around a hearth where a fire of fragrant wood was burning. It was an intimate room, a place to greet friends. Marcellus poured two beakers of liquid from a long-spouted jug.

'Melissa with honey,' he said. 'Elissa's cure for everything. She insisted on sending it with me to ward off the cold. I can't imagine why, it would probably suit her if the cold did away with me.'

Kerin smiled. 'You're too harsh, Marcellus *magister*.'

The haruspex sniffed. 'There speaks a man who has not been married for long. The Cambrian air seems to suit your wife, however; she looked the picture of health when I visited. And quite the leader, according to Publius. We all hope that her abilities won't be called upon for too long, of course. I believe the commander has had a discreet word with Mithras on that score, an event in itself.'

'Well, I hope Mithras was listening,' Kerin said. 'If the women have to go on fending for themselves, it'll mean that quite a lot of us men are dead.'

'You're confident, though?' Marcellus asked. 'Even though you and Vortigern have hatched a plan which Publius Imperator in his wisdom thinks is completely insane?'

'I'm confident,' Kerin said. 'There are things which could go wrong, but even if they do, I think we can overcome them.' He paused. 'Do you have an opinion about the carnyces?'

Marcellus poured more tisane. 'As I've never heard one, my opinion must be qualified,' he said. 'The historian Polybius tells us that they were used to intimidate enemies, and we know that Julius Caesar encountered them in Gallia, as did the Emperor Claudius, when he invaded these islands. But whatever their troops made of the carnyces, it has to be said that both Gallia and Britain fell to Caesar in the end. You'll know, of course, that I've had Publius Imperator bending my ear about this for some time. As a practical man and a military commander of vast experience, he thinks that your druids are charlatans and their carnyces a mere warbling decoration, although of course he's far too civil to put it like that. You, however, are utterly convinced that they could turn a battle. Am I right?'

'You are,' Kerin said. 'From the moment I first heard one in the druids' cave. It was terrifying. And I don't frighten easily, after everything we've had to face this past year. I'm not flattering myself, when I say that if a sound can frighten me, it can frighten any man coming against us. Not to mention his horse. Publius Luca told us that we'd never withstand a cataphract charge because it was like being hit by a moving wall. And I think this could be the same. Except that it'll be a wall of sound.'

Marcellus regarded him thoughtfully. 'You have a rare passion for this, don't you, my young friend,' he said. 'Vortigern, however, sits on the fence, from what I can gather. The Celt in him is with you heart and soul, but the battle commander must listen to his old friend's cold logic and count the numbers. I don't believe that risky military tactics are Publius's only concern, however.' Marcellus's knowing eyes met Kerin's.

'No. He fears that, when the fight is actually upon us, Vortigern will back out in some way. Especially if he has to face Rufus on the battlefield. Publius told me that I should be prepared to lead. I am prepared, and I don't fear it, but I don't want it either.' He paused. The question had to come, whatever his scepticism about Marcellus's methods. 'Do you see anything? For us? For the battle?'

'Blood and water,' Marcellus said dryly. 'You don't need me to tell you that, obviously. I shall go to the temple of Jupiter shortly, to consult further. But whatever the omens presage, as an old man who's hung around on the fringes of quite a few battles, I'd counsel you to have faith. More than that, to show that you have faith. Publius tells me that Vortigern's confidence in you is absolute. Tell me, does that make you feel more or less able to face what's coming?'

'More, of course,' Kerin said. 'It makes me feel invincible.'

'Naturally,' Marcellus said. 'So bear that in mind. As I told you some time ago, Vortigern is not a god. You are doing everything I hoped for, but your task is not over. It won't be over while you both live. Have faith, and bear it like a banner, for all to see.'

There was a tap at the door. 'Lord Kerin,' said the servant, 'Publius Imperator is outside for you.'

Publius Luca was standing in the street holding the bridles of two well-matched grey horses. They were harnessed to a chariot, similar to the ceremonial transports Kerin had seen in Londinium. Its wooden sides were covered in fine ochre-coloured leather, ornamented with gleaming gold plaques.

'This was the best I could find,' Publius said. 'The governors used it now and again, but it needed new wheels, so it got left behind. Far too flimsy and unmanoeuvrable for warfare. But as a means of delivering your men to the battlefront, it should serve. And you'll be pleased to know that I've had a number of Parthian-style bows sent down from Londinium. An old friend of mine had them stored away, along with various bits and bobs of armour and weaponry. Most old soldiers are sick to death of militaria, in my experience, but this man was an engineer, so he never actually fought. I'll get the bows sent over to your lads when they arrive, so they can get used to them.'

'Ashur will be ecstatic,' Kerin said. He inspected the chariot. There wasn't much to it, when seen at close quarters; simply a floor with sides, high enough to shield the occupants from the large new wheels but offering no protection whatsoever from attack. He kept his misgivings to himself. Airing them might have prompted a debate about the deployment of the carnyces. He wasn't in the mood for Publius Luca's scepticism, and he would sooner have walked barefoot to Henfelin than tell the commander about the great wave of the Hafren. 'Who do the horses belong to?'

'To us,' Publius said. 'They're from the *oneraria*. We'll have to use Cambrian horses in battle because they'll be accustomed to the carnyx, but I like these handsome lads. Spoils of war, shall we say?'

'Spoils of war,' Kerin agreed, stroking the neck of the nearest horse. It whickered softly and nuzzled his arm. 'You're not a proper warhorse, are you,' he said.

'They're more like our cavalry horses,' Publius said. 'Bold in action, but docile to handle. I've been riding one myself. I might keep him; Delphinus is well overdue for a peaceful retirement.' As are you, Publius Imperator, Kerin thought; but there were better ways of putting it. The commander smiled, perhaps sensing the unspoken comment. Footsteps were approaching. It was the guardsman who had directed Kerin to the house.

'A message from Master Claudius, lord,' he said. 'Your army will be here within the half hour.'

'To the city gates, then,' Publius said. 'And I shall stand in the chariot, like the sensible retired military commander that I am.' He sounded deeply serious, but there was a glint in his dark eyes which Kerin chose to pretend that he had not noticed. They stepped into the back of the chariot, Publius took the reins and the horses moved off. Behind them, Marcellus slipped quietly out of Claudius's courtyard with a bag containing his ceremonial robes and his knives, and set off for the market to purchase a yearling lamb.

47

The ground was white with hoar frost. It even clung to the jagged brown stumps of rushes, sticking up out of the shallows like decayed teeth. The river beyond was swollen, brown and fast-moving. It was still raining over the hills where it came from, travellers said. There were a few of them about as afternoon slid into evening. A bunch of men on good horses, heading south-west into Cambria. Donkey carts. Some trudging monks. No-one took any notice of the down-at-heel man on the brown mule, riding hunched in the saddle as if his back might be giving him trouble. A robust fellow in his day, probably, but the dark circles under his eyes spoke of recent illness, and the straggling beard didn't help. He kept one hand knotted in the mule's mane while the other clutched the neck of his threadbare hooded cloak, pulling it tight against the creeping cold. He ignored his fellow-travellers, and they ignored him. None of them wanted a dose of lice, or whatever diseases the poor old sod might be carrying. Beneath the cloak, tucked discreetly into one of his boots, was a short-bladed sword. He had two daggers and a garotte at his belt. Kerin had learned the benefits of a good disguise, but there was no point in inviting death before battle was joined.

He had decided to come himself. Whatever the news of Edryd and Cheldric, choices might have to be made. Only he and Vortigern could make those calls, and if Kerin had

420

to gamble with men's lives, he wanted first-hand information. There was not much to be gleaned from what he could see. A thick white fog blanketed the river, obscuring the far bank. He had ridden this road enough times to know that Glevum was close, and his senses soon confirmed what the fog concealed. A continuous low hum which, when dissected, comprised voices both human and animal, traces of music, footsteps, hammer blows, hooves clopping, wheels grinding over cobbled streets. A pervasive smell, common to all cities; wood smoke, kitchens, tanneries and smelters, rotting detritus, the stench of excrement. Soon the old road he was following would meet the Roman highway, one branch heading straight for the bridge, the other running north-west towards Ariconium. He supposed that if he stayed on the old road, hugging the river bank, it would pass the place he was looking for; the shack where the river boys drank and beached their boats.

The bridge came suddenly, a black skeleton rearing out of the thinning fog, looking bigger than it had done in clear daylight when the city walls provided some perspective. A whole troop of guards was blocking the access, twenty men in garrison uniforms, manning a barrier which looked like a slim tree trunk resting on a pair of trestles. As Kerin approached, hoping that none of them would see beyond his clothes and the beard, he noticed a rope attached to one end, fed through a pulley on the bridge's palisade.

'Good day, lads,' he croaked. 'What's all this, then? Last time I came here to see my boy, you could just go straight across the bridge as free as a little bird.'

'Times have changed, old man,' one of the guards said, with a condescending smile. 'The young king's very keen on keeping undesirables out.'

'I'm not an undesirable, sir,' Kerin protested. 'Just a

hardworking, god-fearing fisherman, come to have a jar with my friends. And after that to skip across the bridge to see my son and his wife and the new baby, if you'll be so kind as to let me cross. My son's a good Christian, like me,' he added, as an afterthought. The guard scowled at him. Red tunic, extra gold trimmings on the leather helmet.

'Don't try to butter me up, old codger,' he said. 'And don't get mindless drunk with your scabby friends. Come back sober with a civil tongue, and we might let you cross. Especially if you've got a few sesterces on you.'

'God bless you, sir,' Kerin said meekly, making a mental note of the guard's appearance. 'God willing, we'll meet again.'

The shack was there beside the river, as Edryd had said, but there were no boats on the bank. Kerin dismounted and tied the mule to a dead tree deposited by the river. He found a stick and hobbled into the shack on it. There was no-one inside apart from a skinny man about his own age, sitting on a crate next to a bare table with a cask of ale on it. An oil lamp hung from the roof. The man's hair was thin and wispy, and his skin was white, as if he'd spent most of his life in this dark place. His eyes were bloodshot and he stank of drink.

'Where is everyone?' Kerin asked. The man snorted.

'Ask the young king,' he said. Kerin sat down on a bench.

'Can a man get a jar, then?' he asked.

'Yes, sorry, grandpa. It's not the best, I'm afraid, it's been here a while.'

'Get me one anyway,' Kerin said. It was warm and clammy in here after the chilly fog. He hoped that he wouldn't start to sweat, sending the dark circles of soot running down his face. 'Where's the boats, then? Where's the boys?'

'Gone off downstream,' said the man. 'I'm Pedr, by the way. It's usually my father here, but they've locked him up. He told the soldiers to piss off when they came to move the fishermen on, and they grabbed him. I wasn't here, or I'd have tried to stop it. But I've been in prison myself. That's why I look like a dead man.'

'Why were you inside?' Kerin asked. Pedr grimaced.

'It's a long story. And I don't even know who you are. What are you doing here?'

'Looking for two of my friends,' Kerin said. 'Men in their thirties. One's dark-haired with arms like Goliath. The other one's a deaf mute with straggly fair hair.'

Pedr grinned. 'Couldn't miss those two. But no, sorry, I haven't seen them. By the time I got out, it was all over, and everyone had gone.'

'So why did they move the fishermen on? They've been fishing around the bridge for as long as I can remember.'

'Young king's orders,' Pedr said. 'Have you seen those armoured horses he's got?'

'No,' Kerin said. 'I only just got here. I've never seen an armoured horse in my life. What's that got to do with the bridge?'

'He's going to fight the King – I mean –' Pedr tailed off, with a foolish grin.

'Go on,' Kerin said. 'I don't care either way, so get me another jar of this piss and tell me the rest. Take one for yourself as well.' He tossed Pedr a couple of coins. The ale was disgusting, but he knew he'd have to stomach enough of it to find out what he needed to know. Pedr fetched the ale and sat down beside him.

'I don't owe them anything,' he said. 'They locked me up, and now they've locked my father up and ruined his trade. We depended on the fishermen. No-one much comes here now because of those pricks on the bridge. They come in around midday, when the guard changes, but they just help their bloody selves. That's why I don't bother getting fresh ale.'

'Why the fuss about the bridge?' Kerin asked. 'There's another one just up the river, isn't there?'

'The packhorse bridge,' Pedr said. 'But it's narrow, like the name says. Only just wide enough for a man on a normal horse, or a mule with panniers. You'd never fit those armoured horses across it, and even if you could, it would probably fall in the river. The Romans built this one, didn't they, for huge wagons and legions and things. It could carry anything. And the young king and his friends want to crush Vortigern, so they need to get their cata – catafats, is it? – across the river, and get them back afterwards. That's why they sent the fishermen packing. They don't want anyone near the bridge, in case someone burns it and messes everything up.'

Kerin absorbed the information with a sinking heart. It would be next to impossible to fire the bridge without being seen, except from beneath, as Edryd had planned to do. Pedr brought more ale, in a big earthenware jug this time.

'Help yourself when you're empty,' he said, plonking it down on the bench. 'Better you than those sods on the bridge.'

'Do you see much of the young king?' Kerin asked.

'No. Religious, isn't he. Spends a lot of time with the priests. Nothing wrong with that, of course, but a king ought to be a fighter too. It wasn't prayers that saw the Picts off, was it.'

'Do you think there'll be a fight?' Kerin asked. 'I won't be hanging around if there is.'

'Bound to be,' Pedr said. 'They're spoiling for it in Glevum. Did you hear about the ship that got burned?'

'No,' Kerin said. 'I'm from Blestium. We don't get much news up there.'

'A big ship with horses on it,' Pedr said, spilling some ale as he tried to fill his mug. 'And armour and stuff. Someone set it on fire and it sank with everything on it. So they lost half their catafats. Everyone says –' he paused and swallowed hard. 'Everyone says that the young king wants to go marching into Cambria next spring. There can only be one king, and it's going to be him, he says. God's will, and all that. But you'd have to be off your head to think the King – sorry, Vortigern – would stand back and do nothing. Hit him hard now, they're saying. Then in the spring –' he blew his cheeks out and took another gulp. Kerin, close to vomiting, had managed to pour most of his ale onto the earth floor behind the bench when Pedr wasn't looking.

'I'll be out of here before it all starts, then,' he said. 'Are they guarding the packhorse bridge? My son lives in the city, and I want to pay him a visit.'

'They guard it, but not like this one,' Pedr said. 'All the nasty bastards are on this bridge. The other lot will let you cross, most likely.' There was a silence, then he leaned forward and gripped Kerin's arm. 'I drink over there some-times. In that big place near the bishop's gates. His guards go there when they're off duty. One of them's a good friend. We'd had the news about the victory in the North. Eldof had just come back, and some of his warriors were in there on the cider. Me, I was even more drunk than I am now. Then someone said there'd been a fight between Vortigern and his oldest boy, and it might mean war. The bishop's guards are good lads, but there's a couple of mouthy idiots. One of them stood up and said fuck the son, Vortigern was the best king we'd ever had. I think his friends pulled him down and shut him up, but by then I was standing on the table shouting the same thing.' He grimaced and rubbed his red-rimmed eyes. 'Some of Eldof's boys grabbed me and dragged me outside and beat me. They threw me in a dark hole under the garrison fort. That's where they put the people who upset them. They starve you and beat you until you swear allegiance. I stuck it for ages, until I couldn't stand it any longer. Then I just said what they told me to say.' His eyes filled with tears as the memory bit. 'But I didn't mean it, grandpa. I didn't mean it.'

Kerin felt so sorry for the man that he flung his arms around him and gave him a rough hug. 'Here,' he said, shoving a denarius into Pedr's hand. 'Shut this place down, get yourself to Glevum and bed down at your friend's for a bit. Don't come back until the fighting's over.' He groped for his stick, hobbled out of the shack and leaned against the wall, gulping the freezing air. Then he untied the mule, vomited everything in his stomach into the reed bed and set off for Malan's village.

48

'You can tell Malan and Berget about the land, if they're still there,' Vortigern had said. 'If you follow the Roman road inland from the old fort at Nidum, it'll take you straight there. No-one's living on it, we just graze cattle and sheep there. They can cut enough timber from the woods to build houses and animal pens. I'll send some carpenters over, and a few cattle to get them started. Tell them to head for Isca once they've crossed the rivers. I've told Claudius to keep them out of harm's way until we come for them. If anyone's awkward, they can show this.' He dashed off something on a sheet of papyrus, stamped it with his seal and handed it to Kerin. *Gens Malani in nomine Vurtigurni Regis venit.*

'Malan's people come in the name of King Vortigern,' Kerin said, rolling it up. 'No-one's going to argue with that in Cambria. And it'll be much easier to persuade Malan and Berget to leave, if I have this to show them.'

'The sooner they all get across the river, the better,' Vortigern said. 'Rufus's people wouldn't think twice about killing the lot of them. And that village is on Bertil Redknife's doorstep. It's pure luck that he's stayed at the training camp, for Malan and for us.'

Kerin was eager to share his news, but for the moment, survival was the imperative. Beyond the thickets of holly

427

and blackthorn there should be a welcoming village full of friends and loyal allies; but when the bridge was guarded by cretins who'd fleece a harmless old man, anything was possible. The smell of wood smoke hung in the damp air. It wasn't fresh. Kerin pulled the mule up, wondering if this meant yesterday's cooking fire or a burned village. As he reached for the sword in his boot, something sharp jabbed into his back.

'Get off the mule!' a female voice yelled. Very cautiously Kerin looked round.

'Hello, Berget,' he said. Berget stared hard at him, then creased with laughter. The sharpened stake dropped to the ground.

'Mercy's sake, Lord Kerin. Last time I saw you, you were a bloody monk. Now you're an old beardy man like my father.'

'I'd be dead if I looked like myself,' Kerin said. 'Come on. Make me a brew.'

No-one had burned the village. The remains of a bonfire lay next to the animal pens. Berget led the way to the head-man's house. 'We'll keep away from my house,' she said. 'One of my girls has had a baby, and all the women are in there. Put your mule in the pen with the others, no-one notices a mule.'

Malan lurched from the corner as she drew the blanket from the door. 'Can't a man get some peace in his own house?' he bellowed.

'Shut up and feed the fire,' Berget said. 'Look. We've got a visitor. Tell him what's been going on while I get him a hot drink.'

Kerin took off his damp cloak and tried to rub the soot and stone dust from his face.

'Oh, the gods!' Malan exclaimed. 'I thought you were a

scruffy beggar. Sit down, boy, sit down. Have you hidden your horse?'

'I've got a mule,' Kerin said. 'It's in your pen with Virtus. Why? Have you had trouble?'

'Nothing much,' Malan said. 'But you expect it all the time. You can't open your mouth in Glevum. People get thrown in jail, just for saying the wrong thing. And the bastards are cunning. They've got men in the alehouses and the markets, looking like our own boys. Spies. Dirty, rotten spies, selling themselves for a couple of sesterces.'

'Are Edryd and Cheldric here?' Kerin asked.

'No. We haven't seen hide nor hair of them. Runo's gone to the market with eggs and rabbits like he always does, but Berget was busy with the baby, so he's taken one of the lads.'

Berget came in with a jug full of steaming liquid. 'Here,' she said, filling three beakers. 'It won't get you drunk but it'll get you warm.' She settled down beside the two men.

'Listen to me, now that you're both here,' Kerin said. 'The last time we spoke, I told you that if things got dangerous you should get your people out.'

'Yes,' Malan said. 'Take your people across the river in the dark, you said, and the king won't see you starve. As if I'd leave when –'

'Quiet,' Kerin said, sharpening his tone. 'I told you what happened in Kent. Vortimer's people crucified a Saxon boy, and burned a whole troop of good warriors who'd been sent to keep the peace. You lead this village, you and Berget. And unless you put your pride before your people, you'll get them out before some cut-throat does the same here.'

Malan's eyes closed. 'I'm the headman, Kerin Brightspear. Nothing comes before my people. But I'm Vortigern's man, too.'

'He's sent this message,' Kerin said, pulling the rolled

papyrus from the leather pouch beneath his cloak. 'There's land set aside for you in Cambria. As a reward for the part you've all played, in the rising and afterwards. Over west, not too far from our home. There's pasture, rough grazing, a river full of trout, deer on the moors and oak woods where you can keep pigs and cut timber to build houses. Just a couple of days from Henfelin, for Virtus.'

'For us?' Malan wondered. 'All that, for us?'

'Yes. And it's the king's land, so there'll be no arguments. He said he'll send carpenters to help out, and a few cattle to found your herd.' Kerin turned, hearing a muffled sob. Berget was crying quietly into her hands.

'Sorry, Lord Kerin,' she said, recovering herself. 'I'm supposed to be the strong woman around here. But no-one's ever done anything like that for us before.'

'Vortigern never forgets loyalty,' Kerin said. 'He's a terrible enemy, but if you're on his side, it's like this. So please, do as he's asked, and make ready for the road. Do you have carts? Provisions?'

'Enough to get out with,' Berget said. 'Most of our stuff got looted when we followed Eldof to Londinium.' She smiled, rubbing away the tears. 'Not a bad exchange, though.'

'Half of the families have got carts,' Malan said. 'So that's ten altogether. Just small ones, for going to market. Everyone who's got a cart has got a donkey. Six of the boys have got mules, big strong ones like Virtus. They can carry two people or two big panniers, whatever's needed. We've got goats with kids, two milking cows and some pigs that we'll have to leave behind, unfortunately, because I don't know if you've ever tried to herd pigs in a straight line, but –'

'Fine,' Kerin said. 'When we're done here, feed the animals you're taking, so they're ready for the road.'

'So what about Edryd and Cheldric?' Berget asked. 'And what about Runo? He might be a useless loafer, but I can't just walk out and leave him.'

'He's not a useless loafer any more, as you know,' Kerin said. 'And of course you can leave him. He'll make his own way. You must both swear that you won't tell another living soul what I'm about to tell you.'

'We swear,' Berget said, and dug her father in the ribs.

'We swear,' Malan said hurriedly.

'Edryd and Cheldric have come to burn the bridge. Our plan was to let the armoured horsemen cross, then burn the bridge behind them. Do you know that shack where the river boys used to drink?'

'Yes,' Berget said. 'I've dragged Runo out of it more than once.'

'I'd agreed to meet Edryd and Cheldric there,' Kerin said. 'But now the fishermen have got moved on. Do you know the man who sells ale there?'

'An old boy with one eye,' Berget said. 'I don't know his name.'

'That's the father,' Kerin said. 'They've jailed him for giving the guards a mouthful. The son's there now, a man about my own age called Pedr. He looks like walking death because they've had him locked up for months. He got drunk with the bishop's guards and spoke up for Vortigern. I think that's all it takes these days.'

'I told you, didn't I,' Malan shouted, driving a fist into his palm. 'Bastards! I'll have the treacherous bastards.'

'It'll come,' Kerin said. 'But first I've got to find Edryd and Cheldric, and you've got to get your people out. Tonight, as soon as you can. Just tell them you've had a warning.'

'Done,' Berget said, standing up. 'Go on, father, get the lads together. They can take their tools and weapons but not much else. The girls will see to the food and blankets and kitchen stuff.'

'Give me a bite to eat, then,' Kerin said. 'Just some bread or gruel, anything to keep me going. When you leave here, go straight up the Via Legionis. If you leave soon and travel through the night, you'll come to a bridge just after dawn. If you cross the Hafren there and follow the track west, it'll take you to Ariconium. Once you're across the Gwy, you're in Glywysing. Follow the Roman road down to Isca and ask for the harbourmaster, Claudius Custos. He's looking out for you. If anyone stops you, tell them you're Vortigern's people, and show them this.' He slipped the papyrus back into its pouch and handed it to Berget. 'It says that your father's family are there in the king's name, and it's stamped with his seal. You might as well have God with you.' He paused, hearing an unexpected sound. Hoofbeats, coming at speed. Berget's startled eyes met his. Kerin drew his sword and flattened himself against the wall behind the door. Berget went out. A lad's voice shouted to her. He sounded terrified.

'No!' she howled. 'Why?' Kerin ran outside. 'They've taken Runo,' Berget sobbed. 'They're coming to burn the village.'

'Go,' Kerin said. 'Harness the donkeys, load the carts and get the children and old ones on them.' He grabbed the lad's arm. 'You, come with me.' They went into Malan's hut. 'Tell us,' Kerin said.

'I went to market with Runo,' the boy stammered. 'Some of Eldof's guards just walked up and grabbed him. There was a man with them, tall with fair hair, and he talked funny. He said, "that one there, with the white hairs, he's Vortigern's. And if he doesn't sing like a nightingale, we'll go to his village tonight and burn everyone in their beds."

Then they tied Runo's hands and dragged him away. I didn't know what to do, Headman, so I just jumped on Runo's horse and galloped back here as fast as I could.' He broke off, white-faced and shaking.

'Alright, lad, alright,' Malan said. 'Now, send the men in here, and go and help the women.' He turned to Kerin. 'Runo won't talk. At least not for a while.'

'I'll help you,' Kerin said. 'You have to leave now. It'll be dark soon. If they're coming to burn you in your beds, with luck, they won't look to see if you're in them. They'll just set fire to the houses. But the village can't look abandoned. You'll have to leave most of the animals. Go, get your men together, I'll do what I can.' He ran out to the pens. The women had already taken the donkeys for harnessing and were loading the carts. Apart from the two milking cows and the goats, there were two lame donkeys and a few skinny young cattle. The mules in the next pen, disturbed by the sudden activity, were fidgeting and braying. One of the lads haltered the milking cows while another began saddling the mules. Berget came running, out of breath, but in command of herself now. 'You'll have to leave all these, apart from the cows and the mules,' Kerin said. 'The men who took Runo talked about burning you in your beds. If their leader is who I think he is, he won't hesitate. Are you ready?'

'Almost,' Berget panted. 'Two of the carts are too shaky. We'll just leave them, at least it won't look so deserted.' She forced a smile. Malan came limping from amongst the houses.

'The men have loaded their stuff,' he said. 'Get on the road now, girl. We'll catch you up on the mules.' Berget hugged her father hard and ran for the carts.

'Runo's horse,' Kerin said. 'Do any of them know it?'

'Don't think so,' Malan said. 'It's a good horse for us, but in the end it's just an ordinary brown horse, isn't it. No markings or anything.'

'Leave it here and take my mule, then,' Kerin said. 'When you've gone, I'm going to stay here for a while. But when I leave, I might want to go faster than the mule can go.'

Malan grinned and tweaked Kerin's beard. 'An old grandfather like you?'

'A grandfather led the rising,' Kerin said. 'Now get out. I'll see you in Cambria.'

When everyone else had gone, before the sound of trotting hooves and trundling wheels had faded into the dark wood between the village and the Via Legionis, Kerin went to work. He grabbed a broken rake and dragged piles of dead leaves and twigs across the ruts and hoofprints until they were invisible. He raked up the remains of the bonfire, fetched a brand from the fire in Malan's house, threw on some kindling from the wood pile and set it alight. He would damp the fire down when he heard them coming. Runo's horse, still saddled, was standing in the pen with the lame donkeys. It looked like a Kernow horse; big and raw-boned with hairy fetlocks. Kerin led it into the wood and tied it in a hollow behind a fallen oak. It wouldn't be visible from the village, if it kept still. He ran back to the houses, found the shed where the grain was kept and poured some into all the troughs. In Berget's house, a huge cauldron with some scrapings of stew had been abandoned. Kerin lugged it outside and dumped it at the edge of the fire. At least it would look as if the villagers had had a good feed before retiring to their beds. An owl hooted high above in the canopy. He paused, catching his breath and listening for the answering 'ke-wick'; and then he heard something else.

Hammering up the Roman road; twenty or more sets of galloping hooves. The sound changed abruptly as the riders veered off the cobbles onto the woodland track leading to the village. He had less than a minute. He ran to the fire and kicked dust and leaf mould over the flames, then bolted for the woods and the horse. The startled animal pulled back as he slid down the bank. 'Shh, shh,' Kerin whispered, cupping his hand over the soft pink nose. The riders were amongst the houses.

'Look!' someone jeered. 'They've even left us a fire.'

'Make a bigger one, then,' came the reply. Kerin peered over the rim of the hollow. There was Batraz, sitting on his big white horse while the others split into two groups, some holding the horses, the rest clustered around Kerin's fire. They had come prepared with torches and were lighting them from the dying flames. 'They are as stupid as those fools in Kent,' Batraz said to his companion. 'All drunk or sleeping. So now they burn like those did. And the white-hair, if he does not talk, he will hang like the one Vortigern sent. Slow, with whipcord.'

For a few mad seconds Kerin wanted nothing more than to leap from the hollow and murder Batraz where he sat; but then the madness passed, and he realised that all he really wanted was to live long enough to hold his wife and unborn child again. He clenched his teeth and watched as the men ran from house to house, torching the roofs and door screens.

'What about the beasts?' asked the man next to Batraz. One of Eldof's guards.

'Take them,' Batraz said. 'Give them to your master's kitchen. And kill anything that cannot run. Leave nothing alive.'

The yelling and banging and crack of collapsing timbers

was pierced by the screech of dying pigs and donkeys and the piteous cries of the nanny goats, their kids butchered in front of them as they were driven from the pens with the terrified bawling young cattle. The horse began to struggle and stamp as it smelled the blood. Kerin hung onto the bridle, desperately trying to keep it quiet. Batraz rode around the edge of the village as the animals were herded away from the burning houses towards the Glevum road. 'Search the woods,' he shouted. Kerin leapt onto the horse's back, drove his heels into its flanks and took off through the trees. A chorus of shouts was followed by galloping hooves. Every instinct told Kerin to head north. Any sane man would go where the river was narrower, where there were unguarded bridges and fords which a strong horse could cross. Only an idiot would choose Glevum. But to go north would lead his pursuers straight to a plodding column of mules, people on foot and carts full of women, children and old men; so he made the idiot's choice and headed straight back the way he had come. Eldof's guards, or whoever they were, were gaining steadily. They knew these woods, he did not; and the Kernow horse, although strong and willing, was not fast. Kerin found himself on a clear path. There were hoofprints already, but any half-competent tracker would spot the new ones. The horse slithered down a bank into a stream. Kerin drove it on, following the flow of the water. Behind him he heard shouting as his pursuers real- ised what had probably happened and split into two bands, one chasing him downstream, the other following the path where it emerged on the far bank. His horse stopped dead. Ahead was a waterfall. There was a ford of sorts, with tracks leading away in both directions. And this is where we part company, Kerin thought. 'Thank you,' he whispered, and jumped down into the water, slapped the horse's rump and sent it on its way. The waterfall was about three times his own height. As he scrambled and slithered downwards, he saw that the water fell like a curtain in front of black rock walls grown over with moss and smooth-bladed ferns. Finding a foothold, he inched his way behind the screen of water and held on tight. Above his head hooves clattered down the stream and thudded out onto the track. One, two, three, four riders. He waited until the sound had faded away, clambered up the rocks below the fall and began to run.

It was further to the river than Kerin had thought, or perhaps it just seemed so, to a man on foot. He didn't slow down until the woods had turned to scrub; a jumble of willow, alder and blackthorn intersected by watery ditches. He dropped down in a bramble thicket, gasping for breath. Even if they had managed to follow him, this was terrible terrain for horses, and he was confident of evading them. The mist had risen into the higher air, turned luminous by the moon. Away to his right the distant lights of Glevum were clearly visible. Ahead the scrub merged into saltmarsh. Towards the city the land was better, and he could see cattle lying peacefully in the water meadows. He supposed that if he made his way towards them, it might be possible to reach the river bank without drowning in a mud bath.

The man was standing at the edge of the bank, fishing with a rod and line. His boat was tied to a stake and had drifted to the end of its rope. Kerin was exhausted and frightened and had no time for niceties. He walked up to the man, grabbed him by the arm and said, 'Take me across the river.'

The fisherman pulled free. 'No chance,' he said. 'Look at the boat. It would be off if I hadn't tied it properly. It's hard work, pulling against that water.'

Kerin fished out his purse and showed a couple of coins. 'Please,' he said. 'I've got to get across the river. There are some men chasing me, and they'll kill me if they catch me.' He decided to take a risk. 'I'm no friend of the young king's.'

The fisherman put down his rod. 'They hanged a man from the city gatehouse this morning,' he said. 'An old one-eyed man who used to sell ale up by the big bridge.'

'Pedr's father!' Kerin exclaimed.

'Yes!' The fisherman looked shocked. 'How do you know that?'

'Take me across and I'll tell you on the way,' Kerin said.

The current was ferocious. Kerin was a strong swimmer, but he wouldn't have liked to risk it. 'Are you one of the men who used to fish up by the bridge?' he asked.

'Yes,' the fisherman panted, pulling hard. 'If you know Pedr, you'll know that we got kicked out from there. I've fished there all my life, and my father and grandfather before me. Now we've had to go, because they think someone might burn the bridge to stop those armoured things.'

'Perhaps someone should,' Kerin said. 'There's going to be a battle soon. If Vortigern wins, you'll be able to fish wherever you like.'

'Chance would be a fine thing,' the fisherman said. 'They guard it as if it was made of solid gold.'

'I only met Pedr this morning,' Kerin said. 'I went to that shack looking for a couple of my friends. A powerful-looking dark fellow and a deaf mute.'

The fisherman looked up. 'I know them,' he said. 'Or know of them, more like. They were drinking with us when the guards came. That's when the old man got arrested. We all jumped in our boats and took off before they collared us too. Your friends went back across the river with one of the other boys, but I haven't seen them since.'

The boat butted into the bank on the Cambrian side. Whatever had become of Edryd and Cheldric, Kerin knew that there was nothing he could do about it now. 'Thank you,' he said, paying the fisherman. 'What's your name?'

'Rud. But there's a few of us Ruds about, so most people call me Shorter, because I am. Shorter than my brothers, that is.'

Kerin grinned. 'If you see my friends, tell them that I was looking for them. They call me Right Arm, because I'm useless with the left one.' He got out of the boat into the sucking mud and hauled himself up the bank onto the track he had travelled with the mule. It felt like an age ago, although it was less than a day. He had left the army's encampment at noon, and had reached the bridge at dusk. Now a clear, cold dawn was breaking over the hills east of Glevum. There was ice on the puddles and a cutting wind was driving up the river from the sea. He was wet through, had lost his cloak, and had only the threadbare tunic and breeches he stood up in. Until now he had not had time to think how cold it was. 'Walk!' he told himself, knowing that if he stopped to rest he would either sleep or freeze to death or both. If he were Batraz, he would have at least one man watching the river. He wondered if there would be consequences for the men who lost him in the woods, given that it was a beheading offence to lose a few sets of horse armour.

He was out in the middle of the flat land beside the river, still far from cover, when he saw the rider. He flung himself flat, praying that the man on the low ridge was on his own side, or at least not on Rufus's. The rider slipped from sight. A lookout, perhaps, although it seemed perilously close to Glevum. Kerin stood up. The horse was coming straight at him. There was no point in trying to outrun a galloping horse, and a dagger wasn't going to do him much good, so he picked up a chunk of driftwood and prepared to launch it at the horse's front legs. He braced himself, then the wood dropped from his hand and he fell to his knees. The horse was the Pike.

*

Vortigern had lit a fire in a hollow behind the ridge. Kerin sat beside it, shivering violently inside Vortigern's cloak and trying to get warm.

'You shouldn't be here,' he said. 'On your own, this close to the river.'

Vortigern tossed a log onto the fire and sat down beside him. 'We had this conversation in Kent,' he said. 'Let's not have it again.'

'You're the King of all the Britons,' Kerin said. 'Kings have warbands. Escorts. Bodyguards. Kings shouldn't ride around on their own in sight of the enemy's front line.'

Vortigern passed him a hunk of dried meat. 'I was Vortigern of Glywysing before I was a king. And I've spent my life doing things I shouldn't have done. What happened? Where's the mule?'

Kerin tore at the meat. He was famished, having vomited a day's food into the river and eaten nothing since. 'There's no good news,' he said. 'I couldn't find Edryd and Cheldric. Rufus has tripled the guard on the bridge – twenty men and a barrier on each end. And they've driven off all the men who used to fish under it. There was one half-starved man in the shack. They'd beaten him and locked him up for months, for speaking up for you. All the rest I'll tell you at the camp, except that they've burned Malan's village. Batraz and his thugs. I was there, I'd told Berget and Malan to get out, they were preparing, then this lad turned up scared witless and said they'd taken Runo in the market and if he didn't talk they were coming to burn the place. I gave Berget your letter and made them leave, that moment, but I stayed behind. It was dark in the woods by then. Batraz had to think that everyone was asleep, so he'd burn them in their beds like he did to our lads in Kent. So I covered all the tracks, and lit a fire outside, and shoved a big empty cauldron on it, and fed the animals, and hid the horse – the horse Runo found in the North, a Kernow horse I think, I swapped the mule for it, and thank God I did, because after they'd set everything on fire and butchered the animals and –' he broke off, feeling Vortigern's hand on his arm. He took a breath and steadied himself, realising how frightened he had been, and how obvious it must be now. 'Batraz told them to search the woods, so I had to run for it. I managed to give them the slip, but I had to let the horse go. I found a fisherman who brought me across the river. And here I am.'

'So,' Vortigern said. He got up and whistled for the Pike. 'Edryd and Cheldric are missing. Runo is in prison, being tortured or hanged. Malan and his people are on the way to Cambria, we hope. We have no allies in Glevum now, and no way to set the bridge on fire without being seen. There is some good news, however. Lucius and his cavalry are a day away, and Gorlois is at Corinium. I gave the messenger a fresh horse and sent him straight back. I've told Gorlois to march up the old road and camp in the woodland, as close to the city as possible.' He hauled Kerin to his feet. 'Come on, get on. He doesn't mind you. We'll ride double again.' He legged Kerin up onto the horse's withers and jumped up behind him.

'You sound displeased,' Kerin said, as they set off. 'I don't think there was anything more I could have done.'

'Displeased? If I'm displeased, it's with Rufus and Batraz and Eldof and God. And with myself. I almost stopped you going. I should have stopped you, and sent someone I could spare. Tell me something. After they set the village on fire, and you ran for your life with a bunch of murdering arseholes after you, which way did you go?'

'Which way did I go?'

'Yes. North, south, east –'

'South-west,' Kerin said. 'Straight back the way I'd come.'

'I thought as much. Anyone with half a brain would have gone north.'

'I know. But –'

'I know why you did it. And I don't think there's another man in my company who'd have made that choice. I told you I should have sent someone else.'

49

Most of the leading men had been summoned to the king's tent. They sat in a circle around the small fire as evening's cold seeped in from the flood plain. Lud and his sons, Gwyndaf, Derfyn and Hefydd. They were joined by Varro, just arrived from his stronghold north of Blestium with a warband of thirty tough-looking warriors. Everyone listened intently as Kerin related what had happened to him. After a hearty meal and a few hours' sleep he felt like a new man, and looked like one, now that he had scrubbed away the last of the soot and parted company with his beard.

'Are they ready?' Lud asked. 'Are they waiting for us?'

'No,' Kerin said. 'They're expecting us, and we know the cataphracts have been training outside the walls. But there's no muster. Malan's people or the river men would have seen something. Varro, do you have anyone in Glevum?'

'A hangman, if they catch me,' Varro said. 'But I do have a friend in the merchants' quarter. He deals with Eldof's household and is on good terms there. I have two sound lads who aren't known in Glevum. I could send them with some keepsake that Tobias would recognise. One of them's related to an old soldier in the veterans' community, so he has an excuse to visit.'

'Send them, then,' Vortigern said. 'At first light. I'll see them before they go. They can have two days, no more.'

'Consider it done,' Varro said.

'Your voice,' Macsen said. 'What happened to the croaking frog?'

Varro smiled. 'You should ask Marcellus *magister*. I've no idea what he gave me, but it slides down your throat like nectar. It's killed the pain entirely. I'm not allowed to shout, but my lads tell me that's not a bad thing.'

Vortigern raised his hand for silence. Everyone stood. 'I'll try to make this simple,' he said. 'In the North, all most of you had to do was charge straight at the Picts and kill as many as you could. This is quite different. Rufus has cataphracts, Sarmatian cavalry, British horse warriors and foot soldiers. He'll send his cataphracts first, but anything else is an assumption, so we have to be alert and ready to counter. And the great unknowns? The carnyces, because we've never used them before. And the river, naturally. We know it's flowing fast because of the rains, but fast enough to stop a cavalry charge? We don't know, and we won't know, until either we or Rufus attempt it. I'm going to send Lucius's troop upriver to the ford. They've got the strongest horses. If they can cross and Gorlois rides from the south, anything in front of Glevum will be trapped between them. As for the rest, we know that cataphracts can't swim, so we need the bridge. If we can't burn it, we'll have to take it and hold it. Once the cataphracts have crossed, the spearhead will charge them. At the last moment, our force will turn and divide. Hefydd, you'll lead half back towards the camp. The cataphracts should follow. It's your task to wear them out. Lud, Varro, the rest of us will take on anything else that manages to cross the river. Gwyndaf, you're with me. It'll be chaos at times, and they'll need to see the standard. I'll lead as I always do. But sometimes it's necessary to think beyond it. We'll be fighting up and down the river, perhaps across it too.' He drew Kerin forward. 'You're aware of Kerin's band.

It's up to him to make the calls, in the moment, depending upon what happens. He can't predict this, any more than I can. But know this. If you can't see me or find me, you'll take your orders from him. You have your own bands, who will look to you, but in my absence, this is your battle commander.' He nodded and went out into the darkness. Kerin supposed that he should not have been shocked. But to hear it said out loud, in front of warriors like these, still brought him up short. He didn't even know how to look at these men, all older than him with the exception of Elir and Derfyn. Two of them old enough to be his father, and one of those two was staring at him just as he had done when Kerin was a five-year-old child spilling his breakfast gruel.

'You'll be with the Lord, Lud,' he said. 'As you've always been. You'll be there, and I won't. Macsen and Elir won't, because they'll be with me, killing cataphracts. I can command anywhere on the field, but you can't leave the spearhead. You have to protect Vortigern. You can't be everywhere.'

Lud grimaced. 'If you put it like that,' he said. 'But now I'm going to have a look around. They need to know that the chief warrior's got his eyes open.'

Kerin waited until his footsteps had faded. 'I mean no disrespect to Lud. He was chief warrior before I was even born.'

'We know you don't,' Macsen said. 'But you were right. My father can't be everywhere. And anyway, it's not as it was between him and Vortigern. There'll always be a bond, because of what happened when they were younger. But you're the one Vortigern looks to now. And I know you haven't pushed for it. You were just there, doing the right things at the right time. So keep on doing them. Me and my brother will stand with you.'

Hefydd patted Kerin's shoulder. 'Don't worry about Lud, boy,' he said. 'He knows how the land lies. But it's a nasty old cup to drink, so he's got to have his say. And you'll have no trouble from me and my boys. My father always told me that if a man's good enough, he's old enough. Do you agree, standard-bearer?'

'If I didn't, I'd have gone home by now,' Gwyndaf said.

*

Vortigern was sitting on a boulder on the crest of the ridge where he had sat his horse through the frozen night, waiting for Kerin to come back. Finding the black mare missing, Kerin had come here, to the only place which had any resonance for them both.

'I had to let you deal with it,' Vortigern said. 'None of them would have given an honest opinion when I was standing there. Were there any protests?'

'No,' Kerin said. 'Gwyndaf, Hefydd and Macsen backed me without hesitation. Lud was unhappy, as you'd expect, but I told him it was vital for him to stay with the spearhead. It gave him a reason not to feel belittled, and anyway, it's true.'

'I know,' Vortigern said, not taking his eyes from the blanket of white fog lying over the river. 'He's still a great, great warrior. But hardly a day goes by when I don't thank God that you went to Gwyndaf. He's worth ten men, and his boys are some of the best swordsmen we have.'

'They are,' Kerin said. 'But Gwyndaf has something else. A clear idea of what's happening here, and no scruples at all about how he deals with it.'

Vortigern looked round. 'What are you saying?'

'He was there when you fought Rufus in the North,'

Kerin said. 'Standing back so no-one would notice him, with a stone ready in his sling. If you hadn't caught my sword, he'd have killed Rufus there and then, and we wouldn't be here.'

Vortigern went back to looking at the river. 'I thought he'd cool his head in time,' he said. 'I thought that all this holy fire was a young man's nonsense, and would burn itself out. I thought the risk was worth it.'

'You're his father,' Kerin said. 'But it wasn't worth it, and now the risk is here. So please, if you come face to face with Rufus, don't hesitate for one moment, because he won't. Even though he's your son. Even though he's my blood brother. Because hesitating is what gets men killed. Gwyndaf is ready for it, and so am I, but it's the work of a second, isn't it. The work of a second.'

Vortigern got up and fetched the horses. 'I'm not in-tending to die here,' he said, and looked up at the white disc of the moon, its edge blurred by the thin mist in the higher air. 'Look. It's almost full. Let's find Cynan.'

*

Cynfawr was sleeping in his tent, but his son was sitting cross-legged on the ground beside a small fire of ash twigs. He smiled an acknowledgement as Vortigern and Kerin sat down opposite him.

'How long do we have?' Vortigern asked.

'Two days,' Cynan said, looking upwards. 'The moon will be full, then on the third day, the wave will come.'

'You're sure of this?'

'Yes, lord. Completely sure. It will be a great wave, be-cause the wind is right, the tides are high and the Hafren is full. And it will happen just after first light. If I were you, I would muster by moonlight. When your friends across the river stir from their beds, they will see a mighty force about to strike them. Then they will come, and so will the wave.'

'And the carnyces?' Kerin asked.

'We have studied the river,' the druid said. 'There's a bend downstream from the bridge. My father will stand there with the old carnyx. When he hears the wave approaching, he will begin to blow. I will remain here, out of sight. When the wave is almost upon us, my carnyx will speak.'

'Then we'll have to draw the cataphracts out first,' Kerin said. 'We'll have to make them chase us, just as we did with the Picts in the North. I can do this, with my archers and spearmen. Once they're across, we'll peel off to the sides to start our attack. But all they'll see is the spearhead, coming straight for them.'

There was a silence. 'Now I feel like Publius did in the North,' Vortigern said. 'It's a terrible risk. Some of you will probably die. But I know you're right. And there's one more thing we should have. A man on a fast horse, stationed a few miles downriver, to ride back and alert us before the wave reaches Cynfawr.'

Cynan rose easily to his feet. 'You have your plans,' he said. 'And now I must complete mine.'

'Your father's snoring like a pig,' Vortigern said. 'You should let him lie.'

'I intend to,' Cynan said. 'I am merely going to the woods, to light a few small fires and ask for a benediction. Perhaps you should do the same, lord, whichever god you pray to these days.'

50

Varro took his young warriors to the king's tent. Only four men were within; Vortigern, Kerin, Lud and Gwyndaf. The tension was palpable as they waited for some sliver of information which might mean the difference between victory and ruin.

'Eliud and Danius,' Varro said. Everyone sat. 'Eliud is the one with connections to the Roman community. He'll speak for them both.'

The young men looked eager and excited, much as Derfyn had looked in the North, after Vortigern sent him to spy on the Picts' stronghold. Well-built lads with long limbs and thick curls. Eliud leaned forward on his elbows, eyes gleaming in the lamplight. 'Tobias received us kindly,' he said. 'Your man to the last hair, Lord King. When we explained, he went straight to Eldof's house, on the pretext of offering him a consignment of fine wine. Eldof said yes, he'd gladly purchase the wine, because he'd soon be toasting a victory. Then he introduced Tobias to – well, to your son, Lord King, although they call him –'

'Don't stand on ceremony, boy,' Vortigern said. 'I know what they call him. What happened?'

'Well, Eldof introduced him as the Young King Vortimer,' Eliud said, 'and there were two other men there. Lord Eldof's chief warrior, Belinus, who has replaced Lord Varro, here.'

'He's an oaf,' Varro interjected.

'And the young king's chief warrior.' Eliud raised his eyebrows.

'A tall man with long fair hair and eyes like a fish-hawk?' Kerin asked.

'Yes, Lord Kerin. That's him. Lord Batraz, I think.'

'Well, he's not a lord in this country,' Lud growled.

'Did they speak of their plans?' Vortigern asked.

'Yes, Lord King. Tobias had made sure to give Eldof a big flask of wine to sample, so he was already properly drunk by the time the others arrived. He said that the cataphracts were going to come pouring over the bridge and smash the daylights out of you, with his horse warriors and Batraz's cavalry coming behind.'

'By the bridge?' Kerin asked.

'Probably. The young king was quite keen for some of his horsemen to come straight across the river – he'd done it himself, by the sound of it. But Eldof said no, there was too much water in the river, and they should either ride upstream to the ford or follow the cataphracts across the big bridge, because the foot would be coming over the packhorse bridge. And it's the day after tomorrow. Those armoured men have a bit of Latin. My uncle Virgilius, the army veteran, got talking to one of the commanders. He was tearing his hair because his company was raring to go, but the young king wouldn't have it because tomorrow is the Lord's Day. So it had to be the day after.' Eliud shrugged. 'Up to him, I suppose.'

'No,' Vortigern said. 'It's up to me.'

'There's more, though,' Varro said. 'Tell about the alehouse.'

'There's a place where the guards drink,' Eliud said. 'There wasn't a guard in sight – the landlord said they'd been forbidden – but the place was full of ordinary people, men and women. Carpenters, weavers, farmers and so on. And believe me, Lord King, I've never felt so much raving anger inside one building in my life. Everyone had had someone beaten or hanged or locked up, and now that the guards have been hauled off to join the foot there's no-one to keep them down.'

'It was frightening,' Danius chipped in. 'Frightening. The man we were drinking with told us to get out of the city quick. So we took him at his word, and here we are.'

Vortigern stood up and everyone else followed. 'You've done well,' he said, shaking the young warriors' hands. 'But there's no rest for you. Varro, prepare your men and horses. Feed these lads, then send them back to me. Lud, alert Hefydd and the men of the spearhead, and marshal the foot soldiers. We muster now, to strike at first light.'

Lud marched out, keen as ever now that he had a purpose. Gwyndaf, who had sat silently throughout, gave an evil grin.

'Surely you're not going to lead us to battle on the Lord's Day,' he said.

'It'll be my day if everything goes to plan,' Vortigern said. 'Now, go and prepare your men, and arm yourself with everything you have.'

They went out into the darkness. A huge golden moon illuminated the camp and the shallow valley beyond with the clarity of daylight. 'This wave thing,' Gwyndaf said, looking upwards. 'Can it work?'

'Possibly,' Kerin said. 'And even if the wave doesn't happen, we still have the carnyces. We'll have surprise, because they'll never expect us at first light. And there might even be trouble in the city.' He turned to Vortigern. 'What are you going to do with Eliud and Danius?'

'Send them to Gorlois,' Vortigern said. 'He needs to be ready, and to know what's expected.'

They turned as Derfyn trotted towards them. 'Lucius Arrius and the cavalry,' he said. 'They're waiting a couple of miles away, near that little Roman fortlet we passed. Lucius sent a messenger because he didn't want Glevum to hear a few hundred horses coming down the road. What shall I tell him?'

'They should head up the road behind the fortlet,' Vortigern said. 'There's a good old track which loops round through the woodlands and joins this valley further inland. The ground's soft and the woods are dense enough to muffle the sound. But I want Lucius himself here now, to give him his orders.'

'Done,' Derfyn said. Gwyndaf watched him go.

'Does Lucius know about the wave?' he asked.

'Not yet,' Vortigern said. 'But he should be across the river before it comes.'

'Suppose the ford's guarded,' Kerin said. 'I know it never is, but they'll have lookouts, surely.'

Gwyndaf drew one of his daggers, spat on the blade and tested the cutting edge. 'Permission to go and find out?' he asked, and slipped away without waiting for an answer. After a few moments three horses left the encampment, heading northwards. Kerin heard a familiar sound; slow footsteps, shuffling over the sparse turf.

'Marcellus *magister*,' he said.

'We kept to the ground beside the road to make less noise,' the haruspex said. 'Even small carriages rattle like bone bags. I have found Morvid. He is well prepared, and so am I.'

Vortigern looked round. 'I hope you haven't brought any lunatic Roman generals with you,' he said. Marcellus sighed.

'Well, one did slip through the net. But he's given me his word that he won't fight.'

'Ha,' Vortigern said. 'What's he going to do, then? Tell me how to lead an army? Have a pleasant morning watching the rest of us die?'

'Drive the bard's chariot, I believe,' Marcellus said. 'And perhaps offer a little moral support, if required.' Vortigern opened his mouth to reply, then thought better of it. Marcellus nodded. 'That's what friends do in my experience, Lord King,' he said.

51

The first faint, cold light of dawn edged above the low hills east of Glevum. Tiny dots of lamplight were visible here and there across the silent black bulk of the sleeping city. Kerin stood beside his horse at the head of the arrowhead formation he was about to lead. The sky above had turned from black to a deep, unearthly blue. A huge, paling moon hung over the western horizon. He could see the bridge, but at this distance, not the guards. There was no chance at all that they would be able to see him, although they might have cast an uneasy glance over the low, shallow bank of black cloud behind him, wondering what the weather had in store. The cloud lay motionless across the flood plain, like fog did. The guards would have had to come much closer to see it separate into the forms of a few thousand men and horses. Every mounted warrior and cavalryman was standing beside the animal which would carry him into battle. At the drop of Vortigern's hand, they would leap to the saddle and the cloud would break in thunder.

Kerin stroked Blaidd's neck gently, knowing that he and his warhorse were the first thing the guards on the bridge would see. He hardly knew what he would have done, in their boots; slam the barrier down, or fling it up to release the cataphracts? At least there should be no uncertainty for Lucius's cavalry when they reached the ford. There were no lookouts; they and the token guard were lying dead in a drainage ditch. Kerin looked over his shoulder. Beyond his band of thirty, less than a spear's throw distant, Vortigern was standing at the head of his army. He had spent the night as he always did the hours before battle; moving amongst the men, reassuring the nervous, exchanging warriors' banter, letting them all drink of his confidence. Now he handed the Pike's reins to Gwyndaf and approached Kerin's band. Marc and Ashur were in the first rank behind Elir and Macsen. Vortigern went straight to the boys.

'You remind me of your leader when he was your age,' he said. 'Too brave for his own good. But he survived, and so will you.' His gaze moved over the river and the city beyond. 'It'll be mad out there. Faster than anything you've known. Never hesitate. Kill and go. Don't think, and don't look back. Trust your horses, and remember; every other man in this band fought the Picts, and they're all still here.'

'We'll do our best, lord,' Marc said stolidly.

'If I doubted that, you wouldn't be here,' Vortigern said. 'And my best men are with you. All will be well. Your fathers would be proud of you, and so am I.' He shook the boys' hands, nodded to Kerin and walked away. Macsen gave the boys a wink. Something moved amongst the ranks. Vortigern beckoned.

'He wants us for something,' Kerin said. He led his band back to join the massed warriors. Publius Luca had brought up the chariot. Cynfawr was standing in it, incongruously dressed in a white silken robe and a regal red cloak. His carnyx was beside him, secured in a bracket bolted to the side.

'They're going down to the river bend,' Vortigern said. 'Cynan thinks it's almost time. Our lookout is a mile further down. When he passes them, Cynfawr will start to play. By the time we see the lookout, the other side should be getting frightened. And then you'll go.'

And then we'll go, Kerin thought. Twenty-eight men, two lads and the ten brave volunteers who are carrying the spare spears and quivers full of arrows. He went over to the chariot.

'I have been told,' Publius Luca said.

'About the wave?'

'Yes.'

'I couldn't tell you,' Kerin said. 'Not when you thought we were all mad anyway.'

'In fact, if it's true, it's probably the most sensible thing anyone's suggested,' Publius said. There was a loud rap on the chariot's wooden side.

'Commander, you need to go now,' Cynan said. He reached up and clasped his father's hand. 'Play well. The gods be with you.'

The chariot rumbled off. A fierce tension, almost unbearable, gripped the warriors as the sound faded to nothing and they stood in silence, waiting for the signal which would fling them towards blood and the shadow of death. Vortigern moved to Kerin's side.

'If the wave doesn't come, I've told Cynfawr to play when the moon touches the horizon,' he said. They waited. Brother Padarn came from amongst the wagons and baggage mules.

'Cynan tells me it's almost time, lord,' he said. 'Shall I bless the army?' Vortigern nodded. As Padarn planted himself in front of the quivering mass of men and horseflesh, a sound came from far off; neither hoofbeats nor carnyx, but a low, distant, sullen roar like continuous thunder. A rider appeared, a speck out on the flood plain; flat to his horse's neck as if running before the hounds of Annwn, the dreaded portent of death. Padarn flung his arms to the sky. 'Father God!' he bawled. 'Protect these your children, men of all faiths and none. Give them courage, and shield them with your mighty arm. And please, Lord, if it's your will, let them beat these fools who call you a merciless bastard. You, the God of boundless love, who gave his own son to save our pathetic souls. Amen.'

'Amen!' roared the men of all faiths and none.

'To horse!' Kerin shouted. As his warriors hit the saddle, the boom of the carnyx came rolling across the flatlands. All the fighting horses of the spearhead began to dance on their front feet. Vortigern's arm flew out, commanding his men to mount. He rode up alongside Kerin and seized his shoulder.

'God keep you!' he breathed. Kerin still had no idea which way this would go, so he threw the only stone he had into the balance.

'They hanged Hefin with whipcord,' he said, and hurled his horse towards the river.

The bridge, the bridge. The twenty guards weren't guarding it. They weren't even thinking about the barrier or the at-tackers, they were running back and forth in panic, seizing each other's arms and pointing desperately downriver, towards the terrible noise and its unseen source. Even if some had seen the wave before, it was almost impossible to separate the roar of advancing water from the sound of the carnyx. 'Pick a man, archers!' Kerin bellowed. 'Don't take your eyes off him!' And here was the bearded oaf who'd tried to rob an old man on the way to see his grandchild. The spear flew from Kerin's hand and buried itself in the chief guard's chest. A wall of arrows followed. The barrier was unattended. As Kerin's band reached it, the three sur-viving guards fled across the bridge towards their fellows at the far end. Arrows felled them as they ran. 'Raise the barrier!' Kerin shouted to his spear bearers. The wooden beam flew up. Wrenching his spear free, Kerin led his warband onto the bridge. No-one was guarding the other end, but as they reached the Glevum side the western gates swung open. A mass of foot soldiers headed for the pack-horse bridge. A trumpet shrieked from the training ground, followed by a volley of battering drums. Four abreast, the cataphracts began their advance, charging around the base of the city wall and up the approach road. 'Turn!' Kerin roared. As Blaidd thundered back across the bridge, he glanced downwards. The water was rising, breaking over the banks and drenching his men in spray. The noise drowned everything else, so he didn't know the spear was coming until it slammed into his left shoulder. He cried out with shock, then it fell away and the blood began to run down the inside of his leather jerkin. He couldn't feel the pain yet. Last off the bridge, he galloped straight on as the warriors ahead of him separated into two hurtling bodies and swung out to right and left, just as they had trained to do. He glanced behind. The cataphracts were coming off the bridge. Their front line fanned out, twenty wide. The scale armour gleamed in the cold blue light of dawn and the waning moon. Each one was carrying a lance longer than his horse, and it looked to Kerin as if each lance was aimed at him. But the cataphracts were not alone. Twenty white-clad men of the Sword of God were riding with them, and it must have been one of those bastards who threw the spear, because the cataphracts didn't have them. Please God, let Macsen and Elir have seen them, Kerin thought, because speed alone may not save them. Then the sound came; out of nowhere, it seemed, because Cynan and his carnyx were invisible. There was only the sound, the great, furious, disembodied roar of the war horn. Cynfawr answered it from downstream. The sound redoubled; the chariot was coming back. Behind Kerin's back, the rolling charge disintegrated into a formless melee of terrified, plunging horses. Their riders fought to control them, some of them probably as frightened as their mounts. And then, in their moment of blind panic, the wave hit. It submerged the bridge and the banks, sweeping a score of armoured horsemen into the river and driving back Eldof's mounted warriors. Surging on, it engulfed a troop of Glevum men who were attempting to cross the ford and crashed over the packhorse bridge, sending a mob of foot soldiers fleeing straight towards Lucius's cavalry. Keeping Blaidd running, Kerin turned in the saddle, gasping as the movement dragged on his wound. Some of the cataphract horses had thrown their riders and were careering around loose. The men were struggling to their feet, hopelessly vulnerable despite their armour. He would have pursued them if not for the mounted survivors, close to two hundred of them, circling around their desperate leaders. Their momentum was lost, but the men still had their deadly lances. Kerin hurled his spear, striking the lead horse in the slim gap between head and neckpiece. Macsen appeared at his side.

'You're bleeding like a stuck pig,' he gasped.

'I'll survive,' Kerin panted as they swung right to attack the flank. 'One of those fucking fanatics got me.'

'I know. One of that bunch over there. The one without a spear.'

Kerin glanced sideways. Idris, with sword and spear. Aron, with sword and spear. Rufus with sword and – nothing. 'Jesus Christ!' he choked.

'Go,' Macsen shouted, tossing him a spare spear. 'Take my boys. I've got Gerdan, we'll have those three.'

Kerin went. He knew that he must empty his head or

risk death, for himself and all those he was leading. 'Follow me, lads,' he yelled, raising his spear. As they closed on the armoured horsemen, Ashur galloped along the opposite flank of the formation. The three arrows he was holding flashed from his bow. Two men fell, screaming and clutching at their eyes. Marc, close behind, shot a rider through his unprotected hand. A lance crashed to the ground. The spearmen loosed their weapons. Kerin's shattered another lance. Cadfan's struck a horse mid-chest, bringing the animal to its knees as they galloped out of range. Above the hooves and jingling scale armour, Kerin heard another sound, and it made his heart leap. The Cambrian spearhead was on the charge. The armoured men roared and quickened their pace. Vortigern was riding a few horse lengths ahead of his men. For a petrifying moment Kerin thought he would keep coming, but just short of the lances he wheeled sideways with Gwyndaf and Lud, leaving Hefydd at the head of the front line.

'Come on you devils, chase me!' Hefydd roared. He spun his horse and set off with half the army following. Vortigern and Gwyndaf turned for the river with the remainder. The wave had passed by, a spent force now, but the Hafren was still a heaving mass of brown water. Eldof was leading a band of mounted warriors across the bridge with Batraz and his cavalry close behind. The Sarmatian was still wearing the white tunic of the Sword of God. Elir arrived at the gallop.

'What now?' he shouted.

'Take all the archers, follow Hefydd and the cataphracts,' Kerin panted. 'We've got to see off the Sword and hold the bridge.' Macsen arrived. Someone had slashed his arm, but it was bound up with something which looked like part of a white tunic.

'I killed Aron,' he said. 'And I don't give a damn. The other two got away. Idris killed Gerdan's horse, but he's grabbed another. And I've got Aron's tunic. Keep still for a moment.' He pulled out a length of bloodstained white fabric, rolled it into a pad and stuffed it down the back of Kerin's jerkin. 'There. You're not allowed to bleed to death until this is over. Gods, what's happening over there?'

A ferocious battle had broken out in front of the city's western gates. Eldof's rearguard and the Sarmatians had been caught between Gorlois and the Kernow men, and most of Lucius's cavalry.

'We've got to hold the bridge,' Kerin said. 'That fight can't come over here, and the cataphracts can't go back.' They rode for the river, where the Cambrian army was having its own battle with the horse warriors of Glevum. 'Where did Rufus and Idris go?'

'Back across the bridge,' Macsen said. 'We couldn't stop them, we had our hands full.'

The bridge was strewn with bodies, grotesquely arranged by the force of the water. Kerin and Macsen rode towards the fight, which had edged up to the packhorse bridge. Livius and his troop were defending it so there was no escape for the Glevum foot soldiers. Vortigern emerged, dripping blood.

'What happened to you?' he asked.

'I got speared,' Kerin said. 'From behind, and the wave was coming, so I didn't hear it. I've sent Elir and the archers with Hefydd. They've been magnificent.'

'But now we need the bridge,' Vortigern said. 'We've got the beating of these, they're going to run for it any moment. And we're going after them. We'll drive them all down to the training ground and finish it there.' He glanced back at the fight, disintegrating into ragged private battles, and at the melee on the far bank. 'We could take the city.'

'We don't want the city!' Kerin exclaimed.

'No, we don't. But Eldof has to know that I could take it if I wanted to.' They all reined back as the fight surged towards them, a fluid mass of struggling foot soldiers and horse warriors hacking at each other. The roar of the carnyces resounded across the flood plain behind them. The first of the Glevum men broke away and fled across the bridge.

'Fall back!' Eldof's voice bawled. 'Hold the gates!'

Gwyndaf arrived as the retreat gathered pace.

'We're going across,' Vortigern shouted, above the bellow of the war horns. 'Half the men here with Lud and Varro, the rest with us. Kerin, go after Hefydd, but tell Lud to look out for Batraz and the Sword. They might come out of the north gate and cross higher up.'

Kerin caught up with Lud by the packhorse bridge. The detritus of the battle was lying everywhere; bodies, broken weapons, hacked off limbs, a few dead horses. Livius and his troop had corralled the surviving foot soldiers on the riverbank. Lud gave Kerin a wholehearted grin and shook his fist. He never looked as much in his element as when he was up to his armpits in blood and body parts.

'Where's Vortigern?' he asked.

'Gone to give Eldof a hard time. We're staying on this side. The cataphracts could come back any time.'

Lud licked his lips. 'The ones who got thrown off are in the river. They sank like stones.'

'We're going after the rest,' Kerin said. 'I need everyone in front of the bridge, to stop them crossing. Their horses should be exhausted. But if they're trapped between you and Hefydd and the carnyces, they're going to fight, and I can't tell you how to do it because none of us has ever done it. My lads have killed a few, but close quarters, that's different. You and Varro, one flank each. Drop the horses if you can and go for the gaps, that's all I can say. And look out for Batraz. He could be anywhere.'

Lud grinned. It was completely amicable and devoid of resentment. In an odd way, amidst all this blood and chaos, something seemed to have fallen into place. 'Go and get 'em, then,' he said. 'I haven't got all day.'

The first thing Kerin saw was Mad Mabon, riding flat out down the Roman road. He had a gruesome weal down one side of his face. 'They're coming behind me,' he panted. 'We led them up the valley by the camp. My father said, those archer boys are red hot, if we take the bastards up there, they can go up on the banks and pick them off. And that's what happened. The carnyces started up, the armoured horses went mad and the archers did their work.' He gasped and rubbed his face. 'But if you go up a valley, you've got to come down again, haven't you. There was a bit of a scrap. We lost some men. But not as many as they lost.' He looked away, blinking back a tear. Kerin reached out to grip his shoulder.

'Mabon, that was mad. Mad, and very brave. Like you and your father.' Mabon gave as much of a grin as his swollen face could manage. 'Now, go and tell Lud. He's holding the big bridge. Stay there with him and the warriors.'

The spearmen rode on. They passed three armoured men lying dead beside the road, two with arrows lodged in their eye sockets, one shot through the neck. Soon they heard heavy hoofbeats, coming and going on the light wind. The canter had slowed to a trot. Kerin led his band in a wide loop away from the road. There was no point in engaging cataphracts on open ground. He could feel blood soaking through the pad and running down his back, and the blood loss was beginning to tell. He tried to concentrate, and not to waste energy thinking about where the wound had come from.

'There they go,' Macsen said, as the cataphracts passed. 'Around half of what they came with.'

They rode to meet their own warriors. Hefydd and Elir were leading, with the archers' troop following. 'Magnificent, all of you!' Kerin shouted, raising a clenched fist. Hefydd waved back, cut about the face and forearms.

'Boy,' he gasped, as they rode for the river, 'those lads of yours killed dozens. And you were right, they were nifty enough to keep out of the way. Not like some of us. You've got to risk those lances to get close, and if they catch you, it's over. But my old mare is quick. I managed to stab a couple of the horrible bastards between the helmet and the tunic. Good thing the fight was near the camp, Marcellus and Morvid are with our wounded. What's happening at the river?'

'Gorlois and Lucius have trapped the Sarmatians in front of the city,' Kerin said. 'Vortigern and our boys hammered the Glevum men and chased them back across. They're probably all in the same fight by now. Lud's on this side, with enough men to hold the bridge. Where are the carnyces?'

'Coming behind,' Hefydd said. 'Both in the chariot with Publius. They're going to blow when we get close to the river.' He glanced sideways. 'There's blood all over your back.'

'I got speared,' Kerin said. 'From behind. I didn't hear it coming.'

'He's being polite,' Macsen said. 'But I don't have to be. Rufus speared him.'

Hefydd's bushy eyebrows rose. 'Did he, now,' he said, slapping the blade of his sword against his thigh.

Lud had dropped the barrier and jammed a wagon full of boulders underneath. No-one from Glevum was going to shift it; they were fighting for their lives across the river. As Kerin's force closed on them, the armoured men started glancing behind. The carnyces blasted from the rear, and the steady trot dissolved into roiling chaos. Kerin waved to Elir.

'Get out on the flank. We'll have them surrounded. Just stay back, and do what you've been doing.' He turned to Macsen's band. 'We're going in with Hefydd. Spears, swords, whatever you've got. Now!'

All Kerin could see was a forest of lances springing upright as the cataphracts were forced together, and all he could hear, cutting through the carnyces' roar, was the sound which would haunt him for months to come; the horses in the front rank screaming in terror as riders behind piled into them, forcing them over the edge of the bank to be swept away by the surging water. One of the armoured men was yelling frantic orders. Kerin couldn't understand a word, but it brought a response. All the men at the edge of the company turned outwards, their lances a ring of razor-sharp points. Beyond them, in the shrinking space, horses started lashing out as they got on top of each other. Kerin seized Lud's rein.

'If we can get inside, we can fight them. They haven't got room to use their lances.' Dull Bened gave an ear-splitting roar. He rode to the bridge, slashed the ropes securing the timber barrier, hoisted it in his powerful arms and charged. The first ten men were caught dead as the log smashed into their lances, splintering the shafts. The eleventh man speared Bened's horse in the chest and knocked it flat, but the gap was made. 'Go!' Kerin roared, and the companies closed, hand to hand. Trapped and outnumbered, mad with fear, the armoured men fought like raging demons. Kerin found himself in a frenzied sword fight. Other frantic struggles were going on all around him. The ground grew slippery with blood. With a desperate thrust, Kerin slashed the gap between mail shirt and gloved hand, cutting the artery. A shower of blood drenched him and the sword dropped away, but at the same moment something whistled over his head. He spun in the saddle and saw two things; a pair of eyes gleaming through the apertures in a horse's head guard, and a sword about to fall on him. There was no room, but there was no choice. *'Kill!'* he howled. Blaidd roared deep in his throat and rose on his hind legs. His forefeet smashed into the rider's chest, flattening him over the horse's rump. His jaws closed on the man's arm and dragged him from the saddle. Kerin caught the sword as it arced through the air. Blaidd shook the man savagely, tossed him to the ground and trampled him into the mud. Another horseman, straight ahead. Another gleaming helmet, another blood-stained sword. Kerin raised the weapon he had caught, but the other man froze. The sword dropped from his fingers and he raised his hands in the air. Kerin hesitated. The armoured man slid to the ground and tore off his helmet. A young man, no older than Kerin himself, with long dark hair and jet-black eyes. He fell to his knees in front of Kerin and Blaidd.

'Nos trucidate!' he wept, in broken Latin. *'Nos. Ne equos. Ne bellos equos.'*

It was the same voice which had given the orders. Other men, hearing, began to throw down their weapons and dismount. Lud came barging through the jostling horses.

'I'll finish him off,' he panted.

'No,' Kerin said, staying his arm. 'Look. They're surrendering. They know it's hopeless. He's asking us to kill them, and spare the horses.'

'Well, let's do it, then.' Lud drew his sword.

'Put it away, Lud,' Kerin said. 'I'm not killing a man on his knees, and neither are you. Put it away.' You know what Vortigern said, he thought. But he didn't want to invoke Vortigern's name to make his authority count. He became aware that Varro, Macsen and a group of lesser warriors were standing nearby, waiting to see what would happen. Very grudgingly, Lud sheathed his sword.

'On your head be it,' he said. Kerin turned to the young commander, hoping that the Latin he had learned from Dimos would suffice.

'*Amicum Romanum habeo,*' he said. '*Hic venit. Hic manete, vos et equi.*' The man nodded vigorously and the message was passed amongst his companions. Kerin turned to Varro. 'Fetch Publius Luca,' he said. 'He's right behind us in the chariot. Ask him to talk to this man. Find out who they are, where they're from. Stay here with your boys and keep them in order. Get all the armour off, tie the men's hands and hobble the horses. I'm taking the rest of our lads across the river. We'll probably have to fight some of the men you used to command. I know you'd do it, but I won't ask you to.'

'Thank you,' Varro said. 'But if things go wrong, we'll be across that bridge before you can blink.' Kerin looked around for Bened. He was standing, staring down at his dead horse.

'Bless him,' he said thickly. 'He was a brave old lad.' Kerin reached down and patted Bened's shoulder.

'The lance breaker,' he said. 'We might not have won without him. Now, take some boys and shift that wagon off the bridge. Then help yourself to a horse, take the armour off and find out what's happening across the river. Don't get into the fight, just come back and tell me.' Bened mopped his face and stumped off. Kerin leaned forward over Blaidd's neck and hugged him tightly. 'Thank you,' he whispered. Although it could not be proven, he knew what had sealed the surrender when he looked into the horrified eyes of the young commander.

Elir gathered the archers. No serious injuries, but plenty of cuts and knocks. 'We couldn't hang back once you went in,' he said. 'Are we going across?'

'Yes,' Kerin said, looking towards the city. The sounds of fighting were clearly audible – swords clashing, men shouting and screaming, horses squealing – but the battle had moved on. The western gates were closed, the battlements guarded. The area beneath was strewn with bloody remains. 'Lads, you've done great work. Now, stick together until we know what we're fighting.' He waved to Lud and Hefydd. The warriors gathered. 'We're done here. It sounds as if they're fighting near the eastern gates. Lud, come with me.'

The two men rode over the bridge, their horse warriors streaming after them. The racket grew louder as they advanced. Horses were approaching at speed. A band of twenty men, Bened leading.

'Half the Sarmatians are on the run,' he shouted, shaking his fist. 'Vortigern says it's – what? Tactics. I'm just glad to see the back of them. The other half are still fighting, Eldof and some of his lads too, but the Sword are all inside the city. Vortigern sent us to ride around the walls, in case any of them come out the other side.'

'Can we go with Bened?' Elir asked. 'If they've got archers up on the walls, our boys will be sitting ducks.'

'Do it,' Kerin said, 'but keep your eyes open for the Sword. If they come out, don't take them on, just get back here. And don't shoot the men on the walls unless they're archers.' He wheeled Blaidd and headed towards the sounds of battle. The wound in his shoulder was hurting brutally now that the initial numbness had worn off. It was as much as his left hand could do to hold the reins. 'My left arm's gone,' he said. 'I can fight with my right and throw a spear if someone brings it. But that's all.'

Lud snorted. 'Just as well you're not the king's left arm, then. Stick with me if you can. They won't pass me.' Ahead was a seething mass of human limbs and horses and blood, hemmed in by Kernow men to the right, Lucius's cavalry to the left and Cambrians to the rear. Kerin roared to his men and let Blaidd run. Vortigern beheaded a Sarmatian cavalryman straight in front of him. The horse careered on with the headless body sprawled over its neck. The Glevum men, seeing reinforcements galloping towards them, began to fall back towards their gates.

'They're trying to trick us,' Vortigern panted. 'Most of the Sarmatians are running away down the Roman road. Whoever's in command, they're hoping that I'll split our force and chase them.'

'Are we going into the city, then?' Lud asked.

'Of course we're not. You of all men should know why. They know the place backwards, all the wrong people would get killed. Kerin, you can't move your left arm.'

'Not much,' Kerin admitted.

'Bened said the cataphracts have surrendered. Was he making it up?'

'No. The carnyces terrified them, the wave drowned a few, then Hefydd ran the legs off them. The archers killed a good number, then the carnyces started up again and we drove the rest down to the river. They were getting forced down the bank into the water. Then Blaidd killed a man in front of their commander, and that was that. They gave up and threw down their arms. I've left Varro in charge, but I sent for Publius to talk to them. The commander has some Latin. He asked me to kill them and spare the horses.'

Vortigern ruffled Blaidd's mane. 'You are your father's son,' he said. The Pike tried to bite his child in the neck. Gwyndaf arrived on a Sarmatian horse.

'Some prick wounded my mare,' he said, white with anger. 'She'll live, though, and the stuffing's gone out of them. If we could kill Batraz, they might just go home.'

The city gates were open. All the Glevum men who were close enough rushed through, until someone inside saw the Sarmatians trying to fight their way in and slammed the gates shut. A furious roar came from the cavalrymen. One of them yelled out a stream of abuse. The meaning was incomprehensible, but the blazing anger was not. They turned as one and galloped off eastwards, after their fellows. The remaining Glevum warriors scattered. Gorlois came cantering over, chortling. He was bleeding from a leg wound and a cut over his brow. 'By the gods, I'd have been raving too,' he said. 'But that's Eldof for you. He'd sell his mother. Is all that blood yours or someone else's?'

'Someone else's,' Vortigern said. 'Now, go and round up your men. I want everyone here, where Eldof can see them from the gatehouse.'

'Are we going to storm the thing?'

'God, no. There'd be a bloodbath. Now go and tell Lucius what I told you. And tell him the cataphracts are finished.'

Gorlois gaped. 'Finished? All dead?'

'Dead or captured. Lud, Gwyndaf, bring our men.' Vortigern reached for Kerin's rein as the other men dispersed. 'You can't fight, go and bring Bened and his boys back.'

'The archers are with him,' Kerin said. 'Elir thought they

might have bowmen on the walls. And if that's someone else's blood, why's it dripping off your foot?'

Vortigern leaned on the front of his saddle and laughed. 'I've got plenty left. Now go. I want you there when I give Eldof our terms.'

Kerin rode off along the southern perimeter of the city. The gates were closed. The guards on the parapet had little to look at apart from the few buildings beside the Abona road, all shuttered and barricaded. He was riding towards the point where the wall turned towards the river and the western gate when he heard the crack and the shouting. Hooves hammered over cobbles. Something hard shattered, and a horse shrieked. As Blaidd rounded the corner, he almost collided with Hebog.

'Quick!' Marc bawled. 'Astra's down!' Beyond him, the matched white horses of the Sword of God were turning for the river, pursuing Bened and his band. Kerin followed Marc along the base of the wall and out onto the bare field beyond. Astra was lying flat in the dust with a spearhead and the stump of a shaft protruding from his neck. He must have landed on the spear when he fell, breaking the shaft and driving the point in deeper. Blood was seeping slowly from the wound. Ashur was kneeling beside the horse, cradling his head. Kerin jumped to the ground. As he bent over the boy and the wounded horse, his head began to swim. He dropped to his knees instead, trying to blink the dizziness away.

'One of the white ones did it,' Marc said, from somewhere far off. 'Me and Ashur had got behind, Hebog had something in his foot. They went after Bened, but one of them saw us and speared Astra. Is he going to die?'

'I don't know,' Kerin said. The horse was shaking. He had seen horses die of shock and pain, even if their wounds didn't kill them. 'Did the others see this happen?'

'Don't think so,' Marc said. Now that his head had cleared, Kerin could hear the tremor in the boy's voice.

'Alright. If Bened's got any sense, he'll head round to the eastern gate. Varro may not have seen all this from across the river, so you have to go for him. Get up, Ashur. You can ride double.'

Ashur looked up, tears running down his face through the dust and horse blood. 'I will not leave Astra alone,' he said. 'He is part of my soul.'

Kerin closed his eyes and tried to think logically. A black hole had almost swallowed him as he bent over the wounded horse, and he had no idea how long it would be before it sucked him under completely. But two things he knew. He was incapable of fighting, and if the warhorse had been his, he wouldn't have abandoned it short of death.

'Listen to me,' he said, taking Ashur by the shoulders. 'You're going with Marc. He can't go alone. I'll stay here with your horse. I can't fight, but you can. Now get the saddle off, cut the girth up and tie his feet so he can't move or kick.' He waited, catching his breath, while the boys did as they'd been told. 'Throw the saddle over his back feet to hide what you've done. I'm going to lie across his front ones and look dead. It won't be hard, believe me.' He whistled softly to Blaidd, who came ambling over and shoved him in the chest. 'Alright, Ashur. See if he'll let you get on.'

'But, lord –'

'Don't argue, just do it. That's it. He'll take you.'

'But, lord –'

Kerin sighed. 'Ashur, they have to see this. One dying horse, and one dead man. If they come back, they'll ride straight past. Now go, both of you. Tell Varro to come, and bring one of the big wagons we use for collecting the dead. Jesus Christ, just go!'

The boys took off. Kerin lowered his body gingerly over the horse's forefeet. He drew his dagger, made a pillow of his right arm and laid his head on it, the dagger clutched in his fist out of sight. Lying face down, his back soaked in blood and his hair a tangled mess of gore and dirt, he could have been anyone. Astra had stopped shaking and just twitched now and then. 'Keep still,' Kerin murmured, wondering how much British the horse knew. He tried desperately to focus on something – anything – to stop the slow drift towards oblivion. Gael. His home. The sounds which were starting to disturb the howling silence of that great flat, empty field. Not fighting – and why wasn't there fighting, for God's sake, if Bened had led the Sword of God into Vortigern's arms – but something else. Faint, dulled by the thickness of the city walls, but persistent, and building. Voices. A lot of voices. Footsteps over cobbles. Someone hammering something over the other side of the city. And then the hoofbeats. Heart thudding, Kerin opened one eye just a little and squinted sideways. The western gates swung open and a band of battered-looking Glevum warriors bundled through them into the city, followed by the Sword of God. The gates closed.

'They escaped,' a clipped voice said, a short distance away. 'It is unfortunate.' Batraz. Kerin closed his one eye and tried desperately not to breathe. Two horses came from behind at a walking pace, circled round him and Astra and stopped. Kerin opened his eye to the merest slit and peered through his matted hair. Rufus and Batraz, just a few paces away.

'Bened's stupid,' Rufus said. 'We call him Dull Bened. Stupid, but loyal, and brave. Anyone with any sense would have ridden straight back to strength. But he didn't want to lead us there and make things harder for my father, so he went for the ford instead.'

'He was lucky,' Batraz said. 'That river is for drowning.'

'They know the crossing,' Rufus said. 'And our horses are used to swimming.'

Batraz gave him a withering look. 'Our horses? It is the enemy's horses, no? And here is one of those archers. This one will never shoot an arrow again.' He dismounted and prodded Kerin in the ribs with his foot.

'For God's sake, the man's dead,' Rufus said, in disgust. 'Leave him alone.'

Batraz peered downwards. 'Maybe he is dead,' he said. 'But he has a pretty silver necklace.' He leaned down and grabbed the chain of Kerin's crucifix. With a howl of fury, Kerin rolled over and stabbed him through the foot. Batraz roared with pain and went for his sword. Kerin jerked the dagger free and staggered to his feet.

'You thieving, bloodletting bastard,' he gasped. 'You're no Christian.' He lunged forward, slashing Batraz in the thigh. The sword hummed over his head and nicked his right shoulder. Kerin chopped the other man's wrist, sending the sword clattering to the ground, and went for his throat.

'No!' Rufus bellowed, leaping from his horse. Kerin didn't see him raise his sword for the killing blow, didn't hear the galloping horses; all he heard was the hiss of the arrow in the air before it hit Batraz in the back, and the spear thudding into Rufus's chest. He had heard that sound countless times, when the spear was his own; the dull thump, the agonised cry cut short, the final exhalation. The sound of a man speared through the heart. The sound of instant death. Rufus fell flat on his back. Batraz sank to his knees. Kerin's vision was swimming, but he could make out a band of horsemen galloping from the direction of the river; figures running along the battlements above. A horse blew down his neck from behind. That was where the spear had come from. Kerin turned slowly. The Pike snorted at him. The western gate banged open and Idris came stumbling out, followed by two other distraught youngsters from the Sword of God. One of them was carrying a torn white tunic nailed to a spear shaft; a crude truce flag.

'Please,' Idris sobbed. 'Let us have the Lord Vortimer's body.'

Vortigern stared him down, his face as white as the torn tunic. 'Take it,' he said. 'Bury him in your holy ground.'

Idris pulled the spear out and cast it aside. He and one of the others picked up Rufus's body and trudged away towards the western gate. Their companion followed with his sorry flag. Kerin struggled onto all fours as the gate closed after them, but a hand came down on his shoulder.

'Stay where you are, boy,' Lud's gruff voice said. 'This isn't over.'

Vortigern dismounted and kicked Batraz in the groin. The Sarmatian gasped and rolled onto his side, hugging his knees. Blood was spurting from the thigh wound and the arrow had gone deep, but these wounds would probably not be what killed him. Vortigern squatted in front of him, wound a handful of Batraz's hair around his hand and pulled his head up.

'So,' he said. 'You are the hero who crucifies children, and burns sleeping men in their beds, and hangs good warriors with whipcord.'

Batraz glowered at him. 'They were lackeys,' he spat. 'And you are the devil's handmaid. Kill me, and have done with it.'

'I wouldn't soil my hands,' Vortigern said. Getting up, he leaned on Lud's shoulder and gave his horse a nod. *'Kill,'* he said.

<h1 style="text-align:center">52</h1>

Kerin came to in the back of a cart. It was standing by the road outside the eastern gates. There were horses and men milling around everywhere. Kerin sat up and found Brother Padarn beside him. For a moment he couldn't remember a thing; then it all came crashing over him, like the wave over the packhorse bridge.

'He killed him,' he said blankly. 'He killed Rufus.'

'Yes, he did,' Padarn said. 'To save your skin, according to Lud. No point in mincing words, is there.'

'No,' Kerin said, as the details began to seep back. The thud of the thrown spear. The weeping lads carting the body away.

'I thought I'd better come,' Padarn said. 'The boys were afraid you were going to die. You're not, of course, but that's a nasty wound. I've put some of Morvid's stuff on it and bound it up. Here, drink this. Marcellus said it would help with the pain.'

Kerin emptied the phial of liquid down his throat. 'What happened?' he asked. 'I remember stabbing Batraz in the foot because he tried to pinch my crucifix. Not much after that.'

Padarn raised his eyebrows. 'Batraz pulled his sword on you. He got you in the shoulder. Then you cut his leg open and Marc shot him with an arrow. Vortigern speared Rufus in the chest. Right in the heart, Lud said. Then Rufus's boys carried the body back into the city, and Vortigern's horse killed Batraz. Is that enough for now?'

'Yes,' Kerin said, as disturbing details began to surface. He looked around and located Vortigern, sitting on his horse at the head of his army outside Eldof's main gates. Blood was dripping slowly from his left riding boot. He was leaning on the front of his saddle, whether because of blood loss or the weight of what he had just done, it was impossible to tell. Most of Kerin's archers and spearmen were there amidst the warriors. Blaidd was hitched to the back of the cart. 'What happened to Ashur's horse?' Kerin asked, remembering how the incident had begun. 'Is it alive?'

'The last time I saw it,' Padarn said. 'Marcellus sent some potion to knock it out with. Once it was senseless, Bened and a lot of other big strong oafs heaved it into the death cart and took it back to the camp. And now we're waiting for – well, I don't know what. There was a lot of noise going on inside while you were out cold – shouting and banging and stuff – but then everything went quiet. I think Lud and some of the others would like to batter the gates down, but thank God, Vortigern's got more sense. Now there's something I never thought I'd say.'

Vortigern looked round as Kerin reined in beside him. 'You should have stayed in the cart,' he said.

'You killed Rufus,' Kerin said. 'It was you.'

'He'd swung his sword back,' Vortigern said. 'You were trying to cut Batraz's throat. Rufus was going to kill one or other of you. Probably you. I decided not to take the risk. No, that's not true. You don't decide, there's no time. You do what you do.'

Kerin was battle-shocked and not up to thinking about

the implications. It would all have to wait. But one thing needed to be said. 'I don't know if anyone's told you, but it was Rufus who speared me in the shoulder. Macsen saw him do it.'

'No-one's told me,' Vortigern said.

'What's going on inside the city?' Kerin asked. 'Padarn said there was a lot of noise, then nothing.'

'I don't know,' Vortigern said. 'The place is full of raging armed men who've lost a battle. Something's bound to happen. Nothing much, I hope. If they had reinforcements waiting inside, it would be the end of us.'

Kerin glanced up at the sky. He supposed that it was about midday, but the exhausting, disjointed fight seemed to have been going on forever. He slipped his hand inside his tunic and clasped his crucifix and Gael's ring. Perhaps there was a God, if they had been preserved from Batraz. The sound came then, a familiar echo of Londinium, on the night when Vortigern was crowned; the roar of thousands of voices, amplified by high walls, but this time splintered with bangs and crashes which could have been anything. Something was happening up on the gatehouse. A squad of Eldof's guards lashed a pole to the battlement and man-handled a bound prisoner along the wall, the noose around his neck already. There was no mistaking the lanky frame and badger hair of Runo Whitestreak. A bunch of men burst out onto the battlement, ordinary men in ordinary clothes, not warriors at all, but armed with swords so new and bright that the low sun flashed blindingly from their blades. Two of them grabbed Runo, while two more seized one of the guards and flung him from the battlement. He fell headfirst, arms flailing, and landed on the cobbles with a neck-breaking jolt. Something caught fire near the bishop's house, sending up a pillar of foul-smelling black smoke. 'Down with the gates!' someone bellowed from within.

'God, that's Malan,' Kerin said. Something large and heavy thudded repeatedly against the gates. They burst open and the crowd surged out, sweeping Malan and his black mule down the cobbled road to the point where Vortigern, Kerin and Gwyndaf were waiting. The streets inside the gateway were rammed with people, some carrying torches, a few on horses which couldn't possibly have been theirs. In the middle of it all was a familiar grain wagon, and in the back were Eldof's city guards, held at sword point by a smith and a Saxon cook. Malan rode right up to Vortigern.

'We've brought them,' he crowed. 'We've brought them, Lord King. Eldof's horrible men who were going to hang our Runo.' People had surrounded the grain wagon, banging on the sides and pelting the guards with sticks and stones. Edryd jumped down and fought his way over.

'It all went mad when you gave them a beating,' he said. 'Someone came in bawling that the cataphracts were drowned and you were winning and it was hopeless, so we thought, now's the time. And all the warriors who came back in, when they saw that the whole city was on the move – ' he shrugged. 'Well, that was that, really. The Sword of God have locked themselves in the bishop's house, what's left of them. And Lord Eldof's in his own house with his family, as far as I know.'

'Who's controlling the city, then?' Vortigern asked.

'You are, Lord King,' Malan said cheerily. Vortigern surveyed the crowd. They had calmed down and stopped throwing things at the guards, and were clearly waiting for him to do or say something.

'I want Eldof out here,' he said. Varro moved to his side.

'I'll go,' he said. 'No-one's going to touch me in there. Only Eldof and his cronies hate me. I've got a lot of credit with the people.'

'Alright,' Vortigern said. 'Take your men. I don't want him harmed.' The crowd parted, cheering, to let Varro and his warriors pass through. 'Lud, go for Publius Luca,' Vortigern said. 'He's somewhere near the bridge with the prisoners. I want him here when Eldof comes out. Then send our messengers to Claudius in Isca. Ask him to send a formal note to Valerius Dio, and personal letters to our wives and Gallus Mercator, straight away. Just that we've won, and we're safe. That's all they'll need to know.'

*

Publius Luca rode straight up to Kerin. 'I was wrong,' he said, as Vortigern gathered his commanders. 'And I was the man who told the ordo of Londinium not to underestimate him. I should have taken my own advice. Any number of things could have gone wrong today, but they didn't. It was a magnificent victory.'

'Rufus is dead,' Kerin said, trying to steady his voice.

'I know,' Publius said. 'I was wrong about that, too. Not a moment's hesitation, I'm told; and just as well, or you wouldn't be here. Now put it aside, there'll be time enough to pick over it, if you must. And don't belittle your part in things. Talk to the armoured lads when you get the chance. They won't forget you, or your murdering horse.' He looked round as a familiar rumble and creak announced the arrival of the chariot. 'Or your carnyces. I suppose we'll never know whether they'd have had the effect they did, without the help of the wave.'

'They would,' Kerin said fervently. 'I saw those men, and those horses. They were terrified before the wave got here, and afterwards. Yes, I know the wave made a shocking sound too, but – ' he threw his hands up, unequal to the argument. 'I know it worked,' he said lamely. Publius reached out to pat his shoulder. He would probably never be wholly convinced. Cynan, a better charioteer than anyone had expected, brought his horses alongside.

'Is our part done now?' he asked.

'Yes,' Publius said. 'You did your part, the great wave did its part and every man here fought like a demon. And now it's done, thank the gods, because it'll be a while before this army is fit to fight another battle.'

He reined back, probably to join Vortigern at the city gates, then stopped short. Vortigern was no longer watching the gates, waiting for Eldof to come out. He was talking to a ragged woman on a rangy brown mule, who was waving her arms about frantically and pointing towards the Roman road.

'Calm down, girl,' Vortigern said, gripping the woman's arm as Kerin and Publius arrived beside him.

'Lord King, I'm one of Berget's women,' she blurted. 'Berget, the daughter of Malan, who led the rising.'

'One of her lookouts!' Kerin exclaimed.

'Yes, lord. From out by Corinium. Berget told us to bring word if an army came from the east. And it's coming, lord, thousands of men, coming straight along the Roman road, they can't be far behind me, lord, my old mule's not fast, and they've got warhorses –'

'Steady, steady,' Vortigern said. 'Mounted warriors? Foot soldiers?'

The woman took a breath. 'Mounted warriors, Lord King, and Lord Bertil Redknife is leading them. Lord Eldof's cousin.'

'Bertil?' Kerin said, incredulous. 'The praetor's messengers told us he was camped at Sarum.'

'Well, he's not in Sarum now, lord,' the woman said, with a frightened glance over her shoulder.

'Alright,' Kerin said. 'Get inside the city. We command it now, and Malan's in there with his men. You'll be safe with him.'

Vortigern waved to Elir. 'Get in there and find Varro. Tell him to bar the gates and hold them. I want all your archers on the walls. Then find Malan and Edryd, tell them what's happening and tell them that we have to hold the city. God knows what Eldof will do, but we can't let him join forces with whatever is coming down that road.'

Kerin could hear the sound now. It was odd, hearing the sound of a marching army from outside. Usually he was in the middle of it. The slow, rolling thunder of hooves filled him with dread as it drew nearer. There was no way of knowing exactly what was coming, or of seeing the odds as anything but insurmountable. Bertil's own formidable warriors and his trainees would account for two thousand, even if he had not managed to rally the deserting Sarmatians. Kerin dropped to the ground, throwing his reins to Vortigern. He limped through the gateway as fast as he could, and up the steps to the battlement. There they were, distant but clearly visible in the fading afternoon sunlight; a solid black formation peppered with glinting metal, snaking away out of sight along the gently curving road. Edryd arrived, panting.

'Elir told me,' he said, looking where Kerin was looking. 'Jesus Christ, there's thousands of the bastards. What do you want us to do?'

'Keep them out of the city, if you can,' Kerin said. 'As soon as I'm out, help Varro secure the gates. Do you think Eldof's boys will fight?'

'Don't know. They looked beaten before, but God knows now. We'll do our best.'

Kerin ran. The gates were closing. He heard the thud of the bars coming down and things being piled up against them. Outside, Vortigern had rallied his battered army at the southern gate, invisible to Bertil and his force as yet. The commanders awaited their orders, outwardly calm and resolute at the head of their exhausted troops. Kerin couldn't see a single man who wasn't carrying an injury. Some of those damaged arms would struggle to lift a sword, let alone use it. Gorlois had picked up a wound in his left leg to match the gash in his right. Gwyndaf was bleeding from the neck. Facial cuts had merged into bloody masks, and most of the horses were as damaged as their riders.

'She was right,' Kerin said, hauling himself onto Blaidd's back. 'Horse warriors, as far back as I could see. It must be the men Bertil's been training. I couldn't see any Sarmatians, but he won't need them. Varro and Edryd will try to keep them out of the city. We've got minutes.'

Vortigern turned to his commanders. 'Spearhead, with me. Gorlois, to the main bridge. Lucius, to the packhorse bridge. If you can't hold them, get your men across and burn the bridges behind you. Publius, go with them.'

'You go with them, you lunatic!' Publius Luca roared.

Kerin reached for Vortigern's arm. 'The carnyces.'

'Do it,' Gwyndaf said. 'There's nothing to lose.'

'Nothing,' Vortigern said, as the sound of trampling hooves and jingling bridle rings grew closer. 'Position them, Kerin. We'll draw Bertil towards the river.'

The chariot and Brother Padarn's cart were hunkered under the wall by the southern gate. The three men's faces were a study in bewilderment as the defenders rushed towards the bridges, the spearhead closed ranks and the sound of the advance swelled. Kerin half-jumped, half-fell into the chariot and seized the hands of Cynan and Cynfawr.

'There are two thousand horse warriors coming down the Roman road with Bertil Redknife. We can't hold them. But they're two thousand men and horses who have probably never heard a carnyx. Please, you have to try.'

Cynan grabbed the ancient carnyx from its bracket, threw it to his father and reached for the slim, gleaming neck of Edryd's masterwork. 'Tell us where to go,' he said. Brother Padarn leapt into the chariot and seized the reins. Kerin waved towards the projecting towers of the western gatehouse.

'Get behind there. We'll draw Bertil towards the river. I want his men galloping. When it's time, I'll raise my arm. And for God's sake, if you're seen, lie down flat and run.'

'Our family does not run,' Cynfawr said sternly. Kerin caught Blaidd's mane and struggled into the saddle. The effect of Marcellus's remedy had ebbed away, and the pain in his shoulder was crippling. He was incapable of fighting, but there was one task he could accomplish better than any other man living. Leaning forward he stretched out his good arm, pulled Blaidd's ears and slapped his neck. *I hope you've still got a gallop in you, my friend,* he thought.

The spearhead was wheeling on the approach to the bridge. Kerin fell in beside Vortigern and Gwyndaf as the company broke into a trot. 'The carnyces are ready,' he said. 'Over by the western gate.' Then, without any warning, he drove his heels into Blaidd's flanks and took off. Ignoring Vortigern's shout of dismay, he galloped away from the spearhead, past the southern gate, around the city wall and out onto the eastbound road. The jogging column of horsemen came within sight, and then within earshot. Kerin reined in, cupped his hands around his mouth and bawled at the top of his lungs, 'Bertil Redknife, you useless bastard, you couldn't even keep hold of your daughter!'

A rabid bellow broke from the man at the head of the column. Kerin spun his horse and fled. Flat to Blaidd's neck, he didn't see Bertil lash his mare and launch her into a headlong gallop, or the men behind him draw their swords and follow. But he heard the sudden pounding of hooves, the clamour of fighting men on the charge, the racket of spears hitting the ground behind him as they fell short. You don't have my range yet, he thought, with a brief flash of pleasure. You may never have it, if this works. But Blaidd was flagging, his breathing harsh and laboured, his pace slowing. There was a whole day's fighting and killing in those legs. A spear glanced the horse's quarters, but he kept running. Kerin turned across the face of the advancing spearhead, rode for the western gate and flung his arm high. The roar hit him like a physical shock, even louder than it had sounded in the druids' cave, for the carnyces were speaking in unison now, their voices thrown back and amplified by the overhang of the gatehouse and the towering walls. Breathing hard, as spent as his horse, Kerin reined to a halt. Afterwards, when trying to describe what happened next, all he could draw on was the wave; the great, lethal wall of water rising as it smashed head-on into the unstoppable flow of the swollen river. Deafened by the war horns, terrified beyond endurance, the horses in the front line reared, reeled and were flattened as the hundreds coming behind hit them at the gallop. Men, howling in panic, threw their swords away as they tried to avoid being caught and submerged in the tangle of limbs and hooves. It was probably a mercy that their screams, and those of their felled horses, were almost drowned out by the roaring bellow of the carnyces. The rearguard tried to avoid the bloody chaos, peeling off to right and left; but as the warriors moved, as if by some mysterious alchemy, so did the blast of the war horns. The chariot was skirting the wall unseen. Men fled and were driven into the melee around the southern gate, under the blizzard of arrows and stones falling in deadly showers from the walls of Glevum. Riderless horses began to escape, bolting or limping away in all directions. Kerin saw Bertil scramble aboard one of them and head towards his forests north of the city, followed by his bunch of thugs. Most of the survivors turned and galloped away eastwards, abandoning their fallen comrades to the carrion birds. Vortigern and his commanders simply sat, watching Bertil's army founder and disintegrate under the crushing wall of sound; while the fighting horses of the spearhead, bloodied but unbroken, performed their two-footed ritual dance to the savage music of war.

The remnants of the king's army gathered at the bridge-head. Vortigern slid from his horse, limped to the chariot and clasped the hands of the bard and the druid. 'You are the true warriors,' he said. 'You and the makers of these instruments. Not us, the men of blood. If not for you, we'd have died on this field today. You are the men of power.' He reached up and caressed the pointed ears of Cynfawr's ancient carnyx. It looked strangely quiescent, now that it was silent. Two horses were approaching. Publius Luca and Gwyndaf dismounted. They looked as contrite as a pair of sinners at confession.

'When I'm wrong, I don't mind admitting it,' Publius said. 'And I was wrong today. About these extraordinary instruments, and about other things.'

Gwyndaf cleared his throat. 'We were both wrong,' he said, and gave Kerin a wry look. 'I suppose you're going to make me do what I said I'd do.'

'I am,' Kerin said, with a benevolent smile. 'Back at the

camp, where everyone can watch. I'll ask the cooks to make some gravy.'

Eldof came alone. Kerin was not sure if this was a choice, or if he no longer had anyone credible to bring to his enforced encounter with the king. Varro, his sons and picked men formed a line across the gateway as Eldof emerged. There would be no walking out of this meeting. Vortigern rode forward with Kerin and Publius Luca. The leading men came a horse length behind.

'It didn't work, did it,' Vortigern said. 'My son, who set all this in motion, is dead. His armoured horsemen are killed or captive. His mercenaries have deserted you. Your own citizens have risen against you. I asked their leader who was in control of the city. He said, "You are, Lord King." I could burn Glevum to the ground. I could execute you here, in front of your people, who would probably cheer and thank me. Is this understood?'

'Yes,' Eldof hissed.

'Speak up,' Vortigern said. 'The people at the back need to hear.'

'Yes!' Eldof bellowed. 'Burn the place and hang me, if that's what you want.'

'If that was what I wanted, you'd have been dead years ago,' Vortigern said. 'But there are conditions, to which you will swear.'

'Go on,' Eldof said sullenly.

'Firstly, neither you nor anyone you command raises arms against me or sets foot across the Hafren without my permission. Secondly, you make no common cause with Bertil Redknife or any of Vortimer's associates. Thirdly, there will be no reprisals of any kind against the people of your city. And finally, you release everyone in your prisons, as of this moment.'

A raucous cheer went up from the closest of the onlookers.

'But most of them are criminals!' Eldof protested.

'Not all, then,' Vortigern said, with a bitter smile. Eldof snorted.

'It'll be done,' he said. 'And on your head be it.'

'I'm King of all the Britons,' Vortigern said. 'Everything's on my head. Now, what would you like to swear on? The bible? Or is that only when your brother the bishop is breathing down your neck?'

Eldof's face turned crimson. 'On my children's lives,' he growled. 'I swear.'

'Good,' Vortigern said. 'Let this be an end of it. You've sworn an oath before these men of honour and integrity. But be assured, if you break even one of your undertakings, these men of honour and integrity will return, and batter your gates down, and hang you from your own battlements.'

Eldof's eyes burned with impotent fury. 'Nothing's enough for you, is it, you power-grabbing bastard,' he breathed. 'The crown isn't enough. You have to shame a man in his own city.'

Vortigern rode forward and placed a hand on the collar of Eldof's tunic. 'You betrayed me in the curia after I gave you victory in the North,' he said softly. 'You conspired against me. You came to my own citadel, and shamed me in front of my people. You told me to kneel before my own son. And then you connived in a plot to murder me and my commanders. So don't complain of this, you self-righteous piece of horse shit. You've got off lightly.'

Eldof scowled and straightened his tunic. 'I'll rot before

I forgive you for what's been done here today,' he said sourly. 'But the citizens of Glevum might thank you for dealing with Bertil Redknife. They're better off with me than they would be with him, I promise you.'

'Bertil's daughter told me that,' Kerin said. 'And she told me that you were kind to her when she was a child. That's the only reason you're still breathing. A man who's capable of that might be left alone, as long as he keeps his word.'

Varro and his band surrounded Eldof and moved off. People got out of the way, insofar as they could in a crowded street. A few catcalls and obscenities were hurled, but no stones.

'What now, Lord King?' Malan asked, looking delighted with his efforts.

'Whatever it is, you'll have nothing to do with it,' Vortigern said. 'Do you think I gave you land in Cambria so that you could get yourself killed in Glevum?'

'Your pardon, Lord King, but I couldn't help myself,' Malan said. 'Berget carried on with our families, but I came back. We'd all have been burned in our beds if Lord Kerin here hadn't made us leave. And they murdered the animals. Didn't even eat them. I couldn't let it pass. So I thought, there'll be work for a man with a loud voice. And here I am.'

Vortigern raised his hands. 'Alright. Enough. Get yourself to our camp – you and Runo, Edryd and Cheldric and anyone else who matters. You've all done good work, but the rest can wait.'

Malan scrutinised him. 'Hard fight, Lord King?'

'Hard fight. Go on, get lost. And tell these people to go home. The entertainment's over.'

The crowd around the gates began to thin as Malan rode back, shouting and waving his arms. The men who were carrying weapons put them away, and all the torches were tossed into a heap at the foot of the wall.

'Go back to the camp, both of you, and get your wounds seen to,' Publius Luca said. 'There'll be no hope for the kingdom if the king and his chief warrior bleed to death.'

'It doesn't feel like a victory,' Vortigern said. 'We shouldn't be fighting our own.'

'No, of course you shouldn't be fighting your own. But if your own are too stupid to see it, there's no option. So go and enjoy your success. You owe it to your men, and to yourself.'

Vortigern gave a hollow smile. Publius Luca's face conveyed, only too well, that he knew there was more in play here than military success or the stupidity of the king's deluded opponents. 'Go on,' he said gently. 'Go to Marcellus. You made the right choice out there. You don't regret it, do you?'

'Not for one moment,' Vortigern said. 'But I don't regret fighting it out with the Sarmatian cavalry commander either, and now my leg's cut to pieces. There are usually consequences.' He sighed and gathered his reins. 'I've promised the commanders a midwinter feast. I suppose it would be a shame to die and miss it.'

'Indeed,' Publius said. 'And perhaps there'll be a seat at the table for a lunatic Roman general. Your words, not mine; Marcellus can't keep his mouth shut. Now, I'm going to stay here for a while with Lucius and his men. Just until everyone's calmed down. With luck they'll all go back to their daily lives now that they've proved their point. I'll find out what's happened to the Sword of God. But first I'm going to supervise the release of the prisoners.'

'Do you think that was a mistake?' Vortigern asked.

'Not at all. But there'll be a lot of anger locked up in

that jail. You've told Eldof not to take reprisals. It'll defeat
the object if our side start doing it.' He waved to Lucius
and pointed towards the city gates. Vortigern watched the
cavalrymen assemble.

'We've been here before, haven't we,' he said.

'Yes,' Publius said. 'I managed it without blood in Isca,
and I'll do the same now. You have my word. Put a guard
on the gates, if you will; no-one in or out until I'm done.'

Vortigern nodded an acknowledgment. Lucius and his
cavalry troop followed Publius under the archway and the
eastern gates closed behind them.

'Ask Gorlois to pick a guard,' Vortigern said. 'They've
got less of an axe to grind here than we have. All the exits,
and the wharf.'

Kerin, still stunned by what had happened, was glad to
have something else to occupy his mind.

'Are we done here, then?' he asked. Vortigern's eyes
strayed to the pile of smouldering torches and the un-
blemished gates. A smile flickered, and the moment of
temptation passed.

'Yes,' he said. 'We're done.'

The camp was at peace. Cooking fires burned amongst the tents and rough shelters at the edge of the sparse woodland. It had been like the aftermath of the battle in the North; everyone wanted to go home, but no-one could until the dead had been buried or cremated and the wounded men and horses were able to travel. Now departure was imminent. Dawn would see the breaking of the camp. Kerin and Marcellus leaned on the rail of the horse pen, hastily constructed when it became clear that Astra would live. The horse was standing quietly, nibbling at a feed of oat bran. Ashur was sleeping beside him, rolled up in a blanket. Marcellus had drawn the spearhead while the horse was out cold and stitched the wound with one of the big, curved needles which shepherds used for sewing up bags of fleece.

'I've given one to Elir,' the haruspex said, showing the implement to Kerin. 'I had them in the North, from that shepherd who spoke Pictish for you. I wouldn't want to try sewing horse hide with a physician's needle, any more than you'd have wanted me to stitch up your shoulder with this device.'

Kerin winced. 'Will he make a full recovery?' he asked.

'Physically, yes. He's a young, strong animal. Can they lose their nerve, as men can? I've no idea.'

'Possibly,' Kerin said. 'I've been lucky with horses. Vortigern might know, I suppose.' He looked towards a nearby fire, where Varro's young warriors were sharing a joke with their commander. 'What did you give Varro? He sounds like a different man.'

Marcellus suppressed a smile. 'Honey,' he whispered behind his hand. 'Honey, mixed with a mild painkiller. Although that was chiefly to add a little bitterness, so that he'd believe he was taking some powerful medication. All he really needed to do was keep his voice down. Some men can't help shouting, can they, and if you shout when you have an injured throat, you just continue to aggravate it. I've told him that he has to speak quietly for the rest of his life, which might not be strictly true, but I'm sure there are many people who would thank me if they knew.'

Kerin laughed into his sleeve. This revelation would not be going far. He thought of his last conversation with Marcellus, in Claudius's house. 'Did you see the victory?' he asked. The haruspex looked out across the camp towards the river. His silence disturbed Kerin. For all his scepticism about Marcellus's methods, he would have liked a ready answer. It's probably nothing, he thought, then remembered that the last time those words were spoken, Gallus was talking about the *oneraria*. 'Tell me,' he said.

'Do you remember,' the haruspex said, 'that I once compared consulting the omens to considering the weather before going outside? If the analogy pleases you, you might care to imagine a fine, sunlit sky which nonetheless contains the odd black cloud capable of dumping its contents upon you. Not ideal, but far better than a blizzard or a thunderstorm, wouldn't you say?'

'Yes,' Kerin said. The carnyces had fulfilled his most extravagant hopes. The audacious plan had worked. Vortigern had defied all Publius Luca's doubts, leading from the front as he always did, with the courage and vision which defined him. No-one was under any illusions, every man in the king's army knew that he would have to fight again, but that was months away. For today, at least, it should have been possible to drink deeply of the victory and rejoice. And yet.

Vortigern wandered over to sit by Varro's fire and laughed at a joke the warriors were sharing. Whether the laughter was natural or a strand of some elegant deception, it still jarred.

'You wouldn't think he'd killed his son last week,' Kerin said. Marcellus watched.

'Give it time,' he said.

Kerin remembered the aftermath, and Vortigern shrugging off his battle wounds while blood dripped freely from his boot, and thought: perhaps this is the same. Perhaps, beneath the laughter, you are quietly bleeding to death.

*

It was late afternoon when Publius joined the gathering outside the king's tent. He had returned to a peaceful city for another attempt to trace the Sword of God.

'Someone helped them get away,' he said. 'Varro's friend, Tobias, thinks they probably went by wagon. He saw some big transports heading north-east before the wharf was sealed. He didn't think anything of it at the time – some of his fellow merchants were emptying their warehouses in case of looting. But I think those wagons must have been carrying Idris and his associates. They're not in the city. We've searched all the patricians' houses, and they'd be hanging from the battlements by now if the people had got hold of them.'

Vortigern poured some of the wine Claudius had

brought. The harbourmaster had left Isca for the camp straight after despatching fast messengers to Henfelin and Londinium. Kerin was sure that he felt personally invested in this conflict, in a way he might not have been in the battle against the Picts. Ships had sailed from his port; he had protected the horses; his old friend had been murdered. And Isca was very close to Glevum.

'It can't be helped,' Vortigern said. 'And Tobias shouldn't be blamed. Anyone might have made that assumption.'

'Who'd do it, though?' Kerin asked. 'Not Eldof; I don't think he'll break your conditions. The Sarmatians have gone, and most of Bertil's survivors are probably halfway to Kent.'

'Paulinus, possibly,' Vortigern said. 'He's as mad as they are.'

'What will you do?' Publius Luca asked.

'Wait for them to surface, I suppose,' Vortigern said. 'We can't search the whole kingdom.'

'Will you guard the bridges?'

'No. I shouldn't have to guard the bridges. It would look like a sign of weakness. And we've got enough good men in Glevum to warn us of any trouble.'

Claudius poured more wine. 'I hear the fishermen are back,' he said. 'Those men of yours came to thank me for providing the olive oil. Their friends are back fishing under the bridge, just like they've always done. And the owner of that shack has opened it up again.'

'Then we should visit him,' Vortigern said. 'They beat that man half to death, just for speaking up for me. And then they hanged his father from the gatehouse. He should be thanked.'

Kerin agreed wholeheartedly, whilst hoping that Pedr had something better to offer than the rancid ale which had ruined him on his last visit. 'Let's go while it's light, then,' he said, getting up gingerly from the fireside. The wound was healing well, but still painful. Macsen came trotting from the fringe of the camp.

'There's a carriage coming,' he said. 'It's your carriage, lord.'

'My carriage?' Vortigern said. 'It can't be.'

'Believe me, lord, it is,' Macsen said. 'Dimos Bekuh's driving it.'

The sound of hooves and wheels could already be heard over the many conversations and scattered warriors' songs. The carriage rolled into the encampment and stopped. Dimos jumped down from the driver's seat, smiling, and opened the door. Rowenna jumped out.

'Please!' she exclaimed. 'Do not tell me this is wrong!'

Vortigern sighed and stretched out his hand. 'Come here, Helen of the Hosts,' he said, and took her in his arms. Dimos leaned towards Kerin.

'You'd better come with me,' he said. A small, unexpected sound came from the carriage.

'Oh, God!' Kerin shouted. Dimos opened the door. The shutters were closed to keep in the warmth, and a tiny oil lamp gave the only light. Gael was sitting up, surrounded by pillows and rolled blankets. She looked up as Kerin came in and reached out for him, her face lit by a transforming happiness.

'You have a daughter!' she said. Kerin sank down and put his arms around her and their child, weeping unashamedly at the wonder of it all. The baby, trapped between them, made a small, complaining noise. Kerin withdrew, mildly horrified. Gael laughed and pulled him back. 'She won't break, you know,' she said. Very cautiously, Kerin cupped his daughter's downy head and explored her face and limbs, smiling as one tiny hand clamped around his forefinger.

'She's tiny,' he said, and kissed the top of her head.

'You wouldn't say that if you'd had to bear her,' Gael said ruefully.

'But surely, if she's here already –'

'Yes. It means that she was conceived in my father's house, before you went to the North. But I don't want to share the news with him, do you?'

Kerin stroked Gael's hair. 'Aislinn, if it's a girl?'

'Oh, yes. She's been Aislinn for two weeks now. A few days after she was born, Claudius's messengers brought the news. We were well, so we came. And all's good at home. Tirion's in charge, and Brwyn has been a fine, strong man for us.' Her hand clasped Kerin's neck. 'We met Hefydd on the road. He said Rufus is dead. That Vortigern killed him to save you.'

'Yes,' Kerin said, taking her hand and pressing it to his cheek. The horror came flooding back to invade his moment of pure, golden joy. The thump of the spearhead, the death gasp. 'I'll tell you,' he said. 'But please, not now. Let's not spoil this.'

They clung together in the warm cocoon of Gael's bed with the baby cradled gently between them. After a while, Kerin heard voices and jumped out of the carriage. Rowenna had already shared the news, and most of the warriors had come to investigate. Vortigern flung his arms around Kerin and they stood, sharing an affectionate silence.

'Gael's well?' he asked.

'Yes. She's well, and the child too.' Kerin would have liked to say that Aislinn's birth had filled him with a joy unlike anything he had ever known; but it was not something he felt able to tell a man who had lost two of his sons, one on the end of his own spear. Vortigern leaned into the carriage and kissed Gael's hand.

'I hope she grows up as beautiful as her mother and less trouble than her father,' he said.

Kerin rode with his wife and child in the carriage. Rowenna shared the driver's seat with Dimos, while Publius Luca drove the chariot for Cynan and Cynfawr. It was unthinkable to exclude the victorious carnyces from a celebration, however restrained. Everyone else went to tie their horses to the dead tree where Kerin had tied his mule, the first time he visited Pedr's shack. The river was flowing gently again and the boats were back on the bank outside. Their owners had dragged the benches outside and were drinking beside a driftwood fire in the cool afternoon sunlight. Kerin got out of the carriage.

'Tell Pedr the king's here,' he said, to the nearest of them.

'Pull the other one,' the man said. Kerin nodded towards the dead tree. The fisherman jumped and bolted inside. Edryd and Cheldric came out, propelling Pedr in front of them. He looked as haggard and drained as ever.

'Are you the man who got locked up and beaten because of me?' Vortigern asked.

'Yes, Lord King,' Pedr mouthed. Vortigern took him by the shoulders.

'You're a good man and a brave one,' he said. 'A true warrior. Now bring ale for everyone here. The king's gift.'

Pedr stumbled back inside, calling Cheldric to help him. Gael sat in the shelter of the carriage doorway, cradling Aislinn, as the fishermen gave up the benches and sat on the ground beside them. Edryd came to shake Kerin's hand.

'What now for you?' Kerin asked.

'I'm going to get Malan back to his family, wherever they are, then I'll head home to Calleva for a while. And then wherever you and the king need me. I don't expect you'll be wanting another carnyx, but nobody makes a better sword.'

Pedr and Cheldric came from the hut with tankards of ale and handed them round. Fresh casks were tapped as the light began to dim, and the musicians played the sweet, unforgettable melody which had echoed over Henfelin on the night of Calan Gaeaf.

'What now, for these wondrous things?' Vortigern asked. Cynan smiled.

'When we go home, they will return to their long sleep in the heart of our sacred earth,' he said. 'And if our country should ever be threatened by another enemy who has not heard their voices, they will rise again, and turn his bones to water.'

Kerin sat on the carriage wheel beside his wife and child and drank the good, fresh ale while Gael sipped a mug of Morvid's lime blossom brew, brought from home. Aislinn, full of milk, was sleeping contentedly.

'Will we have peace for a while now?' Gael asked.

'For a while, I expect,' Kerin said. He looked at the gliding river, the quiet city and the bridge. It was almost impossible to believe that he had been fighting for his life in this spot, barely two weeks earlier. Vortigern was standing alone on the river bank nearby. You saved me, Kerin thought. You made the brutal choice Marcellus described; the stark, life-or-death choice which will define my life forever.

'Go to him,' Gael said, kissing Kerin's cheek. 'Deal with everything now. I'm putting this child in her cradle, and then I'm having you to myself.'

'Publius asked me what I wanted to do with the armoured men,' Vortigern said. 'I asked him what he'd do. He said he'd keep them as mercenaries. They're grateful to you for sparing them, so you can deal with them. They're Alans, he said. Related to the Sarmatians, but it's – no, I can't think straight. There'll be other times.'

'I'll ask Claudius to accommodate them in Isca,' Kerin said. 'There's room enough in the fortress. Livius's troop can keep order while we decide what to do with them.' Vortigern's eyes had strayed to the city walls and the closed gates. 'Lord, there's no point,' Kerin said. 'It'll take a while for Rufus's allies to recover, if they ever do. We're going home tomorrow. And tonight, almost everyone we love is here.' He looked back towards the alehouse. Gael and Rowenna were sitting with Dimos and Publius Luca, near the carriage where his child lay sleeping. The women were laughing together, looking towards the river bank. They are waiting for us, Kerin thought.

'You're right,' Vortigern said. 'We've done everything we came here to do. And it was all for this.'

Even days later, after hours of thought, Kerin had no idea why he looked over his shoulder towards the packhorse bridge. But he did, so he saw the hurtling dark horse, the raised arm and the loosed spear. Leaping forward, he brought Vortigern crashing down. The spear landed behind them and skidded along the ground. Kerin had seen the weapon leave the thrower's hand; his practised eye recognised the intended trajectory. It was pure luck that he had seen it coming. Everyone came running as they picked themselves up. Kerin reached for the spear. Something was wrapped around the shaft, secured with a black ligature. A papyrus. He drew his dagger, cut it free and unrolled it. The Latin was simple and stark, intelligible even to him. Vortigern caught his breath.

'I can see you understand it,' he said. He took the

papyrus and read for all to hear. '*It will not be over until you are as dead as your son.*'

'You have to respond!' Publius Luca said, outraged. 'You can't let that stand.'

But there was, of course, no papyrus in Pedr's shack. No ink, and no sharpened quill. Vortigern rolled the papyrus back on itself and laid it flat on one of the benches. He took a burned stick from the fire, obliterated the text with black charcoal and turned the papyrus over. Then he grabbed Kerin's dagger, drew the cutting edge across his left wrist, dipped his forefinger in the running blood and wrote on the back of the papyrus: *V. Rex.* Rowenna, white with shock, rushed to bind his wrist with one of the baby's swaddling bands. Publius Luca, who had probably not expected quite this response to his edict, picked up the spear and secured the papyrus to it.

'I'll take it,' he said. 'I'll stick it in the ground by the packhorse bridge. They're bound to be watching.'

'Commander Publius, wait.' It was Gael who had spoken. Taking the spear from Publius Luca, she ran her hand along the smooth black shaft and examined the finely tooled spearhead. 'This is one of my father's spears. He always has his carpenters stain the wood black before the smiths take it. And look, here. On the spearhead. The drawn dagger, like the emblem on his banner. My father threw this spear.' She turned to Vortigern. 'I am so sorry.'

'Sorry?' he said. 'For what? An accident of blood? You didn't ask to be Bertil's daughter. Rufus didn't ask to be my son. Someone begets you, you grow up, you make a choice. At least you made the right one.'

Gael passed the spear to Publius. He loosed a horse, mounted up and rode for the bridge with Gwyndaf following. Kerin drew Gael close and put his arms around her. 'What will happen?' she asked fearfully.

'Nothing,' Vortigern said. 'Bertil's furious because he failed, that's all. He came here to grab power for himself, and the carnyces put a stop to it.'

They looked round as footsteps approached. Cynan and Cynfawr had brought their instruments of war. 'We should play in anger for that,' the bard said.

'No,' Vortigern said. 'What I've written is enough. It's all they need to know.'

Cynan bowed his head. 'Then let us go back to the camp and play a paean for the new child,' he said. 'A song of thanksgiving for the daughter of two warriors.'

Most of the men were sleeping, oblivious of what had happened at the river. Kerin sat on the narrow bed in the carriage, holding his wife, while the haunting voices of the carnyces wove their heartbreaking song of harmony and peace. There was next to no room in the carriage, but tonight he would squeeze himself into the narrow space between the bed and Aislinn's cradle and sleep on the bare boards. There was no other place on earth he would have chosen to be.

When Gael fell asleep, he drew the blankets over her and went outside. Marcellus was standing by the physicians' tent, examining Vortigern's wrist with a look of utter per-plexity. Rowenna, seeing Kerin, left them and ran to him.

'If you had not been there, would he have been killed?' she asked.

'I don't know,' Kerin said. 'I think the aim was off, just a fraction. But it's possible. Killing Vortigern was Bertil's intention, there's no doubt about that. And he's a very good spearman. But not the best. It was a long throw, and it's easy to lose accuracy when you put that much force into it.'

Rowenna's hand brushed his cheek. 'If you had thrown the spear, Vortigern would be dead.'

'Yes,' Kerin said. 'You can count on that.'

Vortigern left Marcellus to his duties. 'The physician was impressed,' he said. 'A clean, sharp blade. Don't look so worried. It'll heal in no time. And what could I do? There was no ink.'

'You could be dead!' Rowenna protested. 'Kerin says so. And now what? It was Gael's father who made the plot to kill you and your leaders. Father Septimus told us this at Mabli's wedding. And now Bertil is a man full of anger. He will try again, even if Eldof keeps his word and will not help him.'

'Bertil won't act alone,' Vortigern said. 'He was just the same as a boy; full of noise. And now he's lost half his best men, thanks to our carnyces.'

'We should be on our guard, though,' Kerin said. 'He probably hates us more than ever.'

'Oh yes,' Vortigern said. 'You in particular, after that stunt by the bridge. Of course we'll be prepared. But Bertil doesn't know our country. I don't think he's been on this side of the river since we fought the Irish in Dyfed. He'd be an idiot to venture into Cambria. So we're going home. To rest, heal our wounds, celebrate your new child and give a midwinter feast for our brave warriors.'

'And then?' Rowenna took his hands, her eyes bright with anguish. Vortigern touched her fingers to his lips.

'And then, *anwylyd*,' he said, 'it'll be time to fight your father.'

Author's Note

Let's begin with the *Historia Brittonum*, the 9th century compilation of historical record, oral tradition and legend which – according to whom you ask – may or may not have been put together by the monk Nennius. As its name suggests, it claims to be a history of Britain from its foundation onwards. The earliest extant work to mention King Arthur, it is widely held to be the primary source used by the 11th century cleric Geoffrey of Monmouth. His *History of the Kings of Britain* popularised the legends of Arthur and Merlin, imprinting them forever upon British culture and inspiring writers from Geoffrey's day to the present. It would take a very large bookcase to accommodate all the works on the subject of Arthur. From serious historical research through historical fiction, fantasy and the plain barking mad, it's all there. And in one way or another, most of it goes back to the *Historia Brittonum*. 'I made a heap of all I could find', its compiler said, in his preface; quite accurately describing the way in which historical fact and legend got lumped together until it's hard to judge where one ends and the other begins.

The *Historia* has plenty to say about Vortigern, most of it bad. Geoffrey reiterates it in his *History*, albeit with a slightly different slant. After years of investigation I've drawn my own conclusions, but for *High King 3*, my focus was on what the sources have to say about the conflict between Vortigern and his oldest son. Both agree that, for a time, the son was recognised as leader and fought against the Saxons who were settled in Kent after Vortigern and his council hired them as mercenaries. The Britons 'promoted Vortimer to the kingship', according to Geoffrey. He is presented as a devout Christian who deplored his father's marriage to the pagan Hengist's daughter, restored British churches and was supported by prominent Britons who shared his views, as well as by the 'saintly' Bishop Germanus. Both 'Nennius' and Geoffrey inflate Vortigern's employment of the Jutes and his marriage to Rowenna into a ruinous friendship with Hengist, for which he was prepared to sacrifice his people and his country. They frame this as a betrayal, and cite it as the reason for Vortimer's rebellion and his widespread support. I don't find this credible. (No romance here, sorry!) But it is not hard to see why men writing with the benefit of a few centuries' hindsight sought someone to blame for the disaster of the later Saxon invasions, and even some of Vortimer's followers may have believed their own propaganda. 21st Century readers will not need to be reminded of what can happen once a man or woman has been condemned in the court of public opinion.

For the record, my use of 'Rufus' as a nickname for Vortigern's oldest son has no basis in history. Several readers of the first draft of *The West Rises* commented that the names of Vortigern and Vortimer are so similar that it's easy to get confused, particularly in the context of a story which includes many other unfamiliar names. So Vortimer is Rufus to family and friends, whilst remaining 'the Lord Vortimer' to those who need to be reminded of his rank.

Now to the carnyx of the title. This ancient wind instrument is thought to have been used by the Iron Age Celts, between c. 200 BC and c. AD 200. One of the most striking depictions is to be found on the Gundestrup Cauldron, a richly decorated vessel discovered in a peat bog in Denmark in 1891. It is not known where it was made, but the metallurgy and imagery suggest a Gaulish or Thracian origin. On one of its plates, three carnyx players can be seen with their instruments held vertically. It is thought to date from between 150 BC and 1 BC. The animal symbolism of the heads is a deliberate statement of ferocity and aggression. The boar was revered above all other creatures as a savage and terrifying opponent in the hunt.

There are scattered references to the instrument in Roman and Greek texts. Carnyces are reported from Julius Caesar's campaign in Gaul, and from the Claudian invasion of Britain. The Greek historian Diodorus Siculus, writing c. 60-30 BC, said of the Celts:

'… their trumpets again are of a peculiar barbarian kind; they blow into them and produce a harsh sound which suits the tumult of war.'

The Greek Polybius, who documented the rise of Roman power in the Mediterranean in the period 264-136 BC, described how

' … the Romans ….were at the same time dismayed by the ornaments and clamour of the Celtic host. For there were among them such innumerable horns and trumpets, which were being blown simultaneously in all parts of their army, and their cries were so loud and piercing, that the noise seemed not to come merely from trumpets and human voices, but from the whole countryside at once.'

Impressive though this sounds, no physical trace of a carnyx had ever been found until the remains of one were dug up in a field near Deskford, in Scotland, in 1816. Only the bell survives, a boar's head, made almost entirely of brass. It can be seen at the National Museum of Scotland, who have given a date of c. 80-250 AD for its construction. https://www.nms.ac.uk/. The museum's experts believe that it was locally made, as its 'decoration is typical of metal-work in north-east Scotland at the time,' and that it had a peaceful, ceremonial use rather than being exclusively re-served for warfare. The museum also holds a very beautiful reproduction of the Deskford Carnyx, made by John Creed, which appears on the cover of this book.

Further fragments of carnyces were subsequently found in France, Germany, Romania and Switzerland, but the most dramatic development came in 2004, when archae-ologists discovered no fewer than seven at Tintignac in the Corrèze, one of which was almost complete. They appear to have been ritually dismembered and buried soon after the Roman invasion of Gaul. Six of these carnyces have boars' heads, while one resembles a serpent-like creature. French craftsman Jean Boisserie has created a wonderful copy of the almost-complete Tintignac carnyx, made en-tirely from hand-hammered bronze. The European Music Archaeology Project has featured it in several exhibitions along with other ancient instruments. Another splendid reproduction, based on the same carnyx, has been made for the French company Armae - https://armae.com/. It can be seen at the Musée d'Alésia, in the Côte d'Or.

Beautiful as these artefacts are, it was the sound of the carnyx that terrified the enemy – and now we can hear it for ourselves. My first experience of it was in a YouTube video: https://www.youtube.com/watch?v=jRIQp4qZrrE

I have tried to imagine how this sound would have affected men and horses who had never heard it before, and had no idea where it was coming from. But the carnyx was more versatile than its role as a war horn suggests, and probably had ritual and ceremonial purposes too. No-one has done more to bring its sounds to today's audiences than the brilliant musician John Kenny. To find out more, visit his website, Carnyx & Co: https://carnyx.org.uk/

or listen to the CD 'Dragon Voices', produced by Delphian Records. The European Music and Archaeology Project has reams of information about carnyces and other early instruments: http://www.emaproject.eu/

As with the draco in *Under The Dragon*, I have taken a leap of imagination in gifting a carnyx to Vortigern and his warriors. It's generally thought that the instrument had fallen out of use by around 200 AD, so its sound would have come as a complete shock to people hearing it in the first half of the 5th Century. In my story, Vortigern's druids have concealed their forebears' carnyx in a cave for safekeeping. No carnyces have yet been found in Wales, but given the prevalence of other aspects of Celtic culture, who knows what may await discovery?

Acknowledgements

Firstly, thank you to Rebecca Horsfall and Jane Dixon Smith, whose contributions have been as invaluable to this book as to the first two volumes of the 'High King' series. Rebecca, as always, was able to see the wood for the trees and to identify the flaws I was too close to the work to see for myself. Jane's interiors are a pleasure to read, and she has produced another wonderful cover which does full justice to the fascinating artefact of the title, the carnyx. Thanks also to Debbie Young, whose Simply Self-Publish course set me off in the right direction. Her advice and expertise are as relevant as ever.

It would have been impossible to create the cover without the images of the replica Deskford and Tintignac carnyces. Thank you to the National Museum of Scotland for allowing us to use the image of their beautiful Deskford carnyx replica. The museum holds the original carnyx, and if you visit their website – https://www.nms.ac.uk/ - or even better, the museum itself, you can see this and countless other amazing objects. Thank you also to the French company Armae, for allowing us to use the image of their stunning Tintignac carnyx replica, which was made to order for a museum. Armae was founded in 2002 by two passionate history and militaria enthusiasts, who recognised how difficult it was for collectors and reenactors to source beautiful, authentic-looking objects at a realistic price. Do visit their website - https://armae.com/ - where you will find superb replicas of military and other artefacts, from ancient times onwards. And if you happen to be in France, and would like to see the carnyx itself, it can be found in the Musée d'Alésia, in the Côte d'Or.

This would be a lonely journey without the love and support of my family. Thank you all for being enthusiastic, for being patient and simply for being there. And this time, special thanks to my son Gareth, for sending me that first YouTube clip of the carnyx being played at the Festival Interceltique de Lorient. Once I'd heard that, there was no going back!

About the Author

Born in South Wales, S.M. Davies read English at Cambridge, specialising in medieval literature and exploring the history which underlies the spellbinding legends of Early Britain. After graduating she worked as a professional indexer for leading publishers, usually on historical texts – everything from Ancient Babylon to World War Two. Since then she has spent her working life on the Gower Peninsula, first as a farmer, then a hotelier, and finally as a pub and nightclub owner. During these years she continued her research and wrote the first draft of the High King series, much of it based amidst the Welsh landscapes she knows and loves. She still lives on the edge of Gower, close to her children and their families, and shares her home with her sheepdog.

See where it all began …

Thank you for reading *The Carnyx*.

If you have enjoyed it, and would like to know more about some of the characters you have met, go to smdaviesauthor.com/the-foundling to join the High King Readers' Club and receive your free copy of *The Foundling*. This eBook is a free, no-obligation download, available exclusively to members of the Readers' Club, and is not available elsewhere.

The Foundling is a short story about the night, many years earlier, when Vortigern saved the infant Kerin from certain death. Only the barest outline can be deduced from *The West Rises* and its sequels. Vortigern's story is seen through Kerin's eyes, and the young warrior was a newborn baby when these events took place – the foundling of the title.

Members of my Readers' Club will receive an occasional email about forthcoming books, my research for the series and the locations where it is set. I care about your privacy, and it'll be easy for you to unsubscribe from the list should you ever wish to. All downloads are yours to keep regardless.

Once again, thank you for reading my books. If you have enjoyed them, and would like to tell others what you thought about them – whether by leaving a review on Amazon, Goodreads or any e-store, or on your social media – that would be great. Word of mouth matters more than anything to a writer, and any effort you make will be much appreciated.

SMD

Coming Next – the Final Act
High King 4: *The Red and the White*

The struggle for the kingship has been resolved, but peace remains an elusive dream. Once more, Vortigern and Kerin Brightspear must take up arms to protect their homeland and everything they hold dear. Hengist's Jutes return in force to reclaim the land they believe is theirs, and threaten to call in allies from far beyond their Jutland home. Beset by treachery and his countrymen's short-sightedness, the High King faces all-out war with Hengist; but there is more than one threat waiting beyond the sea. In Gallia, amidst the wreckage of Rome's western empire, bitter young rival Ambrosius is biding his time.

Get in Touch!

Thank you for reading my books. I hope that you have enjoyed *The West Rises* and *Under The Dragon*, the first two books in the High King series. If you would like to know more about the historical background, my research, future books or my writing life, it would be great to hear from you. Visit my website, smdaviesauthor.com, where you can contact me – or why not join the High King Readers Club? You will be the first to hear news about forthcoming books, and you'll get exclusive free downloads, as well as interesting stuff about the books, their background and how I write.

Or follow me on social media –

https://www.facebook.com/smdaviesauthor

https://twitter.com/SmdWelshAuthor

https://www.instagram.com/smdaviesauthor

Buy my books from Amazon, or The Great British Bookshop.

www.ingramcontent.com/pod-product-compliance
Lightning Source LLC
Chambersburg PA
CBHW050842210726
48290CB00004B/1048